ALL ABOARD!
PLANET_EXPAT

Why Dedicated Expatriates Seldom Go 'Home'

John Cairns

Illustrations by SARA

ISBN 978-0-9574306-0-0

Proudly Printed by Regal Printing

Published by the Power Publishing Club Ltd
www.allaboardplanetexpat.com

SIGNATURES AND AUTOGRAPHS

Good books really need a special page or two for people to write about their sentiments and to sign when preparing to present a copy as a gift to someone special. In the case of *All Aboard! Planet Expat*, that need magnifies because, as this book suggests, special people live almost everywhere.

Plus if the readers happen to encounter one or more of the highly interesting people featured on these pages, why not ask for an autograph? Definitely, the gregarious expatriates, being always eager to meet new people and to make friends, will oblige.

For that matter, why not collect autographs from anyone mentioned in this book?

MORE SIGNATURES AND AUTOGRAPHS

CONTENTS

CONTENTS...

Contd on next page

CONTENTS...

A FASCINATING WORLD NEEDS EXPLORING

Introduction

Envisioned as a fun project, this book started off as an idea hatched over a few beers at The Junk Pub in Hong Kong's Wanchai District. Looking around, I realized that most of the people in the pub had come from far away. Many of them have moved between countries for decades, working at challenging careers and living international lives. Naturally, they experienced highs and lows, adventures and pleasures, dangers and woes. For millions of people, the world really does resemble one big expatriate planet ready to explore and enjoy.

Long-time expatriates have followed different paths, observed keenly, found friends (sometimes enemies too) and helped to forge the nations where they lived. Normally they may happen to tell a few yarns in bars or at parties, but how does a wide audience learn from them about the benefits of travel, of working overseas and of unique experiences? The more I reflected, the more I realized that a big collection of expatriate stories needed telling in an organized way. Visions of a truly international book, one about people who routinely pack up and cross national borders, often with no intentions to return anytime soon, appealed to me.

Approaching dozens of swashbuckling expatriates, I invited them to participate. Deliberately, I sought out people from different countries, backgrounds and occupations, prodding them to share their often-remarkable stories from as many memorable places as possible. Mostly, the people featured in the following chapters are my friends and acquaintances who have lived abroad for many years and accumulated a treasure trove of tales. Some of these individuals easily could fill their own books, but instead we decided to present many contributors together to maximize the diversity of true stories.

As a guideline, I suggested that each person should consider certain topics: business, travel, culture, jobs, rubbish, lessons, luck, family, countries, dangers, timing, risks of being conned, do-and-do-not priorities, friends, sports, head-offices and other themes of expatriate lives. Through it all, cultural aspects looked likely to play a huge part.

A few basic rules applied. No active politicians or religious nut-cases would be included. Nor would we focus on girlie-bar stories. The participants started by recalling why they had left their original countries. They ended by predicting when, if ever, they will "go home" to live there again.

Soon the Power Publishing Club took shape with a small team of professional people, notably **John Cairns**, a Canadian-born editor/journalist/author living in Hong Kong, and **Sara Seneviratne**, an award-winning cartoonist from Sri Lanka who has journeyed through much of Asia. Then the expatriates ready to tell their stories could write their own material subject to some editing or submit to interviews. It sounded easy, like a pleasant process that they should enjoy as yet another unusual aspect of their adventures and on-the-move lifestyles.

Honestly, the world's habitual expatriates form an entirely different breed. For those highlighted here, this book makes a terrific personal and family keepsake. Usually, too little gets done to record and preserve individual or family histories.

For most readers, the book's contents should prove interesting, eye-opening and even inspiring. They reveal the enormous merits of travel and of exposure to unfamiliar people, places and customs. Everyone, especially young people, should realize with complete glee that such a big, fascinating world awaits them "out there". Putting together *All Aboard! Planet Expat* turned into an enjoyable and pleasing project. We hope that our readers can share in the fun on every page.

We plan to sell *All Aboard! Planet Expat* in shops, on the Internet and as an e-book. Judging by the initial interest, I believe that this first book may lead directly to more and transform into a real business. Many people have said to me, "Hey, Paul! I have dozens of amazing mates too, so how about another book?"

Much more can happen in the grand plan. For now, why not simply get started to discover plenty of unfamiliar places on this expatriate planet by reading the details from some of its most dedicated explorers about what happened to them?

Paul E. Watt

Power Publishing Club Ltd, 2012

info@powerpublishingclub.com

POWER EST 2012 PUBLISHING CLUB

LEAVING HOME SOIL? WHY?

By Michael Harris

Editor's Note: *As an East London-dweller in the 1970s and early 1980s, Michael Harris felt a powerful desire to wander into jurisdictions other than the nation of his birth. Here he tells exactly what happened and how the urge to learn more about other places turned irresistible and propelled him far away. Although some names, including Michael's own, have been changed, all of the stories and details that he reveals are entirely true.*

ENGLAND -- For most people who yearn to live and work overseas, I suspect that there is no single reason why they go, although there may be a single defining moment that triggers each departure. Instead, their life experiences lead them to the inevitable.

For me, a fascination-with-elsewhere began at age 10 during a primary-school trip to France. There, I first saw people who "spoke funny" (well, they were French, for

God's sake) and ate strange food. They drove on the wrong side of roads and had different smells wafting from them. Their shops sold oddly shaped bread or cakes and other things that most people in England never had considered much. Signs in the store windows, being in French, were totally illegible.

My classmates and I did learn quite dramatically that not all of the French people spoke "only" French. A little game that we played consisted of going up and asking people, while pointing at our wrists, "Have you got the fucking time, please?" But our attempts at extra-curricular fun soon backfired badly when one man retorted, "I do speak English, you know." We ran as fast as our feet could go in fear of that angry Frenchman.

So began my desire to see more and different places. After joining several other school trips to Belgium, Germany and Austria, I fully realized that the world offered vastly more than anyone could find in East London alone.

At university, my girlfriend was an Indian and my housemate was a Malaysian. These circumstances led me to a love of Asian food and exotic cultures and then to a holiday, when I was 17 years old, spent hitchhiking through Malaysia and Thailand. There I felt like a kid let loose in a candy shop. The first sensations of being in a tropical climate greatly boosted my dreams. Big differences that I observed all around me from almost everything in Europe sucked me into a new part of the world.

My biggest shock was to learn that so many people, especially in Malaysia, were overwhelmingly friendly and helpful, often buying food for me when I hitched free rides in their cars. I wondered why my own people were not more like that. Later I learned that part of the kindness had resulted from a Malaysian government initiative to welcome tourists, and that people were expected to be nice to visitors. Still, I thought, no such government campaign possibly could work unless the people really felt inclined to be nice. Would the West Ham United football fans back home ever behave so politely and kindly to the visiting-team supporters? Did anyone in the United Kingdom routinely pick up hitchhikers and then feed them too?

As a result of that Asian trip, I immediately chose a career path, as a science teacher with TEFL (Teaching English as a Foreign Language) experience, to allow me to live and work in the largest possible number of countries. My rough plan was to travel and teach in both English- and non-English-speaking nations.

A Chilly Farewell Mood

The essential defining moment leading to my departure came out of the blue (and off the thermometers) three years later on a cold November morning in Chertsey, England. Like most November mornings, it was freezing. Then a high-school science teacher, I struggled to get out of bed for another day at school. Being extra cold, I could not bear to leave the warmth of a blanket so I kept one wrapped around me while grabbing my clothes to prepare for work. I headed downstairs, put on the electric fire and dressed under the blanket next to the fire. When safely prepared, I unwillingly emerged from beneath the blanket, grabbed and munched on some Corn Flakes and then rushed out the door. It was freezing outside!

I got out to my car, a small, yellow Ford Escort, and found that I could not unlock the doors as ice had frozen the locks. So I went back inside, boiled a kettle of water, returned to the car and poured the hot liquid onto a lock, melting the troublesome ice. The car door opened, and I jumped in, already cold but happy that I was going to be on my way.

I WONDER WHETHER THIS PLACE HAS WINE, WOMEN & SONG ?
MAP OF PAPUA NEW GUINEA

Crap! The windshield was frozen over and impossible to see through, so I grabbed the ice-scraper and jumped back outside. With freezing fingers, I gradually scraped the ice away.

Then nearly fully frozen myself, I leaped back into the car. Huh? The windshield remained frozen? Oops, even its inside had frozen. So I scraped at the inside too with bits of snow and ice falling into my lap as I worked.

Finally, I could start the car. As it took a while for the heater to warm up, I headed off still cold. Since the drive to the school took just 15 minutes, the heater barely had time to warm me before I arrived there anyway.

I reached Junction 23 of the M5 motorway, moving down the slip road until I entered the motorway itself. Then I saw a rush of steam erupt from the engine. I stopped the car and jumped out in frozen horror. The engine had overheated because the water plus antifreeze in the radiator was frozen, preventing circulation. As I stood there, the cold ate away at my heart. Worse than chilled, I felt entirely pissed off. In my most energetic action of that day until then, I muttered many of my favorite curses. "Okay," I said to myself. "The time has come for me to contact Voluntary Service Overseas (VSO) and ask for a posting in a warm place with nice food.

A few months later, I arrived in the tropics.

Coming Next: *Michael experiences almost three decades of never-dull life and adventure in Papua New Guinea.*

DEADLY ARROWS, GIANT BUTTERFLIES: DANGERS LURK IN A BEAUTIFUL PLACE

Michael Harris Rarely Has a Dull Moment

Editor's Note: *A British-born teacher turned entrepreneur, Michael Harris has faced big risks while devoting much of the past three decades to advancing education in Papua New Guinea, his adopted homeland. Yet he had hardly even heard of the place before arriving there in the 1980s. Although some names, including Michael's own, have been changed, all of the stories and details that he reveals are entirely true.*

PAPUA NEW GUINEA – A certain magic permeates Papua New Guinea (PNG), a land of ultimate contrasts, but significant dangers exist too. British-born **Michael Harris**, the boss of a small company, who has lived there for a long time, regularly encounters both.

Anyone setting eyes on the immense beauty of PNG's scenery never forgets it. "You see the most incredible natural beauty – remarkable beaches, waterfalls, mountains and islands," said Michael. "Sometimes you encounter huge butterflies that most people do not even know exist. PNG has one of the world's largest bio-diversities, mostly untouched and in its natural state."

Many of PNG's six million people have valid reasons to feel slight confusion. Almost-modern cities, like Port Moresby, the capital, where the businessmen may wear snappy suits and neckties, create a huge contrast to the not-so-distant tribal villages that look much like they did centuries ago. Villagers sometimes travel into the cities merely for the thrills of riding on escalators or elevators.

Amid certain clusters of village huts, rugged men wear penis gourds, shoot arrows with amazing precision and make plans to hunt for wild pigs, tree kangaroos, bandicoots or rats. Tribal menus also feature caterpillars, grubs and grasshoppers.

Untainted by Western Civilization

"PNG is very raw in a sense that most people there remain untainted by the trappings of Western civilization," Michael said. "They never crave for iPads or iPods. Instead, they just want to have good lives with a couple of meals a day and to raise their children. Their idea of fun is to share a few laughs by telling stories to each other. The main entertainment comes from sitting and talking. Mostly the people lead very simple lives, and it usually feels nice to be in that environment, not in the rat-race that runs almost everywhere else.

"Even today, much of the economy is subsistence-based. People use what they have and pass it around to each other. Some catch fish. Others hunt or grow crops.

"Modern developments (the country's only cinema recently opened) and ancient ways appear almost side-by-side. Much of PNG has advanced from the Stone Age to the modern world within just a generation or two. Rapid changes play such a big part in making the country what it is – a place with some people who are very sophisticated, others who are not at all and every variation in between, all very different from everywhere else."

Independent from Australia since 1975, PNG struggles to develop its economy and to forge nationhood. A big place, three-and-a-half times the size of Michael's native England, it occupies half of one massive island and a smattering of nearby islands north of Australia. It shares a land border with Indonesia.

Enormous cultural diversity among more than 800 language groups heightens the confusion. A national language, called Tok Pisin, initially used by plantation owners to address their workers, has emerged from a blend of other dialects.

Mountains create a central highlands covered by tropical rainforest. A dismal road system means that small airplanes give the only access to some places. Even the two biggest cities, Port Moresby and Lae, lack road links to each other.

Highwaymen and Other Bandits

Where usable roads exist, so do highway robbers who "collect tolls" every few kilometers. Often, the "highwaymen" stop vehicles by standing in the way while aiming loaded shotguns or ready-to-shoot arrows in flexed bows.

Similar extortion occurs even in central Port Moresby. "If there happens to be a pothole in one of the side roads, guys will fill it in using a spade," Michael said. "Then they will stand in the road, stopping traffic and saying, 'We just fixed this road so now you must pay us.' They always find excuses to stop the cars and demand money. The conversation stays friendly until the moment when a driver says, 'I won't pay you. Bugger off!' Then the weapons come out."

Disputes often arise between villages, many of them with long histories of fierce tribal warfare. Violent battles and crimes, especially armed robberies, happen almost routinely.

"Once a gang of ex-army guys robbed a hotel where I stayed to run a workshop for teachers," Michael said. "At 6:30 in the morning, I sat in a conference room preparing my material for the day. In walked a guy pointing a pistol at me. Very efficiently, he searched me, emptying my pockets.

"As he examined my wallet, I said, 'Do you mind just taking my money, but leaving the wallet behind because it has some important cards inside?'

"He said, 'Alright.' So he took the money, dropped the wallet and walked out.

"I sat there thinking, 'Well, as robberies go, that was a reasonably nice one.'

"But moments later, the swing doors burst open again. In came an old PNG woman who worked as the cleaner, followed by another armed guy, this one much angrier for some reason. He came over, pointing his gun and saying, 'What is that?'

"I replied, 'My wallet'.

"He picked up the wallet and stuck it in his pocket. Waving the pistol, he said, 'Go outside.'

"As we left the room, I told him, 'Your mate already took my money.' But he had no interest in listening.

"We reached the hotel reception area near where the manager's bedroom was located down a side-corridor. The robber said, 'You lie down.'

WALLET
OR
YOUR
LIFE !

"So I lay on the floor. The robbers held the cleaner nearby. Then several bandits banged at the door to the manager's room, but he refused to come out.

"Furtively, I tried to look around to see more of what was happening, but a foot descended onto my neck to hold my head firmly down. Against my temple, I felt a gun muzzle. From what I could see, I knew that it was an M16 rifle. So I decided, "Okay, I really don't need to look. I'll just lie still right where I am.'

"As the banging intensified, the hotel manager finally opened the door. I heard a conversation, and the robbers said, 'Give us the key to the safe.'

"So I thought optimistically, 'This is not too bad. Once they rob the manager, they will take his money and then piss off.'

"Next a really frantic guy with a hand grenade started to run about, yelling, 'Unless we get that fucking key, I will explode this grenade.'

"Then I heard a robber say to the manager, 'Give us the key to the safe, or we will shoot him in the legs.'

"That got my attention. I thought, 'Oops. He means me.' I was the only other 'him' there.

"The manager said, 'Sorry, but I have no idea where the key is.'

"Knowing that the manager drank a lot, I thought, 'Oh, fuck. He's having a memory lapse.' Already, I felt the most painful burning sensations in my legs as my body anticipated what would happen next.

"Then another guy said, 'No, forget about him. Get her instead.'

"The manager's wife, a PNG girl, had come out from the bedroom, saying, 'Why all the noise? What is happening?'

"When the attention shifted to her, I experienced a flood of relief that no one would shoot me. But I felt sad too because I knew the manager and his wife quite well. It was a funny mixture of feelings.

"Fortunately, she had not been drinking the night before, and so she quickly pointed and said, 'The key is right over there.'

"So the robbers took the key, emptied the safe and disappeared. By PNG standards, it turned out to be a rather good robbery after all because no one got hurt."

Half a World Away....

Years earlier and half a world away, Michael had grown up near the West Ham Football Ground in London's East End. An enlightening schoolboy trip to Normandy in France awakened his soon-perpetual yearning to explore unfamiliar places.

"A little later, at age 14, I had a strange nocturnal dream of floating on my back down a tropical river," Michael said. "Later I experienced the identical real-life moments in PNG. I recognized the river and the trees on both sides as I floated, hearing the same buzzing noises as in my dream. Great moments happen when you realize that you are getting exactly what you want out of life."

Did the river contain crocodiles? "Yes, but not many," Michael said, shrugging. Anyone who has lived for long in PNG grows blasé to a few dangers, even to some with ferocious fangs.

Michael chose to become a teacher of science and English-as-a-foreign-language to facilitate going overseas. After finishing at university, he felt ready for a life of adventure, which PNG has provided in spades.

"I planned to skip and hop, teaching English in non-English countries and science in English places," Michael said. "I had geared up to become an ultimate traveler." Although his career has failed to unfold in exactly that way, he holds no regrets.

Intent on finding work located far away, Michael joined Voluntary Service Overseas (VSO). "Soon I had a job lined up in Flores, Indonesia, but it fell through at the last minute because the employers wanted teachers who could speak Bahasa," he recalled. "So I said, 'Please send me to the nearest available place to there.' I expected to go somewhere similar."

Remote Bush and Huts

Michael's request led him to PNG. "When packing, I envisioned all-night drinking, girlie bars and nice food. I had no clue that instead it would be remote bush and huts. Only just before I left England, when I received some information about my destination, did I start to realize."

Almost three decades ago, Michael first travelled toward Port Moresby on a British Airways flight via Singapore. He arrived in PNG with seven other VSO people, all of them feeling jovial "because in those days you got little plastic bottles (of drinks) on the planes, and we could help ourselves from a tray that the cabin crew had left out for us. We all were completely pissed on arrival."

The newcomers went first to a village in the hills for a week to learn the basics of speaking Tok Pisin. "That week culminated when we put on a singing-and-dancing show in Tok Pisin for the villagers," Michael said. "The show was a spoof of *It Ain't Half Hot Mum* (a 1970s British television sitcom set in India and Burma near the end of the Second World War). For the performance, I wore a dress belonging to a pretty VSO redhead. When I arrived back at Jacksons Airport in Port Moresby still in the dress, it caused a bit of a scene because the people there, just like in most places, seldom saw men dressed up as women."

A Nun on a Muddy Tractor

Michael's first PNG teaching job took him to Walumu (meaning Place of Dogs) in the Nuku district of West Sepik Province. The VSO bosses had done their best to honor his request. The Indonesian border loomed not too many kilometers away – through the bush.

"Going to Nuku, I travelled in a tiny plane, an eight-seater Cessna," Michael said. "It landed on what was just a grass strip.

"To meet me, there was **Sister Joy**, a Catholic nun, with a tractor. Thick mud covered the deeply rutted road, so only tractors could get through to the school. A young PNG brother from the Catholic mission drove the tractor. Sister Joy sat on one fender and I sat on the other for a one-hour journey. I got muddy then, and things stayed quite muddy for my next five years there."

The school buildings had timber frames, corrugated-iron rooftops (helpful to "catch the rainwater"), iron walls and cement floors. "For timber, all of the students helped to chop down huge trees in the forest and then to drag them down a river to our sawmill," Michael said.

"Our school sat in the middle of nowhere, seriously far even from the nearest village and surrounded by hundreds of kilometers of dense rainforest in every direction. There were nine teachers, 250 students and that was it."

A traditional battleground surrounded the school. "Twenty-nine language groups lived in the surrounding region, but none exactly where the school was situated because the villagers used to fight on that bit of land when they had disputes," Michael said. "That neutral place became the school site so that no one could claim, 'Hey! The school stands on our land so you guys should forget about sending your kids there.' "

Was the teaching difficult? "No, it was wonderful and

easy because the students really wanted to learn," Michael said. "They were interested in everything and were the most helpful, friendly and polite children I ever had met, the sort of students that represent a dream-come-true for any teacher."

Most of the youngsters who soaked up enough knowledge and later finished high school could attend university. Invariably, that meant enrolling at UPNG in Port Moresby or at Unitech in Lae.

Village Brouhaha

Before long, Michael witnessed how easily violence could erupt. "I had been there for about a month when a local female teacher said, 'Let's go to my village for the weekend. You can see what we do.'

"So I got to the village and joined an evening 'singsing' with lots of dancing and drinking happening. A beer was put into my hands upon arrival just as the head-teacher for the local primary school walked up to greet me. Suddenly a friggin' humungous rhinoceros beetle – a monstrous thing (the size of a mouse) the likes of which I never even knew existed -- landed on my shoulder. I flinched and accidentally threw my beer over the man. Luckily, no serious harm resulted, and people around me just laughed, although I remained unsure if I had broken any cultural rules.

"As the dance went on, we ran out of beer so a group of us headed off to another village to collect more. Suddenly from the hill where our village was located, we heard loud crackling noises and people shouting. There was an eerie glow of fire in the distance. One of the guys shouted, *'Meri bilong mi! Meri bilong me!'* ('My wife! My wife!'), and he started running back through the bush.

"We all rushed back to find a huge fight raging. Huts were burning, people were whacking each other over the heads with sticks and rocks were flying.

"It was a land dispute. One guy from the village had built a little shelter about a metre inside another village's perceived territory while doing some gardening. That temporary shelter, made of leaves and sticks to keep him dry in the rain, was considered a land-takeover bid. Such shelters, called 'house passengers', also are used by people moving through the forest who build them for sleeping at night. The one causing the dispute stood on the wrong side of a tree marking the boundary.

"Immediately, I went to find the teacher who had invited me to the village. She and the other women in her family were inside their hut trying to wait out the fighting.

"Then a banging noise came from outside the hut. Guys out there yelled for me to *'kam arasait, kam arasait'* ('come outside, come outside').

"So I thought, 'Go outside? Why? Do they want to kill me too?'

"When I went to the door, the men outside said: 'Leave this hut.'

" 'Why?' I asked them.

" 'We want to burn it down,' they said. 'But we can't with you in there because you teach our children too. You have nothing to do with this.'

"My colleague was a teacher too, but she came from that village so they had no concern for her. In contrast, they regarded me as neutral, someone not on their hit list.

"Reluctantly, I said, 'Guys, if you want to burn this hut, then it has to be with me inside.'

"As they thought about that, considering it, a group of other men came up from the side and started to hit them with sticks. The battle raged on, and momentarily, we were left alone.

"My friend, the other teacher, said, 'We should get out of here now.' So we left the hut and descended the hill away from the village, leaving the men to fight. The battle continued for another hour with most of the village destroyed."

Yet Michael soon loved Walumu. "As odd as it was, and so different from what I had anticipated, it turned into a dream place," he said. "Everything there amounted to a big adventure, and we did so much good – constructing most of the school buildings ourselves, growing our own food, and every teacher playing a big part in the students' education. People always talk about crime being a big problem in PNG, but during my five years in Walumu, the front door of my house, which refused to close due to the floor being too high, stayed open, even when I went away during school holidays. Never once was anything taken from inside."

Later Michael moved to a bigger school, 25 teachers strong and one of four national high schools, teaching pre-university children, in a town called Keravat. "That felt like joining an advanced society," he said. "I went from a place with very little structure to one with roads, generators and a much stronger multicultural aspect."

Eventually, Michael advanced to Port Moresby and left teaching to establish a small business. "When a big punch-up erupted with the government over payroll, terms and conditions, I resigned," Michael said. "One week the government abruptly decided to slice our salaries in half. When we received our paychecks, they were for just 50 per cent of the usual amounts. Without discussion, the government simply did that."

A breach-of-contract court case reinstated the salaries. "But then we received letters saying that the government soon would change our terms and conditions, and therefore we needed to sign new contracts. Enough was enough, so I resigned."

Woes Batter Business Plans

For businesses, PNG poses special challenges too. "Anyone going into business there faces an incredible array of problems," Michael said. "For example, you may lose electricity once or twice a day at unpredictable times. The power simply goes off. Water does too. Basic services are unreliable."

As for the police, "You cannot call for them to come because their police-station telephones do not work. Then you go to the station and they have no vehicles so you need to take them to the crime scene in your own car. Often I do not even try to call the police. Instead, I call a security company, its people come and I pay for their work. If I really need the police urgently, then I will send my driver and he brings them in my company van.

"Many things seen as completely basic in most countries do not happen easily in PNG. All of the problems when trying to run a business prevent you from running it normally. But at least everyone faces the same obstacles. Success in business there depends as much on being able to overcome and operate within the many constraints as it does on being a good technician. If you can make sure to have power running, using backup generator sets, and keep your air-cons running and your staff happy, and if they get their salaries each fortnight to feed their families – if you do just those basics – then you can have a business that works there. Many business people try to do these things, but fail. Such are the challenges of PNG that make it exciting and different."

Defending the Compound

In Port Moresby, Michael lives in a house within a four-acre, gated compound containing 29 homes. His company has its headquarters there too. Tenants and staff occupy the other buildings, all surrounded by a sheet-metal fence topped by razor wire.

With PNG decisively split between "haves" and "have-nots", the people needing money and food consistently try to take from others. Security always ranks as priority one. From time to time, prowlers attempt to scale the compound fence or to carve "doorways" in it with big bush knives.

"We have 11 security guards for the compound," Michael said. "They are heavily armed with piles of rocks. We stockpile rocks in different places so that when intruders break in, the guards know where to run to start throwing rocks at them. We discourage hand-to-hand combat or using machetes because we don't want the guards to get chopped. When people try to come in, we prefer to assail, hurt and deter them from a distance. Earlier, our security guards did experiment with bows-and-arrows, but rocks work much better. They are good to throw and usually just hurt the invaders whereas arrows kill them."

The guards never carry guns because firearms are illegal. "Luckily, PNG also has a shortage of ammunition," Michael said. "Some people have smuggled guns into the country, but they often lack ammo. Anyone who does have ammo hates to waste it."

Pointed Guns

Still, Michael has faced guns many times. "On different occasions, you react in different ways," he said. "Sometimes you lie down and beg. Once as I drove up to the compound gate, a guy tapped on my car window. I looked at him and saw a pistol pointed at me. That time, I handed over my money, but a very tough Aussie woman in the car with me immediately leaped out and tossed her handbag over the fence to perceived safety. That angered the robbers, who simply scaled the fence and grabbed the bag anyway, but luckily they did not hurt us."

Another time, Michael had loaded some visiting friends into an eight-seat mini-bus to drive them up a hill for a better view. "After we started down again, I saw a guy walk up from the side of the road in front of us," he said. "It was a quiet dirt road, not a public highway with crosswalks, so I recognized danger. I stomped on the gas, and we started to speed toward this guy. At first, he did not realize that the bus had accelerated. When he turned to face the bus and opened his coat, pulling out a shotgun and trying to point it at us, we were nearly on top of him. So he needed to leap aside before he could raise the gun, and I steered away, trying to escape without hitting him. We sped down a roadside bank and almost rolled over, but I kept the bus upright and drove it back onto the road. When I looked behind us, I saw about eight guys running after the bus. Their plan had been for one guy to stop us while the others came from behind to rob us."

Often the bandits brandishing guns may be bluffing with empty weapons. Michael remembers taking a gamble once by calling such a bluff.

"In the dry season in Sepik, the roads became just barely useable," he said. "We could get a truck out of the school and take the students to play sports at other schools. One drive up to Aitape along the Sepik Highway meant a difficult, eight-hour journey along a dirt road to Wewak, then going through river crossings and continuing for another five hours.

"Once I drove with 40 students on the back of the truck as we returned from a big sports festival. Rounding a bend, we saw a big log across the road, blocking our way, so I stopped the truck. Behind the log, a lot of guys pointed guns at us.

"Two other teachers sat up front in the truck with

me. Making a quick decision, I told them, 'Put your heads down.'

"As they ducked, I threw open the truck door beside me, looked back and started to drive in reverse. For the robbers, it came as a bit of a shock that we did not stop and merely raise our hands. They took a few moments to react before running after us.

"I kept backing up as fast as I could go, looking out the door with my head down, to drive along the narrow road. We went fast, well, faster than the guys could run.

"On the back of the truck, the kids all hung on and screamed: 'We are being robbed. We are being robbed.'

"Each time when I lifted my head, I saw those guys running towards us. The only other things that I watched for were the ditches beside the road, trying to stay out of them.

"Whenever I looked up, I saw the robbers running, but always farther away, falling behind. Luckily, I went fast enough to get away from them. They never did shoot their guns, meaning that they probably had no ammo.

"We returned to a little roadside health centre about half a kilometer back. There we shouted until some guys came out from a village hidden away in the bush.

"I asked a village elder to come with us. Then we drove back to the log blocking the road. By then, the robbers had disappeared, but I wondered if maybe they still hid in the bush.

"The old man shouted out to them: 'Go away. These people are just teachers and schoolchildren. Leave them alone. You tried to rob the wrong people.'

"We moved the log away and I drove through. Then we thanked the old man and off we went again."

Pet Crocodiles and Pythons

In what some people may perceive as a different kind of danger, Michael has kept some surprising pets. "In the Sepik, I used to have up to four crocodiles, small ones, living in my house," he said. "I devoted a whole bedroom to them." He planned to keep "the young crocs" temporarily and then release them.

Unfortunately, "they died when another VSO person, a new arrival in PNG, came by motorbike from another school about four hours away and stayed overnight. She took a look at my pets and thought, 'Oh, how cruel to keep crocodiles on a concrete floor.' Believing that they needed to be in water, she put them into a big sink outside the house. By morning, they floated there, dead, suffocated. She had drowned them. Actually, crocodiles do not live 'in' water, at least not without sticking their noses out. They usually stay on riverbanks, entering the water to eat, swim and cool down."

Do small crocodiles make good pets? "They are fun," Michael said. "They do funny things and make odd noises when you pick them up. Best of all, you can scare people with them."

More recently, Michael adopted two snakes, carpet-pythons named **Erik** and **Erika,** as slithery pets. "They are not poisonous, but they are very big and really strong once they wrap around you," he said. "Erik, the bigger one, measures more than two metres."

Independent-minded, the snakes escaped from their cages and moved into a loft above the living quarters of the house. With Erik loose, "all of my cats suddenly came running down the corridor", Michael said. "Erik had gone a bit wild, and he started to look for food.

"As far as I know, both of the snakes remain up there in the loft, but I have not seen them for a while," Michael said. "They will eat rats or pigeons. The birds especially like to roost in the roof."

Michael also shelters eight cats. "Being unhappy about having snakes in the house, they mostly live outside," he said.

Unwisely, the cats made a blunder that freed Erika. "She escaped after I placed her in a cage outside the house. I would put rats into the chicken-wire cages for the snakes to eat. The cats saw a rat still alive in there because Erika already felt full. So at night the cats ripped open the chicken-wire to get at the rat, which came out alright, but Erika did too. The next morning, I found lots of ginger cat-fur near the hole in the cage so there must have been a tussle."

Bigger Problems Prevail

In the context of life in PNG, any problems with pets look rather minor. The country's much bigger difficulties include blatant discrimination against women and circumstances that deter people from working.

"PNG is not a good place for girls, especially not for local girls, many of whom, if you believe the statistics, have been raped," Michael said. "Discrimination and violence against women tend to be accepted much too readily. Females also do not get jobs easily. All of the best jobs go to the guys. Discrimination even sours the little things. For example, security guards at the supermarkets will take bags and search the women going in, often unpleasantly."

The only form of social security comes from a longstanding system of *wantok* (meaning one language, or people of your language). A matter of attitude, it stipulates that anyone with money or resources should share and help others within the same family or tribal group.

"Any wage-earner needs to look after a large number of non-wage-earners," Michael said. "He or she soon loses the motivation to work hard and to earn money when then obliged to give it all away. People without work also lack motivation because they can rely on the others who do have jobs.

"The *wantok* system definitely has big drawbacks. In a subsistence economy, maybe it works. You are obligated to feed your family and relatives. If you have a pig, then everyone shares. But once a monetary system exists, *wantok* no longer functions quite the same way. Anyone with a job in town constantly has people ringing up or coming into town saying, 'Can we have money for this? Can we have money for that?' People receive their salaries and then need to hand out the money. Often the salaries fail to cover all of the demands, and so then even the people with jobs will stop working. They simply return to their villages because that makes life so much easier."

Why Stay in PNG?

A puzzling issue springs to mind. Amid so many problems and dangers, why does Michael stay in PNG? Why did he not rush to the airport and leave after the first exposure to life-threatening violence?

"Everyone asks me that," he said. "Yes, there are robberies and violent crimes, but the complete opposite happens too. At certain moments, you get more satisfaction in PNG than you could anywhere else. You learn the ways of the local people. They learn about your ways. Together, you make the world a smaller and better place. Ninety per cent of the people in PNG do not rob you because they are good folks who just want to lead quiet, comfortable lives."

Kind deeds balance the hostile ones, sometimes even blending together during the same incident, as in a "heartwarming" robbery in Keravat. "I had been in my house at the edge of the school area, but at 9 p.m. I returned to the science lab for a few minutes," Michael recalled. "When I went home again, I saw that my stereo and other things were gone and a window was ripped open. I had been robbed.

"The next morning, I told a few people about my misfortune. One of our other teachers, **Markus,** a huge, tough guy, said, 'We should go and get your stuff back.' Just like that.

"Then we began to ask people if anyone had been hanging around. They said, "Yes. We saw a certain group of guys near your house at the time.'

"So Markus said, 'Right. Those were the robbers. Where do they live?'

" 'Oh, they live in the settlement near the school.'

"Going to the settlement, we asked for those guys. People said, 'Sure, they live right over there.'

"We approached a house and found several culprits, each about 20 years old, just sitting there, hanging out. Markus said, 'We are coming in to check your place.'

"So we stepped inside. The family's mother moved aside, and there stood half of my stuff. We got that out and then asked, 'Where did the rest of it go?'

" 'Ah, we buried it.'

"We all walked into the bush, and the guys dug a hole where they had stashed more of my stuff wrapped inside a duvet cover. So we retrieved everything from the hole too.

"Returning to the school, I thought that would be the end of the matter. To my surprise, an hour later, someone knocked on the door with a message for me to go to the police station just beyond the school.

"When I got there, a policeman said, 'We have arrested the boys who robbed your house.'

"I said, 'Well, I got my stuff back already. Everything has been sorted out.'

"But the police said that they wanted to discipline the culprits. Next a really old man came up and talked to me. I knew that I had seen him before. Then I realized that a month earlier, he had been walking past my house with his wife and some kids, all of them carrying heavy firewood in bags on their heads. Sitting on my veranda, I had seen them struggling. So I had asked if they wanted some help. 'Stick your stuff in the car, and I'll drive it up to the place for you,' I told them. They thanked me, and we took the wood to their home. What I had failed to realize then was that this old man was the chief, the elder of the place.

"At the police station, the old guy soon started talking to everyone in Tok Pisin, which I understood too. He said, 'You see this white man. He came and helps us in the school. He teaches here, educates our children and once he even helped me to carry my timber. Now, you see these boys here. They stole from him, which is really bad.'

"Then he added, 'Even my own son stole from him.' One of the boys in trouble was his son.

"The old man ordered the police to line up the thieves, including his son, and then he said to them: 'So you want to steal from this man. Well, here, have this instead!' Then he beat them on their backs with a huge stick. Being so angry, he started to sputter and drool. He felt ashamed too – that his own son had stolen from me.

"I tried to tell him, 'It's okay. I think they know that they did wrong.'

"But he insisted: 'No, we must teach them.' Going down the line, he whacked at them all a few times until the police finally returned the boys to a cell.

"Then the old man shook hands with me, saying that he felt really sorry and that if I ever had more trouble it would be dealt with too, but I never encountered any more trouble in that place."

Symbols of Goodness: a Rock and a Pineapple

As difficult as life in PNG gets at certain moments, it also has a way of turning incredibly pleasing. "Good things outweigh the bad."

PNG has plenty of people "who will watch your back if you need them", Michael said. "If you have trouble, they will help or even stand in front of you to take the blows.

"Once a security guard, who had gotten drunk and become upset about who knows what, came at me," Michael said. "Just as he nearly hit me, I saw his eyes go funny, and he collapsed. Another of my security guards, had snuck up behind and struck him on the back of the head with a rock because he tried to attack me.

"The drunken security guard then rolled down a hill and smashed into the metal fence. My other guards picked him up and threw him outside the front gate. We called for the people at a security company to come and take him to the police station which they did.

"The next day the culprit telephoned me, asking ('please, boss') if I could bail him out. I replied by asking if he knew why he was in jail. He said that all he could remember was the police roughly dipping his head into a small pond outside of their station." Understandably, Michael declined to provide the bail money.

As another shining example of PNG goodness, Michael remembers **Hanna,** a student in Walumu. "Once I went along as we took all of the Grade 10 students on a two-day walk across the mountains and down the other side to Aitape," he said. "We had decided to stay for a week at the school there, in part so that our students could see the ocean for the first time.

"All the way through the walk, I noticed that Hanna carried a pineapple. It was hard going. I wore a backpack, struggled to get up hills and plodded through mud. But Hanna still cheerfully carried her pineapple, holding it tightly all the way. For the night, we built little ('house passenger') shelters to sleep in, but they got washed out at about 2 a.m. when the river flooded." No one had a good rest.

"On the second day of walking, I felt exhausted," Michael said. "All that I could think about, for some peculiar reason, was how much that I craved for a cup of coffee with a small Belgian chocolate on the side.

"Suddenly a slice of pineapple came back to me along the line of walkers. After one and a half days, Hanna had decided that the time was ripe to chop up the pineapple that she carried. Then she handed out the pieces to everyone else and ate none herself.

"If I had been the one with a pineapple then, I would have wanted to eat the whole bloody thing at that moment. But amazingly, Hanna gave it away. People in PNG do such thoughtful and kind things. They share.

"In so many ways, PNG's people are incredibly loyal and generous. My protective security guard with the rock and Hanna with the pineapple both demonstrate a remarkable sense of right and wrong, of natural justice. Despite the presence of some rascals (criminals), PNG people are the country's biggest plus. Their sincerity, genuineness and capacity to deal with hardships overcome a lot. Constantly, they surprise you with good things." If Michael had stayed in England, he never could have felt the satisfaction and achievement of assisting so many appreciative people by "helping in education". In Western Europe, "you will not find any really serious problems to fix because someone already did it (albeit perhaps badly) and so life there can turn very boring". But in PNG, "the spirit of adventure stays high. Things constantly happen, and you need to fix problems, which never gets boring. You have a challenging life and gain the satisfaction of fixing things on a daily basis."

An abundant, strong and steady hope beats in the hearts of most PNG people. "By being there with them, I can contribute to that hope," Michael said.

PAPUA NEW GUINEA 'RASCALS' MULTIPLY THE MAYHEM

By Michael Harris

Editor's Note: *After the previous chapter was written, Michael Harris, a former teacher who has lived in Papua New Guinea for almost three decades, revealed even more about his dangerous experiences there. He really did encounter more than his share of "rascals", as the people in PNG almost affectionately like to call those rogues the rest of the world would regard as "criminals".*

AMONG THE RASCALS – Not long ago, I participated in the filming for a training video under production for a security company. The filmmakers wanted to know the details about any "security incidents" that I had experienced since arriving in Papua New Guinea. After they left, I got busy and scribbled down a list.

Off the top of my head, I easily counted dozens of

times when I had faced violent situations. The hazards ranged from M16s (assault rifles) and hand grenades to car chases and car-ramming events.

Here are some of my PNG experiences beyond those already covered in the previous chapter:

-- Men with bush knives levered the louvres out of a window. One person had been tied up in the yard. I jammed one knife in the window by closing the louvres and trapping it.

-- Once I just had arrived back after a long-haul flight from the United Kingdom. Exhausted, I went to sleep starkers. As I slept, rascals entered and tiptoed around the bed, taking all of my best possessions. I slept through the entire incident and even got robbed again later by an insurance company that paid only a percentage of the value of what I had lost.

-- In my residential compound, I accidentally shot my own guard in the shoulder with a flare gun when rascals tried to get in through a kitchen window. After the flare exploded, the rascals ran away. The guard had a hole punched in his shoulder, but please, he did not mind because he had been asleep on the job and felt bad that his lack of watchfulness had given the intruders an opening.

-- Three times, rascals attempted to gain entry into a house in our residential compound where they had targeted a particular tenant. Each time, we chased them off, finally banishing them with rocks thrown by the 10 guards there that night. The rascals jumped and climbed over the fence to escape. The hole that they had cut in it earlier turned out to be too small for them to get out fast enough that way.

-- As I pulled up to the front gate of the compound, a car cut across in front to block me, preventing my entry. Its occupants failed to notice the drain and drove into it, getting stuck. My guards threw rocks and chased them away.

-- Some drunken guys rammed the front gate with

a car, trying to get in on Christmas Day to reclaim their other vehicle that I had locked inside the compound because they owed money. The steep slope was wet so they kept sliding back. Eventually they gave up and returned with the money.

-- A tenant living in the compound and having a domestic dispute with his girlfriend angrily shot off a pistol into the air.

-- An ex-guard wanting more "finish pay" came at me with a knife. I punched him and threw him down the hill.

-- In a beach incident, I was punched in the face from behind and suffered a split cheek. But I learned a lesson that day: do not kiss in public.

-- After a car chase, I was held down onto the counter in a petrol station by the guy I had overtaken. He was upset because when I passed him, I had waved to some pretty girls who rode in the back of his truck. He felt even angrier because when I saw him chasing me I braked in front of him, nearly causing him to crash.

-- One night a gang of guys pulled up, trying to block my vehicle. I waited until they got out of their car and then "gassed" mine. I was gone before they even got back into their car to chase me. Disappearing was easy because I drove a Mercedes V8.

-- On Christmas Eve, a very large, drunk and aggressive female tenant stabbed her English husband in the hand and later threw rocks onto my roof because I had hidden him in another unit for his own safety. When she found out, she attacked me in the car park so I hit her in the head with a torch and took her to the police.

-- After cutting through a fence, a rascal stole a chainsaw from our workshop. Our guards walked down and caught him in the settlement.

-- The drunken friend of a tenant's husband attacked

NO
NOT AGAIN...
this is the 3rd
time you robbed me
this week
Hi MATE!
MONEY OR
YOUR
LIFE
ROBBING
IS A
WAY OF
LIFE
IN
PAPUA

me when I broke up their domestic dispute. In this case, my guard ran away because the attacker was really huge and really drunk. Fortunately, he was so drunk that I had enough time to run away too. He was much too fat to catch us. The next day, we evicted the tenant.

-- A drunken guy pinned me against a wall at a motel restaurant where I had gone for breakfast at 8 a.m. on a pleasant Sunday morning. A waiter, who I knew well, saw the problem, came up from behind and hit the guy very hard on his temple. All I saw at the moment of impact was the guy's sunglasses fly off his face. He stood there stunned. Temple hits are no fun. Then he had to be carried out by his very apologetic friends.

-- A guy with a large rock jumped in front of my car. I drove at him, and he jumped aside. Another guy behind the car hit my back window with another rock, but I drove away.

Probably if I sat and thought for a little longer, I could remember even more unsavoury incidents. But maybe I should leave it at that. Luckily, I also have experienced enough wonderful incidents in PNG to make these bad moments appear insignificant.

BRUCE LEE TO JACKIE CHAN: EXPAT COHORT SHARES IN-THE-MOVIES FUN

Exploratory Trip to Asia Put Jon Benn on Big Screens

Editor's Note: *For decades, American businessman Jon Benn has enjoyed participating in the Asian and Hollywood movie industries. He made friends with martial-arts superstar Bruce Lee and worked with many big-screen personalities. His fascinating experiences even include a non-movie tale about how former Philippines dictator Ferdinand Marcos reneged on a business deal. Jon also tells why he favors living in Shanghai, a dynamic city on the rise, instead of Hong Kong, where urban decay festers.*

SHANGHAI, China – A long-ago, first-time journey to Asia changed American-born **Jon Benn**'s life in a big-screen way. Although perhaps not quite world-famous himself, he has mingled for decades with many of the movie-industry people whose names and faces garner recognition almost everywhere.

Once Jon reached Hong Kong in 1971, circumstances and personal interest conspired to place him in front of rolling movie cameras together with martial-arts master **Bruce Lee**, the most revered Asian film star ever. Since then, Jon seldom has wandered too far from the nearest movie or television sets.

"I happened to meet a movie producer, **Raymond Chow**, at a cocktail party," Jon recalled. "He asked me, 'Would you like to be in a movie with Bruce Lee?'

"At the time, I had no idea who Bruce Lee was. Even so, I said, 'Sure'. I thought it would be a kick to appear in a Chinese movie.

"So the movie people picked me up at 9 a.m. the next morning, and we successfully shot the first scene within about 20 minutes. They gave me a cigar, and I had to sit behind a desk to play a big mafia boss as my assistant explained that **Chuck Norris** (an American action-movie star) was coming to fight against Bruce Lee."

Now 77 years old and living in Shanghai, Jon has made an enjoyable lifetime "hobby" out of acting. He has appeared in 51 movies, mostly shot in Asia, and 14 CCTV (China Central Television) series. A list of his fellow cast-members and the names that sprinkle the stories that he tells resemble a *Who Is Who* guide to the movie world.

Still active in acting, Jon recently worked in a new movie, *The Man With the Iron Fists* (2012), starring **Russell Crowe, Lucy Liu** and **Pam Grier**. "That was a Hollywood production filmed in Shanghai," he said.

Lots of Pretty Little Starlets

Immersion in the world of movies "was not something that I planned, but it is something that I truly enjoy", Jon said. "I get to meet lots of pretty little starlets so it works for me."

Even 40 years later, the movie from which people often recognize Jon on streets or in restaurants is that early one, *Way of the Dragon* (1972), in which he played a mafia boss and appeared with Lee. In the United States, the movie was called *Return of the Dragon.*

"You would not believe how many millions of Bruce Lee fans live in China," Jon said. "Every day as I walk down the street someone will stop me and say, 'Were you in a movie with Bruce Lee?' "

If movie aficionados still recognize Jon after such a long time, then the passing years must have treated him kindly. "I still look the same," he joked. "I had no hair then, and I have no hair now."

Jon shared the screen in no other films with Lee, but that one time "led to a lot of other movies". His ensuing big-screen appearances included parts in *The Clones of Bruce Lee* (1977, playing a professor), *Challenge of the Tiger* (1980, an agency boss), *Death by Misadventure* (1993, himself), *Fearless* (2006, an American businessman) and *Shangdown: The Way of the Spur* (2011, a villain).

Jackie Chan and Jet Li Too

Longevity brings big rewards. Jon has become the only person ever to appear in different films with Lee, **Jackie Chan** and **Jet Li**, a big-three in the martial-arts-movie genre.

"I had a cameo part in a documentary called *Jackie Chan: My Stunts* (1999)," Jon said. "I have known Jackie for a long time. We met in Hong Kong. Recently, he came to Shanghai for a TV interview. I was in the audience, and he came over and gave me a big bear hug so he remembers me."

Jon and Chan, the latter with 100 movie credits, share

treasured memories of Bruce Lee. Early in Chan's career, he appeared in two of Lee's movies, *Fist of Fury* (1972) and *Enter the Dragon* (1973).

Both from Hong Kong, Lee and Chan each have martial-arts themes in their work, but their on-screen dynamics function very differently. "Jackie himself says, 'I am a stuntman. Bruce was a martial artist.' "

Jon appeared with Jet Li in *Fearless*. "In that one, I had a big speaking part," he said.

How do the martial-arts skills of Li, a China *wushu* champion, compare to those of Lee? "Definitely, Jet Li is an extremely good martial artist, comparable to Bruce," Jon said. But most people in martial arts "will say the same thing. A lot of guys tried to top Bruce Lee, but nobody could beat him."

Chuck Norris Concedes

"Once I was in Manila (the Philippines) a few years after *Way of the Dragon* was made," Jon said. "In a tiny bar there, I had a 'little cutie' on each side of me. When I looked up and across the bar, there sat Chuck Norris (Lee's fight rival in the movie) with a little cutie on each side of him too.

"Then we went out and ate dinner together. So I said to him, 'Tell me the truth, Chuck. Who would have won if you and Bruce Lee really had faced each other in a fight-to-the-death?'

"Chuck showed no hesitation in saying, 'Bruce, of course. Nobody could beat him.' And Chuck was a world champion in karate so his opinion counts for something."

Villainous Behavior

Usually, Jon plays the role of a villain. Is that because he is mean, ugly or really a bad guy? "A combination of those factors," he joked. "But still, I am okay with it."

In one non-villain role, "A few years ago, I appeared in a movie with **Fan Bingbing**, one of China's top actresses," Jon said. "It was called *East Wind Rain* (2009), a Japanese-themed movie then the most expensive one ever made in China. In that movie, I played a priest, of all things.

"My movie work always has been part-time," Jon said. "I do it for fun, and it is very enjoyable. Through the years, I have met so many people."

A successful businessman too, Jon operates his own company, Unison China Ltd. As a consultant, he often advises food-and-beverage entrepreneurs about locations, licenses, fundraising and other issues. "Recently, I have been working on a big project -- setting up a Japanese-themed lounge and restaurant underneath the JW Marriott at Shanghai's Tomorrow Square," he said.

At one time, Jon operated three Spanish-*tapas* restaurants in Hong Kong, "the first ones of their kind in all of Asia. They were very successful."

Ferdinand Marcos Reneges

In business, "I have done many things, often import-export work," Jon said. "I used to represent Boeing Military Aircraft in the Philippines."

In that capacity, "I got to meet **Ferdinand Marcos**, then the president of the Philippines. Boeing had a system called 'Flair'. This was long before any GPS (global positioning system). We could have put a device in the car that carried Marcos and others in all of his police cars so that his security forces always could tell exactly where the president was. If a frightening problem arose, then Marcos could hit a button, and boom, all of the cars and the people in them would converge to help him.

"In a large room in the Malacanan Palace (president's

residence), we set up a big screen to display where the Marcos car was situated at all times. It looked like we could close a US$25-million deal. We even were shown a contract that Marcos had approved with his initials in the upper-right-hand corner.

"Marcos himself always collected 25 per cent of any deal that happened in the Philippines. He would stash the money in Switzerland, Hong Kong or wherever else he wanted. We had to set up a special account in Hong Kong for his 25 per cent.

"Then (on August 21, 1983), opposition leader **Benigno Aquino** (the father of the present Philippines president), who had gone to the U.S. for medical treatment, flew back to the Manila International Airport and was assassinated, shot in the back of the head, as he got off the airplane."

A political uproar ensued. The assassination turned into a catalyst inspiring a People Power Movement that in 1986 overthrew Marcos, forcing him into exile. "Aquino got shot, and so did our contract," Jon said. Badly distracted, Marcos never completed the deal.

Six-Month Stay Lasts 30 Years

More than four decades ago, curiosity prodded Jon to visit Asia for the first time. "I had 24 gift shops and six restaurants in California," he said. "For the gift shops, I bought lots of products that came from Asia at the New York, Los Angeles and Chicago gift shows.

"But I never had visited the Orient. So when I finally sold everything, I wanted to go to Hong Kong to see the place for myself where all the money that I had spent buying so many gifts had gone. I decided to stay for six months in Hong Kong and to visit Australia, Japan, Vietnam and all over Asia using Hong Kong as my base. After doing all

JON, I WILL NOT MAKE YOU RICH BUT I WILL MAKE YOU FAMOUS
LET ME TELL YOU GIRLS THAT BRUCE LEE WAS A HELL OF A NICE GUY !
ENTER THE DRAGON
BRUCE LEE
BIG BOSS

of that, I thought that Hong Kong looked like a nice place and so I made up my mind to stay for another year, but I ended up spending 30 years there".

Even when finally leaving Hong Kong, Jon remained firmly in Asia's embrace. He once lived for a few years in the Philippines and has spent the last 11 years mainly in Shanghai.

'Smartest Guy': Bruce Lee Remembered

Jon enjoys sharing his recollections and knowledge of Lee, the late martial-arts-movie superstar: "Bruce appeared in more than 20 movies, starting at age six. His father was an actor too."

Most Hong Kong people have seen Lee's movie exploits. "It was hard for Bruce to walk down the streets because so many fans always wanted to talk to him," Jon said.

Sharing a movie screen with Lee brought potentially frightening risks. It could mean taking some of the fiercest blows that a man could throw. One memorable scene placed Jon on the receiving end of Lee's wrath.

"People used to call me 'One-Take Benn' because usually I could do everything just one time and it was enough," Jon said. "Some other scenes required 20 or 30 takes.

"In one scene, I stood in front of a chair. Bruce was supposed to knock me back into the chair, but he hit me with his shoulder so hard that I fell into the chair, and the whole chair flipped over backwards.

"Apologetically, Bruce pulled me up and said, 'Oh, I am so sorry.'

"In the next take, he put a really big guy behind the chair so that it would not flip over. Then he hit me again, still pretty hard. He never knew the force of his own strength, but I can testify to it."

Lee died prematurely in 1973, aged 32, from swelling and a rupture in his brain attributed to an allergic reaction to medication. "Bruce often suffered from splitting headaches," Jon said. "Usually he just would sit down until they went away, then apologize for the delay and keep on going."

In *Way of the Dragon*, Lee starred and directed. "He never had an angry word for anyone," Jon said, "but as a perfectionist, he kept everyone working until they got things right."

Strangely, "Bruce never used a regular script, only a basic outline of the plot. He directed by the seat of his pants. Everything was, 'Okay, say this next'. So I would say that, and then we moved on to the next lines.

"That may not be the Hollywood way to make movies, but it was the Hong Kong way in 1972." Somehow, the haphazard technique worked.

Lee must have possessed more than just brawn and martial-arts skills. Directing movies without a proper script calls for plenty of on-the-spot creative thinking.

"I would say that Bruce Lee was the smartest guy I ever met," Jon said. "He wrote six books about philosophy. Not only that, but he also was the strongest guy I ever met. And a hell of a nice guy too!

"Bruce joked all the time on the set. Most days I would bring a few girls to the set because they all wanted to meet him. Once he said, 'Hey, Jon. Be sure not to bring any girls tomorrow because my wife will be here.'

"Another time I smoked a cigar just waiting for the lights to be changed for the next scene. Bruce stood by my side, but I did not see him. He kicked and knocked out the ash on my cigar, but the cigar never moved at all. He was that accurate. He could kick near your face -- and you would feel the air move – without his foot ever touching your nose.

"Bruce was an incredible guy. Physically, he did amazing things.

"He liked to show off too. He was the best, and he knew it.

"For the sake of showing off, he would do hundreds of pushups on two fingers or kick hundreds of times. What really killed him, I think, was trying to do too much, going over the top. He had a gym in his home, and he designed a lot of the equipment in it. When on the set for eight hours a day, he would do pushups between takes. He never stopped. Then he went home and spent more hours in his gym.

"I remember one piece of equipment -- a special box that Bruce had made. It had several holes, the biggest four inches wide and then others three inches, two inches and one inch. Edges of the holes were razor sharp. He would push his fist into the biggest hole. Each time, the box delivered an electric shock. He did this very fast. Then he would do the same with the other holes using three fingers, two fingers and finally one finger. Missing meant cutting himself on the edges.

"Each time when Bruce struck at that box, he got an electric shock. That made his reflexes so fast. People on the sets sometimes slowed down the cameras in amazement because no one could believe his fantastic speed. That box was a big part of how he did it." But "he drove himself to extremes, which finally killed him when a blood vessel broke in his brain". If Lee had pushed himself less strenuously, he might have lived much longer. "Yup, I am sure of that." Did Lee teach Jon a few martial-arts tricks? "I learned some basics from him, but I never got into training much," Jon said. "People think that I must know a lot so they never bother me too much."

Welcome to the Bruce Lee Cafe

More than almost anyone, Jon has tried to honor Lee's memory. For example, he wrote a book, *Remembering*

Bruce Lee. In Hong Kong, he also opened a unique museum and restaurant, the Bruce Lee Cafe.

"That was Hong Kong's only museum for Bruce," he said. It was a three-storey place with a bar and the main part of the museum downstairs. There were lots of pictures, original movie posters, *numchuks* (martial arts weapons, each two sticks joined by a short chain or rope), shinguards that Lee trained in and other items, including a replica of a mask that Lee wore as **Kato** in the *Green Hornet* television show.

At first a smash success, the Bruce Lee Cafe operated for several years in the late 1990s and just past the turn of the century. Its menu offered the likes of "Bruce Crazy Toss" (linguine and noodles tossed in other ingredients) and "Bruce's Buffalo Wings" (breaded fried chicken's wings). "More than 20,000 people came from around the world to see the Bruce Lee Cafe," Jon said. "The Hong Kong government even named me as a goodwill ambassador for helping to bring so many tourists into Hong Kong."

Hundreds of news stories about the Bruce Lee Cafe appeared overseas, including in the *Los Angeles Times*, *Newsweek* magazine and the *Financial Times*. "I have six big scrapbooks full of them," Jon said.

Then why did the business last for only a few years? Unfortunately, "it was in a bad location – on Robinson Road in the Mid-Levels (up a hillside on Hong Kong Island). People found it hard to get up there and then hard to find the place."

Stressing Lee's historical and cultural importance, Jon lobbied the local government to help him to secure a better site. "I asked the government to provide some space in Kowloon (near Victoria Harbor) where most of the tourists go," Jon said. "I met with nearly all of the government's top people, and they always said, 'Oh, it sounds like a great idea.' Yet they would do nothing.

"People in the Hong Kong government are not easy to work with if you like getting things done. They took a long time even to erect a statue of Bruce along the Kowloon waterfront. Most Hong Kong people remember Bruce well, but those in the government hardly care."

Before moving to Shanghai, Jon sold the cafe. Now it no longer exists. The location became "a cheap Chinese restaurant", and the Bruce Lee items went into storage.

Why does Jon, an American, try so hard to celebrate Lee's achievements while the Hong Kong government does so little? "Beats me," Jon said. "**Linda**, Bruce's wife, and **Shannon**, his daughter, both visited the Bruce Lee Cafe and told me that they really appreciated what I had done. They also did not know why the government refused to do more."

Shanghai Outshines Hong Kong

Despite Jon's long history with Hong Kong, he now much prefers Shanghai as a place to live. "In the late 1990s, Hong Kong appeared to be in decline," he said. "Many people were selling their properties for low prices."

Meanwhile, "I had gone up to Shanghai several times, and I knew that the place was booming. People called it 'the City of Cranes' because thousands of construction cranes built towers everywhere. Deciding to go where the action was, I moved to Shanghai.

"I like Shanghai much better than Hong Kong. The women are more beautiful here. This is a 24-hour-per-day city too. Every night a big party happens somewhere."

Jon reckons that Hong Kong has declined, becoming overly crowded, expensive and polluted. Even worse, "not many niches remain there. Most things-to-do have been done. Up here in Shanghai, you find a niche around every corner -- so many opportunities, things not yet done that can be done."

What about the U.S.? Will Jon ever return to live there? "Ha!" he scoffed. "That ain't gonna happen. Things are too screwed up over there." How so? In so many different ways!

"I am happy in Shanghai," Jon added. "To me, Asia looks like the best place to be in the world. As Europe crashes and America crashes (economically), Asia just keeps moving ahead."

Born in New York City in 1935, Jon moved often as a boy, first to Illinois at age two and then to a blur of communities in different states. "I attended 11 schools within 10 years," he said.

"My father worked for the J.C. Penney Company. As a successful general manager, he kept getting transfers. He moved around more than the company president did, always getting bigger and bigger stores to manage.

Jane Mansfield by the Pool

As a young man living in California, Jon had the good fortune to know **Jane Mansfield**, easily Hollywood's biggest sex symbol in the 1950s and early 1960s. Jane was the most famous pinup girl just prior to **Marilyn Monroe**. Eerily like Bruce Lee, Mansfield and Monroe both also died suddenly when still young (Mansfield at age 34 in a car-accident and Monroe, 36, after a drug overdose).

"I lived in Beverly Hills, and Jane lived across the street," Jon said. **"Miklos (Mickey) Hargitay**, who was Mr. Universe at the time, lived in a room above our garage. We had a pool, and they would come over. Jane would lie around the pool. Then Mickey (the strongman) would pick her up and spin her around. He ended up marrying her."

Horses in Mexico, Spies in Germany

Prior to arriving in Asia, Jon's favorite adventures happened in Mexico. He first went there at age 18, spent more than three years (not consecutively) and earned an economics degree at the University of Mexico.

"I wanted to learn Spanish," Jon said. "So I sat on a Greyhound bus for six days and six nights, ending up in Mexico City."

Even then, Jon showed a radar-like instinct that guided him to movies-in-the-making. "I used to ride horses everywhere in Mexico," he said. "One time, some friends and I heard a story about dinosaur bones high in the Sierra Madre Mountains. So we rode so far up into the mountains that we met people who never before had seen white people. They did not speak Spanish either – only a local dialect.

"Finally, we reached a place where as far as you could see huge dinosaur bones stuck out of the earth. It was incredible.

"So we picked up a few of the bones and started to ride back. Then soon, away off in the distance, I saw a film set in the desert. It turned out to be **Steve McQueen**, **Charles Bronson, Eli Wallach** and **Yul Brynner** making *The Magnificent Seven* (1960, a western). Wallach needed more horsemen for his posse in the movie so we agreed to ride with him. That was my first-ever movie appearance."

Elsewhere in Mexico, Jon once spotted another movie-in-production. "I had rented an apartment right on the beach in Puerto Vallarta," he said. "One day, I noticed people setting up a movie set down on the beach. It turned out to be *The Night of the Iguana* (1964). **Richard Burton** and **Elizabeth Taylor** were there. I got into that movie too as an extra at a cocktail party."

When living in Hong Kong, Jon often recalled his Mexico adventures. "A good friend of mine was the

Mexican consul-general," he said. "I told him some of my stories, and he said, 'You saw more of Mexico than any Mexican that I know.' I had tried to go almost everywhere in Mexico."

Some real-life drama, as opposed to the movie-reel variety, caught up with Jon. "I was going to be drafted for the Vietnam War, but did not want that," he said. Seeking alternatives, he expressed an interest to learn Russian, which led to spending a year at the Army Language School in Monterey, California.

"From there, I went to Germany to work at a top-secret listening post inside a guarded compound," he said. "There were listening posts set up all along the Berlin Wall. We listened, translated and deciphered. I worked in a section that had to write the final copies that landed on the U.S. president's desk the following mornings. Our equipment was so sophisticated that if an East German general went to see his mistress, we knew exactly who he went to see and where."

On the weekends, "I would drive a German station wagon with an air-mattress in the back (as his sleeping quarters) and go to Paris, Geneva, Stockholm or wherever," he said. "That way, I got to see a lot of Europe."

Later Jon returned to Mexico and helped to set up the country's first English-language radio shows. "There were three million expatriates down there, but no English-language radio shows," he said. "And, of course, television was just starting then.

"We called the radio shows *Anglo-American Hours*. They ran for three hours daily on a local station. We played music, had news in English and interviewed people, especially those from the American, Canadian and Australian businesses operating there. The shows were very successful."

Jon enjoyed Mexico. "Then it was a great place, kind of like Shanghai now," he said. "It was very safe with no significant crime threats. You could walk around at 2 a.m., listen to the mariachi bands and nobody would hassle you."

Now Mexico's situation and reputation have changed. "A few years ago, I returned for a visit," Jon said. "I had a girlfriend who drove a brand new Buick car. For a week I stayed at her parents' home."

One day Jon and his Mexican-lady friend visited Mexico City's most-posh neighborhood. "In broad daylight, we parked the car in front of a friend's house and went inside for a few hours. When we came out again, the whole front end of the Buick had vanished (stolen).

"Much of Mexico has become very dangerous. I have no desire to go back or to live there. Lots of people get killed as the drug cartels take over more of the country."

A Happy Bachelor

Twice married, once on each side of the Pacific Ocean, Jon now describes himself as a happy bachelor. "The first time, I married an American girl whom I had met in Mexico City," he said. "She studied art, and I studied economics. We both were 21 years old, much too young and it did not last.

"That was not a good time so I waited 32 years before trying again. Then I met a beautiful Beijing girl in Hong Kong where she worked, and I married her. Unfortunately, she was 30 years younger than me and wanted children, but I did not care to have kids. We remain good friends. She lives in Barcelona."

Why a taboo on having children? "My two brothers and two sisters all had kids, so I was Uncle Jon. Plus a long time ago, one of my sisters was 18 months old when I was 18 years old. My parents travelled a lot and I ended up taking care of the kids, getting them ready for school, changing diapers and all that crap. So I have had enough."

Foiled by an Amorous Cameraman

Despite no desire for children, Jon still admires many of the actresses he meets. In all of his movie work, which actress became his all-time favorite?

"That is a good question," he said. "The one that I most fell in love with was a dark-skinned, gorgeous Brazilian woman. We were filming a movie in the Philippines about **General Yamashita**'s gold. He was a Japanese general who supposedly hid gold worth billions of dollars somewhere in the Philippines. I played a river-boat captain, but my favorite actress had taken a fancy to the Italian cameraman so I had no chance."

Flying Pizzas, Helicopter Hazard

"Filming in the Philippines always was fun," Jon said. There, he also observed the making of *Apocalypse Now* (1979), a powerful Vietnam War movie directed by **Francis Ford Coppola** and starring **Martin Sheen, Marlon Brando** and **Robert Duvall**.

"I was on the set," Jon said. "My friend was a caterer who provided most of the food, but Francis Ford Coppola insisted on having pizzas flown in from Los Angeles daily because he liked pizzas and disliked the catered food.

"Another guy there, who wanted to produce a different film, hired a helicopter to go looking for locations. The helicopter held just four people, and I was the fifth one so I stayed behind. That particular helicopter hit a high-wire line, crashed and killed all four of those guys. Meanwhile, I am still here so that was some kind of karma."

Nearly the Third World War

Jon accepted a different task when working on the 1982 movie, *Inchon*, about the Korean War and starring **Laurence Olivier, Jacqueline Bisset** and **Richard Roundtree**. "I had met a guy named **Terence Young** who directed *Dr. No* and *From Russia With Love* (both **James Bond** movies starring **Sean Connery**), *Bloodline* with **Audrey Hepburn** and many other films.

"Terence was a well-known English director," Jon said. "I became his assistant and travelled everywhere with him for a few years. During that time I met almost everyone in the movie business.

"Then Terence got a job to direct the movie *Inchon*, then the biggest Hollywood film, costing US$60 million. It was about **General Douglas MacArthur** landing his assault team at Incheon, Korea, which has the highest tides in the world – 32 feet twice a day. Nobody ever imagined that he could land there.

"One day we were out in a field doing a massive battle scene with tanks, 500 North Korean soldiers (actors), 500 South Korean soldiers (actors) and lots of bombs exploding. That happened just three miles from Panmunjom at the North Korean border.

"At 10 p.m. that night, we had 32 big container trucks loaded with 50 soldiers on one, 50 soldiers on another, tanks and all of the equipment. Then we headed back to our headquarters in Seoul.

"I rode in the front truck with Terence, Sir Laurence and Jacqueline. We got stopped at a highway checkpoint. As one problem, we had forgotten about a 9 p.m. curfew, and it was after 10 o'clock.

"Much worse, in the back of our container truck, we had 50 North Korean soldiers. That nearly started the Third World War. We needed three hours and lots of phone calls to do the necessary explaining. That was quite an experience."

More complications arose later. "When that movie was completed, in the can, as we say, the American government refused to allow it to be shown for many years," Jon said. "I understand that it has become available now, but still I never even have seen it."

The U.S. administration had learned that the movie was bankrolled by **Reverend Sun Myung Moon** (1920-2012), the South Korean leader of the Unification Church, often regarded as a religious cult, the Moonies. Notions of any "cult" gaining a voice in popular culture clashed with the American government's wishes.

Despite Jon's involvement with so many movies, he still names *Way of the Dragon* as his personal favorite. "That one brought me the most recognition," he said. "As Bruce Lee told me at the time, 'I will not make you rich, but I will make you famous.' For me, that movie has had the most impact."

When Jon reminisces, he expresses absolute certainty on one point. He has no regrets about that first exploratory trip to Asia. "None whatsoever," he declared.

ADRENALIN RUSH POWERS DOWN-UNDER SCOTTISH NATIONALIST

Thrill- Seeking Colin Mackie Stays in Motion

Editor's Note: *A dedicated advocate of Scottish political independence, Colin Mackie has lived for most of his life nearly as far away from his homeland as anyone can go. Regardless of animosity in London toward Colin's cause, Australia, his adopted nation, has treated him kindly, as do the many places where he travels. Colin reckons that almost nothing can beat the thrills derived from new experiences and unfamiliar places.*

AUSTRALIA – Born up north on the world map in Scotland, a "country" about which he holds vehement opinions, travelling businessman **Colin Mackie** has settled down-under in Australia. At every chance, he feasts on a steady diet of thrills and memorable activities.

Sixty-seven-year-old Colin enjoys the adrenalin rushes and jolts of excitement that accompany his new experiences, especially the most action-packed, slightly dangerous ones. Does he regard any activity as too risky to tackle?

'Birthday Boy' Leaps From the Sky

Showing a "try-everything-with-gusto" attitude, Colin celebrated his 65th birthday in heavenly style. "I have made two skydives and plan for another," he said. "A friend of mine, **Tony Bloom**, and my personal assistant at the time, **Joanna Alexander**, conned me into making my first one. They said that they were taking me out for a special birthday breakfast near the Gold Coast in Australia.

"We kept driving and driving. As we approached the airport, I started to suspect that something might be going on concerning my sister, **Morag Laviolette**, who had planned to visit from New Zealand. I thought that maybe Tony and Joanna had organized that.

"Then we drove straight into a skydiving place, which let the proverbial cat go scurrying out of the bag. By that time, I could not possibly back out. There was no way that I would miss the chance.

"After we climbed into a rickety little monoplane, it went up to 13,000 feet. The airplane really was rickety. Its walls were done in Perspex (clear acrylic material). Six people could ride up in the plane for tandem diving (leaping with an expert strapped to each novice's back).

"There we were -- six people crammed into the back of that plane. Then the plastic along one wall rolled up to create a hole that we could jump through. When the time came, I felt much less timid than Tony and Joanna did. I had to jump out first. Otherwise, they would not have jumped. Wow! The sensation was wonderful. When I dived out, I was at the front with the guy (expert) on my back. I pushed my belly toward the ground and my arms went out to the sides. That got me some wind.

"I fell, but for not nearly long enough in my opinion. It was brilliant, absolutely brilliant. The whole dive took probably four or five minutes, but the free-fall part was much shorter, maybe just 30 seconds until the parachute opened.

"Ahhh!" Colin leaned back in a chair, remembering. "That was so good, such fun.

"When I landed on the ground, about 20 of my best friends had arrived. Then we all went together and finally ate that birthday breakfast."

So Tony and Joanna actually kept their word about treating Colin to a special breakfast. "Yes," he grudgingly admitted. "Mind you, they refused to buy me the breakfast first in case that I got sick on the plane or during the skydiving, in which case they would have wasted their money. They have Scottish tendencies too."

Wild Rides on White Water

Despite the exhilaration of skydiving, Colin enjoys another outdoor activity even more. "My favorite hobby, and I would do it much more often if I could, is white-water rafting," he said.

"I love white-water rafting. One time (circa 2006), I went for an excursion on the Murchison River in New Zealand. With much of the water coming from snow-melt, the river felt freezing cold.

"We had a guide and about nine people on the raft. The guide asked if any of us ever had gone white-water rafting before.

" I replied: 'Yeah, yeah, sure!'

"So he told me, 'Then you can come to the back beside me.'

"Obeying, I went to the back while he continued to get everyone organized. An American lady who sat there too started a conversation with me. 'Oh, you have done white-water rafting before,' she said.

" 'Oh, indeed. Quite often.'

" 'What are the strongest rapids you have been in?' she asked.

" 'Level-seven,' I told her.

"Just then, the guide came to the back and said to me, 'Sir, the degrees of difficulty in white-water rafting only go up to level-four.'

" 'Oh?' I said. 'Is that so? By any chance, did you ever hear of Niagara Falls?' "

Quick-witted Colin never really rafted over the huge waterfalls on the Canada-United States border, but he has struggled along on some mighty rough waters. Even that day's ride on the Murchison River held some big surprises for him.

"I got thrown completely off the raft (by its wild movements) into the rapids," he confessed. Yikes!

"Guides always say that if you get thrown into the water when white-water rafting, then try to lie flat and go feet-first. If you happen to fly off head-first, then you may hit your skull on the rocks and die.

"The other thing that the guides constantly say is to hold onto your paddle. But they tell you that for their own sakes, not for your sake. That day, I tumbled off holding tightly onto two paddles, one in each hand. Going down strong rapids with two paddles and no raft turned out to be an extremely bad idea because the paddles got swung this way and that way, always hitting me. The bloody paddles beat me up more than the rapids did.

"By the time that I could throw away both of the paddles, I must have swallowed almost half of the freezing-cold Murchison River. Somehow I looked back and saw the raft at such a distance away that it appeared to be only about an inch long.

"I thought, 'This is me dying.' I really did.

"So I decided, 'Maybe I just should relax and try to enjoy the sensation.' If I had to die and could do nothing about it, then I wanted to make the most of the experience.

"You see, I have a philosophy that after dying, people go to heaven, which consists of many activity clubs. The arriving people enter the most suitable clubs based on how they died. The biggest club, the most boring one by far, full of snoring old farts, consists of people who died in their sleep. I never want to join that bunch. Smaller clubs, like one for the guys eaten by Tigers in Bengal (or drowned in white-water-rafting mishaps), sound much better – more exciting and elite."

But back in the pounding waters of the Murchison River, Colin missed out on securing a heavenly club membership that day. "Oh, I just lay there, managed to survive and finally got washed up onto the shore. Then the people from the raft came and found me."

Non-Smoker Pushes Smoking Device

Colin, a former Scottish nationalist political candidate, carries several name-cards to reflect his latest work with several companies. For starters, as the international sales and marketing director for an Australian enterprise, Piparette Pty Ltd, he promotes and sells Evo Ezi-Load pipes intended to help people to smoke tobacco less destructively.

While much of the world strives to save lives by going entirely smoke-free, Colin, a non-smoker, marches to a different drummer with a variety of devices to facilitate smoking, albeit with reduced dangers. "We do not promote smoking," he insisted. "I hope that no one will start to smoke because of this product. Only smokers who struggle to pay for their cigarettes should use it."

Slashing the cost of smoking could benefit all smokers,

Air Scot
NO FEATHERS?
Silly old fool
LOOKS LIKE A NOVICE
AMBULANCE

especially those without much money. "My experience suggests that many smokers will find the money for cigarettes even before they find the money to feed their children. Rather than promoting the smoking habit, I say to those who simply cannot give up smoking, try this cheaper, healthier, more environmentally friendly way."

Resembling an easily carried fold-up tobacco pipe, the new product could render paper-clad cigarettes nearly obsolete. "It is an automatic pipe, but filtered and so not for regular pipe-smokers."

A storage compartment holds just enough tobacco for "your 10 smokes for the day". A bowl at the top fills with the amount of tobacco usually smoked in one cigarette.

"Workers in hotels or factories may get only two minutes for a quick smoke," Colin said. "With this, they can stop anytime." Unused tobacco in the bowl can be captured for re-lighting later. That means no wasted tobacco or discarded cigarette butts.

"For smokers, this is much cheaper," Colin said. "For someone in the U.S. who spends US$50 a week on cigarettes, the cost when using this product would plunge to US$12-15, a huge saving."

Colin also works as a managing director for Enterprise 21, which advises people on building and operating franchise businesses. "I have been doing this business, building franchise systems, for about 25 years," he said. "Imagine that a coffee-shop owner wants to expand his business. He asks me how to do it, so I look at the details and advise him. Then, if this is the most appropriate method for him, we can go franchising, after which I put all of his systems and legal documents together and we can take it to the world.

"As another example, I have held meetings recently with some people in Jakarta, Indonesia, who are looking for a way to build good-quality housing, easily and economically, in remote locations. Meanwhile, I also have a client in Australia with a patented, mortar-less building system and a transportable block-making machine. They make for a perfect match."

Among all of the franchised businesses worldwide, Subway sandwich shops have the most outlets – more than McDonald's restaurants or Starbucks coffee shops. Meanwhile, the most franchisees are in the Jani-Clean franchise system, that of a U.S.-based industrial-cleaning specialist.

In a third job, Colin directs ClanTime, a maker of Scotland-inspired jewellery. About six years ago, he wanted a Scottish-flag ring (adorned with a likeness of the national flag). "I went to many jewelers and then had one made, but it was terrible," he said. "Then I discovered a New York Jewish jeweler, a nice guy, with a factory in Thailand who employs Indian cutters to make Scottish rings."

So Colin forged another business relationship. "We are now developing Australia-flag rings too," he said.

'You Have a Grasshopper Mind'

Colin really likes to stay busy. "When I was a kid, my mother used to tell me: 'Son, you have a grasshopper mind – you always jump from one thing to another.' She was entirely right then, and I am exactly the same way today. Without so many things to do, I would get bored silly."

Annually, Colin makes about six overseas business trips, mostly for Piparette. His destinations include the U.S., China, Belgium, Germany, Austria, the Netherlands, India, Indonesia, Thailand, Hong Kong, China, Jordan and the United Arab Emirates. "For some reason, I enjoy Asia the most, without even being particular about which country," he said. "It is hard to say exactly why, but I do appreciate the people. Although I cannot speak their languages, I think that most people in Asia have a good sense of humor."

Humor Eases Business Deals

Despite being unilingual, Colin always finds ways to communicate wherever he goes. Recognizing that an ideal way to win friends and achieve sales is to put people at ease by making them laugh, he gladly tells jokes, even at Scotland's expense. "Not everyone realizes this," he said, "but it was a Scotsman who dug the Grand Canyon in Arizona after he dropped a coin and had trouble to find it again."

Laughter feels good and facilitates business deals. "Humor seems to overcome every language barrier," Colin said. "I just returned from Shenzhen (in China's southern Guangdong Province), and I was able to put everyone whom I met there into stitches (of laughter). In selling situations, I use humor a lot. Luckily, the Chinese and other Asian people appear to understand most of my humor."

Suddenly, Colin takes issue with being called unilingual and demands a correction. "I speak Scottish, Canadian, American, Australian and British – all of those and more," he said.

Colin's "love partner", **Lyndi Edwards**, originally from Burma, often travels with him. She works as an Australia-based interpreter, translator and Burmese-language radio-show journalist. "She has not been allowed back into Burma because as a journalist she has reported on some negative stuff about the government there," Colin said. "But now that the situation in Burma has thawed a little, she believes that maybe she can return.

"Lyndi's father was an interesting person too," Colin added. "He was a Burmese fighter-pilot trained by the Japanese to fight against the British to get them out of Burma, which was then a British colony. After the Brits were thrown out, he next had to fight against the Japanese. Later he became the chairman of a Burmese airline and then the ambassador to Germany."

Intellectual Sponge Soaks Up Sights

For business purposes, travel may not always be as lucrative as one wishes, Colin said. But personally, it invariably proves "ultimately rewarding".

"If I ever stop learning, then please shoot me. I enjoy learning, even if just on a short train ride from Hong Kong to nearby Shenzhen. Always, there will be people, things and situations that I never saw before. It mentally stimulates me, and without mental stimulation, I soon would be in dire straits."

Travel turns Colin into an "intellectual sponge" constantly trying to absorb new information and knowledge. "Wherever I go, I try to soak things up," he said. "I love to wander. Once I stayed in Chicago for five days, and I walked each day from 9 a.m. until 9 p.m., just walking and walking, looking at everything." What could surpass having the time and the freedom to explore in every direction that one's heart desires?

Pa-dump, Pa-dump

A few travel highlights happened in Vietnam. "I went there to do some scouting around (for business) and then tried a home-stay on the Mekong Delta," Colin said. "That was great fun.

"The home-stay turned out to be in a ramshackle shed at the end of a jetty. I could have fallen through some of the holes underfoot right into the Mekong River.

"After sleeping there, I woke up really early in the morning. Off in the distance, I heard, 'Pa-dump, pa-dump…, pa-dump, pa-dump…, pa-dump, pa-dump….' That triggered a concern at the back of my mind, and I wanted to know what caused the noise.

"So I got up, opened the door of the veranda onto the Mekong River and stepped outside. Mist covered the whole river, just like in a beautiful scene in a movie.

"A passing long-boat had been heaped high with baskets of garden produce. An old guy wearing a coolie hat steered it. The boat's long-stroke outboard motor made the sound that I heard. It was the first time for many years that I had heard the noise of a long-stroke motor.

"Pa-dump, pa-dump..., pa-dump, pa-dump..., pa-dump, pa-dump...." The sound vibrated pleasantly along the water.

Into the Bloody Swamp

"That same day, Lyndi and I went on a bicycle ride through some Vietnamese villages, places with just a one-metre-wide concrete strip passing through them. That was fine on the bike, but when something came along going the other way, things got a bit frightening.

"As I cycled along, a motorbike suddenly came shooting in the opposite direction. So I had to stop.

"Before starting out on the ride, I should have adjusted my bicycle, but I had not. The seat was a little higher than I needed it. When I went to get back up onto the seat and put my foot down for leverage, my front wheel just slid off the edge of the concrete.

"Unfortunately, it was a nine-metre drop-off there. As I went rolling down along with the bicycle, I thought that at least I could anticipate a soft landing because I saw nice, green vegetation below. But the green vegetation turned out to consist of lilies on top of a deep swamp.

"I splashed into the bloody swamp, up to my waist in mud and up to my neck in water. All that stuck out was my head and my coolie hat.

"From nine metres up, people looked over the edge, peered down and yelled, 'Are you alright down there?' The water looked filthy black and smelled bad too. Probably it was a cesspool."

Crime and No Punishment

One day several years ago, thieves in the Netherlands snatched Colin's luggage. "That was not much fun," he said. "After attending an exhibition in Dortmund, Germany, I had scheduled an appointment in Amsterdam next so I decided to go there by train.

"I boarded the train in Dortmund. For the previous three days at the expo, I had talked to hundreds of people and collected 30-odd business cards. Sitting on the train, I took out all of the cards, put them into my journal and then added all the information into my laptop. All that took me about an hour to do. Then I put my luggage onto one of the train seats and tried to relax after all my work.

"The train stopped at the station just before Schiphol Airport in Amsterdam. It was one of those upstairs-downstairs trains with seats facing each other.

"A young lad came running down the stairs, banged open the door, ran down the carriage and sat down, looking at me from up the carriage. Then he got up and raced out, but soon turned, ran back in and sat looking at me.

"Suddenly from outside on the platform, someone knocked on my train window. I turned to look outside, and a guy on the platform stood pointing at me. He said, 'You.'

"I replied, 'Me?'

" 'Yeah, you.'

" 'What?'

" He pointed. 'Look.'

"So I got up to look and then heard the other guy run out again."

"Seeing nothing where the guy outside had pointed, I sat down. Only after the train started off again did I notice that my hand luggage had disappeared. My laptop, passport, visa for Vietnam, my notes and all of those business cards were gone.

"When I reached a police station in Amsterdam, no one there appeared all that interested in what I had to say or even in taking a report. For them, it meant doing too much paperwork.

"I told a policeman that I could describe both of the guys perfectly.

" 'Oh, well,' he said.

" 'I need you to file a report so that I can make an insurance claim.'

" 'Ah, right. Okay.'

"Reluctantly, he took a report. Then I said to him, 'Would that train station happen to have closed-circuit television cameras?'

" 'Oh, right. That sounds like an idea,' the policeman said. "So he got on a telephone, talking for a minute or two, and then carried on with the report.

"Soon the phone rang with someone calling back from the train station to say, yes, their surveillance cameras had captured images of those two guys.

"I said, 'Well, good then.'

" 'No, not really,' the policeman replied.

" 'Why not?'

" 'We would have to make an application to a court to view those tapes because doing so entails an invasion of the criminals' privacy. The amount of paperwork involved for us is not even close to being worth it. In reality, all that the thieves will do is take your laptop, sell it for a few bucks and then throw everything else into the canal. For us, it just would create mountains and mountains of futile paperwork.'

"So nothing at all was done about the crime, and I was not encouraged to specify that the two culprits were of

North African appearance. That would have been unfair, but apparently it was alright for them to steal my luggage and get away with it."

'Help, Help, Help'

An old saying goes, "When life gives you lemons (unpleasant experiences), make lemonade." In that spirit, Colin reacted to the train-station robbery by developing a new product, an alarm system for hand luggage. It gives him potential revenge on the two thieves in Amsterdam and all others engaged in similar misdeeds.

"The alarm works a little like many modern cars do. When a person walks up to his car, it knows that he is there and opens up because the driver carries a little sensor in his pocket.

"People in Shenzhen are making a small device for me that can be locked inside of your hand luggage. It has a loudspeaker that goes off at up to 95 decibels, and boy, that sounds loud. This is not for big suitcases. Nobody steals those. Instead, they want the hand luggage with valuables inside.

"Once the device goes into hand luggage, then the traveler keeps a sensor around his neck, on a key-chain or in a pocket. Nothing happens unless the luggage moves more than a few metres away. Then the moment when it does, the luggage starts to scream, 'Help, help, help,' at up to 95 decibels and will not stop. Most thieves in any country immediately will drop such a noisy prize."

The new product has potential value even beyond travel situations. "The ladies who buy handbags costing thousands of dollars – you see them hanging onto them all the time – can put the same device into their handbags for daily use. You also can use it as a personal alarm when jogging, for children or for anything that you want to keep close to you."

Boy Entrepreneur at Work

Colin lives in the Gold Coast in Queensland, Australia. He has travelled far since his birth in the village of Danderhall, just south of Edinburgh, Scotland.

Never idle, he went into business as a boy. "I started my first enterprise when I was 11 years old," he said. "For that, I had to employ a driver, being too young to drive a truck myself. I had a sawmill contract to take away the leftover pieces of wood. I paid a driver to take me there. We loaded the truck with all the bits of wood and took them home. There, I paid somebody to help me to saw them up and then go around to all the doors selling the wood, in recycled potato sacks, as firewood. After that, we got the truck back and made all of our deliveries."

Actually, Colin had tried to enter business earlier. "When I was even younger, I pleaded with my parents that I wanted a phonograph," Colin said. "They bought me one with a handle on the side that needed turning.

"But I got into big trouble. The only reason that I had wanted the phonograph was so that I could set up at a bus-stop playing records (music), with my cap (hat) placed alongside so that people would give me coins. My parents got a bit upset about that scheme – me begging on the street – but actually I did not beg. I offered a valid service. People could enjoy the music while standing at the bus-stop."

An irrepressible entrepreneur, Colin launched his first "proper business", a mobile fish-and-chips restaurant, at age 19. His diverse career in Scotland even included a stint as a mink farmer.

"I carried on with the fish-and-chips business until I was about 26 years old," he said. "After selling it, I went into partnership with a guy whose father had died, leaving him with a mink farm. That diversified into pet-food manufacturing and working as a fallen-livestock contractor."

'Truth' About Scotland... and England

As a young man, Colin's attitude toward Scotland's neighbor, England, hardened after he read the work of **John Prebble**, a Canadian novelist-historian who focused on Scottish history. Prebble's 1963 book, *The Highland Clearances,* depicts violent and unjust past efforts to remove Scottish people from their homes and land.

"I got very angry that the English had misled the whole Scottish population for a long time," Colin said. "Next I started to investigate all of the discrepancies and untruths in what the Scottish people had been told and how they had been manipulated. What the British government had done appeared to be quite extensive."

Indignantly, Colin took a critical look at British politics. "The Scots always were outnumbered in the British Parliament. It really operates as the English Parliament. The way it got manipulated for years was to denigrate the Scots.

"The English showed a tremendous talent to exploit the Scots, just as they did to the people everywhere that they colonized, including in the U.S., Canada and India. The Americans stood up for themselves very quickly. But in other places, like India, Burma and Hong Kong, the people just could not do that.

"The English always adopted the attitude that 'we are God's greatest'. Anyone coming from England could claim to be 'God's greatest', but if you were Scottish, then you were just a piece of non-entity. They treated the Scots like that even in normal television shows. If there was a play on TV, then all of the good guys were English, and all of the bad guys were Scots. That reached the stage that everyone in Scotland suffered from a gross inferiority complex."

No Brains to Run the Country?

Soon Colin "became something of a Scottish national political advocate". He joined the Scottish National Party (SNP), which demanded complete independence from Great Britain, and before long he led its local branch. When in his 20s, he contested elections for the British Parliament.

In those 1960s election campaigns, the Scottish inferiority complex worked against Colin and the SNP. "I would knock on doors and say, 'Hi, I am standing as a candidate for the Scottish National Party. Can we count on your vote?'

"The consistent answer came back: 'No, no, son. We have not got the brains to run this country.'

"Then I would say, 'But Scottish people have run Canada, the U.S., Australia, New Zealand and South Africa.'

" 'Ah, well, they were a wee bit different. We have no got the brains here.' "

Should God Save the Queen?

Even most history books showed a strong pro-English slant, which explains why Prebble's more forthright work had a big impact. "Until then, my parents, who were strong Scottish advocates, knew nothing at all about the highland clearances. After reading what Prebble wrote, my mother, **Bessie**, became an ardent Scottish nationalist. At age 68, she got evicted from a club in Glasgow for refusing to stand during the playing of 'God Save the Queen'.

"In the full and original words of 'God Save the Queen', one verse says 'God help us to oppress the rebellious Scots'. No one sings that part of the national anthem anymore, but my mother refused to accept it."

At the ballot boxes, the SNP faced persistent difficulties. "People did not want to vote Scottish National for three reasons," Colin said. "Firstly, we had only one member in

Parliament, and that was **Winifred Ewing**. Secondly, they had a gross inferiority complex, believing that Scotland and Scots were no good. Thirdly, they saw the SNP as being what they called 'tartan Tories'. Scotland is very left wing and full of working people. The Tories are right wing. Some propaganda had gotten out that we were right-wing Scottish extremists because we wanted to break away from England and from the EEC (European Economic Community)."

Clever politicians find ways to work past such obstacles. "I never even knew the word 'marketing' until I went to Australia," Colin said. Yet he and his SNP colleagues grasped for marketing solutions.

"We could not do much about the inferiority complex until more people got out of Scotland to learn differently for themselves. Since then, much of that process has happened."

Chairman Mao's Hat

As for the "tartan Tories" label, Colin tackled that dilemma personally. "I would stand at the election booth greeting people, and I had gotten myself one of those **Mao Tse-tung** hats. Chairman Mao, the leader of China then, always wore a special hat? So I did too.

"Some coal-miners would walk past, and I would say, 'Can I count on your votes, fellows?'

" 'No,' they would grumble.

"Then I would point to my head. 'Do you see this hat, comrades?'

" 'Yeah, what is that?'

" 'Did you notice my Mao Tse-tung hat, comrades?'

" 'Ah,' they would say. 'Right, Jimmy. Right, Jimmy.'

"Suddenly word started to spread on the streets that Colin Mackie was not right wing, but rather left wing instead, because he wore a Chairman Mao hat."

No Longer 'Extremist'

One problem remained. "How could we convince people that we were not extremists?" Colin said. "We had no money to advertise or for marketing campaigns."

A bold solution sprang to mind. "The best thing was to have another entity that was much more extreme than us. Then suddenly we stood almost in the middle, moderate nearly. So we invented an organization called the Scottish Liberation Army. There was no violence against anyone whatsoever. All that organization was created to do was to appear more extreme than the SNP."

Meanwhile, the sources of friction between Scotland and England multiplied. "Lots of Scottish oil was discovered in the North Sea," Colin said. "If Scotland had been an independent country, then it would have joined OPEC (the Middle East-dominated Organization of Petroleum Exporting Countries) because it produced 11 times more oil than its own requirements.

"Huge natural-gas reserves were found too. The authorities arranged to pipe the gas into Aberdeen and then all the way down, first of all, to Birmingham (England). They pumped Birmingham full of natural gas being sold there at half the price that people in Aberdeen were paying. From Birmingham, the natural gas was piped to Liverpool and then to London and all the rest of it. We were going to be lucky ever to get any. Definitely, we would get none until all of the people in England had all that they wanted."

The grievances continued. "Scotland produces hydro-electricity (from water-power) too, which initially costs nothing to make," Colin said. "That hydro-electricity gets put onto the national-grid system to cover all of Britain. But we paid more for electricity in Scotland than our English neighbors did. Our wages were lower, and we paid more for electricity, but our electricity cost nothing to make because it was hydro-electricity while in England, other electricity came from coal."

Plus "the British government built lots of motorways (big highways)," Colin said. "They had 1,000 miles of motorways in England, but not one mile in Scotland."

Fearing Arrest, Taking Flight

Nationalist activity intensified. Publicity-seeking efforts led to explosions rocking the natural-gas pipeline 13 times. "It was not me who did it," Colin said.

The British authorities alleged plots, illegal undertakings and dangers of lethal violence. Fearing arrest or worse personal consequences perhaps ordered by powerful people in London, Colin decided to flee from Scotland. "I had to get out," he said.

Seeking maximum safety, he left Europe entirely. Then 30 years old, he arrived in Australia. "I went to the Immigration authorities there and said that I wanted to stay, but they told me, 'No way, you have to go back to Scotland.' In those days, Australia only accepted people from certain trades, and I had no trade that the country wanted."

An Illegal Immigrant Expects the Worst

For Colin's first four years in Australia (starting in the mid-1970s), he lingered as an illegal immigrant. "I had gone to Australia on holiday and overstayed," he said. "But I kept getting job offers there."

In one early job in Australia, Colin worked as a clothing company's state manager. "That was fun and kept me fully occupied because everything was completely new to me so I had lots to learn," he said.

A crisis developed after Colin's work success led to promotions. "Then my employer wanted to send me overseas," he said. "When that happened, I got myself all geared up thinking that the Australian government finally would catch up with me and put me into some detention camp or other. In preparation, I told everyone at work that I planned to take a really long holiday.

"Incredibly, my wife and I walked into the Immigration office in Melbourne one day and went up to the reception desk there. Then I said to the lady behind the desk, 'Hi, I am what you would call an illegal immigrant, one who has stayed for the past four years in this country.'

"She went, 'Ohhh! Nobody ever has come in here and said that before. Let me see your passport.'

"So I gave her the passport, and she took it away with her for a few minutes. Then she returned, handed it back and said, 'Can you come back on Thursday? Nobody is here to see you right now.'

"Ha! I really had thought that they would lock me up.

"On the next Thursday, I went back to see a certain guy. After interviewing me, he said, 'The procedure goes like this. You must write a letter telling us exactly why you have overstayed. We will send that letter to the minister of immigration. Then he contacts the police to see if you have a police record. In this case, we also will check with Special Branch in Great Britain for anything on you there.'

"I replied, 'Well, I can tell you right now that Special Branch has a big file on me.'

" 'If so, you will not be allowed to stay in Australia,' the man said.

"So my wife and I went home and started to make serious arrangements to sell our house. Then before too long I received a letter saying that my application to stay in Australia had been accepted."

What miracle had achieved that surprise result? "Let me tell you," Colin said. "We went back to the Immigration office, and the man there said, 'Oh, yeah. Everything looks fine.' Then he started to stamp all of the paperwork, giving me permanent residency.

" 'The letter of explanation that you wrote was one of the finest that we ever have received,' he said. 'Everyone involved commented on it.'

"Under these favourable circumstances, I hesitated to raise the touchy issue of Special Branch in London. But just as my wife and I prepared to walk out the door, I mustered my courage and said, 'Oh, by the way, what happened with that Special Branch thing.'

" 'Well, come and have a look,' the man said.

"In his file, he showed me a photocopy of a letter from Special Branch saying, 'Yes, we have Mr. Mackie on file, but his activities always were of a pro-Scottish nature, and we do not believe that his history indicates he would pose any danger to Australia. If possible, we would prefer if Mr. Mackie stayed in Australia.' "

Place of No Pretension

For the three-and-a-half decades since then, "Australia has been really good to me," Colin said. "I have thoroughly enjoyed the place. It suits my personality. Above all, there is almost no pretension. In Britain, everything demands closed doors and clear distinctions between managers and employees. In Australia, things work much differently.

"My first job in Australia was with Stubbies (makers of 'fashion shorts'). As I walked down a corridor at my new workplace, a guy wearing a T-shirt, torn denim shorts and runners (sports shoes) said, 'Ah, good day, Colin. You will be the new salesman, right?'

"I replied: 'Yeah, yeah. How are you?' I thought he was a cleaner.

"Then when I got taken around on a tour through all of the offices, I met the same man again and learned that he really was the general manager. That reflects the unpretentious attitudes in Australia. The place has no class structure at all. Everybody is everybody.

"In contrast, Britain is all pretension. What made the Brits great for a long time was their enormous skill at convincing themselves that they were superior and letting everyone else believe the same thing. They did it brilliantly by wearing collars and neckties and addressing everyone as **Mr. Smith, Mr. Watt, Mr. Cairns** and **Mr. Mackie**. All of that created an ingenious structure that they thrived on and milked.

"But as much as I appreciate Australia, the situation there can be a negative in some ways too. Back home in Scotland, I (as an entrepreneur and a politician) got treated a little differently than most people. If I got stopped for speeding, the policeman then would apologize for stopping me. He would say, 'Oh, it is you, Mr. Mackie. You have a new car, I see. Do you realize that you were doing 100 in a 30-mile-per-hour limit?'

Is this a true incident? "Well, it happened at 2 o'clock in the morning," Colin said.

"Then the policeman told me, 'It is okay, Mr. Mackie. We know how it goes with a new car. You can continue on your way now.'

"You get no such behavior in Australia."

Colin has two Australia-born children, a daughter, **Elshonner**, who handles publicity for an insurance company, and a son **Mannan** (named for the Celtic god of the sea), an information-technology specialist. Two older children, both daughters, live in Scotland.

When Colin's travels sometimes take him back to Scotland, he feels nostalgia and a sense of history, but no inclination to stay. He never will return there to live.

"On occasions when I go back to Scotland, I feel that

the people and the place are a drab gray. The class structure remains. Everything is contrived. All of the problems that I disliked years ago still fester there."

Final Stop: Sandwood Bay

When Colin dies, the situation will change. Then he wants to return for a last time as ashes to be scattered into the wind on a beach at Sandwood Bay near Scotland's northwestern edge. "The weather gets really cold there, but my ashes will not mind the chill," he said.

Why Sandwood Bay? For sentimental reasons, Colin said. He enjoyed himself there in the past and remembers a remarkable beauty and a sense of closeness to nature. "You drive up, leave your car and walk over the mountains past some inland lochs (little lakes). Then you come to the ocean, and it looks absolutely beautiful there."

Lunatic Enough to Bungee Jump?

Back to the original question: is any thrill-seeker activity too risky for Colin to try it? The answer appears to be a firm "no". From sky-diving and white-water rafting, his attention shifts to bungee jumping.

"I want to try bungee jumping," Colin said. "The idea has terrified me for a long time, and it refuses to stop bouncing around in my head. I always think, 'you would have to be a lunatic to do that'. So I am going to try it. I have made up my mind. I will go to New Zealand and do it."

What better way for a charming and adrenalin-fueled "lunatic" to celebrate another birthday?

NEARLY DROWNED BY TAX DEBT, BUOYANT BUSINESSMAN BOBS TO THE SURFACE OVERSEAS

Paul Watt Sees His Career Rise, Fall, Rise Again

Editor's Note: *Businessman Paul Watt has seen his fortunes surge and plunge several times. By necessity, he learned that making the right move can mean surrendering all the trappings of wealth, even a prized Rolls-Royce convertible, to start again where a different flag flies. Reduced to selling wristwatches on a cardboard box beside busy Asian streets, he realized that the only route ahead pointed upward again. Now after a five-decade business career, much of it on the move, he also has learned something even more profound – that the best motive for wheeling-and-dealing relates mainly to other people.*

ON AN ORIGINAL CHINESE JUNK – When multinational entrepreneur **Paul Watt** stands on the deck of an iconic and much-photographed Chinese junk, the *Duk Ling*, which he substantially owns, he has much to contemplate. The world-famous boat glides across Hong Kong's impressive Victoria Harbor much more smoothly than Paul's career path has progressed.

Already beyond the age when most folks retire from the work-a-day world, the Australia-born Paul continues to chase business deals. Along with the *Duk Ling*, which sails on regular tours and charters, Paul operates The Junk Pub, a small bar on Jaffe Road in Hong Kong's busy Wanchai District. He leads both enterprises with help from business colleagues like **Geoffrey Dart, John May** and others. Lately, Paul also directs the Power Publishing Club, the first book from which anyone reading this most likely holds firmly in both hands.

"Normally, I maintain offices and apartments in three or four cities or countries," Paul said. "I kind of live around." For eight years, he, plus **Emma** and their children, **Pauline** and **Bella**, kept an apartment in Shanghai as their family home.

Several times, Paul's fortunes and prospects suddenly plunged, almost like an attempted-murder victim tossed overboard from a yacht without a lifejacket, unable to swim and with a cement slab tied to his ankles. Indeed, Paul's career once took nasty one-after-another pushes into a sea of destruction from two would-be assassins – a faltering economy and Australia's tax authorities.

Property Magnate Prospers...

Raised on a farm in Duck Creek, near the village of Old Bonalbo in New South Wales, Australia, Paul transformed into a successful property developer, mostly on the Gold Coast. "By my early 40s, I had been flying high, having bought, sold and often developed about 300 properties," he said. "The property market boomed, and I also participated in three stock-exchange listings as the creator and major shareholder. I owned a beautiful deep-waterfront house with a swimming pool and a series of four Rolls-Royce cars, including a convertible that my girlfriends used to like."

...Then Meets the Forces of Doom

In the late 1980s, events took a dramatic wrong turn. "The property market crashed, closely followed by the stock-market crash of 1988-89, after which almost everything halted," Paul said. "It did not matter what you had been doing – at that point, you could do nothing more.

"**Bob Hawke** and **Paul Keating**, two staunch Labor politicians, firmly controlled the nation as it swirled down the shit-hole – to put it mildly. Those were bad times in Australia. The Labor Party stayed in control for nearly the next decade, and the country advanced not one inch in all of that time.

"Taxes induced my departure from the country," Paul Watt said. "My Brisbane lawyer at the time, **Quentin George**, had arranged for a meeting at the Australian tax office. At 2:30 on a Friday afternoon, we turned up there. Quinton had advised me to show protocol and dress down so we did that. I did not even wear a wristwatch.

"We attended the meeting, which lasted for no more than 15 minutes. As we walked out, Quentin asked me, 'What did you think of that?'

"I said, 'Well, I feel really sorry for those taxation people.'

" 'What do you mean?'

" 'Those miserable women we just met look bureaucratic, middle-aged and like they never even had boyfriends. Why would anyone want to look so miserable? I wonder if they even know how to smile.'

"My lawyer said, 'Hang on for a moment, Paul. Do

you understand what just happened at the meeting?'

" 'Yes. They will bankrupt me.'

" 'True,' he said. 'They refuse to allow you more time to pay.'

Joe Cool Vanishes in a Big Crash

"So I had gone from flying high all the way down to bankruptcy, from being **'Joe Cool'** at the top of the economic heap to crashing hard at the bottom," Paul said.

"Remarkably, every second one of my mates (friends) was going bankrupt too. None of us could have foreseen what had happened to the country, and we had failed to make provisions for our tax liabilities. At that point, I owed Aus$550,000 (now about US$575,000), which, I suppose, represents a lot of money.

"My only creditor was the tax department, but I listed my mother as another one for Aus$1,000 so that any correspondence going out to 'the creditors' would come to my attention too. That way, we always knew what was happening."

No More 'Missing the Boat'

A few days after the disheartening tax-office meeting, Paul and his sister **Gail** made a previously planned business trip to Hong Kong. "While there, we stopped in a bar at what is now the InterContinental Hotel in Tsim Sha Tsui (on the Kowloon side of Victoria Harbor)," he said. "That was a fantastic place overlooking one of the world's most spectacular harbors. Well, I hardly could believe my eyes."

As Paul and Gail each had a drink, the Queen Elizabeth 2 (QE2), the planet's most famous ocean liner-cruise ship, glided past. "That was the biggest thing I ever had seen – and no more than 100 yards from where we sat," Paul said. "I felt like I almost could reach out and touch it.

"Then I told my sister, **'I have been missing the boat.'**

" 'How so?' she asked.

" 'Take a look at that!' I pointed to the window. 'By living in Australia, I have been missing the boat. I am going to leave Australia.'

" 'Really?'

" 'Yup'."

Operation Un-Bankrupt

Significantly, Paul also realized something else. "Another wonderful thing had happened too. In discussing my pending bankruptcy with my lawyer, it came up that the Australian bankruptcy laws apply only there. Although bankrupt in Australia, I was not bankrupt in any other country. Therefore, I felt free and decided to move overseas to un-bankrupt myself."

Leaving assets, business wreckage and the remains of bank accounts for his government-propelled creditor to seize, Paul departed ready to start over elsewhere. His next stop happened to be Taipei, the capital city of Taiwan.

Big Men Scramble at the Billionaires' Club

"Wow!" Paul said. "I met some people in Taiwan and learned that the place overflowed with money that investors, who had been released from restrictions in the late 1980s, wanted to move elsewhere – so they were buying up properties and investments all over the place. These guys were very rich. Clearly, they held lucrative interests in a lot of businesses.

"So I talked to them. The Taiwanese, then just learning to bring their money out to the world, did not always know exactly how most other countries worked. Their English sounded less than perfect. The group of guys I met, six or seven of them, invited me to join them as the international white face for their businesses. I was to become the senior executive helping to create an international company for them. They wanted to invest in property, hotels and golf courses. Certainly, they looked at Australia, America, Japan and everywhere. Asian companies starting to look overseas often liked to have a white face in there somewhere.

"We used to meet every day in Taipei, and it amazed me. These guys had plenty of money. With so many business plans, they would say: 'We are interested in this, that and all sorts of things.' But nothing sounded very specific. We ate big lunches in private dining rooms with money being no object. This happened six days a week. On every seventh day, I retired to my favorite little Japanese restaurant for a change.

"At night, we enjoyed grand dinners. Then four nights per week, we went either to the Millionaires' Club or the Billionaires' Club. All of this made an amazing experience for me. We scrambled as to how much money we could spend, and then the Taiwanese bosses scrambled to see who could pay the bill and be 'the big man'. If some of the bills approached the equivalent of US$10,000, no one saw that as a problem.

"Luckily, my role always was that of a guest. It never became my position or duty to pay. Despite my bankruptcy in Australia, things appeared to be going really well for me. I felt like I nearly had bounced right back to the top of the economic world. I thought, 'What a beautiful thing! This has been a lot of fun and not so difficult.' "

After three months of wining, dining, plotting and planning about future business investments, "we were about to start on everything. We had held meetings, meetings and meetings. With lots of potential projects set up, things looked remarkably good."

Back to the Bottom

For Paul and the "big-men" bosses, the situation appeared deceptively good. "One day we had another big luncheon meeting planned," Paul said. "This time the Taiwanese guys failed to turn up, and I sat there by myself for 90 minutes. Then finally one of their drivers, who spoke a little English, appeared.

"I said to him, 'Where are they?'

"He told me, 'They all have landed in jail.'

" 'All in jail? What?'

" 'Mr. Paul, do you really understand what they do?'

" 'No. I have no idea. They told me that they operate a lot of companies and many businesses.'

"Then he said, 'They have been running an underground bank.'

"Basically, that meant that they had operated a Ponzi scheme." (The masterminds of such illegal schemes lure investors with promised high returns, initially paid with the investors' own money or that of others joining later, not with valid business profits. Without ever-increasing numbers of investors, such arrangements soon collapse. They carry the name of **Charles Ponzi**, 1882-1949, an Italian-born conman once notorious in North America.)

Later Paul learned slightly more about his Taiwanese confreres. Reputedly, they had taken in "deposits" that totalled the equivalent of US$1.5 billion.

"There I was," Paul said. "I had gone from the top of the economic heap to the bottom, almost to the top again and then back down to the bottom."

Could Paul have faced arrest along with the others? "Not at all," he said. "I neither knew about, nor got mixed

Mr. Bean, watch this.
Laughter is the best medicine.
What? How did I get in this book?

up in the Ponzi activity. I just had listened to them talk about where to put the money and then offered my advice about that." With Paul's high hopes cruelly dashed, he asked the knowledgeable driver one more question. " 'When will they get out of jail?'

" 'It could be years.'

Lingering any longer in Taiwan made little sense. No longer so richly welcome at the Millionaires' Club or the Billionaires' Club, Paul opted to return to Hong Kong. There he began to wander the streets, wondering "what the hell to do".

Sidewalk Watches

On a crowded walkway in Hong Kong's Wanchai area, Paul noticed a young expatriate man selling wristwatches from the top of a big cardboard box covered by a towel. "He attracted no shortage of customers.

" 'What are you doing?' I asked him.

" 'Oh, I am a backpacker. I travel around the world, and this is how I survive – by selling watches. At night, I go to the street market in Mongkok (another neighborhood) and sell watches there too.'

" 'Where do you get the watches?'

" 'From **Philip Fung** down on Wing Kut Street.'

" 'Well, I could do that too.'

"So I went, found Philip and told him about my new plan. 'Yeah, okay,' he said. 'How many watches do you want to get you started?' "

Survival on a Cardboard Box

Did Paul's new work as a sidewalk vendor sound too small-time, hardly worth the effort, for a past high-roller? "I had to survive," he said. "It was about as far back to basics as a person could go."

Although initially lacking the money to source many wristwatches, Paul secured some and then set up his own cardboard box. "Selling them turned out to be easy," he said. "In those days, people thought about watches much like they do about mobile telephones today. They never could get enough of them.

"Within a week, I bumped into an American named **Bob Goodman**, a former deputy-governor of Nevada who had fallen upon hard times. He was in Hong Kong, and I explained to him what I was doing. I said, 'Bob, I need some capital.'

"He said, 'I need to earn some money.'

" 'I know.'

" 'All I have is US$1,000. What if I invest that much into your business?'

" 'Okay.'

"So he set up another cardboard box to sell wristwatches beside me. Then two of us were in the business.

"We worked for a couple of weeks and did pretty well. I remember Bob telling me, 'I never have struck on a business like this before, one where we sit down for breakfast every morning and have a daily-dividend policy.' We used to eat breakfast at a McDonald's fast-food restaurant. Being an American, Bob liked the ambience there."

As a seasoned three-week veteran of the watches business, Paul made a suggestion, " 'Bob, I think that we can expand this. What if we tried to sell corporate watches, ones with company logos on them? Look at how eagerly these people buy watches. With Hong Kong being a watch capital of the world, who would have thought that anyone could sell so many watches here? It's not so hard, is it?'

" 'Right you are,' Bob said."

Baby-Stroller: 'Blow Me Down!'

Next Paul placed a newspaper ad and recruited a product designer. "A young British man named **Ian Byland** turned up," he said. "I told him that we planned to set up an office and wanted him to join the company.

"So Ian had met a watch salesman on the street, and we negotiated in the cocktail bar at the Sheraton Hotel (on the Kowloon side of Hong Kong's harbor). Then we decided to travel together over to Hong Kong Island.

"About 10 years later, Ian finally told me exactly why he had agreed to join our unproven business. He said, 'As we descended the steps together into an underground-train station, we walked and talked, but suddenly you asked me to wait for a moment while you helped some lady to carry her baby-stroller, with a baby inside, down the steps. Then I figured that you must be a good guy. At that instant, I made my decision to join you.'

"When I heard that story from Ian, I thought, 'Blow me down. How can something so simple and normal have such an impact?' That small action affected plenty. After that, Ian became not only a business partner, but also one of my very best friends. Now he lives in London, and I never go there without seeing him and staying with him, his wife **Sophie** and their daughter **Coco**."

Bottoms Up!

From other sources, Paul garnered more help. "I went around Hong Kong telling people that I was setting up a watches company," he said. "The fact that I really had no idea about exactly how to do it hardly appeared to matter.

"At the Bottoms Up Club, a popular bar in Tsim Sha Tsui, I spoke to **Pat Sephton**, the manager there, and explained what I was doing," Paul said. (An appearance in a **James Bond** movie, *The Man With the Golden Gun*, released in 1974 and starring **Roger Moore**, made the Bottoms Up Club famous until its closure decades later.)

"When I mentioned to Pat that I needed some office space, she told me about one of her friends, an English guy, with a spare room in his office. That sounded good to me. Soon I talked to him and agreed that we would take the room.

"Next I met an English girl, **Sarah Arnold**, who told me about being unemployed. So I asked her, 'Why not come and work with us?' That gave us four people on the team. We established the office, and away we went into business. At first, we scratched along, just getting enough out of it to survive."

An Exclusive Group

By no coincidence, everyone joining Paul's fledgling enterprise came from far beyond Hong Kong. "Expatriates are almost like an exclusive club," he said. "We stick together and try to help each other. As an expat, you always can find great comradeship and enormous help from other expats.

"Being expatriates abroad makes us a minority group. When Asians enter Western countries, they like to stick together too. Sometimes the local people scold them for that, but we do exactly the same thing after arriving in Asia."

Where did Paul live early on in Hong Kong? "I moved around – here, there, in and out," he said. "For a while, I stayed in Chungking Mansions, which was pretty rough, about the lowest of the low-life places. It was not my cup of tea, but I was there purely for survival and economic reasons."(Chungking Mansions, a notorious low-rent complex on busy Nathan Road in Kowloon, attracts down-and-out folks. It provided the setting for *Chungking*

Express, a 1994 movie directed by **Wong Kar-wai** about lonely people in a crowded city. In supreme contrast, just a few short steps away and around one corner, pedestrians find the ultra-posh Peninsula Hotel, a refuge to the rich and famous, complete with a glittering fleet of 14 Rolls-Royce cars.)

Timely Business

The new watches enterprise, called Boss Control, gained traction. "Soon I started to travel and appoint overseas distributors," Paul said.

"We worked with several factories. The watches industry revolves around components. Some companies just make the dials, others just make the cases and likewise for all the bits and pieces. We found everything that we needed and started arranging to put the pieces together.

"Ian and I sat down together and worked out the numbers so that we knew the exact costs to make our watches. Unsure exactly what prices to set for selling them, we settled on a strategy of just doubling the production prices.

"But the real trick to the market was this. The Chinese suppliers work on selling volume and price. Suppose that you run a corporation and need 100 watches with your logo on them to give to customers and suppliers. The Chinese will do a great deal for you provided that you buy 1,000, but you only need 100. So we figured out how to manufacture just 100, or any quantity, at the best possible prices. By giving the customers exactly the quantities that they wanted, we could charge much more per unit than the Chinese did. That was a very straightforward thing."

As another strategic move, Paul approached almost everyone he deemed appropriate with whom Boss Control had a real or a potential business relationship. "I told them that our company policy required them to invest a small amount of money, maybe US$5,000 or more, with us," he said. "That way, I raised a little capital, and wow, we gained more momentum."

Soon substantial, the new company "took me to 50 countries, and I did business and appointed distributors in 43", Paul said. "We had offices in seven countries too. I acted as the front-man, and Ian ran the main office. Everything about it had grown from me just sitting on the street with a cardboard box and selling watches."

In the ensuing years, Boss Control turned into the largest licensee for Walt Disney watches bearing the images of **Mickey** and **Minnie Mouse**, **Donald** and **Daisy Duck** and the two dogs, **Goofy** and **Pluto**. One 16-month period saw the company sell 2.3 million watches in Thailand alone. As another achievement, "Our largest single order was to make one million watches in one go for Coca-Cola, the soft-drinks company," Paul said. "We turned a profit from that order of about US$300,000."

Could one factory handle such a large order? "Yes, it can be amazing how the factories in China operate. Each watch contained 27 moving parts. The factory started with 27 million little pieces and put them all together, 27 at a time, one million times.

"We also made calls around the world, saying: 'We are doing a big order for your company here. Would you like some watches too?' Then we did watches for Coke in another seven countries from New Zealand to Russia."

Paul, the bounce-back businessman, had regained a prized perch high on the economic ladder. "Visiting 50 countries and doing business in 43 represents one hell of a long journey from Duck Creek, Australia, where I grew up milking cows, feeding pigs and riding ponies with my best mate, **Chris Henning**, on our 600-acre family farm," he said.

Camels, Disguised Beer and Poppy Fields

One memorable business trip (circa 1993) took Paul to Pakistan. "I went there with **Lloyd Worland**, who used to work for me," he said. "We did marketing research on Pakistan, India, Sri Lanka, Bangladesh and the Maldives. For a week, we stayed in Pakistan. I always remember riding on camels across the beach in Karachi (Pakistan's largest city, population 25 million). People there dressed the camels to look spectacular in robes, drapes and tassels."

Despite having fun among the camels, these visiting businessmen grappled with a serious concern. "With Pakistan being an Islamic state, most people there do not drink alcoholic beverages," Paul said. "Naturally, Lloyd and I, being Australians, needed a few beers at times. But at first we were told that the country was 'dry' and that no one had any beer to sell to us.

"But a procedure existed. We discovered that Pakistan really has one of the best beers in the world. It comes from a company called the Murree Brewery." (Established in 1860 to satisfy the thirst of British drinkers near a resort site called Murree, this brewery cannot legally sell overseas due to a Pakistan ban on exporting alcoholic drinks.)

"No one was allowed to drink beer in restaurants, and the five-star hotel where we stayed had no bar. But we could order Murree beer in our hotel room, and the staff billed it as something else, maybe fish and chips. The beer arrived, delivered to our room, heavily disguised in black, plastic trash-bags. So we ended up with all the beer that we wanted to drink from the Murree Brewery, which apparently has non-Muslin ownership. It is a mega-brewery and an icon for Pakistan."

Then Paul and Lloyd continued to Lahore, Pakistan's second-largest city (with 11 million people), followed by Islamabad, the national capital (1.2 million people). "One day, we sat in a cab for a few hours, going up north to the border with Afghanistan," Paul said. "We arrived at a place from where we could see across the border. This happened at a time when the Americans were involved there, allegedly as peacekeepers, but mainly backing the Taliban.

"I said to a guy at the border, 'What the hell is this constant commotion and warfare in Afghanistan all about?'

" 'Do you not know?' he said.

" 'No, tell me.'

"He said, 'The war is about the tribes in Afghanistan fighting for control of the poppy fields.' Poppies (used to make opium) are the country's leading industry.

"Since the Americans were there, huffing and puffing as they normally do, I also talked to some of them and asked, 'What are you boys achieving?'

" 'Nothing,' they said. 'We stay busy wasting our time.'

"Ironically, Americans probably rank as the world's biggest users of illicit drugs like the opium that comes from those poppies."

China's Topless Restaurant

Paul reckons that his greatest education came from "learning stuff along the way as I travelled through so many countries. It seems to me that the more of the world that we can see, the richer we become, even when bankrupt, which I may have been in Australia, but not in Asia. The richness that we achieve by travelling and by interacting with the people we meet really has no parallel. The guys featured in different chapters of this book represent only some examples, a few of the friends I have made. Our backgrounds all are so incredibly different yet we form strong friendships because we all travel."

One of Paul's friends, a Hong Kong stockbroker named **David Williamson**, "a Scottish chap", contributed to that "education" with a weekend invitation to visit his three-storey home, part of a gated estate, near Zhuhai on the Chinese mainland. The journey there from Hong Kong took about an hour by ferry.

"At David's home, he asked where we should go for dinner," Paul said. "Since I did not know the Zhuhai area very well, I suggested that he recommend somewhere."

" 'I know of a great topless restaurant just down the road,' David said. "Shall we go there?'

"So I said, 'Well, mate. With you being the host, it's your call.'

"We arrived at the place, a very nice, big restaurant. The dinner tasted terrific, and a Filipino band played. But I saw no topless women anywhere so I wondered what in the hell David had been talking about.

"At nine o'clock, just as we finished our meals, the whole place came to a halt. Then drums rolled, loud music started and people began to march around, almost as if they starred in an MGM Hollywood production. Astonished, I wondered, 'What is happening here?' By then, I fully expected dozens of topless girls to jump out of cakes or to come running from somewhere.

"Then the roof came off the place. The restaurant had a retractable roof that simply rolled back, like the roof on my Rolls-Royce Corniche (convertible luxury car) used to do back in Australia. Suddenly, we saw the stars in the sky above us. That explained the 'topless' restaurant.

"Of course, David burst out laughing. The whole restaurant visit had been a complete joke. To top it all off, he enjoyed the prank so much that he even paid the bill, despite being Scottish. You know how mean that they supposedly are!

"There and then, I told David: 'I will get you back 10-fold for this little incident.' I have not done so yet, but the task remains highlighted in my diary."

Editor's Note: *After deciding to publish this book, Paul stipulated early on that no one featured in it could tell girlie-bar (or girlie-restaurant) stories. Then he brazenly broke the rule himself. Only the publisher could have gotten away with that stunt.*

Gambling Profits

Among Paul's best buddies, he also lists **Dr. Cecil Chan**, his Hong Kong doctor and mate, "a nice fellow who runs a one-man medical practice". In 2008, Paul consulted Dr. Chan about a minor medical complaint. Then they discussed gambling and why so many Chinese people constantly wager away their hard-earned money.

" 'You Chinese appear to be just hopeless,' I told him. 'You cannot help but gamble.'

"He said, 'True, we are a gambling people.'

" 'As a special favour then, I will tell you exactly how to make big money from gambling.'

" 'Really? You can do that?'

" 'I sure can. Now listen closely. At every casino in Macau and everywhere else, the gambling house gets a percentage of the turnover and always wins. The gamblers always lose.'

" 'Yes?'

" 'The tycoons who run the casinos, **Steve Wynn, Sheldon Adelson, James Packer, Stanley Ho** and all the others, know exactly how the games of chance are slanted. So they always get richer, and the gamblers go tumbling in the opposite direction.'

" 'But how can I make money from gambling?'

" 'Let me tell you. Right now, the stock markets have crashed. The shares in the Macau casinos have bitten the dust. Buy those shares and do not gamble.'

"A few days later, Dr. Chan telephoned me, saying, 'Mr. Paul, the next time when you pass by my office, would you mind to pop inside? I need to talk to you just a little more.'

"When I visited his office, he sat me down and said, 'After hearing your advice, I called a family meeting, and everyone agreed that maybe you are right. But please tell me the risk factor in buying a lot of casino shares.'

" 'Alright,' I said. 'The risk factor is that some clever doctor like you may invent a serum to inject and change the DNA of Chinese people to stop them from gambling.'

"Dr. Chan said, 'You are right. It's in our DNA. We cannot help ourselves. Chinese people always crowd into every casino in the world.' So we shared a good laugh and agreed to meet again soon, the next time for beers.

"Now, four years later, the shares in Macau's casinos have increased by 500 to 1,000 per cent. I bought some and sold them away too early. Although I had analysed correctly, I failed to fully practice what I cleverly preached. But I would bet that Dr. Chan and his family still have their shares, and so the student probably has prospered much better than his know-it-all teacher did."

'Don't Know Much of Anything'

From Paul's memories of every country where he has gone, he can mention some unforgettable moments. "When I reached Vietnam for the first time, it turned into an amazing experience. Even as I rode from the airport into Ho Chi Minh City, I thought, 'This place got bombed constantly in the Vietnam War. The people here have had terrible headaches and heartaches, but what a wonderful-looking country!' Of course, Vietnam also has a history as a former French colony with French-looking buildings and plenty of beautiful French bread. The people are so friendly too. Wow! I liked the place and its people.

"There in Vietnam, I recognized for the first time that the more I travelled, the more I understood how little that I really knew. I realized, 'Actually I do not know much of anything about anywhere.' " Definitely, no one even begins to truly comprehend a place without going there, looking around and talking to some of the local people.

An Honest Kiwi Speaks

As a gregarious expatriate, Paul never limits his conversations to locals. "At an Irish bar in Macau, I once met an honest Kiwi (New Zealander)," he said. "I asked him, 'Mate, how do you guys in New Zealand cope with the ongoing invasion of your country by Chinese immigrants?'

"He said, 'We hate 'em.'

" 'Why?'

" 'Let me explain what they do to our country. They come in and work. Can you believe it? Then to add insult to injury, they build up businesses and try to employ people so that more New Zealanders need to work too. It looks hopeless and so devastating.'

" 'Unbelievable,' I said.

" 'You probably know what I mean with Australia being so similar,' he said. "We have developed a culture going back for generations whereby we never need to work. The government pays us not to work. So when misguided people come into our country, work and then try to make us work, we hate 'em.'

"Guess what we did after discussing this problem," Paul said. "We shared a big belly laugh and then a few more beers."

Famous Faces Seen in Passing

When on the move or amid the passing crowds in Asia, Paul sometimes has encountered astonishingly familiar faces, those of past, present or future world leaders. Usually such people behaved amiably enough.

"On our flight to Pakistan, Lloyd and I flew in the airplane's first-class section," Paul said. "We stretched out and relaxed at the front of the aircraft. Directly across from us sat **Jiang Zemin.**" (Then a leading Communist Party of China official, a powerful Politburo member, Jiang soon after became China's president, a position he held from 1993 until 2003. Capable of expressing himself in several languages, including English, Jiang usually wore prominent eyeglasses that sometimes made him resemble an angry-looking owl.)

"Jiang had no security guards with him. It was just him and his wife, **Wang Yeping.** So we showed him our Mickey Mouse watches and told him all about what we were doing in Asia. He seemed like a happy guy, very smiley and extremely polite toward us.

" 'This sounds very good to hear," Jiang told us. 'In China, we want all sorts of Western people to come into the country so that they can work with us and help us to develop our economy.'

"There he was, chatting away with us. Unfortunately for Lloyd and me, this happened in the days long before we carried cameras on our belts so we got no pictures with the guy."

On another occasion, Paul walked down a Hong Kong street in the early 1990s "when coming in the opposite direction, I spotted **Henry Kissinger**". (Born in 1923, Kissinger had been a supreme diplomat. In the 1970s, he served as the United States government's secretary of state and a national security advisor.)

"Kissinger had no security guards either," Paul said. "When he noticed me, the only white face visible in the crowd, he walked up and shook one of my hands, saying, 'Hi, how are you doing?' He spoke to me like I was a long-lost friend."

Soon after that, Paul also encountered Kissinger's notorious former boss, the past American president **Richard Nixon**. (His country's 37th president, Nixon took office in 1969 and won re-election in 1972, but resigned two years later to avoid probable impeachment after being badly tainted in the Watergate scandal involving political dirty tricks. He died in 1994.)

"As I walked past the Mandarin Hotel (in Hong Kong's Central District), Nixon came out of the building," Paul said. "He waved and shook hands with me too. I was formally dressed, and maybe he believed that he should have recognized me from somewhere.

"As best I could tell, Nixon had about two security guards tagging along. These days, leading American political figures have so many security people. But then, Kissinger had none and Nixon had only about two."

Midnight Safety

On the subject of security, Paul appreciates that in much of Asia, personal safety seldom falls into peril. "Japan, South Korea, Taiwan, Hong Kong, Singapore and most of China all are incredibly safe places. In any of them, it usually feels like a pleasure to be there. On the underground-train systems, your wife, girlfriend, mum or daughter, even alone at midnight, will be perfectly safe. Elsewhere, like in Australia, the United States and Britain, you never would dare to allow any woman to take a train alone late at night because of the crime-related risks. That makes a sad indictment of society in those countries.

"One reason for the difference is that these Asian jurisdictions have no unemployment industry. In most of the Western countries, being unemployed activates a big industry. The more that the governments hand out jobless benefits, the more unemployment they have. Since Asian countries give no similar benefits, they have much less idleness. Unlike in the West, nearly everyone in Asia stays busy working and trying to earn money – too busy to terrorize train passengers."

'Something Important'

One way or another, Paul has conducted business for 50 years. "The only job that I ever did when I had to work for someone else was as a trainee hotel manager for about two years when I was a kid," he said. "I never continued on into hotel management because I knew that I could earn more money elsewhere."

Wiser and more open-minded due to expatriate experiences, Paul believes that he has become a better person than the Rolls-Royce collector who went bankrupt in Australia ever was. "My life has moved on," he said. "I really have discovered something important in life – that making people happy can bring a huge sense of satisfaction."

Indeed, "making people happy is what life is all about. The two businesses that I have pursued the most in recent years, the *Duk Ling* and the Junk Pub, both in Hong Kong, have contributed to more happiness for other people than anything else that I ever did in all of my years of business."

Pictures of the *Duk Ling* (meaning "clever duck"), the last original Chinese junk seen in Hong Kong's harbor, appear in magazines, tourism brochures and photo albums worldwide. People enjoy seeing such a remarkable vessel.

If they ride across the water onboard as its three batwing sails billow, then they never forget the experience.

The boat carries up to 40 people, including its five crew members. Famous musicians in the bands Oasis and Green Day have been among the passengers.

"Films and documentaries feature the *Duk Ling* at least once per month," Paul said. "It's a 60-foot, traditional Chinese junk built in Macau as a fishing boat in 1955. Although made from timber, it contains nearly no nails. Little pegs and joints hold it together."

Found derelict in the 1980s, the Duk Ling received an extensive restoration. Two expatriates led the meticulous work, namely **Pierre Couderc,** a French adventurer then in Asia and now living in Chile, and **Alain Zaugg,** a Swiss man-of-the-world since settled in Malaysia. Later, Pierre sold the junk to an enterprise led by Paul on the understanding that he too must treat the precious vessel with respect and maintain it diligently.

"In the 1940s and 1950s, these boats filled Hong Kong's harbor," Paul said. "Now there is basically one left."

Meanwhile, the Junk Pub has thrived, largely thanks to the competence of its past and present managers, including **Mercy Mantala, Maggie Cablayan** and **Lucy Hubahib.** The pub "is a very small space, only 500 square feet, no bigger than most overseas people's lounge rooms. It has a license for 25 people, including a staff of four. At the most, we can have just 21 customers at a time. We serve no food, but our jukebox plays 30,000 songs. The people going there come from hugely diversified cultures and backgrounds. They enjoy laughing and joking. Leading busy executive lives, as they do, they really need a special place to relax, meet with mates and enjoy some beer."

Too Many Miserable People

Paul's learned-on-the-road-of-life approach and his realization that the best business motive is to bring happiness to others make a stark contrast to the attitudes of many business people, those who focus strictly on their own interests. They may insist: "My actions represent business only, nothing personal." Former German leader **Adolph Hitler** (1889-1945) could have said much the same to the internees at his Second World War death camps.

On the other hand, Paul declares that no proper excuses exist to deliberately hurt people, not even for business reasons. "As far as I am concerned, the future situation is that I will not do business, or go into any venture, unless I believe that it will make people happy. Putting smiles on people's faces is a mission that I want to accept.

"The world has too many miserable people, and laughter makes the best medicine. If everyone woke up each morning and thought first of all about how to make 10 other people laugh that day, then the planet would be a better place."

For that reason, Paul greatly admires people who are willing to go all-out in pursuit of laughter. So he describes himself as a huge fan of **Mr. Bean,** a comedic character, kind of like a child living in a grown man's body, played to near-perfection by British actor **Rowan Atkinson.**

As for Australia, where Paul's initial business career rose and fell, he still feels an attachment, but not a deep or profound one. "I still go back there to visit regularly," he joked. "Last year I went for the first time in 12 years."

However, he vows to spend more time in Australia in the future. "I want to go there more often to see my son, **Jason,** his wife **Sharon,** and their children, **Matilda** and **Bonnie.**"

In that case, will Paul return "down under" to live someday? "Never! Of course not," he scoffed, wearing no trace of any smile.

Final Anecdote: After many years away from the wristwatches business, Paul recently visited the Hana Electronic Company, one of his long-ago suppliers. "I wanted to introduce some people who needed watches," he said.

"Seeing my old mate **Winson Chau,** the company's marketing sales manager, I asked him, 'How has your business been going?'

" 'Pretty good,' he replied. Then he showed me his best-selling product.

"I looked at it, and said, 'That looks very ordinary. Why would anyone buy that?'

" 'It has a special timer,' Winson said.

" 'That sounds simple enough. What kind of a timer?'

" 'Parents put the watches on their children, who otherwise stay so busy and focused on playing with video games and computers that they forget to go to the bathroom. The timer reminds the children to take breaks for their bodily functions.'

"I said, 'You must be joking.'

" 'No joke! We have sold hundreds of thousands of these,' Winson said.

" 'What person came up with this idea? Who is your customer?'

" 'Mr. Paul, the guy works as a doctor, but now he has entered the watches business too trying to solve the toilet-break problem that so many of his patients mentioned to him.'

"What an amazing and funny thing – a watch designed to remind children to go and take a shit!" Paul said. "The moral of this story is that no one ever can be certain of what the next big-idea product will be or where it will originate."

RAINE ON THE WAY: PILOT RON GUIDES PLANES FULL OF PACKAGES

Once a Potential Preacher, Ron Raine Retires to 'the Bars'

Editor's Note: *After 43 years as a pilot, notably with United Parcel Service (UPS), Ron Raine, a much-travelled American, plans to settle down to manage two bars that he owns in the Philippines. Here he discusses the joys of living out of a suitcase, the past challenges that he has faced and those still ahead. He even confesses to once studying to become a Christian preacher, quite a strange admission from the proprietor of two raucous Asian drinking establishments.*

IN THE SKIES–Although a self-described "vagabond", **Ron Raine** has shown a few distinct similarities to **Santa Claus.** Like the famous Father Christmas, Ron has white-hair, a rather jovial nature and a long-time habit of flying vast distances to deliver packages. Indeed, Santa, who soars on delivery missions during just one night per year, could take lessons from 65-year-old Ron, an American who has travelled steadily for decades.

A long-time pilot with United Parcel Service (UPS), Ron spoke to *All Aboard! Planet Expat* just two weeks before he retired with plans to settle down and actively manage The Lollipop and Treasure Island, two bars that he owns in Angeles City, the Philippines. Technically, Ron lives there in the Philippines, but he also shares a flat with a friend in Singapore.

A Real Home in Travel Pro City

"I always seem to be moving," Ron said. "My real home has been in Travel Pro City. That's my suitcase. People liked to laugh at me for dragging along a big load of luggage, but I told them, 'Knock it off. This is my mobile home.' "

Flying often from the Arctic to near the equator means passing from one weather extreme to another. Planes usually handle the variations better than pilots do. "Going from a place like Alaska to one like Singapore explains why I always brought along so much baggage," Ron said. "I can get sick easily, being susceptible to respiratory problems when exposed to the cold too much. In the winter, Alaska is not my favorite place."

Ron's final UPS flight, landing at 1 a.m. Eastern Daylight Time on June 9, 2012, took him on a familiar route from Anchorage, Alaska, to Louisville, Kentucky. Typically, each plane that he guided carried thousands of envelopes full of business documents ("they weigh very little – a plane can carry lots") and boxes or crates with diverse contents.

"One thing that always blew people away was when they asked for my personal details," Ron said. "They would say, 'Tell us your address.' So I would mention a mailing address in Anchorage, Alaska, where I started most of my trips.

"Then they would said, 'Oh, so you live in Alaska?'

" 'No, I just get my mail there.'

" 'Oh! What about your phone number?'

"Then I would give that, with a 909 area code.

" 'Ah, southern California.'

" 'Yes, that is my cell-phone number.'

"Finally they would ask for my driver's license, which comes from Florida."

"As they would stare at the license in disbelief, I would say, 'I work as a pilot.'

"And then the person asking the questions would go, 'Oh, okay!' "

Routinely, Ron visited certain cities: Tokyo and Osaka, Japan; Taipei, Taiwan; Incheon, South Korea; Hong Kong; Singapore; Kuala Lumpur and Penang, Malaysia; and Shenzhen, Shanghai and Qingdao on the Chinese mainland.

Despite being unsure exactly how many thousands of flights he has guided, Ron cites one reliable statistic. "I have spent well over 20,000 hours in the air," he said.

Less frequent routes took him to Mexico, Europe (notably Cologne, Germany; and Madrid, Spain), the Middle East (Dubai, United Arab Emirates) and Australia (Sydney). He never flew into India, South America or Africa.

"Dubai has a big airport," Ron said, "but the city failed to impress me. Mind you, its tall buildings and its reclaimed land that forms islands in the shape of ornamental designs are interesting."

Big Bucks to Buy a Beer

Trying to quench a powerful thirst in Dubai always annoyed Ron big-time. "I dislike needing to pay the equivalent of US$10 just for a beer," he said. In Ron's bars in the Philippines, a beer costs just 50-85 pesos (US$1.20-2.00).

Even the beer prices in high-cost Tokyo frazzle Ron less than those in Dubai do. "I know where to find beer cheaper in Tokyo," he said. "When I often went there and stayed at the Radisson Hotel Narita, the beer-vending machines on nearly every floor of the hotel all would sell me an ice-cold Kirin Ichiban for 300 yen (about US$3.50)."

'Anywhere Can Feel Like Home'

At ground level, Ron enjoys mingling with people from different cultures. "I have seen for myself that highly advanced cultures exist in many countries other than just the United States of America," he said. "Sadly, many Americans lack global understanding because they never travel much beyond our own country. That is partly because the U.S. is such a great, huge, wonderful and beautiful country that they hardly need to go elsewhere. But guess what? Travelling widely has broadened my horizons, helped me to understand other people and cultures and revealed different sides of arguments. I learned to appreciate all of the differences, ate great food and enjoyed meeting nice people almost everywhere.

"No matter where I go, I find a way to fit in," Ron confided. "I find what I like, and then enjoy myself. Always, I try to meet and get to know some local people. Everywhere in the world, the people make places special.

"Going to new places and just taking cookie-cutter tours, staring out of bus windows, hardly beats watching a travelogue movie. Getting to know people better is what turns the key to happiness. A family makes being at home special. The friends you meet on the road make travelling special. Once I know some local people and they start to show me the ropes, then I can enjoy every city or country for what it has to offer. Anywhere can feel like home."

Not every pilot takes the same approach. "Many of them stay very conservative in their views," Ron said. "They tend to always go out in groups to eat meals or to shop together, hanging out only with other Americans. They will want to eat at an Irish pub or even a McDonald's -- God forbid – instead of simply grabbing some chopsticks and having good Chinese food with noodles or rice.

"Even worse, there are those we call the 'slam-clickers'. Their hotel-room doors slam, you hear them click the locks and then you never see them again until they return to work. They sit in their rooms, living in their own little worlds. What a waste! What a shame!"

Singapore: the Most Beautiful Place

Asked to name his favorite city, Ron promptly makes an enthusiastic choice. "My favorite city in the world, the most beautiful place that I have seen, is Singapore," he said. "Not only picturesque, it happens to be well run too. People there really have their game on, and everything works smoothly like it should, as if all designed to fit perfectly together. If I could afford to retire to Singapore, then I would, but I do not believe that I can. It really caters mainly to the wealthy of the world. I like to think of it as an idyllic Honolulu of Asia. Singapore makes a big contrast to Hong Kong, another one of my favorite ports of call. But to me, Hong Kong more closely resembles the New York City of Asia." As for a least-favorite city, "I have none", Ron said. "For me, there is no worst place. Definitely, I love all of Asia."

CONTROL TOWER, MY PACKAGES AND I REQUEST PERMISSION TO LAND
HEY PACKAGES, ANY COMPLAINTS BACK THERE?

Follow the Golden Rule

Remarkably, Ron, who was born in St. Paul, Minnesota, once studied pre-theology at the University of Dubuque in Iowa. At the time, he yearned to become a Presbyterian minister preaching Christian gospel. Eventually, "I decided that I had lots of learning to do before I could give strong advice to other people," he said. "You can minister to people in many ways without being part of a church."

Wherever he goes, Ron still strives to apply "the golden rule" that he learned in church as a boy: "Do unto others as you would have them do unto you." Again and again, that maxim proves truly golden by helping him to make friends in disparate places.

Ron retains an "underlying" religious streak, "but it has gotten liberalized over the years. I no longer pound Bibles or point fingers like I once might have been inclined to do as a result of how I was raised. There are many different ways to do good things. Always being pontific does not necessarily carry out the work of any god."

A religious upbringing and early godly ambitions appear difficult to reconcile with owning two raucous drinking halls in the Philippines. "The irony is obvious," Ron said. "Let's just say that my thoughts, values and instincts have changed as I experienced more of life. I realized that I could do good anywhere and follow the same goals that I had as a young man in pre-theology in any walk of life by always trying to do the right things and by applying the golden rule. To me, providing jobs for poor people in the Philippines who want the work is not wrong."

On occasion, Ron's personal life has hit more turbulence than his sky-high career ever did. He married three times – at ages 28, 32 and 42 – and divorced three times. "Three strikes and you are out, so I am done," he joked.

His latest "big divorce" turned final in 2006. "I tell my friends that I worked a long time to give a woman who stayed with me for about 15 years half of everything that I earned," he said. "Then a stock-market crash took half of what remained, which explains why I now need to operate two bars in the Philippines."

With no biological children, Ron helped to nurture those born to his wives in their previous marriages. "Through the years, I had a hand in raising four children," he said.

For 24 years, Ron flew for UPS. Earlier, he served several regional passenger airlines. With the California-based Inland Empire Airlines in 1980, he co-piloted 19-passenger Metroliner (twin-engine turbo-prop) planes and earned just US$700 per month. After joining the rival Sun Aire Lines, he "made captain" and his monthly income reached $3,000.

In 1985, Ron switched to Orion Air, a cargo-carrier on contract with UPS. Three years later, he became a full-fledged UPS pilot. By the time that he retired, he sometimes earned more than 10-times his once-impressive salary with Sun Aire.

No Complaints! Boxes a Pleasure to Fly

After flying planes full of passengers early in his career and cargo later, Ron distinctly preferred the latter. "Over the years, I never received a single letter of complaint from any of my boxes," he said. "If passengers dislike a flight, they often write angry letters, and you definitely hear about it. After going to work for UPS, I received no such complaints. None!

"If the plane got a little too high, I could yank-and-bank a bit to fix the problem. You cannot do that with passengers in the back because they may get air-sick. None of my boxes ever did."

Therefore, "flying cargo really was much more fun, although you did miss the glamor of parading around in a spiffy uniform in front of the passengers. The packages never got impressed quite so easily."

A typical UPS crew consists of a pilot and a co-pilot. For eight-hour-plus flights, a third crew member joins to share the flying duties, allowing the others to take turns to rest. With no flight attendants, "You need to stand up and heat your own TV dinners in a small oven."

Ron's favorite planes are the Boeing 767s, "twin-engine wide-bodies" that he guided late in his career. "The maximum takeoff weight is 408,000 pounds for the plane and its cargo," he said. "The 767 is fun to fly, being smaller than a 747, but comfortably bigger than a 757." Invariably, he prefers Boeing aircraft, and so he quips: "If it is not Boeing, I am not going."

Instrument panels in the cockpits of large planes have plenty for pilots and co-pilots to watch. "Air-speed, altitude, attitude (meaning nose up or down, wings level or banked) and vertical speed – those are the big four instruments," Ron said. "Then the instrument panels show all sorts of peripheral information too. One nice thing about modern airplanes is that they consolidate much of the information on an enlarged screen, making the instruments bigger and so easier to scan and interpret."

As for perilous weather, "Thunderstorms pose the worst threat. Embedded thunderstorms are the worst form – you cannot see them because they are covered by regular clouds."

Foggy or stormy conditions seldom obscure landing visibility all the way to the ground. "Usually we can see the runway at least 500 feet before touchdown."

Although some reported sightings of unidentified flying objects (UFOs) come from pilots, Ron never once noticed flying saucers or anything inexplicable when cruising at altitude. "But I have seen satellites hurtling through space in the distance – and the international space station too, which looks quite magnificent moving slowly across the horizon. At altitude, it is much clearer and easier to see, but you still need to know where and when to look."

Minnesota Milk Cows, John Deere Machinery

Ron spent his youth immersed in small-town America. He grew up in Marshall, Minnesota, a "rural farming community" then with about 7,000 people. "I lived in the town, but my uncle operated a dairy farm just three miles away. I loved the farm and rode my bicycle to spend as much time there as I could. My cousin, who lived on the farm, and I often went fishing in a river or hunted for rabbits and squirrels. It was a great way to grow up."

For years, Ron's father worked as a mechanic at a John Deere machinery dealership, but later took the bold step of buying a restaurant. Many times after that, "he told me not to go into the restaurant business because you never own it – instead, it owns you, and you never can go anywhere," Ron said. "I listened to him about that.

"When I turned 18 years old, I left my home in Marshall and went off to college. I never really went back much, except for quick visits."

Probably Ron will not live full-time in the U.S. again unless his bar-room businesses in the Philippines fail badly. "Then likely I will retire in Florida," he said.

Accustomed to warm climates in the Philippines and Singapore, Ron shivers when recalling the chilly winters back in Minnesota. "My blood has thinned out. When living in Minnesota, I did not like the cold much, but at least I could handle it. Not anymore!"

The Vietnam War formed a sombre backdrop as

Ron became a pilot with the United States Marine Corps. He enlisted in 1969 and entered naval aviation training in Pensacola, Florida, before arriving in 1971 at a U.S. military base in Okinawa, Japan.

"I had no choice about leaving the U.S. for the first time," Ron said. "During my university days from 1965-69, the Vietnam War stayed prominent. The military had a draft, and my student deferment would expire when I finished college. If I had to enter the military, then I wanted to receive training and a career out of it. I could have waited to be drafted into the army and sent to Vietnam as an infantryman, but some of my fraternity brothers ended up coming home in body-bags after doing that.

"So I decided that I wanted to learn to fly. A Marine Corps recruiter had set up a booth at the Student Union in 1967. After horribly failing a statistics exam, I went to visit him and asked about going to flight school."

Unlike thousands of other young Americans, Ron refused to consider avoiding the military draft by fleeing to Canada. "As one of my good friends from high school said to me, 'Ronnie, you were a real straight arrow.' And I was, having been raised very conservatively. Going to Canada to avoid the draft did not appear on my list of options. I would have seen that as being dishonorable."

Learning to Fly 'Very Difficult'

Aviation skills proved tough to master. "For me, learning to fly was very difficult," Ron said. "Some people are natural-born pilots, but not me, closer to the opposite. If not for the war, I probably would have been sent home as a hopeless case, but since the military needed 'cannon fodder', they kept working with me.

"Two things really make you good at flying – eye-hand co-ordination and quick-scanning to see, retain and process information. You need to interpret the details fast and then keep scanning to put it all together to make the plane do what you want. I had to acquire those skills, especially the scanning, through a lot of hard work.

"Then gradually it became almost like riding a bicycle. Once you learn how to fly airplanes, no matter how long it takes, then you never will forget. Before that, luckily I had good instructors who did their jobs well. They taught me how to fly without letting me kill myself in the process."

Bullets Blast, Fear Surges

From a helicopter-carrier at sea, Ron flew just one military-strike mission into Vietnam. That operation drew accurate enemy fire that brought down an accompanying helicopter, one of more than a dozen on the mission.

"We patrolled the Gulf of Tonkin with a Marine Amphibious Ready Group," said Ron, who then flew CH-46 Sea Knights, a twin-engine transport helicopter. On that mission, "we went to drop a squad of South Vietnamese marines into a landing zone. This was in response to the 1972 Easter Offensive by the North Vietnamese and part of a counter-attack by the South Vietnamese. We provided support, hauling no U.S. combat troops, but helping the South Vietnamese."

For Ron, it marked the one and only time in all his years of flying that projectiles fired in hostility hurtled toward him. "We got shot at a little," he said. "Luckily, nothing happened to us (Ron and his military passengers), but we did lose a larger helicopter and all of the souls onboard. It took a heat-seeking missile right up the tailpipe of an engine."

One sensation surges when enemy combatants open fire. "Fear! You think, 'Oh, shit'," Ron said. "But then you do what you were trained for and hope to get the hell out of danger in time. I dropped off the troops, staying in the zone for less than a minute. Then I picked up and got out, hoping for the best."

He could take little evasive action. "The route was planned to be slightly evasive," Ron said. "But after that, you must follow the plan so that the helicopters will not fly into each other. Several helicopters came in to the same landing zone, landing and dropping off troops at the same time."

Ron did two military stints in Asia, from 1971-72 and again from 1976-79. In between, he conducted military flight instruction in Florida.

"If not for the military, I might never have gone to Asia," he said. "Once having done so, I liked it and found it intriguing. My first exposure to the Philippines came while working aboard the helicopter carrier when we often put into the Subic Bay Naval Base."

More Perils in the Sky

Even without enemy actions, Ron has experienced other close calls in military aircraft. On one particular day (circa 1975), "I taught a military student in a single-engine, propeller-driven aircraft above Pensacola, Florida," he said. "We were in a practice GCA (ground control approach) pattern, being radar-guided. Not using instrumentation, we just listened on the radio and followed instructions, turning to different headings and flying at certain altitudes.

"Suddenly, the plane's engine began to self-destruct. It vibrated so hard that the whole aircraft shook. We needed that engine to keep working to get us safely onto the runway.

"So we declared an emergency. Immediately, I took over the controls from the student and maintained our altitude so that if we did lose the engine, we could glide down.

"Going straight in to the nearest runway, not the

one otherwise in use at the time, we reached the ground successfully. The engine kept going, but it was a rough-runner.

"Later a maintenance officer inspected the engine and said that metal pieces filled its oil. The engine had been ready to seize at any moment. That day, we were really lucky."

Maybe the engine had aged too much. "The plane was an old trainer, a T-28 Trojan, with a big nine-cylinder (jug) radial engine. It all came down to the plane's age and to the fact that something broke."

The limping plane had lacked enough altitude for Ron and his student to use parachutes. "We were only about 1,000 feet above the ground, already in the landing pattern to practice approaches," Ron said.

As a pilot, he naturally prefers to stay at the controls and to solve problems there. "When problems arise, it always goes better to ride the airplane in if you can," he said. "Pilots have a saying: 'There is no need to jump out of a perfectly good airplane.' As long as the plane still flies, stay with it."

Another close call happened in about 1978. "I was flying a twin-engine, prop job from Taipei to Okinawa," Ron said. "It was an older airplane still around for utility use. This time, a chip-light came on to warn me that too much metal floated in the engine oil. The oil system had a metal detector – a little magnet. When that attracted enough metal chips, the light came on to indicate that the engine might fail.

"I was out over the ocean hundreds of miles from an air base. To the chagrin of the maintenance department, I chose to land short on an island that had a little landing strip. Then the maintenance people came out, strained the oil, took all the metal out of it and told me that I should have flown all the way back. But at least I stayed alive!"

Ron recalls no "dangerous" situations with UPS or a passenger airline. Luckily, "UPS runs a very safe operation", he said. "I had a few abnormalities, like the flaps getting stuck, but no life-and-death emergencies."

For years, Ron forgot how much that he liked Asia. "When I flew my first trip to Asia for UPS in 1998, I felt an overwhelming sensation of coming home to a part of the world that I really enjoyed," he said.

Significantly, UPS also put Ron on a path to his post-flying career in the Philippines when in 2002 it chose the former Clark Air Base there as its intra-Asia hub. "That was how I got reintroduced to the Philippines – by having crew-rest layovers there," he said.

Ron favors the Philippines for the country's low cost of living, strong business opportunities, use of English and warm-hearted people. "I met some nice people there, including **Dave,** a retired American-educated medical doctor who sold me the two bars," he said. "Once I had met enough locals, I realized that I could feel very comfortable living for a long time in the Philippines.

"I decided that I like the Philippines more than Thailand, for example, because there are more English-speaking natives," he said. "And I think that Filipinos are a warmer, more 'touchy-feely' kind of people than the Thais are."

From Cockpit Controls to Bar-Room Banter

Can Ron make a successful switch from the cockpit controls inside of airplanes to full-time bar-room banter? Time will tell, but definitely the economics involved and the need for entirely new management skills will test him. "I want to improve the efficiency of the bars once I no longer am an absentee owner." Is he confident of achieving that?

"No, but I will give it my best shot.

"Maybe it resembles airline passengers and flight attendants," Ron said. "If so, then I will need to make sure that my people (employees) are happy before I can expect the customers to feel happy. People seething with anger at the company hardly make the best ambassadors among the customers."

Running businesses in the Philippines, amid a culture vastly different from Ron's own, creates more challenges. "I face all kinds of cultural issues with Filipino employees who have problems that sometimes I, as a Westerner, do not even understand," he said. "Then there is the matter of people being very poor and maybe tempted to steal. How can I protect my businesses against that risk and not upset everyone? So far, I still wonder about the answers to these questions, but I will find out. Maybe I can succeed without achieving perfection. If I come out ahead at the end of the day, then why should I worry too much about whether everything looks perfect? Instead I need to focus on the main mission, which is to make a living for myself and for everyone working with me.

"Another issue that I do struggle with is how Filipinos usually refuse to get involved with problems. For example, if I need someone to make a statement to the authorities, the answer invariably will be, 'Oh, I doubt if I can do that.' They know the truth, yet refuse to stand up for it. What should I do? Should I fire otherwise perfectly good employees for not supporting me when I need it?"

In an Emergency, 'Wind the Clock'

When cultural misunderstandings arise, Ron likes to recall "an important lesson" from his early military days. "An instructor told us, 'The most important thing that you can do in an emergency is to 'wind the clock'. Instead of reacting instantly, trying to fix the problem, just reach down and wind the clock.' That means that you should allow yourself some time to figure out exactly what best to do. You never hurt much by winding the clock until you calm down and think clearly. Otherwise, the tendency to overreact causes emergencies to end up worse than they could have."

Sometimes just a little reflection can be enough to narrow what looked like chasm-wide cultural gaps. "When my father ran his restaurant, he used to tell me, 'Unless I watch out, the employees will rob me blind'," Ron said. "That was in the late 1950s and early '60s in small-town Minnesota. So maybe the people in the Philippines in some ways are no different from the American farm-girls."

From constant high-flying and from every city-stay along the way, Ron has gleaned a vital truth. "I have met and made friends with people from different religions and numerous nationalities," he said. "One thing which I have learned is that 99 per cent of the people everywhere in the world just want to get along – get along with each other and just lead happy lives. Nearly everyone has that positive trait in common. Just a few politicians and radical religious nuts try to lead us in the wrong directions."

After most of a lifetime on the move, will Ron face difficulties merely trying to settle down in one place? "That is a good question," he said. "Thankfully some budget airlines do operate regularly from Clark Air Base so I look forward to a few inexpensive getaways when I find that I need to move around."

But on those future trips he cannot fly the aircraft. "That suits me," he chuckled. "I gladly will ride in the back to relax and enjoy myself."

Then undoubtedly he will sleep for a few more nights at what he regards as his real home in Travel Pro City. That's his suitcase.

Added Later (Louisville, Kentucky, United States) -- When the team behind *All Aboard! Planet Expat* emailed a congratulatory note to Ron after his final flight for UPS, he responded to share a few of his thoughts on the occasion.

"Thank you for your kind note," Ron said. "It was very timely as I downloaded your email while sitting in the pilot 'ready room' after that 'last landing'. The final flight went well. It was a beautiful day in Alaska and all across the Canadian Rockies and plains, and then on into Minnesota, Illinois, Indiana and finally into good old Louisville, Kentucky.

"We watched the moon rise as we descended in the evening. I looked out across the panoramic horizon at the bright lights on the ground and the stars in the sky and thought to myself, 'I will never see this spectacular viewpoint again.'

"Then as I talked to friends and well-wishers in the ready room, I decided to check our UPS Flightops Website. I went to the Crew Applications page and then it all hit home when I saw my name together with the words 'No flight assignment found'. Thus I experienced the end of a career and the start of a new chapter in my life."

BULAK AWAKENS WITH THE ROOSTERS AND FIGHTS THEM TOO

Kind-Hearted Wayne Cotton Competes in a Bloody 'Gentleman's Sport'

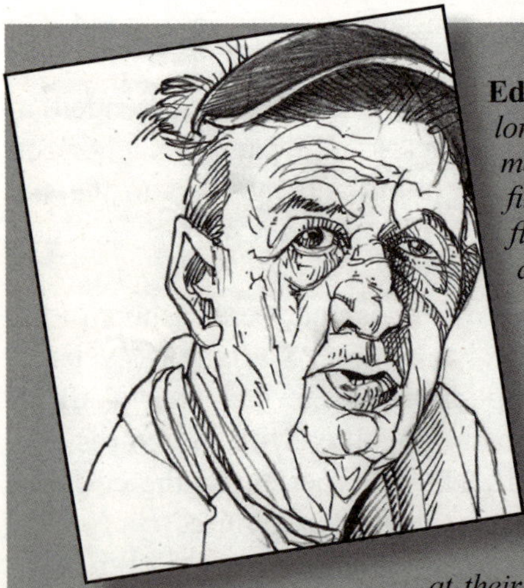

Editor's Note: *Can a long-time plumber, a man focused on pipe-fittings and effluent flows, even survive after abandoning rural roads in the American state of Arkansas and arriving to stay in a populous Asian city? How does a brash newcomer from across the ocean compete and often win against Filipinos at their favorite sport? When a kind man sincerely wants to help a child in need, do things always turn out for the best? A comprehensive chat with Wayne Cotton, alias Bulak, answers these and other fascinating questions.*

NEAR A COCKPIT (not in an airplane this time) – Feel free to call **Wayne Cotton** (nicknamed **Bulak**) a "cocker", a redneck or a hillbilly. He accepts all those labels, enjoys the banter and retorts tartly. But never forget that he also possesses one of the kindest hearts beating anywhere in Asia.

People who encounter 65-year-old Bulak, an American and former Arkansas plumber, in the Philippines say that he distinctly reminds them of **Jed Clampett,** the main character in a classic 1960s television show, *The Beverly Hillbillies.* But he has travelled greater distances, won more friends and done more good for others than the fictional Jed ever did.

A situation comedy, *The Beverly Hillbillies* followed a backwoods family that unexpectedly struck oil, gained huge wealth and moved to California's spiffiest neighborhood, living there happily but badly misplaced. With more modest means, but equally "out of place", Bulak (his nickname comes from the Tagalog word meaning "cotton") gleefully drives a tractor through the streets of Angeles City, his new hometown in the Philippines.

"My tractor is a Harvester, a two-cylinder diesel from China," Bulak said. He drives a car too, but the tractor holds special potential because the managers of local taverns have noticed and want him to use it to pull a trailer adorned with banners advertising their businesses.

Proudly, Bulak rivals the Pinoys at their favorite blood sport, sending cocks (roosters) with long blades tied to their left claws to fight each other. "I have fought cocks (training birds and sending them into battle) for 40 years (first in the United States)," Bulak said.

Also a farmer of sorts, Bulak raises his own roosters to compete in the cockfighting pits (cockpits) of Angeles City and beyond. Long before sunrise each day, normally at 4-5 a.m., he awakens and goes to check on his birds, feed, water and train them. "Now I am a small-time cocker," he said. "At one time, I had 75 birds. Now I am down to just a dozen." But the decline represents mere fluctuation. Bulak has no intention to stop competing. "Not until I die – once a cocker, always a cocker. It gets into your blood."

Children: 'God's Flower Garden'

No matter how much that Bulak enjoys the bird-battles, his greatest pleasure comes from doing favors for the impoverished children he meets. "Children are special," he said. "They represent God's flower garden."

Back in 1972, the affable Bulak married, but his wife left him six years later and he never remarried. Significantly, he has no children of his own.

Since arriving in the Philippines, Bulak has purchased and given away numerous bicycles. "Last Christmas, for example, I took one of the kids at a cockpit into the ring, covered his eyes and then said, 'Bulak, **Santa Claus**'. Then I gave him a brand new bicycle."

Bulak knows that some parents promptly sell the bicycles that he gives to local children. "They could have good reasons," he said. "Perhaps they ran out of money to buy food for their families. On the other hand, maybe the daddies just want to drink more Red Horse (beer) and go to the cockfights."

An urge to help those less fortunate than himself turns out to be a big part of what makes Bulak tick. "Money is just money – not enough by itself to make anyone happy," he said. "God has blessed me, and so I should try to help other people, especially children. Share your blessings. That is my philosophy."

'Blah, Blah, Blah, Bulak'

Children with medical needs often attract Bulak's attention, but his offers to help sometimes misfire. "There was a little boy born with a scar, like a birthmark, and black hair on his face," Bulak recalled. "I knew his parents because they helped to keep my birds at a nearby farm. So I told them, 'We should take the little guy to Manila. Doctors there can remove that scar and graft skin onto his face. It will do him good.'

"They agreed: 'Okay, Bulak.'

"Then I began to check into the details. The operation would have cost about 100,000 pesos (US$2,400). Back then, I had enough money.

"Soon after, I went out to the farm with a friend of mine and began to give one of my birds a bath. The boy's mother was there that day. His father was not.

"My Filipino friend said, 'Blah, blah, blah', speaking Tagalog, in a conversation with the mother.

"Suddenly, I heard the mother say in Tagalog: 'Blah, blah, blah, Bulak.'

"She told my friend that she had no worries at all about the boy's operation because she just wanted the money to start work on building a new house instead. That pissed me off so badly that I moved my birds elsewhere (and never did provide the money). No one ever should use their children's problems to try to benefit themselves like that.

"For a long time, I never saw that boy again. Then six months ago, I visited another farm, and he was there. He had grown a lot, but he still came up to me and said, 'Hello, Bulak'. The scar and the hair remained on his face."

Feathers Fly, Blood Flows

Bulak's eccentricity, enthusiasm, gregariousness and generosity all contribute to winning friends wherever he goes. When he arrives at a cockfighting pit, many participants and spectators yell out his name: "Bulak, Bulak" or "Hey, Bulak". Similar yells ring out when friends or acquaintances notice him on a sidewalk or elsewhere.

Cockfights feature much preening and strutting by roosters and by their owners or handlers. Fluttering, leaping and flying-feathers follow as the birds peck and kick at each other, inflicting the most damage with the knife blades on their left claws.

From near the cockpit, Bulak's voice rings out: "Don't be hopping. Stick the knife in," and moments later, "Cut him, baby. Cut him."

Nearby, two seats down from the boisterous Bulak, looking incredulous at the antics of his countryman, sits **Bruce Moore,** another expatriate American. Bruce wears an artificial limb, having lost his left leg to a logging accident in Washington State. He, too, now lives in the Philippines.

"This all forms part of the spectacle of Filipino poultry," Bruce said. "Most Filipinos cannot afford to buy racehorses so they buy roosters instead, but they love their competitive sport just the same."

The owners of winning birds collect prize money. Hefty wagers hinge on the outcomes too. Before the birds fight, spectators around the pit bellow and gesture frantically to place their bets. "Some people will bet millions of pesos," Bulak said.

"Filipinos have unique styles of betting. They yell and make hand signals." Fingers pointed down indicate thousands of pesos. Fingers pointed sideways represent hundreds of pesos. A raised and rotated hand with the fingers pointed straight up wagers 10,000 pesos (about US$240). After every fight, the losing gamblers wad up thousands of pesos and toss them over to the winners.

On Bulak's best-ever day at a cockpit, he won 100,000 pesos (US$2,400). On the worst occasion, he lost 50,000 pesos (US$1,200).

Prominent businessman and former politician **Robin Nepomuceno,** who owns one of two legally sanctioned cockpits in Angeles City, knows Bulak well. In fact, he has provided a regular parking space on different property that he owns for the American's tractor.

According to Robin, more than 300 people can earn

I WANNA BE MOHAMMED ALI
TEACH ME TO FIGHT LIKE MANNY PACQUIAO!
COCK FIGHTING TRAINER
Cocky

their livings in whole or in part from the regular activities at a single cockpit. Some people collect admission fees. Many handle the birds or the money. Still others sell cigarettes, peanuts or other snacks and drinks at the venue.

The cockpit that Robin owns, located indoors at a former basketball gym, hosts fowl-fights every Tuesday, Thursday and Saturday. Another legal cockpit in town has similar action on the remaining four days per week.

"Anyone who could figure out these birds and always know exactly what they think would become a multi-millionaire and never need to consider working again," Bulak said. "But it really is nearly as hard as to understand what women are thinking.

"With fighting cocks, you never know what goes through their minds. One day, they are primed and ready to fight. Another time, they may just stand there and commit suicide. Maybe it comes down to their moods. Unfortunately, they cannot talk to tell an owner, 'Well, I feel bad today. Awww! My back hurts.' "

A Bird Dies, A Man Cries

Despite the birds' limited life expectancies, Bulak sometimes names those he nurtures and develops sentimental attachments. "I have cried over my fighting birds before," he said. "I have a heart. After all, they are true to me. They fight to the death for me. No one else will do that."

The best fighting bird that Bulak ever had won seven times, but died after an eighth encounter. "I just called him Black Cock, Bulak Cock. He fought for that last time and got cut. We sewed him up, but some of the injuries were internal. He lived for two more days, but then died. I dug a hole and buried him," shedding tears in the process.

Nostalgically, Bulak saved part of a spur clipped from the dead bird. He wears that claw fragment on a necklace.

What made that particular bird so special? "Oh, I hardly even know," Bulak said as the memories brought fresh tears to his eyes. "He would look at me with big, brown eyes. Even during the fights, he would look at me. Then 'Ohhhh', he would just come back, fighting hard, buddy. He refused to give up and was so damn tough. If you ever find a man as tough as a fighting cock, then you know that he is one mean son-of-a-bitch."

Even in the fatal final fight, "My bird did not lose. It was a draw so all the bets were off, but he got cut badly."

The bouts last for a maximum of 10 minutes, but often end within seconds due to the accuracy of flying blades, usually with the loser lying motionless and bloody on the dirt-covered fighting surface. The winning bird probably lives to resume training and fight again another day. Its opponent dies. "Losing birds get sent to a cooking pot."

A Gentleman's Game

Bulak insists that a deep sense of honor prevails in cockpits and among cockfighting people. "It is a good sport -- a gentleman's game. Always, the contest really is between two men. If the other man's fighting bird turns out to be better than mine, then I will shake his hand and congratulate him. We are gentlemen."

But They Will 'Kill Your Ass'

Always, fairness must prevail. "You simply do not try to cheat at a cockpit in the Philippines," Bulak warned. "Otherwise, the people there will kill your ass. They will beat you to death. The same thing if you bet, lose and do not have the money. Then you will die.

"I saw a man try to cheat one time. He brought a cock into the arena. As he started to release it to fight, I bet 1,200 pesos (about US$28). A tall Filipino next to me bet 8,000 pesos (US$190). Then I saw the culprit use a thumb to pop one of the bird's legs out of its joint. His buddies had bet on the other side, see?

"When the guy dropped the bird, I told my cristo (an intermediary who takes bets), 'That bird is hurt.' Sure enough! It got killed right away.

"Then the Filipino who had cheated raced over, grabbed the losing bird and took off out of the cockpit. Well, that counts as strange behavior right there.

"But the announcer acted quickly. He went and grabbed the guy by the neck and brought him back in, together with the dead bird. The announcer held the bird up by its leg. By then, the guy's two buddies who bet on the other side had hoofed it.

"People took the cheater outside, and they beat him and beat him and beat him. They kicked him and kicked him. Then they beat him and beat him again.

"No one has seen that guy since so you know what that means. His remains ended up lying out in a sugar-cane field somewhere.

"People take things seriously here. They do not play around. Life goes like that in the Philippines. If you want to cheat, do not dare to try it at a cockpit."

Cockfights are popular all over the Philippines. "Some people treat their birds much better than they treat their children because the birds can earn them money while the children cost them money."

Enthusiasts must breed and raise new birds to replace those constantly lost in battle. "For my baby chicks, the young ones, I always feed them the yolks from boiled eggs," Bulak said. "That makes them strong."

Part of Bulak's success stems from importing a few U.S. birds. "I flew some over here from Arkansas and Alabama," he said. "They improved the bloodlines of my birds." The winged warriors entering the cockpits usually range from eight months to several years old. Older combatants have an advantage, having seen more, learned more and survived past fights.

Like *Rocky,* Fighters Must Train

Bulak tries hard to help his fighters to succeed. "You never just take a bird and put him in a fight. First you must work with him, training and conditioning him, like a boxer." The training that these birds do resembles what actor **Sylvester Stallone** did in the 1976 boxing movie, *Rocky.*

What precise preparations come before a big bout? "You inject the bird (with vitamin B12, although 'some trainers use steroids'), deworm him and give him a bath. Then you put him into a fly pen so that he can fly up and down, up and down. With my birds, I also spar them. I put tiny boxing gloves around the spurs on their feet so that when they hit at each other, they never get blinded or hurt."

Plus Bulak places a thick pad around one of his forearms and encourages the birds to strike that. "You get a bird riled up, and when he comes at you, hold the pad down. When he hits it, you can feel how many times and with how much power. I hold the pad slightly above him so that he learns to turn upside down and hit upward (more lethal in a real fight). Then when he does exactly the same thing at a cockpit, I will go home with the money."

Filipinos claim to have a 1,500-year history of cockfighting and view their country as the sport's world capital, complete with 20 million fighting birds and 2,000 legal cockpits. Fights happen somewhere "every day, every night". Big showdowns, often in Manila, attract television coverage.

The World Slasher Cup and other global tournaments, some with top prizes exceeding US$1 million, bring overseas competitors and spectators too. Consistent winners in the top tournaments gain widespread fame. For example, **Patrick Antonio** has become a Filipino national idol for winning many World Slasher prizes. He and his family own thousands of birds.

Cockfighting prospers in Mexico, Central America, Peru, Brazil, Indonesia, India, Pakistan and Thailand too. Bulak remembers when the sport also thrived in much of the U.S. "There were cockpits everywhere across Oklahoma, Texas and Arkansas," he said.

In fact, he regards cockfights as a valid part of American history. "People farmed, and on Sundays, they fought their birds against each other for entertainment," he said. "That is how cockfighting got started there hundreds of years ago."

Cockfights Persist on American Soil

Strict laws in the U.S. and in many countries now ban cockfights as needless cruelty to animals, but Bulak sniffs out a whiff of serious hypocrisy. "These days the U.S. has legal UFC (ultimate fighting championship) contests that allow men to break each other's arms, elbows and other body parts, but when it comes to fighting birds, the response is: 'Oh, my God. You are so cruel.' And these birds are bred to fight, not for people to eat. They taste about the same as eating a shoe."

Despite threatened long prison terms for the people involved, cockfights still happen on American soil. According to Bulak, the venues are located out of sight, "away back in the woods".

Born in Jackson, Tennessee, in 1946, Bulak, an only child, moved to Arkansas at three days of age. He went to school in a small town called Gould before relocating to Little Rock and starting a 46-year plumbing career.

Bill Clinton, Hello!

In a McDonald's restaurant once, Bulak met his home state's most famous man, **Bill Clinton,** the governor and later a popular U.S. president. "I shook his hand," Bulak said.

"At the corner of Ninth and Main streets in Little Rock, I went into a McDonald's for coffee. When Bill Clinton came in, I went over to him and said, 'Hi, Bill. How are you doing, sir? I am Wayne Cotton. Good morning.'

"He replied, 'Good morning.' After all, he is just a man like me. He poops through the back end exactly like I do."

What other conclusions did Bulak reach about Clinton? "Well, I would hate to put those into a book," he said.

Huh? No good impression? "Not at all!" Bulak said. "Clinton made his living as a professional politician. He never worked at a real job in his life."

Lucky Old Man

Gradually, Bulak developed a passion for travel. "I have travelled a lot and met many different good people, which is a big part of how I have been blessed," he said. "Where I grew up, many people never even leave the county (much less the country). I have no special education, but I have travelled all over Southeast Asia and other places too. That makes me a lucky old man."

At first, Bulak explored much of the U.S., Mexico and the Caribbean, all while growing more disgruntled at home. "I could see unwelcome changes coming in America with too many restrictions and laws about the likes of fishing, hunting and smoking cigarettes (not to mention cock fighting)," he said. "The country started going to hell, and so I thought, 'There must be a better world out there.' "

'Prettiest Place on the Planet'

By the late 1990s, Bulak visited Australia and then Thailand. "I flew to Cairns, Australia, and loved it there," he said. "To me, that looks like the prettiest place on the planet. Just imagine wild parrots in the trees and delicious mud crabs as big as plates."

Bulak stayed there for two weeks, "just looking at the world, seeing how different people live. After my plane landed, I met some people who own an opal shop, and so I made friends with them. Then I walked down to the pier and made friends with a family who rented fishing boats. Next I met a friend of that family, an older fellow living on a yacht there. A guy named **Richard** owned a tour boat for going to see crocodiles. Another fellow, **Hoppy,** had a boat for deep-sea fishing. People not only kind of took me in, but they also started taking me out on boats and refused to charge me any money.

"When I went out on a diving boat one day, I took me a loaf of bread. People asked, 'Cotton, are you going diving?'

"I said, 'Hell, no. I ain't going in that water.'

" 'So why did you come out here?'

"I said, 'I came out to have a look.'

"So everyone else went scuba diving in different directions while I stayed on the boat. Then I got to throwing bread into the water. Why, hell, so many fish came swimming up that everyone quit diving and returned to the boat. We had a good time."

The next day, "I went out on Hoppy's deep-sea fishing boat. Hell, we caught nothing all morning. At lunchtime, a Japanese girl (a tourist) on the boat sat down, opened her lunch pail and took out a banana.

"Then the other people on the boat jumped to their feet and said, 'Ah, my God! No wonder we caught nothing. Taking a banana on a fishing boat brings bad luck.' Some people believe that down in Australia."

Advised by new Australian friends, Bulak chose Koh Samui, Thailand, as his next destination. "It was really pretty too, but I was in a strange country and did not speak the language," he said. Even so, he made more new friends, who "took care of me and even took me along to a Buddhist ceremony, which was really nice".

'Like a Goat in a Shopping Mall'

On another Asian excursion, Bulak visited Hong Kong, a place with more towering buildings than he could have imagined. "I felt totally out of place, like a goat in a shopping mall," he said. "Without some friends of mine who live in Hong Kong, I would have been completely lost."

Fearful that the skyscrapers might sway and collapse, Bulak entered them reluctantly. He rode on double-decker buses, but considered them unstable-looking vehicles likely to roll and crash. "Those buses scared the hell out of me," he said.

He also rode on the Mass Transit Railway (MTR), Hong Kong's underground railway system. "There I was, 64 years old, and it was the first time in my life that I ever had been on anything like that," he said. "It worked well though. I thought that it was nice, fast and clean."

Despite feeling terrified at times, Bulak gained a positive impression of Hong Kong too. "It is a beautiful city, a very nice place," he said, but as different from Arkansas "as daylight from darkness".

In Hong Kong, Bulak failed to encounter the skyscraper city's most famous resident, **Li Ka-shing,** the richest person in Asia. Otherwise, he surely would have ambled over to greet the property tycoon ("Howdy, sir"), just as he once approached Bill Clinton. After all, Li too "is just a man like me. He poops through the back end exactly like I do."

Bulak first visited the Philippines after feeling bored when in Bangkok, the Thai capital. "So I decided to fly to the

Philippines. Then I learned that the Filipinos fight cocks, and so I started going back." Eventually, "I probably made 20 different trips from Arkansas back to the Philippines.

"It took me about 12 years to gain the respect of Filipinos by winning with my fighting cocks. If you are a winner, then they will respect you. If you are a loser, they will have no use for you."

'Kind of Like Home to Me Now'

Six years ago, Bulak moved full-time to the Philippines, and now he has become a familiar figure in Angeles City. "This feels kind of like home to me now," he said.

He respects Filipinos, much as he believes that they respect him. "It can be a hard world and a tough life here for many Filipino people," he said. "Many of them really struggle to feed their children. You have honest people here, and then you have crooks too, the same as everywhere and every nationality. But, you know, the Filipino people have been really good to me. I have had a lot of happy days here." Bulak vows to stay in the Philippines. "I just want to fight my cocks and drive a damn tractor," he said, planning to enjoy every moment.

"Here, I have different experiences every day," he said. "You never know what you will see. If I sit at the edge of a busy street, sooner or later someone will pass by on a trike (a motorbike with a passenger seat attached) that has a hog in it."

For the Filipinos, Bulak cruising on his tractor makes a surprising sight too. "I drive it around town," he said. "I go to the cockpits on it. Sometimes I use it to haul the feed for my birds. With me being an old farm-boy, it makes me feel right at home."

Even Jed Clampett could not have explained matters any better.

MUSICAL MOVES! EXPAT JAZZMAN MAKES THE WORLD FEEL GOOD

Allen Youngblood Sounds Right on Both Sides of the Pacific

Editor's Note: *A talented jazz pianist born in the Virgin Islands, Allen Youngblood has blazed a musical trail across much of Asia after earlier doing the same in North America. As he explains, each one of his live-music performances unfolds differently. Every city where he has lived and/or played has substantial differences too. Twenty years after arriving in Asia with a plan to stay for six months, Allen remains there. This expatriate piano-man has many tales to tell.*

AT A PIANO KEYBOARD – From notes in mind to fingers on a keyboard and then pleasing sounds filling a room, musical prowess has given **Allen Youngblood** a valuable ticket to ride. Wherever he goes, whenever he sits down at a piano, people eager to listen welcome his presence.

Playing music and the ability of people to enjoy it

transcend international boundaries. "Music has no nationality or racism," said 58-year-old Allen. "It is color-blind. That may not always apply to song lyrics, but the actual music is just music." Significantly, it can open doors on almost every street in any city.

Originally from Saint Croix in the U.S. Virgin Islands but raised in Cleveland, Ohio, Allen has earned a reputation as a leading jazz pianist and composer not only on American soil, but also in much of Asia. Now he lives in Hong Kong, where he has spent most of the past 20 years. The non-musical highlight of his life also involves Hong Kong, where he has a "lovely" three-year-old daughter named **Ruby.**

Music Forms a Common Language

Allen's musical calling can take him nearly anywhere and allows him to prosper upon arrival. "Yes," he said, "and even without knowing the local language because music will be a common language. That is a good thing.

"Of course, I need to stay at a certain level. Otherwise, I would end up almost like a hippie walking around with a guitar and living in a hostel."

For Allen, the essential formula for success comes down to this: "I always have been serious about music. No matter where I am, I put in my best effort, and that is what tends to open doors for me, not just being able to play. Many people can play really well, but they neglect to take care of business properly, and so you never see them or hear them – because they mess up and never create opportunities for themselves."

As part of Allen's "business", he has recorded a stack of CDs over the years. They include: *Selah, New Life, Bloodlines, Digital Cutup Lounge vs Allen Youngblood, Outside the Box, Midnight Odyssey* and *Jazbalaya.*

"I compose music and like to play my own music," Allen said. "I think that I sound better when playing my own music, which is how I learned to express myself when growing up back in the 1960s and '70s. A lot of stuff happened then – the Vietnam War, the Civil Rights Movement, the Cold War and riots. Everyone had to think and to have opinions. In writing music, your opinions are essential."

The Number-One Spot in Town

Leaving the U.S., Allen arrived in Hong Kong in 1992. His first job, the one that lured him across the Pacific, was to play nightly at JJ's, then a wildly popular nightclub at the Grand Hyatt Hotel.

"Back then, JJ's was so popular," Allen said. "It was the number-one night spot in Hong Kong. Many people from the entertainment industry came in there. They would ask me, 'Can you do this, this and that?'

"And I said, 'Yeah, of course.' Mostly, it involved daytime work. So I would end up getting some students to teach, and things kept on going well."

Later Allen played long-term at the LA Cafe, the Conrad Hotel, The Jazz Club and other Hong Kong venues. For the past 15 years, he has appeared regularly at the Foreign Correspondents' Club.

His relationship with the FCC cemented when the club's downstairs area became Bert's Bar, named for **Bert Okuley,** a long-time FCC member and another jazz pianist. "That is a multi-purpose room, but it looks like a nightclub," Allen said. "I became the musical director there. We have a band program on Tuesdays, Thursdays and Fridays, and sometimes a guest artist on Saturdays."

'A Trip' With Martha Reeves

Soon Allen joined the FCC's New Charity Ball Committee too. Subsequently, the first charity-ball guest star turned out to be **Martha Reeves,** a famous Alabama-born vocalist from the Motown group, Martha Reeves and the Vandellas. In the 1960s and early '70s, her group recorded many hit songs, including "(Love Is Like a) Heat Wave", "Jimmy Mack", "Dancing in the Street", "Nowhere to Run" and "Quicksand".

"For me, meeting Martha Reeves was a trip," Allen said. "Personally, I always liked Martha and the Vandellas better than their big rivals, **Diana Ross** and the Supremes.

"Martha and her musical director were scheduled to come to Hong Kong. So our committee chairman, who had a car, and I went out to the airport to meet them.

"When Martha got off the plane, the first thing that we asked her was: 'Where is your musical director?'

" 'Not here! He never showed up at the airport for our flight.'

" 'What?'

"So I had no choice. Immediately, I became Martha's temporary new musical director. I felt nervous about doing it, but then again, since our eight-piece band had rehearsed and knew the music, it should have been no problem.

"On the way back from the airport, as we crossed the Tsing Ma Bridge, Martha freaked out. (Then new, the Tsing Ma Bridge ranks as the world's longest double-deck suspension bridge.) 'Wait until I tell my son about this,' she said. She hardly could believe the size of that bridge. It fascinated her."

Apparently, Martha's interest in public infrastructure later led her in new directions. From 2005 until 2009, she served as an elected city-council member in Detroit.

In fact, even before Martha arrived in Hong Kong, Allen had struggled to overcome a big problem. "Earlier, I had called Martha's agent in New York. With a lot of these agents, once they get your deposit, then you just cannot find them again. But I reached this guy and told him, 'Look, I need copies of Martha's music so that we can rehearse it. When

I am a
VIRGIN
islander
PLAY IT AGAIN
AND AGAIN AND
AGAIN ALLEN
FCC
JAZZ
KiNG
JAZZ
CHINESE
US
PIANO

she arrives, there will be a sound check and no real rehearsal, so it behooves you to send the stuff, which covers a lot of musical arrangements. That way, we can prepare and sound professional.'

"The guy said, 'You call her.'

"I argued that it was not my job to call her. 'How would I address her? Miss Reeves? Mrs. Reeves? Martha?'

"Anyway, I called her. I had to because I was convinced that it was the only way to rehearse the band in advance so that 'Boom', we could play with her.

"For about 45 minutes, I talked to Martha on the telephone, pleading with her. I understood her concern. She did not want to send me the music because, based on what often happens in Hong Kong, what would stop me from taking that music, copying it and then having an imitation Martha Reeves and the Vandellas band? After all, I have seen an imitation Supremes band here?

"Solemnly, I gave Martha my word, telling her all about my history and that my father was a church preacher. I told her that I did not want to steal her music, that I respected her and had grown up listening to her.

"So she actually did send us the music, original stuff. I felt so happy that she did." Then Allen and his band rehearsed.

"That rehearsal made all the difference. Once Martha arrived, she was really cool, and we did a really good show, one with lots of energy. Later she wrote a letter back to the organizers saying, 'Thank you for the genius of Allen Youngblood.' From her, that really meant something. She knows that she was right to trust me. I handed back all of the music, the show went really well and she had a great time here."

Serving on the FCC's charity-ball committee gave Allen other musical highlights too. "Since then, through Martha and by being on that charity committee, I have met The Temptations, The Beach Boys and others."

Staying in a Hotel Room Gets Old

During Allen's earlier days in Hong Kong, seeing certain familiar faces could come as a big surprise. "One time in The Jazz Club, I turned around and saw some guys who I knew from Los Angeles," he said. "They were wearing tuxedos and sitting behind me. I yelled out to them, 'What are you doing here?' I hardly believed my eyes.

"They were in Hong Kong to play at the Conrad Hotel. So I would go over there, check them out and hang around. Then their piano player – he came from New York – had to go home, and they wanted me to play.

"But I dislike playing in the hotels. It gets boring because usually you have to play six nights a week. You really cannot do anything else, except maybe to teach a few music lessons in the daytime.

"Then I learned that I could get a so-called 'expatriate package'. That meant that I would be paid, the employer would pay the taxes on my money and I would get a hotel room, three meals a day and my laundry done. Basically, everything would be free unless I was stupid enough to use the telephone in my room or to eat or drink from the mini-bar. For a telephone, I could buy a phone card, and when the card ended my conversation would be over. If I wanted a beer, I could go to the 7-Eleven store and buy six beers for the cost of one from the mini-bar.

"For two years, I lived at the Conrad Hotel. Everyone thinks that would be cool, but staying in a hotel room gets old really fast. You cannot open the windows. People always want to clean your room at the wrong times. Often I tried to tell the hotel people, 'No need to clean this room. I am not that sloppy. Let's make a deal. When I need something, I will call you.' They never would agree because that is not the way that hotels work."

North to Shanghai

Still following his musical instincts, Allen roamed north for a short time in 2011. He spent five weeks in Shanghai, playing at the Peace Hotel and the Cotton Club.

"That was my chance to see if I wanted to move to Shanghai," Allen said. "I know many people who left for Shanghai during Hong Kong's SARS (Severe Acute Respiratory Syndrome) outbreak in 2002 and 2003, and they stayed there.

"Shanghai has a lot of music – all different types," Allen said. Even so, he returned to Hong Kong, lured back by his history and the people he knows there.

South to Singapore

In 1996, Allen left to spend a year in Singapore. There, he played at BJ's, a popular venue in that city's Conrad Hotel, but he did not go willingly.

"One day, I played as usual at the Conrad Hotel in Hong Kong when I saw the place's European general manager gesturing to me, almost like waving. I wondered what he meant. At first, I thought that he might be waving goodbye.

"So I walked over to see what he wanted. It turned out that his gesture had been a Swiss-German one that meant, 'Come here'.

"Until then, I never had realized that he also acted as a vice-president for all of the Conrad Hotels in East Asia. He told me, 'I want you to go to Singapore.'

"A new Conrad was almost ready to open there. I had no desire to go to Singapore. If I went anywhere, I wanted to go home to the U.S. But the general manager spoke in such a way that suggested if I did not go, then I might not have the job in Hong Kong for much longer either."

Life in Singapore brought some interesting times too. "A funny thing happened there," Allen said. "I hired some friends of mine from Los Angeles and Seattle to come to Asia, but then I had to let the bass player go because he really got on my nerves. I knew that **Victor Gaskin,** a world-famous jazz bass player from the Virgin Islands, happened to be living in Malaysia. So I got him as a replacement. When my Mom back in the U.S. heard about that, she freaked out, which started to freak me out too."

Best to See History Happen

Deliberately, Allen returned to Hong Kong shortly before its 1997 handover from British control to Chinese sovereignty. "I wanted to see that history as it happened, not just to read about it," he said.

Of course, new musical opportunities waited for him too. Just by chance, "I wandered into a Dan Ryan's restaurant, which I hardly ever do because I am good friends with the people who own Grappa's, another restaurant," Allen recalled. "Usually, I go to Grappa's.

"Hardly anybody was in that Dan Ryan's then. So I sat at the bar eating a Reuben sandwich and watching basketball on television.

"Suddenly, a group of people came in and sat down right next to me, which was okay, but I thought, 'Nobody else is in here so why do they need to sit so close to me.' Maybe I am a paranoid American.

"They started to talk about the Cannes International Film Festival in France. The man seated the closest of all to me mentioned something about **Robert De Niro,** whom I really respect as an actor. So I started to ask the guy questions. Our conversation went on and on. I told him that I was a musician who played the piano.

"Then he leaned toward me and said, 'Well, you know, I happen to be a member of the FCC.'

" 'Yeah? What is that?' I asked.

"He meant the Hong Kong Foreign Correspondents' Club. Okay, I knew what that was, but I had never set foot inside the place."

Apparently, "a guy named **Larry Allen** (no relation), a piano player and a living legend in Hong Kong for 50 years, wanted to return to his home country for health reasons." So Allen Youngblood soon agreed to take over Larry's place at the piano in the FCC.

"The next day, a guy with a Hong Kong radio show telephoned me. He wanted someone to play with a singer at The American Bar in the Peninsula Hotel. So I got two jobs, one right after the other."

At the Peninsula Hotel, Allen played, but only temporarily. "I do not like working in (posh-hotel) environments like that," he said. "Everything becomes too sterile. People treat the music like furniture."

Mutt, Jeff and Snake Venom

Back in the early 1980s, Allen's music took him to Kobe, Japan, for one year. "That was my first experience in Asia," he said.

With 1.5 million residents, Kobe is Japan's fifth-largest city. A decade after Allen's time there, on January 17, 1995, a massive earthquake rocked the city, destroying property and killing 6,400 people.

News about the earthquake jolted Allen too. "I used to live right where that happened," he said.

When in Japan himself, Allen's "biggest scares" came from "people eating weird stuff. Most of the Japanese food looks and tastes fine. Still, when you stay in a place for one year, then you start to see some unusual things, especially since many people would come into where I played and then want to take me out to eat."

In those days the Japanese economy rippled with

strength, and many of its people enjoyed immense affluence. "I met some unusual people," Allen said. "I remember a submarine designer and a pearl jeweler. They were like **Mutt** and **Jeff,** one guy tall and the other guy really short." (*Mutt and Jeff,* an American cartoon strip, created by **Bud Fisher** in 1907, features two mismatched friends. It stayed in syndication until 1982.)

"Those two guys came to the club where I played nearly every night," Allen said. "It cost the equivalent of US$100 just to get into the place, plus, plus, plus (for consumption when there). But they were nice guys."

When Japanese friends or acquaintances took Allen to restaurants, he always made one thing abundantly clear. "I told them that I disliked snakes and so I would not eat one. I did not even want to see one."

On some outings, "everyone wanted you to 'milk' a snake and put the venom into little shot-glasses and then kick that back". To that idea, Allen delivered a consistent response: "No!"

Misfortunate Monkey, 'Disgusting' Demise

Allen's most startling food experience in Japan involved a small monkey. "That was an absolute culture shock, away out there!

"We sat at a table with a round hole in the middle, and I wondered what that was for," Allen said. Then people "brought out a drugged-up (live) monkey, whacked off the top of its skull and poured some hot oil inside." With the misfortunate monkey positioned so that its head stuck up through the hole in the table, the delicate diners could reach right in to help themselves to morsels of the animal's warm, soft and accessible brain.

"I did not eat any," Allen insisted. "I was appalled. Honestly, I hardly even could believe what had just happened. It was shocking. Even looking at that sight….

"Maybe if somebody had made a pate out of monkey brains, then I might have tried some. But this monkey simply had the top of its head whacked off and hot oil poured inside. I wanted no part of that. It was disgusting.

"One guy got angry with me when I refused to eat any. He said, 'That always is the trouble with you Americans. You never appreciate anyone else's culture.' That is some culture!"

A Whale of a Time

At times in Japan, Allen and his fellow musicians found unusual dining experiences on their own. "In the area where we lived in Kobe, we often went to a Chinese restaurant," he said. Usually, but not always, the idea was to take a break from Japanese food.

"If we had wanted Indian food or something like that, we could have found it, but it would have been very expensive," Allen said. "So we liked that Chinese place. It was run by a family, and soon all of the family members knew us and what we did. The little kids there thought that we were amusing.

"One time we told the people at the Chinese restaurant that we wanted to eat some of what they liked to eat. We made arrangements and went to the restaurant at a certain time for a special meal. Guess what! There stood the whole family, lined up in a row looking at us.

"First, they gave us some prawns. In the U.S., you seldom see the heads still on prawns when they are served, so I thought that these ones looked a little too prehistoric.

"All the time, those little kids were priceless, giggling and laughing at us.

"Next we had a brown, blubbery, broth-like thing. It smelled good, but it turned out to be whale, just like blubber with sandpaper on top." The special meal ended there. "We insisted on going back to the normal dishes on the menu," Allen said.

Who Appreciates Good Music?

Looking beyond mealtime dilemmas, Allen rates the Japanese people as "number one" for appreciating good music. "They have a very deep understanding of other cultures besides their own," he said. "Speaking about jazz because that is the music that I most like, Japan has produced some very good jazz players, some very good jazz clubs and some very good audiences who appreciate jazz.

"Recently, I visited Tokyo. As I walked along in the streets, I heard jazz blasting from different places. Suddenly, I would think, 'That sounds like **Miles Davis.** Where does the music come from?' The city has put up speakers, and they play jazz. That takes the appreciation of jazz right over the top. Everywhere that I went, in every restaurant, and even at a ski resort, I heard jazz."

Elsewhere in Asia, Allen's favorite music genre struggles much more. "Recently, we had a special show in Hong Kong with **Ernie Watts,** a two-time Grammy Award winner," Allen said. "A friend of mine who lives in Singapore was playing the bass. So I asked him about Singapore: 'What happened to all of the jazz places there? What happened to Harry's Bar? What happened to Southbridge Jazz?' They are all gone, closed."

Likewise, most professional musicians will complain, sometimes bitterly, that Hong Kong offers far too little live music. "Where is all the live music in Hong Kong?" Allen said. "You tell me."

In fact, "most of Hong Kong's live music takes place in the hotels. So it will be a certain kind of hotel-type music. I do not even see many rock-and-roll bands."

Why does Hong Kong endure this live-music shortage? "Because most people are not greatly interested," Allen said. "They focus too much on business and money. They work hard and then like to eat. Karaoke stays popular because many people prefer to sing and to participate as fun."

High rents hit hard too. Live-music venues face potentially crippling costs. "A number of places are in the process of closing right now because the landlords jacked up the rents by 30 per cent or more. Then no one can do anything, and the places are small anyway."

In a few countries, like the Philippines and Thailand, people show an intense and undeniable interest in music. "I have attended and co-organized at jazz festivals in Puerto Galera in the Philippines," Allen said. "There are many musical people there, but perhaps not so many professionals. By 'music professionals', I mean people whose jobs and money come 100 per cent from music. That means other people must be willing to pay to hear them. Of course, some music people and places do exist in Manila, but everything still tends to revolve around the pop music played in hotels."

No Two Cities the Same

Allen's travels for short-term stays and performances, often "corporate gigs", have taken him to Vietnam, Malaysia, Taiwan, Thailand, Macau, the Chinese mainland, Greece, the United Arab Emirates, Scotland and Australia. All those journeys happened as a direct result of living in Hong Kong.

Among so many places where Allen has played, he refuses to name a "favorite" city or country. "They all are different," he said. "For example, I enjoy Hong Kong now that I have been there for so long. When I visited Tokyo, I enjoyed being there. Tokyo has a lot of energy all over and around. Hong Kong has financial energy. Personally, I would like to see Hong Kong with more cultural energy."

Knowing that no two cities are the same, Allen believes that far too many travelers and even expatriates, "especially the American ones", make a serious blunder. "They expect to just go from point A to point B and back again," he said. "Maybe they want to swim in a swimming pool when the sea waits right there. They fully expect everything to be just like back home. Sometimes I really want to say to them, 'Why did you come here? Instead you just should have taken your money, headed for the best hotel in New York City and lived it up.' Anyone who goes from one place to another needs to try the food, learn the lifestyle, do this and do that."

Facing the Crowds

When in front of audiences in any city or town, Allen tries to focus on what he needs to do and on doing it well. "If I am playing my own compositions, then I do my best to interpret what I believe each song is about," he said. "The kind of music that I play has lots of improvisation."

Listeners may not always react. For example, "people in Hong Kong seldom clap very much, but I do not care. Musicians who play for applause tend to showboat. That is never my motivation to play. I know perfectly well if my band, or me personally, messes up. I do not need applause to tell me that. It never bothers me whether people clap or not because I always know what just happened on stage.

"Besides, some people just do not clap." At other times, "I have seen people clap for stuff that I think is really horrible, but maybe looks show-biz". Indeed, audiences that clap constantly may "look stupid for clapping at the wrong times".

Yet some musicians hunger for applause. "Audiences in Japan (and Hong Kong too) clap mostly at the end of songs or sets," Allen said. "Some musicians think that something must have gone badly wrong if the audience fails to clap at every little thing. I always ask them, 'Why are you thinking that way? You should be concentrating on what you are supposed to do.' "

Basketball Theory of Jazz

At every chance, Allen likes to teach too. He often leads jazz clinics or workshops and offers technical advice about music. As he tells his students, the improvisation in jazz resembles basketball. "A referee throws the ball up, and a game starts," he said. "Every game goes differently within a familiar framework, which is why people gladly pay to watch."

In jazz, as in basketball, the performances vary. "You play according to how you feel, never exactly the same. If you have the flu, you do not sound the way that you would if you had just gone swimming and felt all refreshed."

The music has an ebb and flow. "Songs are the framework. What a musician does with them is like a sports game. That adds the exciting part and explains why so many people always want to see and hear live music."

Meanwhile, Allen makes no attempt at one particular aspect of music. "I do not sing," he said. "If I could sing, probably I would be a rhythm-and-blues guy."

'How Much Money Do You Make?'

Although music serves as a universal language, sometimes the reactions to musicians can be typical of certain places. "When I visit schools in Hong Kong on music programs, the little kids, the students, always ask me the same question," Allen said. "Every time they want to know, 'how much money do you make?' So I tell them, 'None of your business.'

"Then I try to turn the question around to my advantage by telling them how much money that they may be able to earn by following the different avenues in music.... Some musicians, like those who have toured with **Michael Jackson, Madonna** or whoever, make good money. Usually they live in Los Angeles. When they leave one top musician, then they go to someone else. **Gerry Brown,** a guy that I worked with the last time when I visited the U.S., was **Stevie Wonder**'s drummer for 14 years and then became Diana Ross's drummer. That is where the money is, the top of the game."

If the students want to become wealthy from music, "then they had better pay attention now". They must become capable, well-educated musicians and good business people. "They will need to know how to read fly-shit (written music)," Allen said.

"Sometimes working in music is not about what you like. Music is a business. If **Quincy Jones** (a famous American musician and record producer) tells you that he wants eight measures of a country-and-western guitar solo, then you had better do it. Otherwise, you will be out, and someone else will do it. Plenty of other musicians are out there just waiting for their chances."

Beethoven Shares a Special Day

Born in 1953, Allen always chuckles when his birthday arrives on December 16. He shares the same birthday as **Ludwig Van Beethoven** (1770-1827), a German musician long famous on piano and maybe the greatest composer ever.

"As a kid, I took piano lessons," Allen recalled. "When I was about eight years old, I read a good book, *Meet the Composers*. First, there was a section about Bach (another German composer, **Johann Sebastian Bach**, 1685-1750). When I reached the part about Beethoven, I learned that I was born on his birthday."

Naturally, Allen admires Beethoven. "To this day, I almost cannot believe that somebody could be deaf (as Beethoven was) and still write *The Ninth Symphony*. That is amazing.

"On my birthdays, I always blast Beethoven's music. Usually, I never play music at all after certain hours at night out of respect for my neighbors. But sometimes I hear my neighbors playing mahjong, even at three in the morning. Bam! Clack! Click! Then I think, 'Okay, folks, just wait until December 16.' Then I will blast Beethoven all day long."

Cleveland: Musical Hotbed

The son of a church preacher, Allen moved to Cleveland as a child. There, he learned much of his music. "We had really good music programs there," he said. "Many people regarded the Cleveland Orchestra, led by **George Szell** then, as the world's best orchestra. There also were lots of city-wide music programs, like the Cleveland Music School Settlement. In high schools, the music programs were great too."

Other notable professional musicians emerged from Allen's "immediate class" in high school. One, **Debra Byrd,** has been the vocal coach on the *American Idol* and *Canadian Idol* television shows. Another, **Irwin Reese,** has spent a quarter of a century with the New York Metropolitan Opera. Obviously, Cleveland's ability to nurture musical talent stands as a good reason to justify why the Rock and Roll Hall of Fame settled there in 1995.

As a teenager, Allen played the trumpet and the piano, but the piano eventually became his main instrument. "Everyone always needed a piano player… so I usually ended up playing that.

"My first little gig was with some friends at a girls' Catholic school. We actually got paid, and to perform for all those girls. I enjoyed doing that."

'One Teacher Pissed Me Off'

Allen graduated from Wittenberg University in Springfield, Ohio. Surprisingly, he secured a degree in history and philosophy, not music.

"I went there as a music-major," he said, "but most of

the professors did not teach me anything. That music program turned out to be so disappointing. I needed to play Bach only so many times, no offence to him. That kind of thing only gets you so far.

"There was one teacher I did not like, and he did not like me either – because I could play all of the stuff. Plus I had been trained in music theory. By then, I held a keen interest in church music, Motown and all the 'black-music', rock, like **Jimi Hendrix** and **Led Zeppelin,** and jazz too. That guy (the teacher) just kept dismissing all of this great music with disdain. He pissed me off.

"At the same time, I played in bands with my friends. We would leave the school and go to open big shows for professional musicians, maybe seven-piece Earth, Wind and Fire-type bands. So I got paid and learned more about music from doing that than I did from sitting in the university classrooms.

"It got to the point that I just switched my major. But I continued with the piano teacher, who was the head of the music department. He was from Chicago and understood my reasons."

As a working musician in the U.S., Allen lived mainly in Seattle and in small-town North Carolina. "For a number of years, I participated in artists-in-residency programs," he said. "That means that you go into a community as a professional musical artist to work with the community and to help with programs for schools, churches, Rotary Clubs and other groups."

Behind Prison Walls

"One time in Seattle, which is called 'the rainy city' for a reason, I sat around with the guys in my band," Allen said. "It rained hard, and so we just messed around, talking about all kinds of stuff. So I said, 'Do you know what I hate? I really despise all those people who just complain and complain, yet do nothing. At least they should suggest some solutions.' "

Inspired and prompted by his own remarks, Allen then called the Department of Corrections to ask about performing and teaching music in prisons. "Which I soon did," he said.

"You know, sometimes musicians have big hit-songs. Then they receive lots of attention and money. But those rewards are not the most important things. What a person really needs to do is to give back to the community. So my bands and I often used to go into the schools for autistic children and play there for free. Plus when you can see people who are so much less fortunate than yourself enjoying the music, then it makes you play better."

Allen's queries about taking music into prisons helped to prompt the Washington State Arts Commission to start a relevant program. He became one of the first musicians to participate. "It meant going in there (behind prison walls) for six hours a day and teaching two- or three-hour classes about music as a profession. A lot of the prisoners would get out of there someday, and music could be a viable career option for them. So I brought in equipment, set up a little recording studio and made them work together. There was a little theory involved too.

"The classes had about 30 people in them. I knew that those guys were prisoners, but I never wanted to hear any of the details about exactly what any of them had done to get in there. Otherwise, it would have affected how I taught."

What It Is All About

When Allen moved to North Carolina, he paid special attention to local musical history. "**John Coltrane,** a wonderful saxophone player, was born in Hamlet, North Carolina. **Dizzie Gillespie** was born nearby in South Carolina, and another famous guy, **Woody Shaw** (trumpet), came from Laurinburg, North Carolina." So Allen spent much of his time in those areas.

"I was able to bring in a lot of my musician friends from New York, or even Seattle, to perform and do workshops," he said. "That was good for them. Of course, some of them just wanted to play, but I said, 'No, you also need to tell the people here about your experiences.' They all did. No one ever should hesitate to talk about musical or other work experiences because you just never know which little kid may be affected or inspired by what you have to say, and that is what it is all about."

In 1991, Allen signed on with the Southern Arts Federation touring roster. Based in Atlanta, Georgia, the federation helps to book musicians to play at festivals and other events. Those festivals created some thrills. "In Birmingham, Alabama, there was my trailer next to those for **B.B. King, Albert King** and the Neville Brothers. Yeah!"

British Territory, Bruce Lee and Cheap Stuff

Allen's earliest travels, before he relocated to Asia, took him across the U.S. and to the West Indies, Mexico and Canada. Inspiration for a move to Hong Kong came as he ended his stay in North Carolina and elsewhere in the American South.

"All that I really had to do right then was to drive from Virginia back to Seattle," he said. "I had a trailer full of equipment, and one way or another I needed to get that past the Rocky Mountains. So I decided to go through Mississippi. One of my best friends lived in Dallas, Texas, so I drove there next.

"After that, I had to drive, drive and drive. I headed for Los Angeles. Another good friend lived there so I could stay at his house and then make the trip north to Seattle.

"Along the way, I received a message from another

friend, an agent in Seattle. But he does not book musicians for the U.S. He books them for Asia, including Tokyo, Kuala Lumpur, Jakarta, Seoul and Hong Kong.

"He constantly had asked me to go overseas, but I always used to tell him, 'No, I am busy.' But that one time on the road, I was not so busy. All that I needed to do was to finish my driving.

"When I contacted him, he said: 'Allen, what about Hong Kong?'

"So I thought, 'Hong Kong? Hmm! Okay, that means British territory, **Bruce Lee** and cheap stuff.'

" 'For how long?'

" 'How about staying there for three months with an option for three more?'

Allen agreed and made plans to spend six months in Hong Kong. Twenty years later, he still lives there. Why? What does he like so much about the place?

"The big thing about Hong Kong is that I meet different people from different places every single day," he said. "In the rooms where I play, I can talk to people not only from Hong Kong, but also from the Chinese mainland, Norway, Denmark, Greece, Indonesia, Pakistan, the Philippines, the U.S., Britain and everywhere else. I always enjoy talking to lots of people about their cultures and countries, which definitely beats just reading. For example, if I have questions about things that were mentioned in the news concerning Greece, and you are Greek, then I can get your real insights and learn your opinions, no matter what I read in the newspapers. I love that about Hong Kong."

At times, Allen still thinks and talks about returning to live in the U.S. again "someday…, eventually". Yet the prospect of doing so stays on a back-burner.

"I did not leave the U.S. because I had to go," he said. "To me, I took a sabbatical, but 20 years have passed."

As a musician eager to reach as many people as possible, Allen has another perspective too. "More people live on this side of the world (in Asia) than on the other side (in the Americas)…. Living and playing in Asia have allowed me to go to places that otherwise I might never even have thought of any possible reasons to visit."

Final Note: Music fans hungry for a big helping of jazz well done may wish to watch for Allen playing live, listen to his CDs or see him play in video on YouTube. At the time of writing, Allen plays most often in Hong Kong at Bert's Bar (downstairs at the Foreign Correspondents' Club), at Peel Street Fresco (a club in Central District) and at Grappa's Cellar (a restaurant in Central).

CHARISMATIC CANADIAN SWAPS WOEFUL WHINES FOR HAPPY-BUSINESS WINES

Garry Benny Wants Everyone to Find a Favorite Flavor

Editor's Note: *Once a potential policeman and then a silver-tongued lawyer, Garry Benny turned expatriate after winning a Canadian lottery and celebrating with a huge party that carried him away to the Turks and Caicos Islands. Seeking new challenges and fresh locales, usually at five-year intervals, he became a business trouble-shooter, launched his own enterprise and then entered China as a wine merchant and master vintner. Amid bottles of wine or kegs of beer, Garry shares true stories that range from the Canadian wilderness to Chinese wineries.*

FUJIAN PROVINCE, China – Trained as a lawyer, Canadian **Garry Benny** might have used his impressive gift-of-gab to reap the riches of a brilliant career in and out of courtrooms. Instead this gregarious Canuck wearied of hearing the tales of woe linked to his clients' legal problems. Choosing a new path and new places, he has moved to China where he makes and markets wine, a commodity that inspires much happier stories.

Fifty-eight-year-old Garry thrives as a master vintner and the vice-president operations with Bellavita Fujian Winery Co Ltd, based in Yongtai, a county administered by Fuzhou City in China's Fujian Province. Under the GOLRIDGE label, he is the Master Vintner behind the production and sales of an array of wines. No wonder that so many of his Asian-based friends call him "Garry, the wine guy".

For Garry, a successful career means having "the greatest time" and seldom working. "If you enjoy what you do, then it almost never feels like work, right?" he said.

Trapped Underground

When Bellavita expanded to Hong Kong, Garry started to spend time there too. Almost immediately, he and his wife **Elizabeth** became incarcerated in an underground cavern – albeit by mistake.

One night the Bennys consumed a really late meal and a few drinks on Hong Kong Island. As Garry recalls: "When we looked at the time, someone told us, 'You really should hurry because the MTR (Mass Transit Railway, the city's underground train system) will close soon.'" (Late each night the trains stop until early the following day.)

Garry and Elizabeth rushed to the nearby Wanchai District MTR station and descended the stairs into its underground halls. Meanwhile, an MTR employee locked one station entrance and walked around outside (not inside to check for straggler passengers) locking the other entrances, each also an exit, and then departed.

"But we had gone inside," Garry said. "All of the turnstiles showed bright red lights, and nobody was around anywhere. We had missed the last train.

"We walked back upstairs to the entrance/exit and found it locked (with a sturdy metal-grille gate slammed and solidly secured across the opening). So we were trapped inside the underground-train station and had to start thinking about spending the night there.

"I yanked on the gate and yelled out toward the street, 'Hey, hey, is anyone there from the MTR?'

"A bus pulled up outside, and I yelled, 'Hey, come here.'

"When the bus-driver approached, I said, 'We got locked in here.'

" 'I cannot help,' he said. 'I work for the bus company, not for the MTR.' And away he went, leaving!

"Going back downstairs, I looked all around. I spotted a fire alarm, but figured, 'Pulling on that might be a little too much.'

"Finally, I went up to another exit and stood there, waiting, yelling and grabbing on the gate.

"Elizabeth said to me, 'Maybe we just should find a bench somewhere in here for the night.'

"Then a police officer walked by so I waved and waved toward him, but he just waved back happily and continued right past. 'Shiiiiit!' I said.

Pedestrians strolling within earshot failed to react to Garry's pleas bellowed in English. "As people passed, I started to yell, 'Does anyone speak English?'

"I also tried to send text messages, but failed, being slightly drunk and unable to read much without my glasses.

"Finally, a guy came by wearing the MTR logo. He looked at me and started to talk: 'Wah, wah, wah', something in Chinese.

"I looked at him and said, 'Wah, wah, wah to you too. Get us the hell out of here.'

"He moved away and got busy on a telephone. Then

Point of Law
Cheers from China!
WINE
Gan bay! Gan bay!
Onion Wine

the next thing that we knew, an MTR car, a little green vehicle, pulled up, and a guy came running out from it. He had keys, and he struggled, jiggling them, trying to find the right one. Finally, the lock opened, and we stepped outside, free after being trapped in there for an hour or so.

"The man with the keys spoke no English either. He tried to question us about 'where the hell we came from?' And I tried to give him shit because the MTR had locked us in there."

Double-Barreled Tactics

In more routine activities, the Bellavita Fujian Winery receives leadership from Garry and his Chinese-Canadian partners, business-savvy brothers **Peter** and **Ephraim Tsang** and Peter's sister-in-law **Nancy Kwan** (not the famous actress with the same name who starred with **William Holden** in the acclaimed 1960 movie *The World of Suzie Wong*). The company takes a double-barreled approach.

Firstly, it invites individuals who enjoy wine to come and "ferment on the premises" to create their own favorite varieties at a fraction of the cost to buy wine in stores. "We bring in the pure natural juices and show people how to make wine, and then they make their own," Garry said.

Secondly, with its own production, the winery sells to bars, restaurants, stores and event organizers, mostly in Fujian Province and Hong Kong. Exporting to the whole world forms no part of the company's immediate plans. "Our micro-winery concept works really well," Garry said. We are the number-one (and only) wine-maker in Fujian Province."

Much beyond that, long-distance "logistics in China are a nightmare. Too many shipments end up broken, damaged, soaking wet, nasty, and I am so angry."

Although Bellavita owns more land in Fujian and plans to open another winery there eventually, "we still do not aim to expand too much and get all crazy", Garry said. "We want to keep everything compact. I prefer to risk running out rather than to have tons of stock. Maybe extra stock should not be considered a totally bad thing because aging wine is aging wine, but you never have enough storage space."

Fruity Niche Found, Tea-Wine Tested

With a firm foothold in Fujian since 2009, Bellavita has widened its scope by renting premises, creating a do-it-yourself winery and "testing the market" in Hong Kong. "We seem to have found a niche there with our fruit wines", Garry said.

The company's wide variety of fruit wines proves that Garry really tries to create something for everyone. The list includes: Peach Chardonnay, Seville Orange Sangria, Cranberry-Apple Chardonnay, Banana Pineapple Viognier, Green Apple Gewurztraminer, Canadian Riesling Ice-Wine, Strawberry White Zinfandel, Raspberry White Zinfandel, Kiwi Melon Pinot Grigio, Blackcurrant White Merlot, Blackberry Merlot and Pear-licious. As for which ones sell the best, strawberry and peach consistently lead the list.

"We want to bring up the sweetness -- the flavor actually is in the sweetness," Garry said. "Take strawberry for example. We mush up strawberries, heat them and bring them down to form thick syrup. Then I make a Chardonnay and add that syrup to reach a level at which you still taste the Chardonnay, but wow, this is strawberry, and it is sweet."

With Asian (especially Chinese) consumers in mind, Garry even created a special tea-wine from fermented tea leaves. "I believe that I am the first person on the planet to make tea-wine for sale commercially," he said. After all, the Chinese love tea. "There is tea toothpaste, which I once got by mistake thinking it was lime," Garry said. "Then there is that delicious lime ice-cream, but, oh, my God, no, that really is green-tea ice-cream. This is a tea-society with tea-everything."

Bellavita soon must expand into bigger Hong Kong premises to produce more wine, especially the popular fruit wines. "Rent levels in Hong Kong are totally nuts, completely insane, for what you get," Garry said. "In Fujian, we have 15,000 square feet and pay the equivalent of US$6,000 per year." No such attractive deals exist in Hong Kong.

As Garry and his team network, news of their expertise spreads, and they receive invitations to help with outfitting other new wineries. "China looks like a good place for us to work," Garry said. "People in Guangzhou (the biggest southern city) want more wine too. We just need to continue putting together all the pieces of the puzzle."

Fake Wine: Kool-Aid in the Bottles

Some wine merchants lack honesty. "France produces 50,000 bottles of Beaujolais wine each year," Garry said. "The Hong Kong and China markets take probably 20,000 of those. Yet the sales figures in China show close to 100,000 bottles.

"Definitely, fake wine has become a huge thing. Always look at the labels. If they say 'Produit (sic) of France', the chances are high that the contents of those bottles never really came from France. Spelling blunders like that never would happen at a legitimate winery.

"The taste provides another clue. China has plenty of people mixing Kool-Aid and alcohol in bottles, sticking on labels and selling it as expensive wine."

Different Places, Different Ways

Garry has started to learn about China's enormous diversity. Doing business in Fujian varies big-time from in Hong Kong. "One of my pet peeves is government," he said. "On the Chinese mainland, the government can be impossible to deal with. Any part of the government that you must interact with presents a horror show. But when we want to open a new place in Hong Kong, still part of China, the government will pre-register us and preview us business licenses. On the Chinese mainland, it took us eight months to get a license. Government bureaucracy in the two places is amazingly different.

"So are the people and their ways of drinking. In Fujian, I recently went to an eight-person dinner party, took 14 bottles of wine and all 14 got consumed. At dinner parties in Hong Kong, somebody will bring out one bottle, and later a guest ends up taking part of it home. People will sit and constantly play with their wine.

"Enjoying wine is like taking a pleasant journey. After finding a wine that you like, please drink it, not play with it."

Secret Ingredients: Leprechaun Urine and Bullshit?

Garry regards wine-appreciation as simple – not the complex process that many alleged "experts" suggest. Too many people make exaggerated claims, like "The Andalusian oak that I used from the enchanted forest, pissed on by leprechauns, makes my wine the best.

"Honest to God – here is what wine is. Wine consists of water, flavor, alcohol, and the seldom-mentioned fourth component, bullshit. The wine business bulges with bullshit. Some people insist that if you have a big punt (inverse indentation) in the bottom of a bottle, then that wine will be the best. Oh, wait! If you have a big punt with writing in there, that tastes even better. If you use this kind of cork, that kind of cork.... it all is bullshit.

"Honestly, the grape is good or not good. The taste is good or not good. If the grapes grew on the west or the east side of somewhere means nothing. The heaps of hype that surround wine (especially in Hong Kong) are phenomenal. That big bullshit factor really pisses me off, especially when I see groups of guys with their noses stuck up in the air and hear them talking about wine and saying things that are complete lies."

Two-Buck Chuck: 'Grab It Fast'

Garry encourages people to experiment with wines and learn what they like. Personal preferences should prevail, not what the "experts" praise. No one should feel ashamed for liking Two Buck Chuck, a supremely cheap variety. ("**Charles Shaw** from California looked around and thought, 'Hey, look at all these grapes unused at the end of the season. They just will get mulched up.' So he decided to buy all of the leftover grapes from different places, took them to his processing plant and gave orders to make wine. Wham! Out came delicious wine! Two Buck Chuck! The price has risen to US$5 per bottle, but within two months, every bottle sells. Get it quickly!")

Notice that the world's leading wine critics, like the American commentator **Robert Parker,** originally from Baltimore, Maryland, never tell other people what to like. "I have met Parker several times," Garry said. "He rates any wine and tells why he likes it or not. He never professes to say that you should like it too."

Sadly, wine-drinkers in Hong Kong taste precious little variety. "The market constantly gets flooded with French wines, mostly Cab Sauv (Cabernet Sauvignon, from a famous grape variety), often not very good," Garry said. "Everyone always flogs the same stuff. Too many Hong Kong people fail to understand the immense variety of possibilities. I can make more than 1,000 varieties of wine just from the ingredients that we have and put together."

Grimaces Give the Verdict

So Garry strives to educate everyone. "Go to a table in China and watch the people sitting there. The men all will say, *'Gan bay, gan bay* (cheers)!' The women will reveal whether they like the wine by their faces. Always watch the faces. You never even need to ask what they think. If they dislike the wine, a little grimace always appears. Then persuade the people who grimaced to try a different wine. If a woman tastes some red wine and shows you 'the face', give her some banana-pineapple fruit wine. A wine exists for everyone. You just need to find it.

"I want to convince people to forget about the bottle, the top, what experts think – all of that. They should pay attention only to their mouths. Do they like the taste? If not, then do not drink that wine. If they do, then drink. Then they will have found a suitable wine. It means nothing what the label says – Chateau this, Chateau that. All that counts is what their mouths tell them."

Most people never realize one disadvantage about being a master vintner like Garry, someone who knows all the techniques and decides how to perfect the wine-making process. "As a master vintner, I always must be able to detect things, especially in my wine," Garry said. "So if I go out drinking casually, I will drink beer, vodka, scotch, rum, rye or gin, but not wine. Red tannin in wine dulls the palate." So he drinks wine strictly for professional purposes.

Happy Business and a Frozen Hell

Garry's partner, Ephraim, age 56, also enjoys the wine business. "I find it very interesting," he said. "The people I meet all feel happy and look forward to enjoying their wine. People who drink wine become happy. You never see people crying while drinking wine. This is a happy business."

A past computer-systems analyst and IT teacher, the

Hong Kong-born Ephraim once worked for Nortel (Northern Telecom), then among Canada's largest companies, long before it collapsed into bankruptcy in 2009. He lived in the Toronto area for more than a decade before returning to Asia. He has two daughters, **Jacqueline,** born in Canada, and **Jane,** born in Hong Kong.

"I may return to Canada someday," Ephraim said. "I adapt to new places quite easily. Some people go to Canada, and they hate it, especially the cold weather. 'Crazy!' you hear them saying. 'This place is like hell' (if hell had frozen over, presumably).

But Ephraim takes a different view: "Life in Canada flows so easily, so simply. On weekends, you can go fishing or attend barbecue parties with friends. The houses are big and comfortable. You may get off from work at 5 p.m. and sometimes then sit at home wondering what to do. Maybe you end up going to bed at 9 p.m. But in Hong Kong, you may not even leave work until 9 p.m. and there always is action. The lifestyles are totally different, but I can adapt to either one."

Where Does the Best Fun Happen?

Meanwhile, Garry regards Hong Kong as being a tough place to make steadfast friends. "Most people never invite anyone to their homes because they live in apartments that are too tiny," Garry said. "Much of the social interaction happens in restaurants and never reaches the level of down-to-earth, hell-slapping fun. Instead, it means watching what you do, or 'we need your table now'. In many cities or countries, you always have the best fun at someone's home. In Hong Kong, most people never get to enjoy that kind of interaction."

Garry and Elizabeth divide their time between Fujian Province and Hong Kong with occasional visits to

Canada. Their sons, **Tyler** and **Adam,** have families near Orillia in Ontario (Canada's most populous province).

Five-Year Plans

When Garry lingers beyond five years on any career path, he turns restless. He begins to crave new places and fresh challenges. "For some reason, everything with me happens at five-year intervals," he said.

When growing up in Toronto, he anticipated becoming a police officer like his brother. "I planned to walk the streets, righting wrongs, and putting the bad guys behind bars where they belong."

Once accepted by a police academy, Garry felt "ready to rock-and-roll as a police officer", but "a probationary police officer got shot about two months before I was supposed to start. Then all of the Canadian police forces dropped their probationary programs. No one younger than age 21 was allowed by law to carry a gun, and the Police Commissioner believed that probationary police no longer could wander around without guns since one of them had been shot."

At the time 18 years old, Garry faced a long wait so he decided to study law. "I ended up having so much fun drinking my way through law school," he said. Luckily, "I had the ability to stand up in mock court and just go crazy (performing well)."

To help pay for his tuition and other expenses, Garry even worked as a private investigator, gaining "a background in snooping around, along with being good at law". Soon he joined Dun and Bradstreet, a huge credit-report company (where Elizabeth toiled as a business analyst) that gathers and provides information for clients to use in credit and supply-chain-management decisions.

"It was cool and everything, but it was corporate law. I could get people into or out of any contract, and I also specialized in regaining money from companies that owed it." But after five years, the Toronto-based job badly bored him.

Lady Luck Funds a Big Bash

One stroke of luck, the likes of which many people constantly fantasize about, turned Garry and Elizabeth into expatriates. They won a substantial prize (Cdn $250,000, now worth about the same in US dollars) in the popular Wintario lottery. In a festive way, that good fortune washed them ashore in the Turks and Caicos Islands, a British overseas territory in the West Indies.

"The first thing that we did was have a huge party," Garry said. "When a television reporter started to interview me about winning the lottery, I ignored the first question. Instead, I said: 'For anybody who knows me, a huge party will begin on Friday night, this date, this time, and continue until Sunday night (at the Benny home in Orangeville, just outside of Toronto). It will be catered with German food, all you can eat, all you can drink.'

"Then the reporter said; 'Now can we interview you?'

" 'Yes, as long as you promise to include what I just said.'

"So the party turned out to be massive with people I had not seen for years and many more I did not even know, who just showed up. During the all-weekend party, 24 hours a day, about 1,000 people came and went. We even had a beer truck parked outside."

Empty Briefcase Fills With Plans

"At the party, I apparently met someone who talked to me about a project in the British West Indies. Two weeks later, a telephone call came in, and then my secretary told me that I had a meeting scheduled with the people from a Czechoslovakian glass company.

"Great! My secretary and I both searched through all of our files, but we had no idea who those people were and found no trace of them. So I went to the meeting carrying an empty briefcase.

"When I sat down, one guy grinned and said, 'Garry, you threw quite a party.'

" 'Thank you,' I replied, staring and blurrily starting to remember talking to him."

The Czech company represented a group of investors who had been struggling with a real-estate project, one with 24 luxury homes around a big pool and a tennis court, which was badly stalled in the Turks and Caicos Islands. "None of it was finished," Garry said. "A total of US$5 million had gone into it, the project had not been completed and next to no receipts had come out, but the money was all gone."

To investigate, Garry and Elizabeth headed to the sunny Turks and Caicos Islands (population 45,000). "What an absolutely incredible place!" Garry said. The island of primary interest, Grand Turk, two miles wide, five miles long and with 5,600 residents, has an airport runway across its entire width.

Liking what they saw, Garry and Elizabeth moved there and salvaged the real-estate project. "We stayed for five years (naturally). We pulled the development out of the paws of the people who had it, found out where the money went, could not retrieve most of it, but got some back, had the investors inject more, finished the project and opened it. Then we stayed on and managed the project."

Unlike friends back in Canada, "who actually had to work for a living, I rode a motorcycle around a warm island having a great time", Garry said. "We travelled to Miami, Haiti and the Dominican Republic. Every few weeks, we travelled somewhere. We always went to the Governor's mansion for his parties too. Often we were the only white people invited who spent the entire time at the parties together with the black guests. All of the Brits always stayed on the other side of the huge room with a big gap down the middle."

Boat Fails to Float on a Busy Street

Again growing bored, Garry relocated his family back to Ontario. "One thing that I bought in the Caribbean to take to Canada with us was a 28-foot, live-aboard boat," he said. "I got that beauty at a drug-proceeds auction. Someone had been running drugs in it, and so the authorities sold it really cheaply.

"When we got the boat to Miami (by ship), we put it onto a trailer. No more than 20 minutes outside of the port and within sight of the hotel where we stayed, we turned a corner and the trailer's tandem wheels hit the curb, bent around and the whole thing – the boat with all of our stuff, that we were moving back to Canada, inside it – dropped to the street at 4 p.m. on a Friday right in downtown Miami. Unbelievable!

"I looked around, considered the situation and thought, 'Things could not possibly get any worse than this.' So I started to laugh.

"The police came and asked me, 'What will you do?'

"I told them, 'I don't know. Our hotel is right over there. Do you think that we could get the boat there.'

" 'No.'

"That really heavy boat, filled with all of our possessions from the Caribbean, rested right on the ground. We had to arrange for a construction crane to come, scoop this thing up and place it onto a flatbed truck. By then, night had fallen.

"Next we flew down the highway going I-had-no-idea-where. The flatbed-truck driver pulled in at the

Horizon Trailer Company. A little Italian guy opened the gates, and we drove inside.

"The boat turned out to be too heavy even to take off the flatbed truck. We needed to leave it there and pay for the truck to stay overnight. The little Italian guy told us: 'Just come back in the morning.'

"We went to the hotel, collapsed and returned by cab the next day. As we walked in, I could see my boat with workers busy building a huge, beautiful-looking trailer underneath it.

"The guy supervising the work told me: 'Your boat is so heavy.' He kept adding more springs into the trailer. Then he added hydraulics, a braking system and an extra tire.

"I thought, 'This will kill me. My American Express-card bill looks headed through the roof.'

"Elizabeth and I, carrying our six-month-old baby son Adam and with our seven-year-old son Tyler, walked into the trailer company's main office and sat down. I said. 'How do I pay for all of this? What does it cost?'

"A woman in the office said, 'Hang on for a moment. Our owner wants to talk with you.'

"Reluctantly, we entered the owner's office, and, hey, it was the little Italian man again. He smiled and asked us, 'Are you guys okay? Did you spend the night alright?'

"Then he said, 'The cost for the trailer will be US$1,200.' He felt sorry for us and charged us just that much for a US$18,000-20,000 trailer. When he had seen the boat come in with the trailer totally destroyed and noticed that we carried a baby and had a young child with us too, he had decided to be a really nice guy."

Later after finally crossing the border into Canada, Garry floated the boat on Ontario's Lake Simcoe. "Then the boat was perfect, and we used it," he said. "Later I sold it and made a profit, which always feels good."

Up-North First Nation Beckons

For an encore, Garry tackled "legal problems" at a location totally unlike the Turks and Caicos Islands, namely the Kasabonika Lake First Nation, a small native Indian community 1,500 miles north of Toronto. Being "away up there toward the Arctic Circle", the place lacked even reliable roads. Only small airplanes consistently reached it.

After a few weeks, the First Nations community leaders asked Garry to stay for much longer than he had planned: " 'No other white man ever has assimilated here. We think that you should do some things with us.'

" 'What things?' I asked.

" 'Well, what would you like to do?'

" 'Ohhh!' I said. 'Let me tell you. The federal government offers you lots of money, but you guys never use it properly. We could design a new school, put in a recreation facility for the children and build new homes.'

" 'Great,' they said. 'Stay and do it.' "

Toilets Untended Along an Airport Runway

Repeatedly, Garry noticed something disturbing at Kasabonika Lake's airport. "Beside the runway sat lots of hot-water tanks, toilets and bathtubs, just sitting there and rotting. So I sat down with the chief and the council and said, 'Guys, I hate to tell you this. You may have heard it before, but I am one of the Canadian taxpayers who paid for all of those things. What is the problem? Why do you just let them sit there and deteriorate?'

" 'Well,' they said, 'what should we do with them?'

" 'Put them in your homes. Use them. Get those toilets installed. Throw out the old ones.'

" 'We have no toilets,' they said.

" 'What do you mean, no toilets?'

" 'We have no toilets and no running water, no sewage system.'

"A posh, little hotel where I stayed had everything, but the local houses had nothing. So I said, 'Well, get those things off the edge of the runway. Put them inside a warehouse.'

" 'What warehouse? Where do you see a warehouse? We have no warehouse here.' "

So Garry suggested arranging for a chat with the appropriate federal-government people. At the ensuing meeting, "I gave them hell. 'You accuse the Indians of wasting money, but you are the guys who brought in all of this crap. Basically, you unloaded a plane at the edge of the runway and left everything. Then we get the bad press. So now you need to install a water system.' "

At first, the bureaucrats balked. They tried to dismiss Kasabonika Lake as being just a few hundred people "in the middle of nowhere", but "soon we received Cdn $4 million for the water system. Every house got running water and a working toilet."

In Garry's time there, "we also built a new school and a police station. Again, I had the time of my life. We even bought a fire-truck, and I became the fire chief." He drove in the fire-truck on a winter-only road across the icy muskeg and frozen lakes.

On a Chase With the Chief

"What a great time I had!" Garry said. "I remember the First Nations chief one day approaching me at 10 a.m. and saying, 'Come. You must come with me.'

"He took me down to a lake. 'Get in the boat,' he said.

"Then he started the outboard motor and away we went. 'Where in the hell are we going?' I asked him.

" 'Oh, we can do some fishing and then have a shore lunch.'

"For three hours, we travelled. There were fish everywhere, right? But he had a special spot in mind.

"Finally, we threw a line into the water and started to pull out fish like crazy. The chief cooked up a big lunch. Then he wanted to do some hunting.

" 'We should get back soon,' I said. 'I have stuff to do at the office.'

" 'Oh! We should be back at 4 or 5 p.m.,' the chief said. "But he meant two days later. We had no sleeping bags or anything. He liked to take a bag of sugar and one of salt and just go. Two days later, we finally returned."

Towering Task Tackled High

Once, the Kasabonika Lake leaders had a brainstorm. "They decided, 'Do you know what? We want to use mobile telephones up here. The rest of the world has them.'

" 'Okay, why not get them?' I said.

" 'But you know, Bell Canada and those big companies never will want to install the infrastructure all the way up here.'

" 'We could get our own.'

So Garry prowled south to Toronto, and despite not being the slimmest or most agile guy, he "climbed high up on a cell tower. There was a ladder surrounded by metal hoops. If I had fallen, I would have bounced back across the hoops and probably somewhat survived.

"At the bottom of the tower, everything had been sealed. I found no information there, and no one would have told me anything. The most important part was a big drum-like thing on the top. So I scrambled up there and saw some name-plates telling me which company had made the equipment and where it all came from, namely Motorola in Scottsdale, Arizona.

"I contacted Motorola and said, 'We want a cell tower.'

" 'Where are you?'

" 'At the Kasabonika Lake First Nations in Northern Ontario.'

" 'Sorry! Nobody will install a tower away up there.'

" 'We will. Sell us one – the tower, equipment, a whole bunch of telephones and everything that we need.'

"It was crazy. Soon I went to Scottsdale and spent two months learning everything that the people there could teach me about mobile phones and the systems. All of the necessary equipment came to Kasabonika Lake. We put up the cell tower, sold everyone their cell phones, put them on little cell-phone plans and now the First Nations band generates money using the cell-phone equipment. Hunters out in the bush can call their wives: 'Hi, honey! I just caught another caribou.' "

After five years in Northern Ontario, Garry met a group keen to open a First Nations casino in Orillia, part of populous southern Ontario. For five years, he joined that project, first as a legal representative and then also as the "slot-department manager".

Secret Sips Behind Trees

"After my casino stint, I wanted to do something totally different," Garry said. "When I had worked with the First Nations in Northern Ontario, I spent a lot of time in the woods. The community had been controlled by the chief and the council. One of their edicts banned alcoholic beverages. Northern communities that brought in alcohol often became disaster areas. I saw plenty of terrible examples. Much of my time had been spent flying to a place called Sioux Lookout (population 5,000) to try getting chiefs or elders out of jail.

"If people never have been taught to drink in moderation, it can be almost insane what they do. Some of the First Nations people would get off airplanes, and within four hours, I would receive phone calls from the police to say, 'We have this person, and that one, in jail' (for alcohol-fueled offences). Or 'Somebody is bringing up blood on the street.' They drink, drink, drink and drink. Not many have the concept of drinking half a bottle and saving the rest. Instead, their policy calls for 'drinking it all and then getting another one'.

"So the chief and the council declared, 'No drinking. This place stays dry.' Well, great! It was a peaceful, wonderful community with no locks on the doors. Great friends, good people and amazing hunters all lived there.

"But when I went off into the woods, I found people there making their own wine – not moonshine because that process required a still and cooking things down, which they had not done before -- but wine-making, wow! Of course, it was all natural because no chemicals were up there. I spent lots of time watching and seeing exactly what they did."

'Could You Do This in China?'

Ready with his backwoods knowledge, Garry opened a make-your-own-wine business in Orillia. He helped the customers to produce favorite varieties of wine for as little as Cdn $3 per bottle, a big saving versus at least $15 in liquor stores. "For $4 or $5, they could make a $50 or $60 bottle of wine.

"I also had the bizarre habit of doing my own TV commercials and being open 24-hours-a-day, seven-days-a-week, by appointment, which means that I was not really open constantly, but all the media took notice," Garry said. He even started a TV show called *The Friendly Fermenter.*

The landlord for Garry's business, Peter Tsang, later became the president of Bellavita Fujian Winery. "One day Peter said to me: 'Do you think that you could do this business in China?'

" 'Sure, I can do this anywhere if I have a backer and proper facilities.'

"He said, 'Alright.'

"Then we flew to China and spent three weeks travelling to pick a spot." They chose Yongtai in Fujian.

From No Talk to Verbal Diarrhea

Life in China brings distinct pleasures and challenges. "Almost none of Yongtai's 25,000 people speak English," Garry said. "I have a best friend there, but we never have had a direct conversation. Not once! He picks me up in his car and drives me into the mountains to meet his parents and grandparents. I even agreed to become a godfather to his son's child. But I never have spoken directly to any of these people. If my interpreter has gone elsewhere, then we just laugh and joke, say *'gan bay, gan bay'*, party and eat.

Luckily, no one necessarily needs perfect conversation to enjoy the benefits of Chinese hospitality. "I have a motorcycle," Garry said. "When I drive up into the mountains, people drag me into their homes and feed me – because they figure that I look like I need something to eat, right? They give me tea too, but I never understand a single word that they say" (and vice-versa).

That language barrier posed "an unusual challenge that I looked forward to with gusto, but it has started to get a little old," Garry said. "When I go to Hong Kong, I find that I have verbal diarrhea. Then I cannot stop talking because I have so many things that I want to say. When I talk to people and they actually talk back to me, I think, 'Oh, my God! That is away too amazing!' "

Does Garry, the chatty "wine guy", miss his past life as a lawyer forced to listen to whiny clients lament about their legal worries? "Not at all," he said. "In courtrooms, I sometimes had to do things that I did not want to do. I could be known to say to clients: 'What you did was wrong. Just because we found a way to get you out of it does not mean that I need to be the one doing it.' "

But can Garry persist with wine in Asia beyond the five-year limit that has applied to his work elsewhere? "I do not know," he said. "I love Asia, and I love wine so I will try to stick with both of them for as long as I can."

As many expatriates learn, "Things come and go. The wind blows, and a door opens. Then I say, 'Yeah, great! I want to go there and do that.' "

Final Note: How unusual are some of the wine flavors that Garry develops? Maybe readers will want to watch for one of his latest – tasty onion wine.

GUNSHOTS ECHO ACROSS DECADES, CONTINENTS

Dallas Drake Sees RSL Help Veterans and Others

Editor's Note: *If Australian military veterans face woes in the Philippines, then Dallas Drake and his colleagues in the Returned and Services League of Australia (RSL) stand ready to help. They make a point to assist sick children and others too. Here, Dallas tells how the many RSL activities can make a difference between life and death. He gently reminds that wars not only kill people, but also scar many others in ways that never heal. Along the way, he recalls his own experiences and tells a few odd, but true, stories.*

IN THE WAKE OF WAR – Once a soldier has survived during warfare, then peacetime should make for easy-going. Too often, that turns out to be a premature assumption, which explains why **Dallas Drake** stays active on an important military-related mission.

An Australian who first left his home country as a soldier bound for the Vietnam War, Dallas still dodges the echoes from that and other conflicts. Now 68 years old, he devotes much of his time to the ongoing charity work and assistance to former military people undertaken by the Returned and Services League of Australia (RSL).

Post-traumatic stress disorder and many other emotional or physical consequences from military skirmishes never go away, said Dallas, the honorary secretary for a 400-member RSL sub-branch based in Angeles City, the Philippines. The presence of a network of people who understand the problems and the accompanying distress can be essential.

'A Very Important Organization'

"The welfare of veterans ranks as the RSL's primary objective," Dallas said. "To me, the RSL is a very important organization because it provides interaction between military veterans and forms a safety net to stop guys from falling out or even killing themselves. A lot of Vietnam veterans have committed suicide. For some reason that I fail to fully understand, quite a few children of Vietnam veterans have done the same.

"Many people may need help sometimes. The only sure way for us to be in the right position to provide it is by getting them together and socializing. Otherwise, I can talk to someone and maybe not even know that he is a veteran. He will reveal nothing, but then may go through a distressed period. People who have made a habit of communicating very little throughout their lives, and still have no one to talk to, may do some stupid things."

Established in 1916 (amid the First World War), the RSL, a military-leagues club, has 1,500 sub-branches in Australia. Only four sub-branches exist outside of the country – in Washington, D.C., in Papua New Guinea and in Subic Bay and in Angeles City, the Philippines.

The Angeles City sub-branch began in 1994, established by Korean War veteran **Doug Slide.** Military people from Australia's allied nations can join too. So can non-military people as affiliate members. Membership costs 700 pesos (US$17) per year.

Members in Angeles City keep a permanent clubroom and meeting site in the Ponderosa Hotel there. They communicate by new-age means (with a blog, Facebook page and Twitter account) and by more traditional ways (a monthly newsletter). "Some veterans remain isolated, but they may communicate through some of these systems," Dallas said.

When Australian veterans face difficulties in the Philippines, Dallas and his RSL buddies want to help. "Guys have fallen sick and gone into hospitals, but in other locations," Dallas said. "Then the Department of Veterans' Affairs in Australia tells us, 'A veteran is hospitalized in Cebu and cannot do his paperwork. Can you assist?' And we say, 'Okay.' Then we go and assist.

"We help on pension and welfare issues too. If a veteran gets robbed and has no money, he never will receive assistance from anyone else in the Philippines. But if he is a member with us, then he can obtain a little financial assistance to keep him going. If he is slightly invalid, we will send someone to go and clean him up in bed and provide some food. We can supply communications back to his family too."

While striving to help veterans directly, the RSL also works indirectly by organizing regular charity events to benefit others. "We do a medical mission almost every month in Angeles City, supplying free medicines to 1,000 children on average," Dallas said. While helping children, "this also keeps veterans busy and allows them to see life from different angles. They can contribute to the community and to their own well-being while feeling good about themselves."

The sub-branch conducts twice-weekly charity raffles for prizes donated by local businesses. Members also enjoy themselves in other ways. "We have fun with bar-hops every week," Dallas said. "Actually, the idea is not to get everyone pissed out of their minds, but to provide communication and bonding. Once the guys get to know each other, then when someone has a big problem, we will hear about it much sooner."

In death, the RSL makes a crucial difference too. "When a veteran dies, we are the ones who provide a military funeral," Dallas said. "We are the ones who put a flag on the coffin. Probably we are the ones who notify the next-of-kin. We can provide the documents through the police and hospitals for the transport of remains back to Australia."

War: Nasty Business

Advancing technology may change the ways in which people fight wars, but the entire process remains stressful and nasty. "The modern War on Terror may not qualify as a real war in historical terms, but for many of the soldiers it often gets more intense than the Great Wars were," Dallas said. "The soldiers stay on active lines all the time. In the Great Wars, guys were prepared to push forward and go into battle followed by a break. There was no continual threat of infiltration of your position by insurgents, combatants or terrorists. Today, war has become a continual thing. Guys experience the conflict in Afghanistan with no breaks, no little holidays in between."

Every war creates countless tragedies. Sadly, "I doubt if any way to avoid wars even exists," Dallas said. "They always happen. Ever since men first arrived on this planet, they have been at it in one way or another. There never has been an entirely peaceful day."

BOMBS AWAY
MORE WASTED AMMO...
Blam Boom DONG
SAi GONE
AMMUNITION
HIGHLY FLAMMABLE
Made in China
AMBASSADOR TASMANIA
War-Washup Philippines RSL

Several poignant questions always stay relevant. "Why do we send our sons (and daughters) to war?" Dallas asked. "Why is it that God always stands on our side?"

Born in 1943, Dallas hails from Hobart in Tasmania. His family has a military history. "My grandfather was serial number three in the First Tasmanian Contingent to go to South Africa for the Boer War (1899-1902)," he said. "Other members of my family, two of his brothers, went to that war too."

Dallas attended technical college and received more training after enlisting in the Royal Australian Army in 1965. Initially, he served at a base near Albury-Wodonga, an Australian town split between the states of New South Wales and Victoria.

"My project there was working on Centurion tanks, getting them ready to go to Vietnam. We rebuilt the tanks from scratch. The old ones were pulled apart, sandblasted and repainted. Then we put on new wheels, bearings and chains -- the whole lot. Specifically, my job was to inspect the finished products. Whatever came out of the workshop, I inspected it, together with a team of other people, to make sure that everything was in working order."

What were the chances that the inspectors would miss something important? Minimal, Dallas said. "We had gauges, equipment, checks and balances to make it highly unlikely that we would send away anything that was not quite right without someone realizing it."

'Free' Ticket Overseas

Unlike most travelers, Dallas first left his country on a "free" ticket. "The Australian government sent me to the Vietnam War. That was my first overseas experience."

Dallas served in Vietnam in 1968 and 1969. Never a front-line combat soldier, he specialized in engineering, electrical mechanics and gunsmith work. "I fixed up weapons and made sure that they were safe for the guys to use," he said. "Provided that they pointed the guns in the right direction, there should have been no problems. Generally, soldiers take care of their own weapons, and all of the guys were trained to do that, but the parts of any weapon will wear.

"Also I did general engineering work, which could involve fabricating buildings or repairing gas stoves, hot-water tanks or anything that broke down. In fact, we had no hot-water tanks provided by the military so we made our own from 44-gallon drums. We used salvage materials to put together heating devices so that the guys could take hot showers."

Enemy Fire Rattles Rubbish Dump

Often enemies outside of the Australian encampment tried to inflict damage. "When we came under mortar attack from the Viet Cong, projectiles would be in the air and sirens would go off to warn us of the incoming fire," Dallas said. "Mostly, the mortars hit our camp's rubbish dump. We used to take all of the rubbish from our 5,000 people there and burn it as the best way to maintain a healthy rubbish pit. Smoke always wafted up from the burning there. I think that the Viet Cong probably thought that the smoke came from our kitchen, so they ended up aiming all of their mortars at our rubbish dump."

Apart from incoming mortars, the Australian base never attracted fierce attacks when Dallas served there. "I used to sit on top of a bunker and listen for the mortars," he said. "You could hear a difference between the incoming and the outgoing. If one came in extra close, I could yell out to warn the guys nearby. It was not as if the incoming missiles meant that we stopped everything and hid in holes."

'Almost Everyone Must Have Been on That Shit'

Dallas remembers "a trading mission" when Australian soldiers in Vietnam visited an American military base there. "We went to trade slouch hats and boots. Some of our equipment was better than what the Americans had, and we wanted some of their stuff.

"Military vehicles escorted us out of our zone. Moving through our secure area, we felt happy – no problems. Once we reached the American zone and they took over the security aspects, then things looked a little slacker. Naturally, that made us more careful in keeping our eyes open for anything that might cause us greater concerns.

"At dusk, we reached the American base. Inside, there were blazing mercury-vapor lights and a four-lane highway with a nature strip down its middle. Growing all the way down on the bloody nature strip was a lot of marijuana."

So the American soldiers had a sideline farming special plants? "It became even more obvious when we looked around over the military-camp area. Under those blazing lights, a pall of marijuana smoke hung low above the whole place. You could smell it too. Almost everyone must have been on that shit."

When eating an evening meal in the American mess hall, the Australian soldiers raised their eyebrows again, this time at a perceived security breech. "The Americans had Vietnamese girls there working as waitresses and looking after gaming devices (poker machines)."

At the Australian military base, things worked much differently. "We never had any Vietnamese civilians come into our zone at all," Dallas said. "The only Vietnamese who ever got inside were prisoners.

"Our base was a secure one. Basically, it was situated inside a rubber plantation so we were under cover. We had no blazing lights to tell everyone where we were. We relied on a protected perimeter area.

"Maybe we had some Australian soldiers who smoked grass too, but it was not a big activity at our base at all. The only case that I ever knew about involved our cook, who went a little crazy, and so we locked him up inside a 20-foot sea-container for a while. Technically, that was a storage area, but it made a good prison too."

'Paul Revere Is Coming'

Dallas did have some American neighbors in Vietnam. "Next door to my unit's camp, there was an American signals unit (to facilitate military communications, including air-to-ground, and to learn from enemy transmissions)," he said. "We used tents, but these Americans had prefabricated accommodation units. From my unit, I used to go down to the sergeants' mess for a few drinks. On the way back, I loved to terrorize the Americans. I would open their door and have a look inside. It was a long structure with double-bunks all along. Then I would run straight through yelling, '**Paul Revere** is coming.' (An 18th-century historical figure, Revere warned colonial forces about advancing British soldiers at a strategic juncture in the American Revolution. Allegedly, he yelled from astride a galloping horse, 'The British are coming. The British are coming.')

"Sometimes I yelled other things too," Dallas said. "Then I would be out the other end of the building and gone before anyone could stop me. I doubt if the Americans living there ever really knew exactly who I was."

In consistently playing this prank, Dallas refused to let the American soldiers outfox him. "I think that they wanted to 'get me' somehow," he said. "If I believed that they were waiting for me inside, I would get up onto their roof and run along there, yelling at the top of my lungs on top of the bloody roof."

How wise was the notion of playing tricks on anxious soldiers? After all, they had weapons at hand and good reasons for jittery trigger fingers. "At the time, we all were young and physically fit," Dallas said. "Nothing was wrong with a bit of game-playing, even involving one unit against another. Things always went on that someone or other could have gotten into trouble about."

Tragedy of a Red-White-and-Blue Dog

Nevertheless, young men in stressful military situations do not always exercise the best judgment. "The Americans in that signals unit were a little different," Dallas said. "They had a small dog that they shaved and painted red, white and blue (colors of the United States flag). The poor little bastard died because of the paint all over its skin."

Definitely, the war experience brought some life-threatening times for humans too, and various friends that Dallas made died in Vietnam. "The guys involved in the combat certainly had lots of very bad experiences. Yes, I lost friends."

Five hundred Australian soldiers died in the Vietnam War, a surprisingly small figure among the 60,000-plus who served. Many more suffered injuries, maybe hit by "bits and pieces of shrapnel".

"I had shrapnel go through me there," Dallas said, pointing to his left shoulder and upper arm. "It was friendly fire that ricocheted, came back and punched a hole through me."

No Happy Returns

Dallas endured a more disheartening wound, a deeply emotional one, when he least expected it – after returning to Australia. By then, an international anti-war movement had gained such momentum that many Australians reacted to the sight of military men with displays of angry contempt. Returned soldiers "had tomatoes thrown at them. The press, the politicians and the public all expressed hostility.

"The anti-war movement had built up so much that anything to do with the Vietnam War was considered bad. There were big marches and demonstrations against the troops. People thought that Australian soldiers should not have been in Vietnam. They wanted to know why the guys still fought there. In fact, our soldiers went and fought simply because the government had sent them. But nobody ever spoke up to defend the soldiers." Nobody at all!

Many soldiers took the direct exposure to back-home hostility personally, worsening their stress from the events in Vietnam. "After going back to Australia and finding out exactly what the attitudes of Australians were toward Vietnam veterans, I would have liked to return to the war," Dallas said. "I felt not happy at all.

"We received no welcome back – just the opposite. This issue always has played a part in my feelings about living as an expatriate. Mind you, I get more relaxed as I age."

The way that many Australian soldiers returned from Vietnam, often arriving individually, with little or no help to readjust, left much to be desired. "We came out of a war zone and were dropped into Sydney," Dallas said. "Suddenly, everything was totally different. At the time, I felt used to hearing certain noises and had learned to react to those. When someone slammed a door, I might almost have a heart attack. Still being acclimatized to Vietnam, I reacted differently to lots of things than most other people would, which often attracted some curious glances. There I would be, still ready to fight, even when sitting quietly with groups of civilians. Until then, I had been living among my friends and fellow-soldiers, people I could trust. Suddenly, it felt like I could trust no one. That created a very unusual and most uncomfortable situation!"

Like Alaska, Only Hot

In the 1970s, Dallas settled in Darwin, then a much smaller place than now, almost like a frontier town. His marriage had crumbled when he was in Vietnam, but he gained custody of his children. He has had four children (one eventually entered the military), leading to 11 grandchildren.

Diligently, Dallas stayed in Australia until his children matured. Still active in engineering, he worked for a supplier of pipes and related parts for mining, storm-water drainage, sewage-works, irrigation and cattle farming.

"For me, those were good years in many ways," he said. "I went to the most remote places in the Northern Territory – every cattle station, every mining community and every island. It resembles Alaska there, only with the reverse climate, being hot instead of cold. The U.S. has its frontier in Alaska. Similarly, Australia's frontier is the Northern Territory.

Suddenly, a dramatic turn of events led Dallas to Indonesia. "The Northern Territory government planned to send a trade delegation to Jakarta," he said. "One position in the delegation related to the beef-cattle that the Northern Territory exported. My previous work had educated me about the cattle business, and so when the delegation went, I said, 'Well, then, let me go along with you.'

"We arrived in Jakarta on a week-long mission. We met with government officials and business people from different sectors, having breakfasts, lunches, dinners and talk-fests together. At the end of the week, I looked around at the other delegation members from Australia and asked them, 'Did anyone sell anything?'

"Nobody had sold anything. So I made a bold decision. I told everyone right there and then, 'Leave me here. I will stay until I sell something.'

Pineapple Bits, Cattle Bites?

"I wanted to sell something, anything, but actually I had my eyes on a project in Timor involving 11,000 hectares of land where people planned to grow pineapples. When pineapples get processed, their skin and cores become waste products. All that waste could become useful feed on cattle lots. When eating the residue from pineapple factories, some cattle can gain up to 1.8 kilograms per day. Unfortunately, the pineapple project never happened. People kept talking about getting the land, but eventually East Timor erupted into a war."

As wheels spun futilely on the notion of fattening cattle on pineapple leftovers, along came a man "with a big coat that he opened up, saying, 'Hey, I have watches for sale.' " That visitor from Hong Kong needed a distributor in Indonesia for "corporate watches", those with printed logos or messages for promotional purposes.

So Dallas became a watch merchant leading a Jakarta-based company called Bossindo Promotama, a task that he pursued throughout the 1990s. "My first client was the Hyatt Hotels," he said. Indocement became another leading client, as did Blue Bird Taxis (Indonesia's biggest taxi company) and the Golkar political party led by **President Suharto.**

Gradually, the product line widened to also feature ball-point pens, clocks, garments and special items. "I expanded the office to create a sewing area for making T-shirts," Dallas said.

Although never active in feeding pineapple debris to cattle, Dallas later did visit East Timor and secure business there. "I was not supposed to go because there was insurgency," he said. "With some family friends, we got two four-wheel drives and went across from the Kupang side of Timor. Freeport-McMoRan, an American enterprise, operated one of the world's largest copper mines there.

Part of its goodwill efforts among the local people was to provide gifts to the area's children. So they had us supply about 1,000 soccer balls, ones with **Mickey Mouse** and **Donald Duck** on them, to the local kids."

Big Wedding, Big Deal

One memorable business order required 10,000 Rolex-style watches for a high-society marriage. Large crowds gather for Indonesian wedding parties, and often everyone who attends must receive a gift or souvenir. So in Indonesia, a big industry swirls around marketing products for weddings.

"Anyone can go to wedding receptions there, even without an invitation," Dallas said. "A lot of people went from wedding to wedding, always eating and collecting gifts. They would think, 'Ah, a big wedding is on at the Grand Hyatt. We should go there for a good feed.' "

One Street, Five Number-One Buildings

Altogether, Dallas and his company sold a few million watches. "My first employee in Indonesia was a young lady named **Murdiana,**" he said. "She had just one word in her name, a common thing there. After my intensive training, she became the country's business woman of the year.

"Soon we had secured a license for doing Disney products. With the marketing that we did, Murdiana acted as the front-person for the business. Foreigners like me usually tried to stay in the background. First, Murdiana appeared on a list of the top-50 business women in Indonesia. The next year, she landed in the number-one spot."

So Dallas had chosen well to hire his first Indonesian employee. What had impressed him about Murdiana? "I liked her ability to solve problems and to understand what was said to her," he recalled. "When seeking someone to work for me, I set a test in the advertisement. The street that I lived on was called Asem Baris Raya (Salty Tree Street). The building was Number One on Asem Baris Raya, but the street had five buildings marked Number One. The test was for the job applicants to find the right place, which would show a degree of intelligence. The real Number One had to be the first building at the beginning of the street, not the imitators. Murdiana quickly realized that and passed my test."

Why would a single street have five buildings with exactly the same address? "That too is part of how things work in Indonesia," Dallas said. "Everyone wants to be number one. They think, 'If I am in Number One, then that definitely is the best house.' "

Hence, the building numbers along many Indonesian streets are badly repetitious, out of sequence and confusing. "It makes for a total mess," Dallas said. "If you want to find someone, then you must stop to ask local people in the neighborhood. When I lived there, my visitors would ask, 'Where does that foreigner live?' And everyone nearby would know."

After leaving Indonesia, Dallas had short stays in Hong Kong, Taiwan and South Korea, all to seek business deals. "I have a good friend who had been active in real estate during the building of Hong Kong's original Mass Transit Railway (subway train) system," Dallas said. "Later we travelled together in search of more opportunities to become involved in real estate.

"My friend has enormous experience in the property business, but is completely dyslexic. When we went to South Korea (where almost everyone in the entire country shares just a few surnames), people from the firm of Kim, Kim and Kim took us around in their big Mercedes. They would say, 'The next building that we will show you is called such-and-such.'

"Then my friend would speak up: 'Ah, yes! That building has so many square feet of available space. Its efficiency is 82 per cent, and the other details are….'

"He already knew all about every building that they took him to see. The information came straight out from the top of his head. I have no idea how he does that."

A Meal Costs US$14,000

There in South Korea, Dallas once participated in an unforgettable five-hour dinner. "The most expensive meal that I ever ate happened there," he said. "It cost (the equivalent of) US$14,000 for five guys to eat. Luckily, I was not the one paying the bill.

"One of our hosts, **Mr. Kim,** was determined that we should see and experience some of the best places in Seoul. Among the spots where he took us was the first geisha house ever opened in South Korea. When the Japanese occupied Korea, they opened some geisha houses, of course, and we went to the oldest one. At first, I felt a bit surprised and disappointed. For some reason, the management could not afford chairs, and so we had to sit on the floor.

"We were forbidden from using our hands to touch the food or drinks. The geisha girls did all of that for us. We each had our own girl to feed us. Basically, we just sat there and opened our mouths at the appropriate times. The food consisted of some lovely delicacies -- traditional Japanese things, a lot of very small dishes.

"The young ladies there appeared to be intent on trying to get us drunk by giving us whiskey shots in beer. Then we were allowed to sing, of course. And then we were allowed to dance, but no romance. No funny business!"

Did the host hesitate when pulling out his wallet to pay? "No," Dallas said. "My understanding was that he had the good fortune to own about five hotels in the U.S.

"But I did notice one interesting thing. The geisha-house ladies took clever precautions right away to make sure that we could not run off quickly at the end of the meal. When we first arrived, they took away our shoes. We got them back only after the big bill had been settled."

Tasmania Ambassador Welcomed

In 2001, Dallas arrived in the Philippines, where he retired and plans to stay. Not surprisingly, he retains the same sense of humor that led him to play tricks on the American soldiers in Vietnam. These days, he may try to spoof some higher-ranking people.

"One of my best friends, **Henry Sawaya,** recently went back to Lebanon after 27 years in the Philippines," Dallas said. "For a long time he owned the Prince of Wales Pub in Makati (Manila). Every year, he still comes to the Philippines for a few weeks.

"Henry has strong connections with the Middle Eastern diplomatic community in Manila. One time, he said to me, 'Dallas, I want you to come to the Lebanese national birthday party at the Hyatt Hotel.'

"So I said, 'Thanks, Henry. I would love to go.'

"Then he added a catch. 'But I want you to do something for me when you get there.'

" 'What?' I asked.

" 'I want you to pretend to be the ambassador from Tasmania." (An Australian state, not a country, Tasmania has no diplomats.)

" 'Alright,' I agreed. 'No problem.'

"When I arrived, wearing my best barong (an embroidered formal shirt), at the celebratory event, Henry stood at the front of the reception group. 'Mr. Ambassador, how are you?' he began.

" 'Ah, quite well, my dear friend, Henry,' I said. 'May

I offer my most sincere congratulations on the Lebanese birthday festivities?'

" 'That is very kind. Thank you, Mr. Ambassador.'

"Then Henry rather formally introduced me to a group of Middle Eastern ambassadors. 'We have not seen you here before,' they said to me.

" 'No,' I told them. 'I arrived only recently.'

" 'Wonderful! Welcome then. We are pleased to have you here.'

"The conversation continued for a long time. Finally, Henry confessed to the real diplomats that we had played a joke on them. By far, the funniest part was that none of the ambassadors had a bloody clue where in the world that Tasmania was, and none of them had bothered to ask me either. Instead, they just welcomed me onto the scene to represent my 'country' as the new ambassador."

Still Kicking in Battle

Pranks aside, "The Philippines has been a good place for me, in part because it has so many military people," Dallas said. "Of course, the U.S. military was based there in large numbers for a long time. So I easily can interact with many people because we share military backgrounds."

Dallas stays busy on RSL work. The importance of the RSL and the satisfaction that it brings for him and for others make him unlikely to consider leaving his adopted country.

But significantly, even for Dallas, the rumblings of war still take a toll all these years later. His long-time Filipina spouse, **Ara Palapar,** helps him to cope.

"I do have a problem," Dallas confessed. "When I sleep, I have nightmares and can become aggressive, hitting out, punching and kicking. In my dreams, I fight frantically, but once awake again, I remember nothing.

"But Ara successfully controls that. She stays close to me so that when I start to move too much and too violently, she can hold me even tighter and calm me down."

Obviously, the explosions of war reverberate through time, leaving deep and lasting scars. "They certainly do," Dallas said.

SAFETY EXECUTIVE STARTS ON THE ROAD TO SUCCESS BY PINCHING MOM'S MONEY

Tony Smith Helps to Build Big Projects

Editor's Note: *A dash of desperation took Tony Smith away from his British home and along a winding path to an impressive career as a corporate executive focused on the quality and safety aspects at sometimes-huge construction sites. Despite preaching the need for safety to others, Tony at times has faced big hazards himself. Remarkably, his story begins with deep discord and a disgruntled decision to grab some money and run.*

ON BUILDING SITES – Being responsible for quality, safety and environmental issues on big construction projects, British-born corporate executive **Tony Smith** takes his job seriously and works diligently. Nevertheless, he has endured some close calls, frights and phobias surrounding his own safety, all following a dubious start to his career.

"At age 16, I did not get along well at all with my parents so I ran away from home," said 41-year-old Tony, now a corporate QSE (quality, safety and environmental) director with Dragages Hong Kong Ltd. "I nicked 20 quid (20 British pounds, now equivalent to US$32) from my mother and went down to the pub. Then I hitchhiked to London (about 150 miles away) where I slept rough on a park bench for six months and started to work on building sites."

So began his career, explained Tony, now a long-time resident of Hong Kong. "I was a very naughty boy when I started."

Dragages Hong Kong excels as part of the Paris-based Bouygues Group, one of the world's biggest construction enterprises. Tony endeavors to guard the safety of more than 2,000 workers toiling directly for Dragages and about another 6,000 for its subcontractors. "We do a lot of work, and I have a serious job," he said. "This year, we have had two construction fatalities. I deal with the families and many other issues, which is not always easy."

Despite Tony's best efforts, the safety precautions at many Asian construction sites fall short of perfection. "Safety issues are not firmly enough placed in people's minds," he said. "Construction laborers in Hong Kong are seen as standing at the bottom of the economic tree. Most people prefer to work in offices or at banks. So it happens that many of our workers are Chinese-mainland immigrants, Filipinos or Nepalese. Trying to pretend that they resemble **Superman**, they will stand on top of 35-storey buildings and not care about the safety harnesses. We provide all of the tools to make our construction sites safe. We use good equipment and take safety precautions in line with every international standard. Getting all of the workers to use all of the safety equipment all of the time is a different matter."

Despite being an established British expatriate himself, Tony does not necessarily approve of every other expat he meets. "Some Brits come to Asia and never fit in here. Too often, they start to demand everything: 'I expect this and that.' And I also dislike when they try to point fingers. I never want to hear, 'Yeah, things went wrong because of that Chinese guy.' I hate finger-pointing."

Since arriving in Hong Kong, Tony has followed an action-packed career with related travels to Jamaica, Cuba, Canada, the United States, Cyprus and much of Asia. Yet for a long time, even the notion of air travel terrified him.

Park-Bench Sleeper Visits the Royal Box

Tony's first big move happened 25 years ago when he stole the 20 quid in his hometown of Sheffield, England, and then set off hitchhiking. "When I arrived in London, I had no national security card. Nothing! And I thought, 'What the hell will I do?'

"I had nowhere to stay so a little park bench became my home for about six months. That worked nicely until winter arrived and snow began to fall.

"At first, I got a job with Blue Arrow Ltd, which is basically a labor-supplier. You go there – druggies and alcoholics do – and the company will pay you a minimum wage to do cleaning jobs in buildings. The big consideration for me was that I could pick up my cheques at Blue Arrow's office and so did not need a mailing address.

"My first job ever turned out to be cleaning up the royal box at Wembley Stadium (England's top football venue). No royalty was there at the time, but I never even had seen Wembley Stadium before so I thought: 'Brilliant – getting paid to clean this place!' "

Once Tony had earned a few pounds, a friend

introduced him at Tarmac, a construction company. Despite "no qualifications", he began to work at building sites.

Four years passed before Tony ever contacted his parents. "There was a big thing about runaway children in *The Sun* newspaper (owned by media tycoon **Rupert Murdoch**), and my mum arranged to put my picture in there. I did not read *The Sun* much, but all of my mates suddenly told me, 'You need to call your mum.' So I called her – out of peer pressure."

Was that an emotional mother-son conversation that followed? "Well, I guess so," Tony said.

Scared Stiff Going to Asia

After a stint at a materials-supply company, Tony, then aged 20, joined Lagan Holdings, an Irish builder. "Lagan got a job to do the runways at Chek Lap Kok (a massive construction site that gradually transformed into the Hong Kong International Airport)."

That planted a seed of interest for Tony to reach Hong Kong, although he arrived, then 24 years old, with Fugro-MateriaLab, a testing company for construction materials ("asphalt, steel, everything"). "They offered me more money."

For years, "I felt scared stiff of flying", Tony confessed. "When I took my first flight on that airplane to Hong Kong, I thought, 'Well, that does it. Probably I have eaten my last meal.' For the entire 11-hour flight, I gripped the back of the seat in front of me."

The plane landed at the old Kai Tak Airport beside Hong Kong's Victoria Harbor, a place notorious for its tricky aerial approach route amid the tall buildings in densely populated Kowloon. "That terrified me," Tony said. "From my seat on the plane, I almost could see televisions flickering inside the nearby apartments."

Full of You-Know-What

Promptly, Tony started to work. At the airport-construction site, "I was lucky enough to stay in the workers' accommodations, a massive block of rooms that I shared with about 10,000 mainland Chinese and Filipinos," he said. "Six people lived in each room. There were bunk-beds and no televisions.

"The toilets were fantastic too. Another building held all of the showers and toilets -- with (Chinese style) squat-toilet after squat-toilet and shower after shower. That place got cleaned out just once a day so by late at night, the toilets always were full of you-know-what. God! Disgusting!"

Even so, Tony rated those lodgings as "five-star" compared to the park bench back in London. True, there were delicate moments. "The first time when I went out on the town in Wanchai (Hong Kong's most famous nightlife district), I got drunk, returned to the workers' accommodation and then came down with diarrhea," he said. "Of course, I needed to use those squat-toilets. So you can imagine what happened. Oh, boy!"

In the early-to-mid-1990s, many of "the bosses" arriving in Hong Kong to help build the new airport "made up their CVs" on the fly. Often they scribbled out the "bullshit" details while on airplanes bound for Kai Tak. Once, "the QA (quality assurance) manager at the airport-construction site got found out because he actually was a welder. He had no real qualifications at all for his job in Hong Kong, and people told him, 'You have no idea what you are talking about.' It all led to a big process of vetting the Airport Authority staff much better."

Tony soon left MateriaLab because his boss also appeared ineffective, whereas "I had not lied on my CV". Some deft job-hopping took him to IP Foundations and then to a Japanese contractor, Nishimaksu Construction, as a quality manager. During two years with the latter, he worked on "everything from the train station at the airport to the ferry pier for boats to the Chinese mainland".

Repeated job advancements allowed Tony to move into an apartment in Wanchai, much preferable to the airport-workers' rooms. "There was a building boom in those days that made it easy to move up at work," he said.

What a Wise Man Taught

Building boom or not, Tony attributes much of his success to advice and help from people he met along the way. For example, "When I moved to IP Foundations, I was lucky to work for a wise expatriate named **Tony McDonald** who taught me some important things.

"A month after I moved to live in Wanchai, we had an important meeting with a government auditor. For me, it was the first time to meet that guy, and my boss wanted to introduce me.

"But I had been out in bloody Wanchai all of the previous night and stayed at a Thai girl's place. When I got to work in the morning, she had tried her best to iron my shirt, but it was dirty. My necktie was a mess. I had not shaved and still stank a bit of alcohol. So I thought, 'That's it. The boss will kill me.'

"Late that afternoon after we had met with the government man, I learned my lesson when Tony McDonald pulled me into his office. 'Right,' he said. 'Shut the door.'

" 'Oh, fuck!' I thought. 'Now I will have no job.'

"But he said to me, 'You are a smart lad. I will train you and teach you how to be a good manager, but you never again will do what you did today. I am not angry because I have done similar things myself. Instead, I feel disappointed that you were not better prepared.'

"Then he opened the top drawer of his desk and

PLANE PANIC
HELP!
MOM's 20 BRITISH POUNDS
HK TO PARIS
HELP!
BRITISH PRISON
SIBERIAN EXPRESS
WELCOME HOME!

pointed inside. 'What do you see?' he asked.

" 'Oh!' I said. 'It's an electric razor and a toothbrush.'

" 'Right.' Then he opened the second drawer. 'What is that?'

" 'That's an extra necktie.'

" 'What about over there hanging on the wall?'

" 'Ah, a clean jacket and a shirt!'

" 'So you see,' he said, 'if I accidentally fall down or have been out all night, then I can go into the bathroom, spruce myself up and look fine. In the future, you need to be fully prepared too.'

"I learned a lot from that guy. He taught me well."

On and On: Riding the Rails

Eventually, Tony Smith joined Dragages. In his 15 years with the company so far, he has faced some crisis situations. Early on, "my boss told me to go to Paris and make some presentations to show everyone at the head office exactly what we had done. I replied, 'You want me to fly to Paris? No way!' "

Coping with Tony's fear of flying called for a huge effort. "When my boss then insisted that I absolutely had to go to Paris, I felt so scared of flying that I took two weeks off from work before the business conference so that I could travel by train on the Trans-Siberian Express." Reaching Western Europe that way took nine days, and Tony saw plenty of geography as he peered out through the train windows.

"First, I went from Hong Kong to Beijing by train, which took two days. After a day there, I went from Beijing across the rest of China, through Mongolia and into Russia. The journey across Mongolia and Russia turned out to be a bit boring because it took a long time, but the train itself was a nice one with a good restaurant at the end that sold proper restaurant food. At every stop, local people tried to sell stuff to the passengers.

"After reaching Moscow, I switched onto a less-comfortable German train. The train to Moscow had been an older one with more space, proper radiator heaters and more character."

With five days still to spare before his scheduled presentations in Paris, Tony continued on by train to England so that he could visit his family. "Do you know what the worst thing was about the trains?" he asked. "Not one unscheduled stop happened all the way from Hong Kong to Europe and through the Channel Tunnel (between France and England). Then soon after we reached England, the passengers heard an announcement: 'There will be a two-hour delay because we have experienced signal problems.' I thought, 'Jesus Christ! That represents British Rail at its absolute worst.' "

Sudden Stop in a British Jail

Surprisingly, Tony still nearly missed his business obligations in Paris. "On my first day back in England, I took my mum and dad out shopping," he said. "When lunch time came, we went down to the local pub.

"As it happens, my uncle is the head of the Hell's Angels (a notorious motorcycle gang) there (in Sheffield), and my cousins are a bit wild too. Together with my parents, about 10 family members gathered at the pub.

"Soon my relatives started to drink a few bottles of vodka that I had brought from Moscow," Tony said. "So we drank the vodka and stayed at the pub until about 8 p.m. Keep in mind that although I did nick that 20 quid from my mum, I never had been in trouble with the police in my life.

"Finally I came out of the pub, quite pissed. I saw a policeman standing outside, but paid no attention to him. Instead, I walked straight to the road, waved my hand drunkenly and yelled, 'Taxi, take me to Wanchai', although

I was in Sheffield then, not in Hong Kong." After enough vodka, anyone can make a mistake in geography.

A bigger blunder happened next. "The policeman came up behind and grabbed me by the shoulder," Tony said. "Without even looking to see who it was, I shrugged my shoulders and lifted my arms trying to brush him away. I did not punch him, but the policeman still claimed that I had assaulted him.

"The next thing that I knew, I woke up the following morning in jail and had to appear in front of a judge. A duty lawyer showed up and told me, 'Oh, no problem. How much money do you have? Probably you will get a 200-quid fine.'

"Soon I got into the dock in the courtroom. Then the judge said, 'Oh, you came from Hong Kong, huh? Drunk, were you? Do you think that you can do whatever you please here? Well, I sentence you to seven days in jail.'

"When I reached the Doncaster jail (nearby), everyone inside there behaved really nicely to me. They all knew my uncle. Luckily, I was released after three-and-a-half days. Then I had to make a mad rush straight to Paris and right into the business conference."

Reluctantly, Tony later returned to Hong Kong by plane. Yet his fear of flying persisted.

Clap and Sing For Jamaica

When the construction business in Hong Kong entered a slight lull, Tony's company sent him to oversee quality and safety at a highway project in Jamaica. He stayed there for much of 2002 and 2003.

"The bosses told me, 'You will love it there with the beaches, bright skies, blue seas, ganja (marijuana) and Red Stripe beer.'

" 'Sounds great,' I replied.

"But I still despised flying. To reach Jamaica, I had

to do an 11-hour flight to Heathrow Airport in London and then 10 more hours to Kingston, Jamaica. And the bloody boss there was a nightmare character, who had told me, 'We go economy class.' So I could get no sleep for that entire journey.

"The Jamaicans on the plane were loud too. Just as we came in to land, they all started to clap and sing, 'Come on. We are in Jamaica. Let's dance.' I thought, 'Oh, fuck! My head hurts.'

Tony felt greatly relieved to plonk his feet firmly back onto solid ground, but his joy soon subsided. "I arrived in Kingston at 11 o'clock at night," he said. "The airport looked as scary as hell, hardly even like an airport at all. It was dark without nearly enough lighting. I collected my bag, stepped outside and came face-to-face with a lot of six-foot-tall black guys, all of them saying, 'Come with me, man. Come with me.' I almost crapped myself then because I knew nothing about the place, wondered if it was safe to get a taxi and could see guns almost everywhere. I thought, 'Oh, God. What have I done by coming here? This looks nothing like a nice sandy beach, does it?' "

Going from Hong Kong to live and work in Jamaica triggered a considerable culture shock. "Our boss in Jamaica then had a reputation as the hardest boss we had," Tony said. "Previously, he had worked in Nigeria for 10 years and gotten used to taking that approach. Among other things, he put our office right in the middle of Trench Town, the ghetto, because it cost us almost no money. In Trench Town, you see all little shanty houses. It is not a nice place." (Trench Town also was reggae music's birthplace and the home of Jamaican music's biggest star, the late **Bob Marley,** who in 1981 died prematurely from cancer.)

'Just a Stupid White Guy'

Criminals posed one danger. "At a certain stage, Jamaica ranked worse than Nigeria with more murders per year – normally some every day. News about murders sounded normal to the people there, and the country really does not have such a huge population (only 2.9 million)."

Dealing with the police represented another hazard. "After I arrived in Jamaica, the boss told me, 'If you ever get stopped by a policeman, do not try to bribe him directly. The police here do not care about you at all. Actually, they love to shoot the white Westerners.'

"Instead, the best strategy was to tell the policeman, 'I am very sorry. Being just a stupid white guy, I hardly know what I am doing.' The police like to hear that. It amounts to a type of reverse racism. Some people think that white people may be racists, but in Jamaica it goes completely the opposite way. There, being white makes you a second-class citizen, which can be a good learning curve because you soon find out exactly how discrimination feels.

"Then you say to the policeman, 'Can I invite you and your family out to dinner?' Next you give him some money and add, 'Oh, please go ahead and book a restaurant. I will call you later.' Finally you take his telephone number and leave. Otherwise, he will lose his temper and you will face serious trouble."

'No Weed, No Work, Man!'

Tony reckons that marijuana, a miracle drug of sorts, helps many Jamaicans to stay calm. "On my first day there, I walked down Knutsford Boulevard, the main street in Kingston, and almost everyone I saw was smoking it," he said. "When coming back from a shopping center, I noticed three policemen with a huge reefer on one corner. I thought, 'Oh God! Even the police smoke it.'

"Then I attended my first safety meeting at work. That got really interesting. By then, I had been in Jamaica for just two weeks. All of the workers were unionized, a bit like in Australia that way."

But some of the union demands sounded nothing like those commonly heard in Australia or England. All of the labor leaders were Rastaferi (part of a Jamaican spiritual movement inclined to use marijuana religiously, wear dreadlocked hair and worship former Ethiopian leader **Haile Selassie,** who died in 1974, as a reincarnation of God).

"My boss, knowing that I arrived so recently, had written out an agenda for me to use at the meeting," Tony said. "The first agenda item was: 'No weed (marijuana) at the work site.' So I read that out.

"Then the union leader, a Rasta guy, sat down and spent about two minutes rolling the biggest joint that I ever saw. He took a puff, exhaled the smoke and said, 'No weed, no work, man!'

"My jaw dropped. I looked at my project director, and he looked back at me. Then we both shrugged, and the director said, 'Okay! Moving along, the next agenda item up for discussion is….'

"Jamaica really was amazing. You saw marijuana everywhere that you went.

"The project that we built there was a 20-kilometer highway with lots of bridges. Each bridge had a group of workers. I would turn up at the worksites and the smell of ganja always was unbelievable (even outdoors)."

Three Murders and a Mishap

Despite Tony's endeavors as the safety manager, not all of the Jamaican workers survived. "We had three murders and one fatal accident pop up in my first few months there," he said. "It was a bit of a baptism by fire."

In one case, "a road through the sugarcane fields led to a quarry. The drug people often went speeding through there. One of our truck drivers came around a corner and got shot in the head. At 2 a.m. on a Sunday morning, I received a call from my boss. He asked me, 'Oh, Tony, can you just pop down and see what has happened?'

"I replied: 'Do you really want me to go wandering out to the cane fields where a guy just has been shot?' Not to mention that I would have needed to pass through Spanish Town, another rough part of Jamaica. Never run out of petrol there, especially not at 2 a.m."

"Short tempers", a local trait that Tony consistently noticed, triggered another murder. "Two truck drivers clipped wing-mirrors on their vehicles. One guy climbed down and accused the other, 'You damaged my truck.' They started to argue. One driver just pulled out a gun and shot the other fellow through the head – all over a wing-mirror.

"The third murder happened in a drive-by shooting. One of our flagmen, a man responsible to stop the traffic, died when somebody speeding past did not stop and sprayed bullets all over him."

More random, but equally deadly, the fatal accident occurred when "a truck hit the back of an excavator, burst a tire and then fell straight over on top of an unlucky guy".

Fortunately, Tony enjoyed some good experiences in Jamaica too, especially when he finally found his way onto the sandy beaches. "I learned to scuba-dive there, which I never had expected to do, and that was great," he said.

"Eventually when you can take some time off and start to get used to the Jamaicans, then you like them. They are naturally loud (boisterous). Often, they sound aggressive, but really are not. They are nice people, and Jamaica is a beautiful country. I would not hesitate to go back there, especially since I already have gotten used to the place."

No Fear of That Airplane

Maybe best of all, Jamaica supplied a badly needed fix for Tony's fear of flying. "After being in Jamaica for just six months, I had been exposed to those three murders, a fatal accident and even a gunfight outside of my house at Christmas," he said. "The police chased some drug-dealers up to the crossroads, and then the shootout started. At first, I listened and thought, 'Ah, fantastic! That must be festive fireworks.' In fact, what I heard were the sounds of semi-automatic machine guns coming from just outside.

"So the next time when I went to the airport, I realized, 'Hey, I have no fear of that airplane. None whatsoever! I face much greater dangers simply by walking across the street in front of my house.' After that important risk assessment, I never again felt afraid of flying. I can go up and down with no concerns at all."

Dances in Castro's Shadow

Grasping a new fly-anywhere-at-anytime sense of freedom, Tony used his base in Jamaica to make several pleasure visits to another fascinating place, Cuba, then still led by **Fidel Castro,** the ultimate revolutionary. "Going from Montego Bay in Jamaica, I could reach Havana, Cuba, within an hour in a propeller airplane."

Tony greatly enjoyed Cuba. "Havana is amazing," he said. "I consider it as one of the world's most beautiful cities with old buildings, old cars and lots of traditional stuff. I had my first beer after arriving there at the Bodeguita del Medio, the bar where **Ernest Hemingway** (1899-1961, an American, winner of the 1954 Nobel Prize for Literature) wrote some of his books. I also had a mohito (a Cuban classic cocktail that Hemingway loved) with his signature on display right behind me, and I thought that it was great – a really good mohito."

People go to chat, swim nearby, fish or even party on

Havana's "sea wall", a popular street along the waterfront. "On Friday nights, all that most of the Cuban people want to do is party," Tony said. "Many of them take their drinks and guitars to the sea wall where they can dance and enjoy themselves.

"I had hired a taxi driver and his car for a week in Cuba. He told me: 'Just get yourself a bottle of rum, go down to the sea wall and you will find loads of friends.' Everyone felt happy there. It was great."

For anyone fully familiar with Cuba, taxis may prove unnecessary. "I went to Varadero, which is a seaside resort there," Tony said. "Then I learned that in Cuba, it is considered illegal not to stop for hitchhikers. With no proper public-transport system, Castro simply had said, 'Okay, if you drive a car and have empty seats in it, then you must pick up those people who need rides and take them as far as possible along your way.' That appears to work well."

'Careful! Secret Police'

One negative aspect darkened almost everything else in Cuba. "It was difficult to meet girls (and impossible to discuss politics) because everyone felt terrified of the secret police. The people are very nice, but absolutely terrified of the secret police, who they believe lurk everywhere. I heard the same thing so many times: 'Quiet! Be careful -- secret police!' What a strange situation!"

Shadowy authority figures may accuse women of prostitution for becoming too friendly with visitors. They also tend to make certain individuals, those who speak too freely or dare to criticize Cuba's government, to disappear, often forever.

No one even wanted to mention the name Castro. "Absolutely not," Tony said. Instead, the Cubans preferred to tell him about their island, its geography or attractions and about their personal concerns. "They feel very proud of their country."

Did Tony fear the Cuban secret police too? "No," he said. "I was not likely to disappear. It would have been others, the Cubans."

Chilly Shivers, Top-Alert Trembles

Despite the usually bright skies of Jamaica and Cuba, Tony did feel a winter chill once. "The steel for the bridges on our job in Jamaica came from Canada," he said. To ensure its quality, he flew to Miami and then north to Montreal.

"Being in Miami felt nice because the temperature there hovered at 30-plus degrees," Tony said. "But in Montreal, it was minus-whatever with snow and ice almost everywhere. You know, I really thought that I might end up catching a bad cold!"

Apart from making Tony shiver in the outdoor chill, Montreal looked like a "nice place, perfect to enjoy some good food", presumably with Quebecois flavors. When he went south again, the shivers from the cold turned into fearful trembles.

"On the way back to Jamaica, I missed a flight and ended up with an eight-hour stopover in Miami," Tony said. "So I began to imagine having a lovely day at the beach there. But then I wandered into a little bar where a television showed the news. Suddenly, the newsreader announced a top-level red alert for Miami (under the U.S. Homeland Security Advisory System signaling a severe risk of a terrorist attack). The authorities thought that terrorists would try to blow up a nuclear power station."

Startled, Tony nearly toppled off his seat. "I thought, 'Fuck! I do not fly out of here for another six hours. I want to leave right now.' Oh, boy! I tell you."

Fortunately for Tony and for everyone else in Miami,

no terrorist assault happened that day. "But it was a little unnerving to say the least." Hence, Tony has no real desire for a repeat visit to the U.S.

Back to Asia

Unexpectedly, a resignation in Hong Kong prompted Tony's return to Asia. Then he directed his attention to the AsiaWorld-Expo, a new conference-and-exhibition facility near the Hong Kong International Airport.

Later Tony moved to Macau for a year as Dragages worked on The Venetian, a massive casino-hotel project, now the biggest single-structure hotel-building in Asia. The Venetian even has indoor canals complete with gondola rides and Italian-singing gondoliers. "We did the waterproof concrete for the canals," Tony said.

"Actually, I do not like Macau very much now," Tony said. "When I went there soon after first coming to Hong Kong, it reminded me of the settings in old **Bruce Lee** movies. In those days, walking around near the old Lisboa (casino-hotel) was amazing with little rabbit-warren streets and Russian ladies standing everywhere. Then you went into the main casino and everyone smoked, rolled dices and made lots of noise in Chinese. It really resembled an old movie.

"When I returned to work in Macau, almost everything had changed to westernized casinos and more modern appearances. I liked the place a lot more as it looked before."

Cyprus: Like a Soap Opera

For another year, Tony went to the Republic of Cyprus, part of the third-largest island in the Mediterranean Sea. There, a Green Line buffer zone keeps a Turkish-controlled section of the island off-limits. "We were building new terminals at the Larnaca and Paphos airports (both on the

Greek-dominated side of the line)," Tony said.

Cyprus holds a strategic location just east of Greece, south of Turkey, west of Syria and Lebanon, northwest of Israel and north of Egypt. Many British people choose to retire there.

"I absolutely hated the place," Tony said. "Maybe you know about *Coronation Street* (a famous British soap-opera TV show). Cyprus reminded me of that. I would go into any pub, and the people inside would be arguing endlessly over who had shagged a next-door neighbor's wife and other disputes. It really sounded melodramatic. The people in the pubs were all retired and so bored. They would talk: 'Blah, blah, blah, he grows better flowers than I do' or 'Oh, look at the great patio that I have.' After living in Asia, where most guys hold down good jobs and do not care in the least about who has the biggest television, listening to chatter like that proved tough to take."

Politically, Cyprus, with just 1.1 million people on the whole island, stays "interesting". Since the Berlin Wall fell in 1989, Nicosia in Cyprus, perched on the Green Line, has been the world's only remaining divided capital city.

"You have the Turks, who invaded, and you have the Greek side of the Green Line," Tony said. "Nicosia exists as a city cut in half with United Nations vehicles on patrol in the buffer zone. You cannot go past the Green Line. It all makes for a very strange city."

Small Comforts Best

An oddity arises as Tony compares Cyprus to Hong Kong. "In Hong Kong, a person strangely gets used to living in a small apartment," he said. "My apartment in Wanchai measures just 650 square feet.

"When I moved to Cyprus, the company gave me a five-bedroom house with a huge living room, American-style kitchen, big swimming pool, nice garage and garden. I took my Indonesian girlfriend at the time there, opened the door for her and asked if she felt impressed at all. She took a quick look around and said, 'Do we have to clean all this? No thanks.'

"When we stayed there, we used only the smallest bedroom, the kitchen, which was nice, and that was all. Having lived in Asia makes me so used to small accommodations.

"A lot of people who come to Dragages from France arrive with their wives, who take a look at the size of typical apartments in Hong Kong and then promptly decide to return to France. They prefer not to stay.

"But I have gone entirely the other way. I am so used to a small place that I prefer less space. I feel happy to have a convenient layout and to keep everything nicely within my reach."

Equally "tidy", Tony lives directly above his favorite Hong Kong bar, The Junk Pub in Wanchai. "Since I work as a safety director, I decided to avoid the risks of crossing any busy streets (after visits to the bar)." Instead, he merely steps into a lift and rides that home.

Always busy, Tony has no intention to return to live in England. "By now, Hong Kong has become my home," he said. "I see no reason to go back.

"I like Hong Kong as a base, but I would move elsewhere again if the company asked me to go. You see a lot of expatriates who retire to the Philippines or Thailand, and soon they die from drinking too much beer or other bad habits. Maybe I already drink a little bit too much, but could you imagine if I retired in Thailand? That would be it – goodnight for me. So I plan to stay in Hong Kong and to keep busy. When I finally do want to retire, I can leave the company, but continue on with some consultancy work."

Long before that, Tony expects more big challenges.

His employer has gained a strategic role to help build a massive bridge to link Hong Kong, Macau and nearby Zhuhai and also tunnels for Hong Kong's high-speed-rail links to the Chinese mainland.

Considering that Tony began by stealing money and running away from home, his career has turned out remarkably well. "Yes, I think so," he said. His parents long ago forgave him for the missing 20 quid, their initial distress replaced by a fierce pride.

"I have worked hard, had some good luck and been quite brave to move about," Tony said. "Probably if I had stayed in the United Kingdom, I still would be bashing concrete somewhere. Everything would be totally different."

HIGH-FINANCE MAN STUDIES ASIA AT STREET-LEVEL

No Average Banker, Singapore Pete Cooks, Listens and Learns

Editor's Note: *Hardly a typical financial industry doyen, indeed no run-of-the-mill anything, Peter (who asked to be called Singapore Pete, his nickname) hails from Birmingham, a struggling industrial city in England. Now a long-time resident of Asia's financial capitals, notably Hong Kong and Singapore, Peter may wear a business suit to work, but he refuses to talk like "a suit" or to behave entirely like one. Instead of balance sheets, interest rates or investment returns, he prefers to discuss his belief that financial wealth has little impact on achieving real happiness. Personally, he often pursues happiness the most successfully by exploring Asia or by listening to music (although seldom to rap music).*

INSIDE THE FINANCIAL TOWERS – Not many people stepping briskly through the global financial industry's halls of power describe themselves by quoting from **Yogi Bear,** a long-popular cartoon character. Then again, any chance to meet a big-finance player quite like **Peter** (alias **Singapore Pete**) probably happens just once in a lifetime.

On TV screens, Yogi often declared, "I am smarter than the average bear." Similarly, while referring to that famous picnic-basket-loving cartoon bruin, 50-year-old Peter, a high finance, risk-management specialist based in Hong Kong, insists, "I am no average banker." Any candid conversation with him readily proves the point.

"I spend my life in one world during the working days, and in another world the rest of the time," Peter said. "I like to separate the two.

"Soon after I first arrived in Hong Kong in 1995, I met a Canadian guy named **Walter** who said to me, 'Peter, you look like a suit, and you desperately do not want to be one.' With that sentence, he summed me up perfectly."

Happiness Carries No Price-Tag

With perhaps unusual views for a man active in high finance, Peter entirely understands that money and happiness function as very independent entities. One never needs to depend on the other, despite many people believing to the contrary. "A big reason why I like Asia so much is that you see so many people smiling," he said. "Some of my best experiences in life have come from meeting and interacting with many of the poorest people. Often they are the happiest ones with the most optimistic outlooks.

"On the streets of India, in Bombay (Mumbai) for example, I have seen the extremes of poverty and yet the biggest smiles on people's faces. Many children there grew up amid poverty, begging on the streets, and never knowing anything different. The same goes for Thailand and other countries. Some of the poorest places in Asia actually have many of the happiest people."

In much of rural India, typical work-days revolve

around gathering firewood and toiling in fields. "It looks like an agrarian society with high levels of happiness, which I found to be really refreshing," Peter said. "As a Beatles song declares, money 'can't buy me love' or happiness." (In 1964, The Beatles, a famous British band, released that insightful song, "Can't Buy Me Love". The credits for writing it went to **Paul McCartney** and **John Lennon**.)

"No one necessarily needs very much money to be happy," Peter said. "People do need somewhere to live, and it poses problems to live in Hong Kong without a certain amount of money because the place always stays so damn expensive. But you can live in a shack in many other locations and still be really happy."

As for Peter's personal "art of happiness", he believes that an ideal situation might be to grow carrots (producing his own food) and to work as a postman (enjoying the outdoors in a low-stress job). So does this guy really even fit into the realm of financial pooh-bahs? "At work, I have been called many things," he said. "Being labelled as a 'heretic' may be the best comment that I ever received from any of my bosses. I never have gone along easily with any system – and never will."

Trailing President Hu into the Presidential Suite

When Peter once unexpectedly found himself surrounded by astonishing luxuries, he treated the windfall not with any sense of entitlement, but with joviality. "For eight years, I lived in Singapore and travelled to Hong Kong for one week each month," he said. In those days, friends nicknamed him "Singapore Pete".

"Altogether, I stayed at the Grand Hyatt Hotel (on Hong Kong Island) for 650 nights, nearly two years of my life. When I arrived there for my 100th stay, the hotel management upgraded me to the presidential suite, totally free of charge, for five nights.

"Most people have no idea about such luxury. The presidential suite occupies a high floor with a secure access route. The president of China, **Hu Jintao,** had stayed there the previous week, and then I showed up next.

"Immediately, I looked all around that presidential suite. It had three double-bedrooms, an enormous kitchen, a huge wine cabinet full of very expensive wines, a baby-grand piano, a table that seated 12 people and a private sauna. The suite measured 285 square meters, rather a lot for hotel accommodation.

"So I decided to enjoy myself. I went to The Wanch (a live-music club), met a bunch of musicians and brought some people back to visit in the presidential suite. I had some of them playing the piano there.

"**Bill Clinton** (a former United States president) has stayed in that same hotel suite too. One of Hong Kong's top jazz musicians, **Allen Youngblood,** has played the piano for Clinton in that very room.

"For me, the worst move that I made was to fall asleep in the sauna there. Quite a few people had been sitting in the sauna, and I just fell asleep. Everyone else left me there." Peter awoke feeling very warm indeed.

"When I checked out after that hotel stay, the Grand Hyatt staff asked me, 'How did you enjoy your time in the presidential suite?'

" 'Only one problem,' I told them.

" 'What? You had a problem in the presidential suite?' They looked puzzled.

"So I told them, 'On every other occasion that I have stayed in this hotel, when the time came to leave, I could look in the bathroom and then look in the bedroom area and know that I had repacked all of my belongings. In that damn presidential suite, I had to walk around for a long time, looking

FROM BIRMINGHAM
TO THE HONG KONG
GRAND HYATT.
DID I FORGET
ANYTHING?
WALL ST.
YOGI BEAR
INSIDE
BOB
MARLEY
S'PORE
PETE
HAPPINESS
HAS NO
PRICE TAG
BUFFALO SOLDIER

here, here, there and there. Even after all of that, I still wonder if I left anything behind.' "

From Birmingham to Big Banks

Originally from Birmingham in England (just a short drive southeast from where the Beatles originated in Liverpool), Peter, came to Asia in the mid-1990s. He then worked for 16 years with a leading investment bank before recently starting a new job.

"I have done some contract work too," he said. "That means going in and trying to tell bankers how to run their businesses properly. If you look at the news headlines these days, the leading bankers really do need plenty of good advice. As a risk-management person, I try to keep them out of jail. When it comes to financial people not always doing the right things, then I need to say the right things to them and hope that they will follow my advice. I say whatever I can, but often the issues come down to points of principle. If they continue to ignore what I say, then I will need to leave, and I have done that a few times.

"An ex-boss of mine once told me that we truly could find out where all the risks were in banks only by going into the boardrooms, sitting down with the senior management and asking them. They are the ones supposed to orchestrate everything.

"But most financial markets are fixed in some way. In high-frequency trading, options or futures expiries and everything else, the financial institutions fix things to settle at certain points such that their trading desks make money. Too often, the senior management leans back in the soft boardroom seats and really does not know quite everything that happens. Now the resulting problems are starting to come and torment them."

Do the people ambling along on the busy sidewalks

outside of the big-city banking towers need to worry about misdeeds and miscues in the financial world? "Normal people should worry because too many of the people running the whole thing hardly care," Peter said.

Much that happens in the financial world has little real connection to economics. "What has been going on about trying to save the euro really amounts to a political spat between Germany, France, Italy and Spain. When it completely blows up, who knows what will happen? And it will blow up because much of the situation looks unsustainable. The financial situation in the United States will explode too. Can people there sustain many trillion dollars of government debt? No!

"These financial problems circle most of the world. The really interesting thing is that Asia somehow for the time being has remained resilient and resistant."

National Leaders 'Fear the Reality'

Even China endures "a slightly troublesome time. Its leaders invested loads of money into infrastructure a few years ago in response to the global financial crisis and to create local jobs. Now the country has reached a point of wondering what to do next because its leaders do not want to have too many unemployed people around. They already have built all of the cities that nobody lives in, all of the roads that nobody drives on and all of the airports that nobody uses.

"Former Chinese leader **Mao Tse-tung** (who died in 1976) found his support from poor people in the rural areas, not in the cities," Peter said. "He went to the cities and found very little support. Revolution came from the poor people. I believe that the DNA from that era remains within the Chinese government, and so the national leaders still fear the reality that they now have 1.3 billion people. Only a few individuals drive around in Ferraris (Italian sports cars) and live in big houses in Shanghai, Beijing or elsewhere. Loads more people out in the provinces see their land confiscated and then have nothing to do. When that situation blows up, the whole world will rattle and shake."

Advantage Singapore: Hong Kong's Filthy Air

Officially, Peter has divided much of his time between offices in Hong Kong (1995-2000), Singapore (2000-08) and Hong Kong again (2008-present). "For work purposes, I prefer to live in Hong Kong," Peter said. "For family reasons, I prefer Singapore. The size of typical accommodations, affordability and pollution issues all make Singapore a better place to raise a family.

"I know many people who have left Hong Kong entirely because of its worsening air pollution and returned to their original countries. They felt unwilling for their families to stay, continually inhaling the bad air. I never have met so many people suffering from respiratory problems anywhere else.

"But Singapore is different. It has no such serious pollution problem, and people there can follow more family-oriented social programs. In Hong Kong, life often revolves around work and guys in bars. Life in Singapore has a lot more to do with groups of people going out or to private homes for dinner. Many times in Singapore, I cooked meals in Indian, Italian or French styles for 10-12 people. One of my passions is for cooking. I can make an onion bhaji that would beat the hell out of anything at most Indian restaurants." But in Hong Kong, Peter's enthusiasm for cooking wanes in "the tiny kitchens. Everything is so small."

All Intrinsically Asian

As much as possible, Peter likes to step outside of the financial towers and study the real Asia amid the nitty-gritty activities at street-level. He has explored nooks and crannies across much of the continent.

"I have had the privilege of travelling across the entire Asian world, which probably is the best thing I ever experienced," he said. "Culturally, every country -- China, Taiwan, Thailand, Indonesia, Malaysia, Singapore, Laos, Vietnam, Cambodia, Burma, India and elsewhere – has differences. In nearly every country, the people, culture and food are different, yet all remain intrinsically Asian in their own ways."

By contrast, the Australians to the south sometimes yearn to be regarded as a vital part of Asia, but are entirely different. They have little in common with Asians.

Lee Kuan Yew: 'Bloody Good Job'

"Asia looks like the most vibrant place commercially, but also has the greatest disparities," Peter said. "In India or the Philippines, the biggest poverty appears right beside some of the greatest wealth, which never fits well together."

In Singapore, more equity and fairness prevail. "Although many average Singaporeans may say some less than polite things about their former leader, **Lee Kuan Yew,** having been a benevolent dictator, he did take Singapore from independence in 1965 and turn it into a First World city," Peter said. "Despite being a very small place, it stays vibrant and wealthy. Average Singaporeans are well looked after with excellent health services, transport and housing. Lee Kuan Yew did a bloody good job and achieved a lot of the right things for his people.

"Many Singaporeans may wonder about what comes next. Their freedoms of speech and what they can do socially remain restrictive, but not as bad as when I first went there. A significant number of people doubt the credentials of **Lee Hsien Loong** (Singapore's present prime minister, Lee Kuan Yew's son). The elder Lee fought for political causes from away back. Now his son holds political power just through birth-right.

"What comes next for Singapore? I wonder about that too. I do not expect anything too dramatic, but it will be interesting to watch. People will carry on, yet I really believe that they want changes."

Biggest Con-Trick in History

When Peter first arrived in Asia, Japan was fairly dominant. In the financial industry and beyond, dealing with Japanese interests may pose problems. "The Japanese can be quite insular," Peter said. "They believe that they know best and are perfect in many ways. You can face difficulties to tell, ask or advise them about anything because they know that they are perfect. Therefore, it is, at times, challenging trying to manage staff in Japan. Things are very hierarchical too. Most of them will not act autonomously and need to be instructed from the top."

More recently, the balance of power has shifted tremendously with the rise of China and India. "The Chinese know greed better than almost anyone," Peter said. "They care mainly about dominant positions, an attitude apparently built into them almost from birth. Their attitude will be 'Get out of my way. I have got to get ahead.' It even extends to riding on subway trains or in elevators where each day you experience problems trying to exit while the crowds pile inside. A person feels like saying, 'Excuse me! Do you mind terribly if I get out alive before you all stampede in here?'

"Business people in China also want knowledge. Although seldom prepared to pay for it, they consistently ask for 'technology transfers', hoping and expecting that the biggest American and European companies will give them technical expertise – essentially, teach them what to do for free. It makes for some really interesting exchanges and interactions because the Americans and the Europeans always anticipate lots of business coming back in their directions. 'If we give them this, they will give us that.' When overseas business people look at the 'China market', they quickly can get badly blinded by their own greed. Then the Chinese side seated across the boardroom tables outplays them in this business-themed game of chess. The situation, as it continues to unfold, may one day be regarded as the biggest con-trick in history."

Street-Level Lessons

In unfamiliar cities or districts, Peter enjoys walking and then strolling, followed by more meandering. "When I travel, I love to walk through cities," he said. "In New York, I have walked from the World Trade Centre (when it still stood prior to the notorious terrorists' attack in 2001) all the way to Central Park (about 7.5 kilometers away) and then back. All that walking took me about eight hours to do, but it felt wonderful. From the street level, when walking (not riding in a taxi), you actually can see, experience and learn about places. You experience aspects of the culture, sights, smells and sounds, including the wackos yelling at each other -- things like 'Get a job, you bum.' I never go anywhere to see the buildings or monuments. Instead, I travel to experience places and things. With peripheral vision, I can absorb the details about buildings, but the experience of being in a place and walking through the middle of it counts for the most.

International experiences also have given Peter some valuable insights into how best to deal with people. "Nowhere in the world should anyone pre-judge someone else. Never presume that what someone looks like or what you imagine that he or she does represents what that person really is. If you indulge in pre-judging, then probably you never can find out exactly what that individual is all about inside."

From an Economic Typhoon to a Real One

Peter moved to Asia because a British "economic typhoon", one blowing in "spectacularly high interest rates", prompted him to seek significant changes. In London-based newspapers, he often noticed the words "Hong Kong", a place then teetering on the verge of exclusion from the British Empire and facing the perils of Chinese sovereignty.

Extra motivation came from a friend already working in Hong Kong. "When I telephoned him, he said, 'Why not come here on holiday for a week?' So I did."

Peter first landed in Hong Kong as "the tail end of a real typhoon", one with torrential rains, raging winds and flying debris, swirled away. Within a few days, he also landed a job.

Singapore Splashes

Peter and his wife **Jackie** have three children, 18-year-old daughter **Jordan,** 15-year-old son **Nathan** and 12-year-old daughter **Eden.** All three children now live and study in the United Kingdom, thereby avoiding the risks of hazardous exposure to Hong Kong's chronic air pollution.

The youngsters enjoy competitive swimming. When living in Singapore, they received expert guidance as members of a swim-club led by the national-team coach, **Ang Peng Siong,** a former Olympian and an Asian Games gold medalist once ranked as the world's fastest swimmer in 50-metre freestyle.

Top swimmers in Singapore learn "perfect techniques", Peter said. "Ang Peng Siong is a lovely guy, a 50-year-old icon who runs one of Singapore's top swim-clubs. The coaching is first-rate and you often see the coaches in the water leading the youngsters up and down on their typical daily two-hour training schedules.

"Each year, an Asia-versus-Australia swimming competition for young athletes takes place at the Challenge

Stadium in Perth, Australia. When my children participated, 400 others turned up too – all serious swimmers. The level of competition was spectacular."

As Peter fondly recalls about that competition one year, "the funniest thing was the coaches. The last event consisted of a coaches' relay race. The Australian coaches looked quite young and the Singaporean squad reasonably old. What the Australians failed to realize (at their peril) was that Ang Peng Siong, a former world-record holder was there, and a few of his other coaches came from similar backgrounds." No prizes will be presented for guessing which group of coaches won that race.

Then Peter mentioned **Ye Shiwens,** a 16-year-old swimmer who smashed a world record to win a gleaming gold medal for China in the 400-metre individual medley at the 2012 Olympic Games in London. Some observers insist that she must have used performance-enhancing drugs to achieve such unexpected and remarkable success.

"I know what children like her go through," Peter said. "Actually, they love it (the training and competition). My own children used to climb out of the swimming pool after going hard for five kilometers in training, and then they just wanted to go to McDonald's for more fun."

Long-Term Industrial Decline

At age 18, Peter departed from his hometown. "I left Birmingham carrying an Adidas bag and a rucksack, and I seldom returned," he said.

"Actually, I needed to get away from there. I disliked Birmingham. Many problems had arisen from the long-term decline of British industry. Birmingham had been at the center of British car-manufacturing. My grandfather used to work for Lucas Industries." (A famous producer of automobile parts, Lucas Industries began in 1860, long before the invention of cars. Initially, the company made metal merchandise, like pot holders, scoops and buckets. **Joseph Lucas,** the company founder, previously had sold paraffin oil from a barrow cart on the streets, much like **Paul Watt,** a modern businessman featured in another chapter of this book, formerly sold wristwatches from on top of a cardboard box.)

"Birmingham was built upon manufacturing which to a large extent has disappeared," Peter said. "The place fell into serious urban decay, "probably much like Detroit has in the United States. Although still England's second-biggest city, it had descended into long-term decline."

Reggae to Rap

As a favorite hobby, Peter exalts in listening to music. "I have 74,000 songs on my computer at home," he said. "My favorite genre is reggae."

Yet Peter never has visited Jamaica, the birthplace and spiritual home of reggae. "But every time when I play reggae songs on the jukebox at The Junk Pub (one of his preferred Hong Kong bars), my friend, **Tony Smith,** who once lived in Jamaica, starts to enjoy himself, moving to the beat and saying, 'Ohhh! I feel like drinking a Red Stripe (Jamaican beer).' "

Peter also favors "old" music from the 1950s and '60s. "I have introduced some music to the jukebox at The Junk Pub that other people there never had heard before, songs like 'North to Alaska' by **Johnny Horton.**" (From the country-music genre, "North to Alaska" became a hit in 1960, the same year when Horton, an American, died in a highway accident. He also had recorded other historical ballads, including "The Battle of New Orleans" and "Sink the Bismarck".)

As another public service in music appreciation, Peter familiarized his Junk Pub friends with the song "Paddy McGinty's Goat" by **Val Doonican.** (Born in 1927, Doonican, an Irish singer most popular in the 1960s, appeared often on British television, notably with his own long-running show. Known for singing and playing guitar while seated in a rocking chair, he made the most of comic Irish songs, also including "Delaney's Donkey", and "O'Rafferty's Motor Car".)

When Peter lived in London (where he first entered the financial industry), one of his neighbors vigorously played drums in Fun Boy Three, a successful new-wave-pop band most active from 1981 to 1983. Fun Boy Three scored six top-20 British hits, including "The Lunatics Have Taken Over the Asylum", "Tunnel of Love" and "Our Lips Are Sealed".

"The musician lived next door, and he drummed loud, loud, loud," Peter said. "The noise almost drove me crazy so I went around and yelled straight into his face, 'Will you shut the fuck up?'

"Starting the next day, I heard much softer drumming. He had bought some drum pads, the sort that you can put on drums to keep the noise down."

Although Peter loves music, "all sorts of it", one exception exists. "The only music that pisses me off is rap. I cannot deal with rap, which resembles not so much music as political rants, just gangster stuff.

"Did you know that the American rapper **Snoop Dogg** has changed his name to **Snoop Lion** because he visited Jamaica, suddenly appreciates reggae and now wants to sing that? Ha!"

Chatting With Freddie Aguilar

"When travelling, I always like to find the best local music bars," Peter said. "I enjoy listening to live music. I just fit in there.

"Recently, I visited the Philippines and listened to **Freddie Aguilar** play. I have known Freddie for a long time from going to Manila where he has his own music bar called Ka Freddies."

Born in 1953, Aguilar, a folk-rock songwriter and musician adept on acoustic guitar, towers among the most-talented people in Pinoy music. His song, *"Bayan Ko* (My Country)", helped to inspire the 1986 People Power uprising that toppled dictator **Ferdinand Marcos**. Another Aguilar song, *"Anak* (Child)", one with remorseful lyrics addressed to parents, has become the country's all-time bestselling piece of music.

On Peter's latest visit, he and Freddie spent two hours together at Ka Freddies, drinking brandy while debating Filipino and global politics. "Where are all the protest songs these days?" Peter wondered. "In the late 1970s, a time of massive unemployment, punk songs emerged as big protests. In the 1960s, the Vietnam War and student riots inspired protest songs. Where are the new protest songs now?

"Not many people appear to have much fight left in them anymore. To me, the absence of protest songs suggests that the Western world has lost its ambition and sense of endeavor. **Joe Six-Pack,** sitting on his sofa in front of a television in America, may not have much of a future. The Asian world will gobble it all up.

"Of course, Freddie has written and performed a protest song, 'Maguindanao' (about the province in the Philippines where 57 people, including journalists, died in a 2009 pre-election massacre). He sings that song with massive passion.

"Freddie also says that **Manny Pacquiao,** the champion boxer turned politician, has little chance to achieve meaningful political change, that he may already be spent from a political point of view, and that the deeply flawed Pinoy political system quickly will swallow him up.

"Above all, Freddie shows immense integrity. He sings some very political songs. To me, he resembles a Philippines equivalent of **Bob Dylan.** I would recommend for anyone to visit his bar in Manila to hear him play on a Friday or a Saturday night. And Freddie's son, who plays guitar in the band, even may sound better than **Eric Clapton** does."

Cold Hands, Rough Rides

When younger and still living in England, Peter also loved motorbikes. "Sadly, I gave up that hobby when I left there," he said. "I used to ride motorbikes everywhere. After Jackie and I married, we even went on our honeymoon by motorbike. Until age 34, I never even held a driving license for cars. I only got one then because our daughter, Jordan, had been born, and she did not fit very easily onto the back of a motorbike."

Riding motorbikes in the British winter brought some discomfort. "It got cold," Peter said. "Sometimes I would get off a bike, and my hands, despite being inside gloves, would shake violently because they felt so cold. Then I could not get the keys out of the bike because my fingers shook so much. Meanwhile, the keys to the house, where it would be warmer inside, hung on the same key-ring. Riding through the winter meant dealing with ice, snow, temperatures of minus-15-to-minus-20 degrees (Celsius) and the wind chill factor. It could get a little dangerous too. I did slide a few times.

"One of my strangest experiences on a motorbike (in warmer weather) happened as I went to the house of my **Aunt Iris** in Kent (a county in southeastern England)." At the time, Peter was about 24 years old.

"I knew exactly where I was going," he insisted. "I had been there before, and so I expected a certain road to go straight down and then up with a left-hand turn at the top of the hill. But I had miscalculated and taken the wrong road. As I accelerated and travelled at about 80 miles an hour, away too fast, I unexpectedly came to a bend in the road.

"Suddenly I saw roadside gravel coming up at me. The

bike and I went into (what seemed like) a slow-motion slide. Then I noticed a gap in a fence and went straight through that into a farmer's field where I bounced along at high speed. Somehow I stayed upright on the bike and finally got it stopped. When I had recovered a little, I restarted the bike, drove slowly back out onto the road and then continued on my way."

Missing-Motorbike Muddle

Unfortunately, British criminals often preyed on Peter. "I had four different motorbikes stolen, all when I lived in London," he said. After one theft, "the police came around and said, 'We found your bike.'

"I said, 'Oh, great. What condition is it in?'

"A policeman said, 'Well, the bit that we found looks fine.' " The authorities had found the motorbike's frame abandoned on Greenwich Common. All of the other parts had been stripped away.

Thieves nabbed another of Peter's motorbikes, a Suzuki 750, off the street and carried it away in the back of a truck. "I was in the local pub when a guy told me, 'I see that you had your bike sent away for something.'

"I said, 'What?'

" 'A lorry just came, picked up your bike and took it away.'

" 'What? What?' "

Then Peter started to take extra precautions. "After I got another motorbike, this time a VFR750, I knocked down the outside wall of my basement flat in Camden (part of inner London) and bolted the bike to the floor inside. I had a builder put some bolts right into the concrete in the floor. He told me, 'No one ever will get those things out.'

"The renovation work pissed off my neighbors. The people who lived upstairs yelled down at me: 'What do you think that you are doing?' But no one stole that motorbike from me."

Even without more wheeled valuables to protect, will Peter eventually return to live in England? "I have no idea," he said.

"Honestly, and notwithstanding my previous commentary, I may end up living in Australia. My wife has Australian citizenship. I actually like the place, and my children do too."

New expatriate experiences, ones with entirely different flavors and musical soundtracks, may wait for Peter there. Perhaps he will continue to work inside the office towers of urban financial districts, but still learn more from walking through the streets elsewhere. Maybe he will take an entirely different route toward achieving more personal happiness by becoming an Australian postman, or even a carrot-farmer.

FROM A TINY SWEDISH VILLAGE TO A BIG GLOBAL ADVENTURE

Robert Hoffberg Feels at Home on Any Part of the Planet

Editor's Note: *Like thousands of businessmen from almost every country, Sweden-born Robert Hoffberg sources products from Asian factories for import into overseas markets. But Robert, who spends 80 per cent of his time away from Europe, hardly qualifies as any ordinary wheeler-dealer trying to buy low and sell higher. His edge, a big ace-in-the-hole, comes from how much he loves staying on the move, making friends and enjoying himself "everywhere". With his life unfolding as a constant adventure, he feels nicely satisfied.*

SWEDEN – Not much surprises **Robert Hoffberg** anymore. As a globetrotting businessman, he spends just a fraction of his time in Sweden, his birthplace. After years of seeing astonishing sights, bumping into usual people and learning valuable lessons, he feels equally relaxed strolling along the chilly Baltic Sea or dipping his toes into the more tepid South China Sea.

"Everything in my life turns into a big adventure," Robert said. "I never know for sure in exactly what city that I will wake up the next morning." But fortunately, "I am happy everywhere."

Fifty-one-year-old Robert has followed a meandering career path. Now he works as the president of Primal Home Concepts Industrial Corporation Ltd. From factories on the Chinese mainland, Taiwan or increasingly Thailand, Primal buys bathroom and household products for sale mainly into the domestic markets of Sweden and its Scandinavian neighbors, Denmark, Norway and Finland.

"I plan to move more of my business toward sourcing from Thailand," Robert said. "China gradually has become too expensive and, in my opinion, no buyer properly can control what happens at the factories there. Too many companies in China refuse to follow any laws. Do you know any of them that conduct business without engaging in double book-keeping? I do not. In Thailand, the situation looks much better."

'QC Bitch' Saves the Day

Sales results seldom soar unless the products involved satisfy high quality standards. To ensure that they do, Robert always seeks help from a certain type of person. "I like to work with a QC (quality-control) bitch," he said. "I have one in China. She resembles a rattlesnake. No one gives her any shit. I call her the 'QC bitch' all the time, although she dislikes the name."

Relying on a tough-minded, female quality-control person gives Robert a strategic advantage. Most similar companies send QC men, often from their headquarters in Europe or the Americas, to visit factories in China. At moments of difficulty when the quality looks the most dubious along the production lines, the factory bosses may try to distract such people by hosting big meals for them at fancy restaurants, escorting them to exotic nightclubs, pouring an endless supply of alcoholic drinks and surrounding them with beautiful women.

Then probably the quality-inspection work receives scant attention. Maybe it never happens at all. "When I return from QC trips, sometimes I hardly even know where I have gone," Robert said. "In those cases, I really should have stayed at home."

Invariably, "the QC bitch" saves the day. She has sharp eyes, a fierce determination and little inclination to drink intoxicating beverages. The factory people have "no ways to stop her from doing the job".

As for raw materials, Primal favors wood, mainly medium-density fiberboard (MDF) or bamboo, and steel (everything from regular steel to stainless steel). Applying his home-market knowledge, Robert orders and obtains shelves, medicine cabinets, bathroom mirrors, toilet seats, shower hoses, wall-hanging dust bins or toilet brushes and much more.

People Run in Tunnels

Active as a consultant too, Robert helps other entrepreneurs and companies with advice on business issues. "Many people rush too much. They 'run in tunnels', unable to see beyond what appears right in front of them. So they ask me, 'Is this possible to sell?' and 'What price should it have?' We discuss a lot. They are smart and good guys who need to see things from many sides. Anyone who looks at just one side of things always makes serious mistakes. Everyone needs to figure out exactly what can go wrong in the future."

For 10 years, Robert has kept an office in Hong Kong and appeared there regularly. From that vantage point, he can

ABBA
MONEY
MONEY
MONEY
ALBUM
WHISKY

supervise work and visit the factories in China, Thailand and elsewhere. After every month or two in Asia, he likes to return to Sweden for at least a few days.

Luckily, "I have a very good assistant back in Sweden," Robert said. "He has worked with me for about seven years. We think in nearly the same ways now, and he understands most of my strange humor and sarcastic jokes. We get along."

Meanwhile, Robert refers to his Chinese assistant in Hong Kong as "so honest" and reliable, but also "the shiest person I ever met in all of my life. For the first six months that we worked together, I heard not a single word that she said."

Hacked Fish Still Swims

No matter how long that Robert lives, he never will forget an eventful few hours that transpired in 2002 after he arrived in Hong Kong for the first time. "I just came for a few weeks," he said. "I knew nothing about Hong Kong. Well, I knew that we were on an island, but not much more."

After Robert had checked into "a really nice hotel suite", he and a colleague went searching for a meal, "but not hotel food". So they wandered onto the neon-sign-filled streets of Hong Kong Island at night.

"We went down the Electric Road (in the Tin Hau area). Soon we saw a fish tank. My friend said, 'Come on. We can order some fish.'

"After we did, the restaurant staff cut off pieces from a big fish and then put the still-alive fish back into the tank. A quarter of the fish had gone, but there it was, still trying to swim. I thought, 'How can anyone do that? No one would try that in Sweden. Well, maybe such things are considered normal here.' "

Lifejacket Needed in a Hotel Bed

After the meal, its flavors enhanced by a bit of whiskey, Robert returned to the hotel. Soon he went to bed and fell asleep.

"Late at night, I heard a sound: 'drip…, drip…, drip….' At first, I thought that maybe it came from somewhere in my dreams. Even so, I got up and checked around everywhere in the hotel suite. I still heard the noise, but found nothing wrong. I checked the shower, toilet, sink and everything. There was a big Jacuzzi (whirlpool bath) there, but it looked alright too.

"So I went back to bed and fell asleep again, but only for a few minutes. Then the noise got louder and faster: "drip, drip, drip, drip'. I wondered, 'What the fuck? Is something wrong with my head or what?'

"Worried, I got up and looked around again, but then returned to bed. Then the dripping got really fast: 'drip, drip, drip, drip, drip, drip'.

" 'Jeez!' I thought. This time I jumped up and spent an even longer time to check absolutely everywhere, but still saw nothing wrong.

"Suddenly the dripping sound stopped. Then I saw a stream of water start to dribble down from the ceiling and go into the Jacuzzi. 'Shit,' I thought. 'What has happened? A pipe or something must have broken.'

"Quickly, I pulled on some clothes and telephoned to the hotel's reception desk. 'There is water leakage in my suite,' I said.

" 'Ah, no problem!' the hotel person said. 'We will take care of that tomorrow.'

" 'Yeah, but it does not come from the faucet or the shower. It leaks from the ceiling.'

" 'No, no, no. That would be impossible.'

"At that moment, I heard a huge splashing noise from the other room. 'What was that?' I said.

"Rushing to look, I saw that the stream of water had become a thick flow, the size of a tree-trunk. Now this was serious water -- cubic meters per minute -- pouring down into the suite.

" 'Oh, shit!' I yelled and ran back to the telephone. 'You need to send someone up here right now.' This was on the 24th or 25th floor at about 3 o'clock in the morning.

" 'No problem. We will go there tomorrow.'

" 'Tomorrow really will be much too late – that is for sure. Now the place is flooding."

" 'No, sir. That cannot be true.'

" 'Send someone up here immediately.'

"By the time that a hotel-night-staff person came to my door, the Jacuzzi had filled and overflowed, sending waves of water across the bathroom and bedroom floors. In retreat, I had moved all of my belongings to the next room.

" 'Sir, what is the problem?' the hotel person asked me.

"To demonstrate, I opened the bedroom door and so much water came flowing out. Then the hotel people started to take my complaint seriously.

"Apparently a big pipe to the main water-tank had broken. Two entire hotel floors ended up needing total renovations. Definitely, it was the worst water damage to a building that I ever saw. But for me, it all became part of my fantastic experience when first arriving in Hong Kong.

"A year later, I returned to the same hotel and learned that the two floors remained 'under construction'. I believe that workers had to clear out everything and rebuild almost from the beginning."

Canton Fair Drive-Away

Robert's first visit to the Chinese mainland's biggest trade fair, the Canton Fair (alias the China Import and Export

Fair), also in 2002, produced another memorable incident. This huge business event routinely attracts thousands of international buyers to Guangzhou, the largest city in southern China.

"I took a short flight from Hong Kong to Guangzhou," Robert said. "The airplane went up and back down again, all within 20-some minutes.

"The plane landed at the old airport (Guangzhou Baiyun International Airport, named the same as the present one) inside the city," he said. "I thought that probably someone at the airport should speak really good English. Well, not much, I discovered, so welcome to China. It looked like a big challenge ahead to find the exhibition.

"So I started to ask people: 'Can you help? I want to attend the big exhibition?'

" 'Oh, it is quite close,' someone said.

" 'Yeah? What direction?' But the person walked away.

" 'Well, that was a rude one!' I thought, wondering if all of the mainland Chinese would behave like that.

"Then I stopped another person. 'How can I go to the exhibition?'

" 'Follow me,' he said. 'No problem at all.'

" 'Fantastic!' I thought. 'This guy behaves really politely. Not everyone here insists on being rude.'

"The guy went to a car. 'Get in. I can drive you.'

"Suddenly I felt slightly suspicious. 'How much will this cost?'

" 'Only 200 RMB (about US$25).'

" 'Two hundred RMB? That sounds quite expensive.'

"But I believed that I had to move quickly because already it was the final day of the annual fair with only six hours left on the schedule. So I climbed into the car.

"The driver went for less than three minutes and circled

back to drop me off almost right across the street from where we had started. It gave me a good lesson on how easily I could get cheated in China."

Even when Robert arrived at the doors of the Canton Fair, his woes continued. "I tried to pay the entrance fee, but I was told, 'There is no entrance fee now.'

" 'What? No entrance fee?'

" 'Right! Just walk inside. The exhibition has closed.'

" 'Closed?' But the schedule showed six hours left.

"I rushed inside and saw almost all of the exhibitors busy packing away everything in their displays early. A few of them already had finished packing and just sat there, some even sleeping, while waiting for their transportation."

Although deeply disappointing, Robert's first visit to the Canton Fair did not flop entirely. "My purpose had been to learn more about how things work in China," he said. "For sure, I learned a lot."

No Worries on Any Part of the Planet

When Robert diverts his attention from business matters, he likes to enjoy himself. Fellow patrons at various pubs appreciate his generosity to buy rounds of drinks. "I have a lot of friends," he said. "Almost every day, I bump into people who become good friends."

As a happy result, "I could be dropped off on any part of the planet without any worries", he said. "It is easy for me to make new friends, even if at the beginning some of them will think that maybe I am a little bit peculiar. Later, of course, they will know for sure."

Robert regards China, Taiwan and much of Asia as fertile ground to win friends. "The people always feel curious and want to know if things look greener on the other side of the world."

But unfortunately, most of the Hong Kong Chinese

cannot be classified as being among the world's friendliest folks. "When I say 'hello' or 'good morning' to people in Hong Kong as we stand together on lifts, they never answer me, even though I may have seen them once or twice a week for many months," Robert said.

Who Likes to Eat Mud?

In Europe, Robert follows a completely different pursuit. He passionately enjoys racing, mainly motocross (on motorbikes along off-road circuits), but originally in cars too, a hobby that he has loved for most of his life. "I always have been addicted to racing," he said.

Back in Sweden, he keeps a collection of 13 motorbikes. He sold his last rally car in 1983 when switching permanently to two-wheeled racing vehicles.

Some tough lessons learned when vying for position in motorbike races also apply in other realms. For example, Robert likes to surge ahead and stay in front of his rivals. Otherwise you end up constantly "eating mud" and dirt thrown up by the leaders and everyone else. "No one likes to eat mud" – not in a race, business or life.

Mastering such lessons meant accepting all-too-frequent pain and a big element of risk. Twice, Robert broke his neck in serious racing accidents, but he made remarkable recoveries. "I have had so many crashes," he said. "Almost everything has happened to me. Some people believe that I must have nine lives," with many of the nine already expired.

His first serious neck injury happened in 1986. "It was so bad that a doctor told me that I never should race again," he said. "Of course, the accident gave me a real brain-shake too. For one month, I could not smell anything. I also could not see properly, especially in the dark."

Later a physician lambasted Robert, calling him "an asshole", for refusing to heed medical advice. But the plucky

Swede resumed racing after three years.

Seen from a competitive perspective, that particular accident had transpired at a bad time. "It happened in the last race of the year," Robert said. "I had good scores from before and only needed to finish the final race to become the local champion. But instead I broke my neck and ended up in third place for the season."

Sounds Perfect, Right?

In racing (as in business), Robert constantly forges friendships, often with past rivals. "I have at least 100 really good friends living around the world, who are racers or racing engineers," he said.

Sometimes familiar faces appear unexpectedly. Recently, Robert spent a few days in Thailand after failing to secure a timely ticket back to Hong Kong. "It was about 9 a.m. on a Friday, and I had just come to Chiang Mai in northwest Thailand from Shanghai, China," he said. "As I walked through the airport, I noticed someone, wearing a backpack and about 30 meters away, who looked really familiar.

"That guy started to focus on me too. He came closer, looked at me and said, 'Robert, are you still alive?'

" 'Oh, yes. Who are you?'

"It was **Micke Lyden.** I know him from racing in Sweden, but had not seen him for 14 years. No matter where you are in the world, you absolutely cannot predict who suddenly will come walking along at any moment. You never know where or when that you will meet people.

"So I said to him, 'Where are you going in Thailand?'

" 'I don't know,' he said." (Micke was on a business mission in unfamiliar territory and had the weekend to spare.)

" 'You don't know? Then where will you stay here?'

" 'I don't know.'

" 'Okay. So what do you know?'

" 'I don't know anything,' he said.

" 'Welcome to Thailand, my friend.'

" 'What about you?' he asked me.

" 'The same as you,' I told him. 'I do not know. I cannot go back to Hong Kong yet.'

"He tilted his head and looked at me. 'It sounds perfect, right?'

" 'Yeah.'

"So we decided to take a taxi together. 'Where to?' we asked each other.

" 'South?' I said. 'Why not south?'

" 'Okay, south. But first we need to wait for **Morgan'** (another acquaintance then about to arrive from Sweden)." So they waited, and the Swedish duo turned into a trio.

Did the old buddies from Sweden's chaotic and noisy motorbike races have a pleasant weekend in Thailand? "More than fine," Robert said. "We ended up out in the middle of nowhere.

"Our taxi-driver spoke good English. 'Okay, I will go south somewhere,' he told us.

"We drove on small roads, small roads and more small roads.

" 'Where should I stop?' the driver finally asked.

" 'Find a small hotel,' we said.

" 'In the end, we found a hostel, a place with eight rooms, along a muddy road. It looked ideal. Almost everything about the place was outside -- two plastic tables with parasols on top, a big plastic shelf, three bottles of liqueur, all half-finished, some beer inside a refrigerator and a pool table, of course. Two girls worked there. What a funny place!

" 'We stopped and asked, 'Do you have rooms?'

" 'Yes, we have eight rooms.'

" 'Okay, what is the price?'

" 'Maybe you want to see the rooms?'

" 'No need.' The rooms were alright. Of course, it was no Shangri-La. But we paid only 200 baht (less than US$6.50) per night.

"The owner of the hostel stayed sleeping in a corner with a beer all the time. A few naughty girls came out a bit later. They were sisters who cleaned up the rooms, threw out all of the biggest cockroaches and stuff like that."

Evidently, another variety of insects avoided expulsion. "When I returned to my place in Hong Kong, my travel bag turned out to be full of ants," Robert said. "Without meaning to, I had imported them from Chiang Mai, Thailand. After I opened the bag, they climbed up onto the ceiling and then disappeared."

So Robert had learned another valuable lesson -- that a businessman always on the move should strive to avoid importing more than intended. Looking on the bright side, destructive termites from Thailand would have made much worse houseguests.

Three Swedes Walk Into a Bar....

Another of Robert's "strangest" experiences happened in Shanghai. "I was there not long ago," he said. "My life fills with coincidences, and this amounted to a big one."

Robert had planned to meet a friend who has lived in Shanghai for a decade. He telephoned the man.

" 'Where are you?' I asked him. 'We should go out together and drink some beer.'

" 'Yes, I will be there soon.'

" 'There soon? What do you mean?'

" 'I am in Hong Kong now,' he told me.

" 'What? I just came to Shanghai yesterday.' "

Unexpectedly left on his own, Robert ambled into a bar near his hotel. "I sat down," he said. "Some girls working there saw me and wanted to know where I came from. I was in a good mood so I enjoyed the beer and did some paperwork.

"Soon I chatted with the girls a little more. Then another one came along. They all seemed very curious. Eventually, I told them that I was Swedish.

"Already I had a feeling that one of the girls liked me perhaps a little bit too much – it happens sometimes – and so I tried to maintain a safe distance. But soon she told me, 'I am divorced already.'

" 'Oh!' I replied. 'Thanks for the information.'

"Suddenly a blond man walked into the place. I looked at that guy and knew right away that I had met him somewhere before. What was his name? I had it right there on the tip of my tongue. **'Nicholas**?' I said.

" 'Yes,' he said. 'That is right.'

"Then he said my name, 'Robert, from near Kisa, Sweden, where have we met before?'

"I had no idea. We did not know and still do not know. Definitely we had met before, but neither of us had a clue about exactly where or when.

" 'So what should we do?' Nicholas asked.

" 'We need to celebrate, of course!'

" 'The girls found the situation very funny too and started to laugh. Some of them sat down with us. They spoke perfect English.

" 'Do you want drinks?' we asked them. 'What would you like to drink?'

" 'I want Sex on the Beach," one girl said. (Sex on the Beach is the name of a popular cocktail.)

Robert swivelled his head, taking a quick look around. " 'I see no beach here,' I told her.

"Then one girl mentioned that another Swedish guy sat in the bar too, just three tables away. 'What?' we said. At first, we hardly believed her.

"No other people were in the place – just the girls working there and three Swedish customers.

"So we asked the other guy, 'Are you sure that you come from Sweden?'

" 'Yeah,' he said. A big man with lots of muscles, this fellow came over to our table and took a closer look at me. Then he opened his mouth and started to speak in a special dialect (from a region of Sweden).

" 'Where did we meet the last time?' he asked me.

"I knew exactly where: 'It was in 1993, after a race (motorbikes through the forest), on the winners' podium.'

" 'You fucking shit! You beat me by two seconds. You were number one, and I was number two.' "

The big world sometimes looks decidedly small. Against astronomical odds, three familiar Swedes had stumbled into the same bar far from home amid the vastness of China and its 1.3 billion people.

Settling a Sensitive Stomach

Robert also takes a special interest in food. "I love to cook as a hobby chef," he said. Then he boasted about feeding a former houseguest "who once stayed with me for only one week but gained 3.5 kilos".

When travelling, "sometimes I am a bit sensitive to Asian food", Robert said. "I have a sensitive stomach. Whiskey, that always is perfect! But often the food can give me problems."

Once on a business trip to Taiwan, Robert and some cohorts took time to go out for lunch, which included pieces of unsavoury-looking, discolored fish. "It must have been dead for at least a week," Robert said.

" 'Should we eat this?' I asked the others.

" 'You must try a little,' they told me. So I did. Within just a few minutes, I began to feel really ill."

When the group returned to a company showroom where

they had been working, "I was so sick and sweating a lot."

The other people tried to help. " 'Why not drink something?' they suggested. 'Should we bring you some tea?' Maybe they thought that hot tea would kill the bacteria.

"When all of the Taiwanese had left the room, I remembered that earlier I had bought a bottle of whiskey. Better yet, I had it with me in my bag. Good then! No problem!

"I dug out the whiskey bottle, lifted it to my lips and just had started to drink (wetting his whistle, as the saying goes) when the showroom door suddenly opened." An unfamiliar Taiwan business executive entered.

" 'Oh, hello, Robert,' the newcomer said. 'Are you Robert?'

"So that image with the raised whiskey bottle became his first impression of me. Quickly, I made the excuse that I had experienced some serious stomach problems. Of course, he believed me, I suppose."

Small-Village Charms

In the 1960s and '70s, Robert grew up hundreds of kilometers south of Stockholm on a farm, "with cows, pigs and everything", near a tiny Swedish village called Bjorkfors. With only about 100 people, the village hardly qualifies as worldly. "The farmers there might use tractors when they want to go somewhere…," Robert said.

The nearest "big city" is Linkoping, "the science city of Sweden", best known for its university and burgeoning high-tech industries. Even there, the population totals just 105,000 people.

Yet Bjorkfors possesses certain powerful charms that continue to lure Robert back regularly. He also has three children in Sweden and owns property there. Family concerns, together with the immense natural beauty of evergreen trees, clean water and bright-blue skies, "explain why I did not give up living in Sweden totally", he said.

Each morning when Robert awakens and peeks out a window in Hong Kong, he sees a parking lot and a big sign for the Galaxy nightclub. Back in Sweden, where forests and lakes dominate the surroundings, he wakes up, peers outside and sees a pristine lake surrounded by trees. "That looks more beautiful," he said, putting it mildly.

Such different places mean dramatically different lifestyles. Therefore, taking business calls from Asia when in Sweden can lead to some odd conversations. Once when Robert answered a mobile phone, the caller heard him huffing and puffing, breathing heavily.

" 'What is wrong?' the caller asked. 'I hope that I did not disturb you. It sounds like maybe you have a girl there with you.'

" 'No.'

" 'Then what are you doing?'

" 'I am in the forest.'

" 'What? You have a girl in the forest?'

" 'No, no. I am chopping some firewood.'

" 'What? Firewood?' "

Actually, Robert appreciates Hong Kong in large part because it has so many vast differences, as seen in lifestyles, experiences and attitudes, from the less-populous place where he grew up. Regularly spending time in both locations sprinkles the spice of variety into his life.

New Orders to Pick Up Trash

Robert left school at age 18. Then in 1980 and '81, he performed military service, which entailed plenty of training in the Swedish countryside and forests.

Although known to enjoy beer and whiskey, Robert takes a dim view of non-medicinal drugs, an attitude that formed during those soldier-in-training years. "I am totally against people using illegal drugs," he said, recalling one day when a drug-impaired Swedish military-service trainee pointed a gun at another trainee and fired. The victim "died before he could get to a hospital.

"Of course, drugs were involved," Robert insisted. Otherwise, "no one aims a gun from 30 centimeters away and pulls the trigger like it was a joke. The next day, we got entirely new orders." Instead of more firearms training, "we had to go into the forest and pick up trash."

Robert also remembers the amazing powers of certain military gear. "We had really strong binoculars – so strong that you could see a pile of dog shit at long distance," he said.

One night when rather far from the military camp, "I remember looking around using binoculars. The image was so sharp…. Suddenly, I saw something (back at the camp) that really surprised me. 'What's going on? I see dozens of police cars, and dogs everywhere.'

"The next morning, 40 of our friends were missing. They had been arrested as drug-dealers or users. The dogs had checked everyone and everything. Those 40 guys never came back (to military service)."

Delightful Digging

Early in Robert's working career, he regarded himself as "a handyman". He always enjoys studying products and deciding how to improve them, or mulling problems and finding solutions. By no coincidence, he holds more than 40 patents.

Robert excelled in the 1990s when working on heavy trucks and excavators, "making special tooling, hand-made". One of his best innovations helped to perfect the rototilt, allowing the digging buckets on excavators to turn through 360 degrees while tilting and maneuvering more effectively.

"Then you can dig sideways, backwards or any way

that you like," Robert said. "I made it for fun to help a friend and was so stupid. I should have registered a patent on that one. Now every such machine in the world has that feature."

Robert benefits from possessing "a photographic memory" that allows him to "take an engine apart, throw all of the pieces aside, take a good look at everything and then put it back together again", all without reference to a manual. Obviously, that same potent memory helps him to handle import-export business details too.

Eventually, Robert's thirst for new sights, experiences and knowledge meant that he had to move far beyond his home village, its region and even Sweden. After all, the entire country has just 9.5 million people.

For a while, Robert worked a lot in Italy, Spain and Portugal. "I spent quite a bit of time in Porto (second to Lisbon among Portugal's biggest cities)," he said. "Portugal is a nice country, except for the food poisoning that I get every time when I go there."

So Many Countries

Decades ago, Robert clung to nationalistic sentiments. "Not anymore," he said. "I have been to so many different countries that I know very well each one of them has both good things and bad things about it."

By now, this inquisitive guy from one of Sweden's smallest communities has made the entire world his new village. In doing so, he accepts everyone on the planet as an interesting neighbor and a potential friend or business partner.

Naturally, his travel schedule rarely allows him to rest for long. "Soon I must leave for Sweden because I promised to take my daughter to the Baltic Sea for a few days," he said. "Then I will come back to Asia to attend a wedding."

By no means has Robert finished wandering the globe.

"My girlfriend is Indonesian, and I am very curious to visit Borneo," he said. "At age 16, I worked at helping a famer, but at night I still found the time to read a book about a minority group in Borneo who did not love people so much as eat them up (cannibals)." Now cannibals may be in short-supply even in the most remote areas of Indonesia, but Robert still senses a chance for new adventures.

"Many people ask me: 'Where will you settle down?' " he said. "Honestly, I have very short roots. Probably I cannot settle down anywhere."

Robert's travels consistently earn him precious friends, adventures and memories. To him, those things represent greater wealth than anything that happens to his bank account from buying and selling household products.

Final Notes: When telling about his own adventures, Robert made glowing references to some of his very favorite movies. "Have you seen the movie, *Cast Away* (2000, starring **Tom Hanks,** about a FedEx employee stranded alone on a remote island)?" he asked. "Maybe it sounds strange, but I would love to be in that situation. I like daily challenges. In a sense, I am cast away a little bit every day. For me, each day is different and challenging."

Repeatedly, Robert also praised another cinema selection, *The World's Fastest Indian* (2005), a biographical film starring **Anthony Hopkins,** about speed-bike racer **Burt Munro** (1899-1978), from Invercargill, New Zealand, and a much-modified Indian Scout motorcycle. At the Bonneville Salt Flats in Utah during the late 1950s and early '60s, Munro repeatedly set land-speed records for bikes with less than 1,000cc engines. "Everyone should see that terrific movie," Robert said.

NO NEIGH-SAYER: HARRY THE HORSE HEE-HAWS ABOUT ADOPTED HOMETOWN

Jim Dale Straight-Talks to the World

Editor's Note: *An online publisher, Jim Dale has ties with two of North America's most exciting cities: New York and Las Vegas. Yet he chooses to live in a less famous, but dynamic, Asian community. Also known as Harry the Horse, Jim uses the Internet to tell the world about the people and businesses, blessings and foibles, of Angeles City in the Philippines. No event has etched itself more deeply into his memory than the time when the nearby volcano, Mount Pinatubo, erupted, trapping him amid chaos and destruction.*

IN A VOLCANO'S SHADOW – A career in the United States military and a lifetime of observing fellow humans, chatting, telling jokes and writing have taken **Jim Dale,** more widely known as **Harry the Horse,** from the Big Apple on the East Coast of America to a hotspot in

Southeast Asia.

Retired from the military since 1984, the 74-year-old Jim has become a long-time resident of Angeles City in the Philippines. For more than a decade, his written words, published first in a print magazine and then online, have presented his adopted hometown and many of its people to the world. "I try to put my feelings about the town into writing and to point out its pitfalls," he said.

A team from *All Aboard! Planet Expat* listened intently as Jim spoke. The small group had assembled for a late-morning meeting inside the popular Phillies Bar on Fields Avenue near the center of Angeles City.

Jim's popular Website, titled *Harry the Horse, The Man About Town,* updated and maintained from an office in his home, attracts impressive readership totals, including from overseas. As Harry the Horse, Jim writes everything from feature stories to snippets about selected Angeles people and tourists. He even lets loose with some "political rants". Apart from the Philippines, his biggest readership clusters are in Australia and the U.S. He welcomes new readers

(at www.harrythehorse.asia).

Never Pulls a Punch

"Really, I hardly even consider myself as being a writer, and I often wonder about exactly how Harry the Horse got to be so popular," Jim said. "Usually people say that they like to read how I tell it like it is. I write what I feel and never pull punches.

"I just write. Honestly, I have no wild ambitions for Harry the Horse. My only thing is that I enjoy doing it. Beyond that, mainly I try to promote Angeles City because I love the town. So I write about the good, the bad and the ugly of the place. Since I am so blunt, the police sometimes ask me why no one has shot me yet. I don't know. Maybe I just am lucky."

Do the readers include many Filipino people? "I am not sure just how many," Jim said, "but I do receive emails from Filipinos who read Harry the Horse."

How did Jim get his nickname? "A thousand people have asked me that," he said. "When I used to live in Thailand, I did a magazine for the NCO Club, and the magazine's most popular section was a gossip column called 'From the Horse's Mouth'.

"When I came to the Philippines, an editor at the local *TV Guide* asked me if I would like to write a column. Wondering about a good gimmick to stay anonymous, I came up with Harry the Horse. No more exciting reason for the name exists. I could have said **Scotty the Horse** or **Joseph the Horse.** But Harry the Horse came out of my mouth.

"Nearly a year passed before anyone connected Harry the Horse to me. That turned out to be a reader who knew me and how I talked. So finally he said to me, 'You are Harry the Horse.'

"At the time, I had tried to keep my identity secret. I enjoyed listening as people talked and asked each other, 'Who the hell is this Harry the Horse guy?' It was fun. I would sit back and say nothing."

An Incurable Illness

Jim often warns about a potentially lingering illness. "Once you come to Angeles City, no matter if you stay for a day, a week, two weeks or more, you catch what I call the 'Angeles City Virus'," he said. "It is completely incurable! You fall in love with the women, the place and the atmosphere. No matter who you are, or where you come from, you never get Angeles City out of your blood again. A guy just wrote to me who has been away living in the U.S. for 20 years, but he still laments, 'I miss Angeles City'."

Victims of that virus regularly read Harry the Horse. "In doing so, they grasp at the memories of Angeles City," Jim said.

Cupid's Arrow Hits Home

While many people enjoy and appreciate Angeles City, others fall in love with someone they meet there. Sometimes Jim even likes to dabble at matchmaking. "Twaaang!" goes the sound when **Cupid**'s arrow takes flight.

"As a matter of fact, I had one case in which Harry the Horse was essential," Jim said. "A couple I know asked me to put their relative into my column. The lady they told me about had been raised by a military father who was very strict so she had been sheltered and unable to do much. Then the father passed away so she wanted to break out of her shell. So I got a picture of her, interviewed her and wrote up the details, saying: 'This lady is perfect for somebody. She is one you need to court. She is educated, a professional person.'

"After reading that, an Australian guy wrote to her and they clicked. He came here. They met, fell madly in love and got married. Now they live in Darwin, Australia. I really am proud of that success story."

Like the Wild West

Neither Jim, nor Harry the Horse, ever will run out of fascinating topics and material. Jim likens Angeles City, with its surging prospects and bar-room culture, to a boomtown in America's Wild West of the 1800s. "Years ago, I predicted that Angeles City would develop and explode economically, which it is doing now," he said.

How far has the boom advanced? "Actually, you can

buy a house more cheaply in much of the U.S. than you can here," Jim said.

With good news, bad elements arrive too. Along with legitimate tourists and business visitors, "Angeles City has become a magnet for expatriate con-artists, again like in the old West," Jim said. "We get shady characters along with the good people. For example, be careful if someone wants to sell you a share in a bar when he already may have sold 207 shares."

For that matter, "not all Filipinos are wonderful people" either. "Never fall for the constant propaganda put out by the Philippines that everyone is wonderful and nice. Many people here really are like that, but you need to be aware that exceptions do exist. Sometimes I sense what I call a phony Catholicism whereby certain people go to church on Sundays, but then steal from you on Mondays anyway."

Many of the modern "saloons" in Angeles City, like those 150 years ago in the Wild West, have signs on the doors warning the patrons not to bring guns inside. Yes, some people carry guns. But "the signs are directed mainly at the police," Jim said. "Even some regular stores have signs that say 'no guns allowed'. Usually the police are the ones who carry their weapons inside, maybe have a few too many San Miguels (beers) and then start shooting at each other."

From the 'Real' New York

Unabashedly, Jim declares that he comes from "the real New York", meaning the borough of Queens. "I always consider that area, the Bronx, Brooklyn and Queens, as the real New York. I say that the people from out beyond that are elitists. Those in the real New York are the working classes, common people. We know nothing about wine,

WE SURVIVED MT. PINATUBO
IS HARRY A HORSE?
YES!
HEE, HEE

gourmet foods or any of that stuff, and we do say what we think. If anyone asks me, 'Do I look fat?', then I will reply, 'Yeah, you look fat. You should lose weight.' We are not always nice. Never ask a New Yorker about anything unless you want to hear the honest truth."

Actually, Jim's connections to New York City have stretched thin. "I went back last April," he said. "I had not been there since 1984. The weather was cold and terrible. I decided never to go there again at the wrong time of year."

When Jim travels to the U.S., his favorite city happens to be another action-packed place, Las Vegas, where he also lived for a time and still has a house. "I love Vegas," he said.

At age 18, Jim joined the military. "Thank goodness, or else I might still be in New York," he said. For 28 years, he served the air force, not as a pilot, but "just a common enlisted man, a desk jockey".

His work took him for stays in several countries, notably England, Thailand, the Philippines (1977-81) and Germany. He travelled even more widely, "all over Europe and the U.S.", as a performer with the Air Force Tops in Blue (TIB) talent show appearing at military bases and community theatres. "My talent was as an MC (master of ceremonies) and comedian," he said. "I like to talk."

Jim returned permanently to the Philippines in early 1985. "There were a number of reasons," he said. "I already had purchased a house and my girlfriend **Divina** (now his wife) was there.

"But, you know, I love Thailand too. My original intention was to make the Philippines my home base and then travel back and forth to Thailand. During the four years that I had spent in Thailand, I did not love every minute – I loved every second. I loved my job and the scenery. Also I was an MC for floor shows at the NCO Club, did the club magazine, bowled five or six days a week, wrote about bowling for the *TV Guide* there and participated in Toastmasters International."

Jim first met Divina, who worked at a dress shop, when he acted as the MC for a fashion show at an NCO Club in the Philippines. "She was there to model some of the dresses. Later when I moved to Germany, we kept on communicating. She is a good lady who takes fine care of me. We make a good team, and I could not ask for more."

Mount Pinatubo Turned Nasty

The incident that most frightened Jim and proved that Angeles City may be too much of a hotspot at times happened in June 1991. Nearby Mount Pinatubo, a usually mild-mannered volcano, blew its top, sending clouds of ash and dust high into the sky. The ash and lahar (volcanic mudflow and debris) descended as people sought shelter or fled from one of the largest volcanic eruptions of the 20th century.

Jim waded through the mess and dodged destruction. "At the time, I worked on the American military base as a civilian," he said. "When Pinatubo erupted, it was something that you never forget. It was horrible, but then again, afterwards the recovery was amazing.

"See, I made a big mistake. We had some leftover goods from charity work so after hearing on radio that a church across town needed donations of goods because people were gathering there, I told my wife, 'Load up the truck. Whatever we have left, we will take it there.'

"We tried to cross one bridge, but it had collapsed. Then we decided, 'Okay, let's try to get over the Abacan Bridge', which is the main one here in town.

"As we went over that bridge, I saw cracks coming up, appearing in the bridge. I told my wife, 'We have to hurry. I hope that we can deliver this stuff and get back.'

"I don't know why the bridge was cracking. Probably it had something to do with the volcanic ash, the heat and the lahar flow coming down.

"Fortunately, we reached the other side. By then, the sky had completely darkened, and this was in the afternoon.

"We dropped off the goods. It was chaos at the church and everywhere else. Confusion reigned. People ran in all directions.

"Next we started to drive back, trying to get over the same bridge again, but it had collapsed already. By then, the sky had turned pitch-black. Mud rained down. Stones rained down. We kept driving.

"Since we had relatives in San Nicolas down in the middle of town, we decided to try reaching them. Meanwhile, people were jumping into my truck. They did not care where I was going. More just kept jumping into the back. There were lots of them. I never took the time to count. Mass confusion reigned.

"Then I could not see where I was driving. The mud and ash were so thick that it became impossible to see through the windshield. I had to stop at a gas station to get water and clean off my windshield.

"Luckily, I found some water. Then we got down to San Nicolas where the people finally got out of the truck when it stopped moving. We needed to consider if we should try to stay there.

"But then I decided, 'Okay, let's try to get home by going through Carmenville. That was a subdivision that perhaps we could cross and reach the other side.

"We tried to make progress, but could see hardly anything. Still, we went through Carmenville and got to its back gate. There, a little concrete structure crossed a creek.

A car already had put a tire onto that and it had collapsed. The car remained there in front of us so we could see that. Otherwise, we might have run into the same problem and maybe gotten stuck.

"To make a long story short, we stayed overnight with my wife's brother because we could not get back. All night, the brother stayed up shoveling lahar. Rain made the lahar thicken, harden and stick like concrete. That was why so many roofs and buildings collapsed. A lot of the roofs were made of tin.

"The next day the city looked exactly like a bleak moonscape. Everything was gray. The sky was gray, the ground was gray, everything. There was absolute silence.

"Then we took the truck and again tried to find a way back, but could not. So we parked the truck on the other side of the river and walked across into the Diamond Subdivision and back home.

"When we walked across the Abacan River, it was dry, all ash and mud, but not too sticky. We were able to walk across, but it was scary. The whole thing was scary."

Although surrounded by devastation, Jim and Divina's home had stayed mostly intact. They never forget the sight of houses in some neighborhoods nearly covered by lahar and ash, some "with only the roofs showing. People climbed onto the roofs of buried homes and tried to get their goods out."

Angeles City had turned into "a place of devastation. There was no electricity. Roofs had collapsed. Lahar lay all over the place. Most gas stations and businesses were closed.

"But even in that situation, as with all tragedies, people in the community shared whatever remained and worked together. There were sad times, but also some fun times and funny times."

For a long time after that, "I watched Angeles City rise from the ashes", Jim said. Literally, the city and its people together "rose from the ashes".

No One More Contented?

When Jim first settled in Angeles City, the only real English local periodical was a *TV Guide,* which is where Harry the Horse first appeared. In payment, "I used to receive a discount on my cable-TV and they gave me – this is the funny part – 30 copies of the *TV Guide*. At that time, the *TV Guide* cost 20 pesos (about US$0.50) per copy. I had a little motor-scooter and so I went around and did home deliveries of the *TV Guide,* earning a few pesos that way. I cannot say why, but it was fun to do."

When the *TV Guide* got a new editor, "he disliked the notion of an American writing, I guess. So he stopped the column. But then people asked, 'Where did Harry the Horse go?' They wanted to read something."

At first, Jim did nothing to satisfy the need. Then a popular Website asked him to provide Harry the Horse content. After a few years, new management took over there, and Jim migrated to his own site.

During breaks from writing, Jim spends time with Divina and their 13-year-old son, **Jason,** at La Case Pension, a small guest house that they operate together. "Online, I refer to my wife as **Priscilla the Horse,**" Jim said, "but people tell me that she hates that. They say to her, 'Oh, you must be Priscilla.' And she insists, 'No, I am Divina.' "

Jim even finds time for charity work. "Every Christmas time, I have my own charity projects," he said. "People donate clothes, candy and other goods, and I appear as **Santa Claus** at some malls and schools to raise needed funds. We then prepare packages that we deliver to hospital charity wards on Christmas Eve. Each patient gets a food package, candy and some money, plus a stuffed toy for the sick children. We also have a special day set aside for a Christmas event when we host 120 to 150 children and parents from extremely low-income families. Each child receives a personal gift from Santa, and we enjoy a day of games, prizes and lunch. Our last project is to prepare packages of food (oranges, apples and more), candy and clothes to be delivered to an Aeta community (indigenous people) during the week before each New Year's holiday."

Another positive factor about expatriate life in the Philippines is not sliding into debt. "If I ever moved back to the U.S., I would fall into debt up to my ears," Jim said. "Finances are easier to handle here. Things are getting more expensive, but it remains possible to live at a higher level than I could in the United States.

"I do not want to give the impression that there are no negatives to living here. There are some, and one has to learn how to deal with them, but it all forms part of the choice that one makes when deciding to live in a foreign country.

"One word of advice is that people never, ever should sever the ties with their home countries. All of America, especially Las Vegas and the New York Yankees (a highly successful professional baseball team), remains a big part of my life."

Sounding happy and fulfilled, Jim says that he would return to live in the U.S. "only if there was a serious medical need". On that front, he has valid experience, having survived a recent battle with cancer of the vocal chords for which he received treatment in Las Vegas. Due to the illness, his voice has deepened so much that he anticipates "getting a part in *The Godfather 4* movie".

Slightly critical of some of the fellow expatriates he observes, Jim scolds them for shortening their lives with bad habits, like too much drinking and smoking. "I do not drink alcohol or smoke which helps to keep me alive," he said.

Much happens in Angeles City, and Jim enjoys keeping watch on almost everything. As Harry the Horse, he plans to keep galloping onto computer screens for a long time. "You probably could not meet anyone more contented with his life than I am," he said.

As with many expatriates, another issue prevails too. "Not a day goes by when I can say that I am bored," Jim said. "Every day, every month, here, something changes. I am living, witnessing and even becoming a part of the history here as the city develops.

"Back in the U.S., most people live in their neighborhoods – middle class, lower middle class, wherever they fit in – and nothing ever really changes. They seldom even know their neighbors. They get up in the mornings, follow their routines and then look at their budgets wondering if they can afford to go to a movie or to eat in a restaurant.

"Here, something always happens that is exciting and interesting (affordable too). Until the day when I die, I am seeing the history of Angeles City unfold in front of me. What could be more exciting?"

INSIGHTFUL IMAGES PROPEL ARTIST ACROSS BORDERS

Hard-Hitting SARA Wields Mighty Power of the Pen

Editor's Note: *No stranger to newspaper and magazine readers, Sara Seneviratne comes originally from Sri Lanka (formerly Ceylon), which he regards as Paradise Lost. He travels the world and often lives overseas following a path determined by his artistic talent and passion for caricatures and political satire. By lucky happenstance, he also has illustrated this book.*

SRI LANKA – When **Sara Seneviratne**, alias **SARA,** reaches for a pen, despotic dictators and tyrannical tycoons, even those hiding far away in luxurious surroundings behind thick walls, may twitch nervously, perhaps without understanding exactly why. But everyone else finds nothing to fear, and much to admire, in what SARA does.

Almost by instinct, SARA, an artist extraordinaire who takes immense pleasure in creating caricatures and political satire, uses his robust talent to defend the downtrodden and to torment anyone who abuses power. "The pen holds greater might than a sword or a gun," said SARA. "Caricatures and cartoons make a powerful art form often capable of achieving change or even toppling governments."

An award-winning cartoonist and multimedia veteran, SARA has journeyed across much of the planet as a consultant and artist. His work appears in leading newspapers, magazines and online. This satirist who specializes in political, social and human-rights issues won Amnesty International Human Rights Press Awards in 1996, 1997 and 1998.

Although intensely proud of receiving those awards, SARA believes that they have caused him prolonged problems. "Being recognized as a defender of human rights created serious difficulties for me to continue finding media work in Hong Kong after its 1997 handover to Chinese sovereignty," he said. "The media began to self-censor, especially about China and its terrible human-rights record."

'Dirty Business': Monsters or Angels

"Many politicians, especially those in the United States, Sri Lanka and Hong Kong, know me as a controversial political cartoonist," SARA said. "Any kind of politics can turn into a dirty business. If I believe that I should punish certain politicians because they do a bad job, then I can do it with my hands (holding a pen). When doing caricatures, I can exaggerate. I can draw someone as a monster, or I can draw that person as an angel. I do a lot of political cartooning and try to make the world understand exactly what the politicians have been doing.

"Good cartoons can pose a serious threat to the powerful guys who play dirty political games. I am talking not just about in Sri Lanka, but around the whole world.

"Sometimes my cartoons make certain people angry. Then I may receive threats. I used to scratch my head and think, 'Freedom of the press – is it real? Is it there?' "

In Hong Kong, SARA once resigned from a newspaper after its bosses told him to stop drawing **Tung Chee-hwa,** the city's first local leader under Chinese sovereignty, as a "pineapple head". But "that was how I saw him so what else could I do?"

Like a Banana Republic

In Sri Lanka, questions about freedom of the press ring with life-or-death relevance. There, journalists who push too hard for the truth or turn into thorns in the sides of powerful people have a way of encountering "fatal accidents". Stories circulate on the streets about mysterious "white vans" (not ambulances) from which burly, well-paid thugs emerge to threaten, beat or capture those who speak too loudly or critically about authority figures. If a white van cruises into sight, dissidents may disappear, their voices silenced forever.

"Sri Lanka is a beautiful island with scenery that makes it look almost like the ultimate paradise," SARA said. "But certain aspects of it, especially the limitations on media freedom and corruption in high places, make me ashamed even to say that I come from there. It resembles a banana republic. I much prefer to call myself a citizen of the world, a man from the global village who feels sympathy for all people and with the spirit of every place and every ethnicity flowing in my body."

The more that SARA ponders events in Sri Lanka, the

more he wishes that the island nation just to the south of India never had secured its independence from Britain. "Countries that formed a part of the British Commonwealth probably should appreciate their past much more," he said. "In Sri Lanka (called Ceylon until 1972), the British influenced us towards tea, rubber, cricket and greater discipline.

Later "our freedom from British rule (starting in 1948) brought us one disaster after another. The day when we achieved independence from Britain turned out to be the same day that we buried our real freedom. We still can't find it again.

"Some people in Sri Lanka may choose to call me a traitor for speaking out (vocally and artistically)," SARA said. "But I regard myself as a big patriot."

Friends in High Places

In dealing with more liberal-minded public figures in other places, "the people I have criticized later become my friends," SARA said. "For example, **Lord Chris Patten,** the last British governor of Hong Kong, became very friendly with me."

After leaving Hong Kong, Patten accepted a post as the European Commissioner for External Relations from 1999 until 2004. As such, he visited Sri Lanka and encountered SARA again.

"At a press conference in Colombo (the Sri Lankan capital), I asked Patten about the 'one country, two systems' concept by which China rules Hong Kong and whether something similar should apply (for the Sinhalese and Tamil areas) in Sri Lanka," SARA said. "Probably the idea could have saved many thousands of lives.

"Patten said to me, 'Why not? But, of course, it's up to you guys, to the people here in Sri Lanka.'

"On my way out of the building after the press

ANOTHER DAY IN
A BANANA REPUBLIC...
DICTATORS!
BEWARE!
DON'T ABUSE
HUMAN RIGHTS
STOP ABDUCTIONS
NO TO WHITE VANS!
WE FIGHT FOR
FREEDOM OF THE PRESS!
WE FIGHT FOR HUMAN RIGHTS
REALLY?
WE FIGHT FOR ANIMAL RIGHTS

conference, another journalist challenged me," SARA said. "That bugger accused me of 'still polishing the boots of the British'.

"So I told him, 'I don't mind. British leaders always appreciate my work so much more than those in Sri Lanka do.' "

SARA's images have attracted appreciative letters from the offices of prominent people, notably the British monarch **Queen Elizabeth,** former British prime minister **Tony Blair** and past presidents **Bill Clinton** of the U.S. and **Fidel Ramos** of the Philippines.

The Queen received an album of SARA's work, depicting the British royal family, when she visited Sri Lanka in 1981. "Her Majesty is touched by your thought for her and will value the gift," said a thank-you letter to SARA from Buckingham Palace.

"Due to my power of the pen, I also once had the privilege to dine with President Clinton and his family," SARA said. "I am just a guy born in Moratuwa (a suburb of Colombo). I never imagined that I would go quite so far.

"After Clinton was exposed for a (soon well-publicized) sexual affair with **Monica Lewinsky** (a White House intern), I published lots of related cartoons in the *Hong Kong Standard* newspaper," edited by **Mike Lynch**. "When Clinton came to Hong Kong (where SARA then lived), I gave him a book of my cartoons. He really appreciated it."

The Tug of Talent

Constantly, SARA follows the tug of his talent across borders, pursuing his own creative projects or reacting to the demands from employers or clients for his artwork. "Major clients engage me for my caricaturing work," he said.

An impressive career already spanning decades has allowed SARA to spend significant parts of his life in far-flung cities, including Colombo, Rome, Singapore, Bangkok, Hong Kong, Kathmandu, Sydney, Paris, Los Angeles and New York. "I seldom stay in one place for too long because I get assigned by clients in different locations, hiring me as a caricaturist," he said. "Today, I am in Colombo. The next week I may be in Paris and then in Hong Kong. My art has become a very exciting kind of a job that takes me all over the world." Does SARA have a favorite city? "I like Hong Kong the most," he said. "It's an absolutely cosmopolitan place full of people from everywhere in the world. It's fascinating and unique with a hectic pace of life. I never tire of poking fun at its excesses." In Hong Kong, Singapore and elsewhere, SARA has worked not only in the mainstream media, but also as a creative director for advertising companies. When Singapore's *Straits Times* newspaper hired him, its bosses forbid him, as one would expect there, from drawing political cartoons.

Back in 2001, SARA's travels took him to the United States as a consultant to the Freedom Forum, a foundation dedicated to "a free press, free speech and free spirit for all people". When in New York, he visited the Twin Towers of the World Trade Centre just a few weeks before their destruction by terrorists who hijacked airplanes and crashed them into the huge buildings. "I felt a strange, but powerful, premonition that something terrible soon would happen there," he said. "Sometimes I experience such sensations, almost like foreseeing the future." Worried and wary, he never returned to the Twin Towers.

A Crazy Idea For a Better World

Like nearly everyone else, SARA wishes that the world could become happier and entirely peaceful. Unlike most others, he has a strong notion about how to achieve that.

"My crazy idea is that the whole world should consist of just one country with one government and everyone speaking the same language, probably English," he said. "Then people everywhere would face so many fewer problems. They would understand each other more and get along much better."

SARA's "one-country" concept would mean "just one ruler for the whole world. Ideally, it must be someone who loves freedom of the press. Maybe Chris Patten or Bill Clinton, the two politicians I most admire, would be willing to take the job."

Real-Life Angels

For a time, SARA provided the creative force behind a small art gallery deep in the heart of Hong Kong's Central District. His wife **Menaka** worked tirelessly as the gallery's director of operations.

Much of SARA's creative inspiration, whether he depicts certain world leaders as angels or monsters, comes from the presence of "two real angels" active in his life. "My wife, Menaka, and our daughter, **Minka (Su)**, are the most angelic people I ever met," he said. "They always give me enormous encouragement."

Elvis Presley's Example

Decades ago, SARA and Menaka exchanged wedding vows at a chapel in Las Vegas. "We followed the example of singer **Elvis Presley** (1935-77)," SARA said. "I always admired him.

"When I was young, I also wanted to become a professional singer," he added. "For my 16th birthday, my father gave me a guitar."

In those days, SARA endeavoured to look like a future music star. "I grew my hair down to my shoulders and wore

T-shirts that said, 'Make Peace, Not War'," he said.

"Several times I entered Radio Ceylon talent contests," SARA said. (Established in 1923, Radio Ceylon, later renamed as the Sri Lanka Broadcasting Corporation, ranks as Asia's longest-running radio station.)

"Consistently, I reached the talent-contest finals by singing hit songs from Elvis Presley or **Engelbert Humperdinck.** (Born **Arnold George Dorsey** in Madras, India in 1936, the romantic crooner Humperdinck had a long career that peaked in the 1960s and '70s. Among his best songs were "Release Me", "The Last Waltz" and "The Man Without Love".)

"In those days, I admired many famous singers from the West," SARA said. "I loved the Beatles a lot too." His multi-genre list of listening favourites bounces from **Frank Sinatra, Sammy Davis Jr.** and **Louie Armstrong** to **Hank Snow** and even **Roy Rogers** to **Abba** and **Celine Dion.** One of Snow's hit songs, "I've Been Everywhere", makes a good theme-song for SARA's always-on-the-move career.

SARA's early interest in music came from his parents. "My mother and father both were Christian missionaries from Ceylon who lived and worked there," he said. "My father played piano and trumpet, often in a Salvation Army band. He had a talent for music."

On Familiar Turf

Unlike most seasoned expatriates, SARA recently resettled in the nation of his birth. In large part, he wants to celebrate the 2009 end of a three-decade civil war that pitted the Sinhalese majority against Tamil separatists.

At the same time, SARA can participate in his homeland's economic rebirth. Properly applied, his artistic talent has the potential to help push Sri Lanka along the path of advancement and progress.

Much of SARA's best work has appeared in *The Sunday Leader* newspaper, based in Colombo. No other publication has dared to criticize the regime of Sri Lankan president **Mahinda Rajapaksa** quite so openly.

"Our outstanding former editor, **Frederica Jansz,** has been one of the world's most courageous journalists," SARA said. "I proudly have worked with her on the only Sri Lankan newspaper telling the truth to the country's 20 million people."

But any glance at SARA's career history suggests that he may not stay "at home" in Sri Lanka indefinitely. Having indulged in expatriate discoveries and adventures in the past, he almost certainly will hunger for more. "I am sure that I will go elsewhere again," he confirmed.

Terror in Traffic

Possessing tremendous talent as an artist hardly means that SARA shows enormous skill at every task. Despite how deftly he manoeuvres any pen, he also has been described as one of the worst drivers ever to grip a steering wheel anywhere on Planet Expat. "With difficulty, I have started to drive a car in Sri Lanka," he said.

A recent visitor there who for several days rode as a passenger when SARA drove describes the experience as "terrifying". The excitable artist has a habit of bouncing about in the driver's seat. Through the nearest window, he constantly waves a fist at other drivers and pedestrians. Simultaneously, he gestures toward the windshield, converses with his passenger and fiddles with a mobile telephone to call his wife. "He never drives in reverse either," the passenger said. "I doubt if he even knows how to back up."

But SARA retorts that the visitor's account sounds "highly exaggerated". Furthermore, "maybe anyone from around the world who wants a really exciting experience should come for a ride in my car".

Early Inspiration

For as long as SARA can remember, he has loved to sketch or paint. "Even as a tiny tot, I used to walk around the house carrying a pencil or a crayon and drawing anything that caught my attention," he said.

Along with testing his musical mettle, he also toyed with notions of becoming a medical doctor, one with art and music as powerful hobbies. But clearly, his skills as an artist surpassed all others.

"I started my career as a teenager working for a newspaper called the *Weekend Sun*," SARA said. "My ability to do caricatures soon took me in the direction of political cartoons."

Not all of his training came "on the job". He holds diplomas in graphic art and animation, plus a fine-arts degree.

When young, did SARA look up to any professional heroes whose work fanned his creative spark? "I always admired **Jack Davis** from the United States," he said. (Born in 1924, Davis, a 2003 inductee into the Comic Book Hall of Fame, excelled as a cartoonist and illustrator. A founding artist for *MAD* magazine, he also did magazine covers, film posters, record-album art and comic books.)

"As a kid, I used to enjoy looking at the political satire and caricatures by Jack Davis that appeared in *Time* magazine," SARA said. "Unbelievably, in 1999, I met him when he took a seat next to me at a media-industry event in Pennsylvania. Amazingly, a man I had appreciated greatly for such a long time, in whose footsteps I had tried to follow, simply sat down beside me."

Cheap Ticket to Moscow

SARA's political cartoons soon had an impact and commanded attention. In the 1970s, he illustrated a series of political booklets perceived as highly critical of **Sirimavo Bandaranaike,** the long-serving prime minister, then one of the world's few female leaders.

Suddenly, SARA became an expatriate – albeit reluctantly. "Very quickly, I had to go into exile," he said. "The authorities searched for me and threatened to take me into custody. The government forcibly closed down my newspaper."

Capture surely would have led to torture and imprisonment. "If I had stayed in Sri Lanka, I would have faced the same fate as **Aleksandr Solzhenitsyn** (1918-2008) did in the Soviet Union," SARA said. (A famous dissident writer, Solzhenitsyn drew world attention to Soviet human-rights abuses, notably with his most-famous work, *The Gulag Archipelago,* which filled three volumes from 1973-78. Long imprisoned and then exiled, he returned home in 1994 after the Soviet Union had collapsed.)

As for SARA, "then in my early 20s, I never had travelled outside of Sri Lanka before". But he needed to depart quickly.

Ironically, he escaped initially to the Soviet Union, the very place where the national government persecuted Solzhenitsyn. "The first city that I visited was Moscow," SARA said. "I arrived there on Aeroflot. That was the cheapest airline and the cheapest ticket."

Going into exile looked like a daunting prospect (but much less dangerous and potentially painful than staying in Sri Lanka). "With hindsight, my exile turned out to be a blessing in disguise," SARA said. "Everything good that happened to me later resulted from my departure."

Favors a Funworld

One of SARA's long-time ambitions has been to sustain *Funworld*, a satirical magazine "with lots of funny stuff" under his direction that would feature talented artists and writers while taking aim at corrupt political or business heavyweights. Issues of the magazine have appeared sporadically in cities where SARA has lived. He wants to build *Funworld* strong in the style of the U.S.-based *MAD* magazine. (*MAD*, an influential humor periodical founded by editor **Harvey Kurtzman** and publisher **William Gaines** in 1952, achieved a peak circulation of 2.1 million during the 1970s.)

"I want to create the first international magazine, a very humorous and artistic one, to come from Sri Lanka and with a Sri Lankan point of view," SARA said. "That's my vision."

As another important aspect of SARA's power of the pen, he recognizes that laughter makes a potent tonic for nearly all ailments. Unlike most people, he can distribute that precious medicine in massive doses. "We stay in this world for a very short period," he said. "Why should we make ourselves miserable during that valuable time?" He prefers to strive for the opposite effect.

Final Note: Readers keen to see more of SARA's work may visit his Website: www.sarasene.com.

CROWDED CITIES, SMALL SPACES WIDEN HORIZONS

Past Cow-Herder Ian Watt Ponders Big-City Deals

Editor's Note: *As a boy, Ian Watt grappled with Australian farmyard problems, like how to coax a little extra warm, rich milk from each of the mostly Guernsey dairy cows that his family raised. As an adult, he worked hard for decades in his home country. Only after age 50 did he "go expatriate", suddenly facing all of the related challenges and adjustments. Now he tussles with much different dilemmas, like how to coax a little extra viability from business deals in some of Asia's most dynamic cities.*

FAR FROM THE FARM – After growing up on a dairy farm and spending his first half-century in Australia, an abrupt adjustment to the daily activities typical in some of Asia's leading cities at first had **Ian Watt** doing double-takes, blinking in disbelief and shaking his head in amazement.

For Ian, arriving in Asia a decade ago felt almost like starting a new life on a completely different planet. The hundreds of animals that he remembered from back on the family farm suddenly looked tiny in numbers versus the human crowds teeming along on Asian sidewalks.

"Everything was certainly different," Ian said. "I came from living on the east coast of Australia – with nice blue sky, fresh clean air, a small population and lots of space.

"Then I arrived in Hong Kong, which is a vertical city with lots of people. One of the biggest shocks was to see the small apartments where people live, and the high volume of apartments, while trying to grasp the fact that seven million people all live in such a very confined area."

'A Big Eye-Opener'

"The whole situation was a big eye-opener and took some adjustment. I needed a few weeks to settle down (in Asia) and to gain a better understanding of what actually happens in this part of the world".

A company director, 61-year-old Ian has spent the past decade dividing his time mainly among the Philippines, Hong Kong, Shanghai and Macau. He specializes in scrutinizing business-compliance issues.

Ian works closely with his older brother **Paul,** who left Australia and came to Asia almost a quarter-century ago. As Paul pursued diverse business activities, he ultimately needed a fellow director whom he could trust implicitly. So he urged Ian to embrace the expatriate lifestyle too.

"I also had other reasons to leave Australia," Ian said. "At the time, the country's political scene was unfavorable, the economy struggled and unemployment ran high. For me, going to Asia sounded like an ideal chance to clear my head and start afresh. That was my goal.

"My original intention was not to stay away for too long." But as with many expatriates, his early notions of soon returning home to live have lost momentum.

Crowds of Commuters a Little 'Scary'

Hong Kong, although startling for this Australian newcomer, may have been a good place for Ian's early Asian experiences. "In getting around the city, I became impressed by the public-transport system," he said. "I found that everything moved quickly. It amazed me to see how easily that everyone moved from their apartments to their offices and back home again, and how everything ran so smoothly despite such a huge population in a small place.

"The first time when I saw so many people commuting to work during the morning peak hours, they scared me a little. I wondered where they all were going and how so many of them could fit all at once onto the MTR (Mass Transit Railway). It looked so vastly different from anything that I ever had seen in Australia, with its smaller volumes of people, although Sydney, Melbourne and Brisbane can get busy at times. The miraculous part is that Hong Kong's public-transport system always works so extremely well."

Most Amazing, Best Thing

Although Ian stays routinely on the move between cities, his main address is in the Philippines. There, he cherishes the most tangible result of his Asian experiences – a new family. His wife, **Josie,** a Filipina whom he met in Hong Kong, lives in Angeles City, together with their five-year-old daughter, **Angelica,** and four-year-old son, **Jerico.**

"To start a new family, at my age, surprised me, and it certainly would not have happened in Australia," Ian said. "That has been the most amazing and best thing. My new family responsibilities motivate me to live, if possible, all the

"BESSIE, HERE WE ARE IN MACAU. SHOULD WE GAMBLE ON THIS PLACE?
LET'S MILK IT DRY
The Casinos
THE GAMBLERS
WIN! WIN WIN!
LOSE LOSE
CASINO
MILK
MILK
Casino

way to age 100-plus."

As evidence of exactly how international Ian's life has gone, he stresses that everyone in his Asian family was born in a different jurisdiction: Ian in Australia, Josie in the Philippines, Angelica in Hong Kong and Jerico in Macau. That diversity makes Ian "very proud".

After travel-flavored childhoods, Angelica and Jerico probably will pursue international lifestyles too, sending expatriate ways strongly forward into a new generation. "Where my children will end up is anyone's guess," Ian said, "but I believe that they will become globally minded people."

For work or pleasure, Ian also has visited Thailand, Singapore, Malaysia, Britain, South Korea and Guam. All these journeys sprouted from his presence in Asia.

Shanghai: Another World Again

For several years starting in 2003, Ian spent much of his time in Shanghai to focus on food-and-beverage business prospects and procedures there. "Because of the huge opportunities on the Chinese mainland, we wanted to have a big presence there," he said. "The potential in China is enormous. People need to go there, live there and do business there to grasp the enormity of it.

"For me, Shanghai was another world again. It had an enormous 'Wow' factor, so much that it could be almost overpowering with such large numbers of people. Anyone who goes there for the first time, especially from a small town (and compared to Shanghai almost everywhere else resembles a small town), must keep his wits about him."

No wonder that Ian felt impressed. With a population of 23-million-plus, the city of Shanghai has more people (and more skyscrapers) than the entire nation of Australia does.

"I saw enormous growth and rapid development that amazed me," Ian said. "You fly into the Shanghai Pudong

International Airport and then take the Maglev magnetic (levitating) train into town. That train does 430 kilometers per hour, which creates an unbelievable experience. At first, it feels disconcerting to move so fast on land."

When forging business plans in unfamiliar cities and countries, nothing can substitute for taking proper advice from leading local expects. Ian especially appreciated the sage advice that he consistently received from Shanghai accountant **Jason Xu.**

"What made my life easier in Shanghai was that our accounting and legal advisors were particularly helpful," Ian said. "We had the right people behind us to guide us through the complexities so that no doubt ever existed about our ability to get things done.

"You hear incredible stories about deep-rooted corruption in China. But during my time in Shanghai, we never paid a single bribe, nor did the subject even arise."

Increasingly, the world's biggest enterprises go there. "Shanghai welcomes all the international companies," Ian said. "Its leaders have relaxed a lot of policies to make the place more user-friendly."

Indisputably, Shanghai ranks as a leading international city. "Lots of big supermarkets are there," Ian said. "Any food that you buy in New York, London or Sydney, you can get it there too. Any wine is available from all over the world. Everything is there. Shanghai is more affordable and spacious than many leading cities. You have more parks and gardens. It is easy to get around too."

When asked to name his favorite city, Ian immediately replies, "Shanghai", adding "The enormity of the place and how quickly that things happen there almost defy belief. For example, its elevated freeways, railways and buildings – these projects go ahead seven days a week, 24 hours a day, until finished. Of course, China has all of the manpower that it needs, and the labor costs are affordable, so these things can proceed quickly.

"People in Shanghai are very efficient too. They are driven by earning money and notions of moving ahead. The place pulsates with an overwhelming sense of urgency to equal and surpass everywhere else. Even the people on the streets, especially the young people, have that urgency about them. They all work hard wherever they can and learn as much as they can.

"The most exciting part is that anyone who goes there and does business with the right people, those who are moving forward, has a really big chance to become extremely successful."

Although Hong Kong people like to regard their hometown as China's leading city, the folks in Shanghai have no inferiority complex, nor do they fixate on Hong Kong as a significant rival. "Absolutely not," Ian said. "In all my time of doing business there, I never once heard anyone in Shanghai express any desire to go and live in Hong Kong."

Essentially, Shanghai people pay little attention to Hong Kong because they stay much too busy as pace-setters. "They want to be number one," Ian said. "Beijing may be the number-one city politically, but economically, Shanghai easily leads the way."

Gambled and Lost on Macau

After Shanghai, Ian turned his attention to Macau for nearly five years (circa 2004-09). Unlike the positive impressions that he gained in China's largest coastal city, his ambitions for new ventures in Macau, the world's latest gambling capital, turned into a big wager that failed. "It was a huge challenge trying to make progress there," he conceded.

"I went to do some due diligence and to work with lawyers to see how difficult it would be to set up a company and start to conduct business in Macau," Ian said. "We were attracted by the casino-industry expansion with the issuing of more licenses, apart from the two dozen casinos operated by business tycoon **Stanley Ho**."

Immediately, Ian noticed a higher language barrier. "Most people in Macau are Chinese, and they speak Chinese," he said. "They do not know a lot of English. By comparison, many of Hong Kong's Chinese people do understand some English, and so I can communicate. But in Macau, I had much more difficulty.

"Unless I had certain things written down for me in Chinese, like the addresses to show to cab-drivers, it was extremely hard. When hopping into Macau taxis, the easiest thing always was to carry brochures or name-cards for the places where I wanted to go. Otherwise, I soon could need a big drink or several drinks. Still, I tried to overcome the problems in most situations by being very patient and understanding.

"Another big challenge when entering Macau was the large volume of people at the ferry terminals, which often meant waiting in queues for an hour or 90 minutes just to pass through Immigration. That was the norm, and naturally almost everyone tried to rush off the ferries, racing for places near the front of the lines."

Then a fascinating spectacle took shape as huge new casinos and rapid development transformed the Cotai Strip, previously "little more than mud-flats. It was all reclaimed land. Contractors came from all around the world.

"After seeing the first stages of development on the Cotai Strip and then observing its progress, I witnessed the launch of Macau as the world's new gambling capital," Ian said. "The place went from being a sleepy, little backwater to an international city within little more than a year. That was exciting, and I watched as history unfolded in front of me."

In 2006, Galaxy Entertainment's Grand Waldo Hotel

became the first casino to open on the Cotai Strip. A year later, a Las Vegas Sands project, the massive Venetian Macau, followed.

As the gambling industry soared, the needed extra city infrastructure and services lagged. Plans for vastly upgraded bus and taxi services, better ferry terminals, light-rail transport and other improvements fell behind schedule.

Initially, Macau's business and political leaders, together with newly arrived American casino-operators, looked poised to turn Macau, into a supreme international gambling destination. Soon it really did surpass Las Vegas based on total wagering activity.

Even so, Macau's leaders failed dismally in some respects. Actually, the city remains not much of a global attraction. Instead, it lures mainly gamblers from China and from overseas Chinese communities.

"Macau relies heavily on the Chinese mainland people crossing the border from Zhuhai," Ian said. "The original proposal had called for truly international tourists in Macau to be served by a raft of international businesses, but instead the place has become almost a straight-Chinese gambling den. The business people who geared up to cater to more international visitors have suffered serious disappointments and severe setbacks. Most of them stopped doing business and moved away. Many lost a lot of money."

When Ian first arrived, Macau deliberately pursued a policy of welcoming international entrepreneurs and encouraging them to bring key executives or employees from overseas. Ian also liked the fact that most property in Macau then cost only about one-third of that in Hong Kong.

Seeing the emerging business situation as almost ideal, Ian began to work on plans for pubs (Australian, British and German varieties), coffee shops, coffee, wine and jukebox distribution businesses and property deals. As construction workers built the city's huge new gambling halls, "we planned to launch small businesses to complement the casinos", he said.

Abruptly, the Macau government then switched policies to make staying there much more difficult for expatriates. "The government suddenly changed its mind and decided that new businesses could not bring the necessary expatriate employees into Macau," Ian said.

After that, all the jobs had to go to Macau people. "We faced big problems to renew work visas for the expats we had there," Ian said. "The Macau government wanted all local people, not expats, and so it reviewed everyone's position. Our intention had been to employ local people, but we also needed some expats to train the locals in exactly what we did. There were too few skilled locals. Without being able to bring in at least some expats, we could not operate the businesses as we wanted."

Fear, maybe racially motivated, had gripped Macau's 500,000 people and their leaders. "When so many expatriates, including Americans, British and Australians, began to arrive, we were sort of different," Ian said. "Our arrival may have been a little too much for the local people to handle. It badly scared them. They thought that we posed a serious threat, would continue to come in and could take over the place."

How Things (Don't) Work in Macau

Worsening matters, Macau, a former Portuguese colony that became Chinese territory in 1999, has a legal system based on ancient Portuguese laws that, in practice, grind slowly, little faster than glaciers move. For anyone trying to work within those laws, they prove "archaic, difficult and frustrating". Luckily, Ian could rely on valid advice from a prominent local lawyer, **Porfirio Gomez,** and his firm.

"All the legal documents in Macau were in Portuguese

and Chinese, which had to be translated into English too," Ian said. "So forming a company there felt more like forming three companies with a Portuguese version, a Chinese version and an English version, complete with three different company names.

"One day, our lawyers gave us a revealing example of how things work in Macau. The lawyer who handles the firm's court work said, 'We never know if we are winning or not.'

"I said, 'Why is that?'

"She said, 'Consider a simple case in which a driver has crashed into a parked car. The driver should be at fault. As a rule, that would be a very straight-forward situation, but not in Macau.

"After arguments in court, the judge will say, 'Okay, I will hand down my decision later.' Fifteen months later, he finally does.

"The simplest thing takes 15 months for a decision. With anything complex, you could be looking at five to 10 years. It goes like that."

When the 2008 global financial crisis hit, business prospects worsened and new problems loomed. Soon Ian's management board decided to backpedal right out of town. "We decided not to risk putting any more money into Macau," Ian said.

Did Ian like Macau on any level? "I could see some good things there," he said. "We were close to the international airport and to the Chinese mainland, which is never more than about 10 minutes away from anywhere in Macau. Being able to go into Zhuhai in Guangdong Province was very attractive because a lot happens there. Actually, Macau occupies a really good location within easy reach of the Chinese mainland and of Hong Kong. With less than two hours of travel time, I could visit all three jurisdictions."

Except for the language barrier, Ian found nothing

wrong with the day-to-day surroundings and the lifestyle in Macau. "We lived in a nice apartment conveniently close to the shops and banks. Whatever we needed was never more than a few minutes away. The rents and our food all cost much less than in Hong Kong."

Workaholic Ways Never Change

Born in Lismore, New South Wales, Ian had a childhood focused on farm-work. The Watt family, led by **Ted** and **Yvonne,** along with their five children, operated a 600-acre soldier-settler dairy farm (acquired under special arrangements initiated by the government after the Second World War). Along with about 300 dairy cows, and a mix of Hereford beef cattle, the farm raised horses, pigs, chickens, ducks and geese. "It was real pioneering stuff and the norm in those days," Ian said.

Caring for the milking cows and other animals meant rising early each morning to work hard. Some habits learned when young always remain, no matter where a person goes. "The seven-days-a-week, workaholic lifestyle never has changed for me," Ian said.

Once a soldier, Ian reaped good fortune when the Vietnam War, in which Australians fought on the side of the Americans, ended before he could be sent overseas into the fray. Then he settled down to a career in Australia with much of it devoted to sales, marketing and hospitality. In the period prior to leaving for Asia, he managed a motel/apartment building in the Gold Coast.

Along with his brother Paul, Ian has three sisters, **Gail, Linda** and **Cheryl,** the latter three still living in Australia. He also has two adult children, **Katina** and **Timothy,** there from his first marriage to **Deanna,** a nurse.

Proud of all his family members, Ian advises that Katina and Deanna both work for the Australian Red Cross Blood

Bank. Katina hopes to join humanitarian aid work overseas. Her son, **Joseph,** studies lighting, stage and show production, while also visualizing an international career. Timothy, a multi-skilled tradesman and a former child sports star, dreams that his own tiny son, **Laughlan,** eventually may become an international sportsman.

"Deanna provided the main parental support for Katina and Tim during my absence," Ian said. "Of course, everyone must consider that sort of thing when it comes to having two families and going overseas."

Despite Ian's initial disorientation and the moments of wonderment that persisted for longer, he knows that going expatriate has brought him big gains. "Absolutely," he said. "It made me appreciate many things more. As people experience more in the world, they become better off within themselves. Those who just sit in Australia, as many do, and assume that the rest of the world is much like Australia, are quite mistaken.

"Having travelled around and stayed in different places has been almost unbelievable. Having experienced so much makes me better able to appreciate life and being alive. I have learned so many things, all that I never could have done by staying in Australia, that it almost boggles my mind."

Of course, not everything happened easily. "Asia has given me big challenges, and I had to learn on every step of the way," Ian said. "Since the very first day when I stepped down from an airplane in Hong Kong, I always have worn my learning cap. After learning so much -- about different cultures, how things work and what it takes to deal with people – now I probably could cope with moving almost anywhere in the world."

WOOLY ADVENTURES: FROM CARPETS TO COBRAS

Roy Beckwith Follows the Textile Trails

Editor's Note: *A career textile-business executive, Roy Beckwith has worked in a long list of countries. His travels have taken him almost everywhere from Ireland's Atlantic coast to the South China Sea. To say that his experiences have proved interesting puts it mildly.*

WHERE THE TEXTILE ROAD LEADS -- With a little imagination, **Roy Beckwith**'s busy career in the textile business, which routinely carried him across international boundaries, resembles a magic-carpet ride. Along the way, he has learned plenty about carpets – and about clothing too.

"In the past 40 years, I have worked on almost every aspect of the textile pipeline – fibers, yarns, fabrics, knit and woven, dyed and finishing, garments and right through to branding, retail and promotion," Roy said. "I dabbled in them all."

World's Best Carpets Need New Zealand Wool

Questioned about his career, Roy mentions one intriguing detail after another. For example, few people may realize that much of the wool in the most elaborate and expensive hand-knotted carpets sold in Turkey, India and Nepal actually comes from New Zealand. "For the highest-quality such carpets, you can be 90-per-cent sure that they contain New Zealand wool," Roy said. "But otherwise, Nepalese carpets, Indian carpets and Turkish carpets are quite different, each with distinct ethnic designs. My work really has been interesting."

As for a clothing-related oddity, Roy once worked for an enterprise making polyester fiber from corn instead of from oil. "But the fiber melted at 130 degrees Centigrade, meaning that you could not iron it," he said. "Any clothing-iron placed on it went straight through the bloody thing so the plug got pulled (in more ways than one). These days, polyester fiber from corn remains used extensively, but mainly for packaging."

Sixty-eight-year-old Roy still works as a textile consultant. Based first in his native England and then in Hong Kong, he has travelled widely.

"For a long time I worked with the International Wool Secretariat (IWS)," Roy said. "Our objective always was to build the demand for wool. We were financed by the wool boards from Australia, New Zealand and South Africa. Consistently, we bridged the gap between the sheep farmers there and the mills, fabric-makers and brands in each country where we worked."

Roy focused on "developing countries" and often visited India, Nepal, Turkey, Mauritius, North Africa (mainly

Egypt), Israel and elsewhere. "I enjoyed the travelling and different countries," he said. "It was a big challenge, and I really relished it, plus they paid quite well.

"By simply driving from one textile mill to another, I could pass within a stone's throw of the Pyramids near Cairo, or the Blue Mosque in Istanbul or the Golden Temple in Amritsar (India). I also could see vast extremes – from the snow-capped Himalayas in Nepal to the silver beaches, turquoise lagoons and palm trees in Mauritius."

Within the textile industry, Roy has observed remarkable contrasts too. In certain regions, the work transpired as a cottage industry. In Nepal, he often noticed washed wool spread along the roadsides to dry in the sun before being hand-spun into yarn.

"You cannot fail to be impressed by what is virtually an art form, carried out under primitive cottage industry conditions," Roy told a journalist who reported in the June 1992 issue of *WoolReport* magazine. "But the products end up in North America and Germany, which are among the most sophisticated markets in the world."

In Mauritius, Roy once presented a plaque to Floreal, a company there, honouring its achievement in having produced 50 million Woolmark garments. Globe-trotting Roy flew in to mingle at a reception that also celebrated the company's 20th anniversary.

The *Gweilo* Image

People in the emerging economies tended to regard Westerners as business experts. "For everything that we did, there always was lots of interest," Roy said. "We could get the media onside with no problems whatsoever. Journalists would turn up in droves. Everyone loved having a token Westerner there too. Some local people, in India for example, knew so much more about the relevant textile trade than I did, but we went to meetings and all of the questions would come to me.

"This tendency has benefited Western expatriates in nearly every developing country. People from there look up to the fashions, technologies, designs and everything else in the West. They think that having someone there from the influential, high-fashion and high-tech world instantly adds a lot more credibility to what they do."

A Westerners-know-business-best philosophy long prevailed in China too. "To a degree, it still does, but such thinking has diminished," Roy said. "The *'gweilo'* (foreign devils) image lacks the great power that it once had."

Roy pinpoints some familiar economic patterns. For example, Mauritius "has followed the classic developing-country cycle of industry", he said. "It starts with agriculture and food, shifts to textiles and then moves on to the likes of electronics and jewelry. Now the textile mills from there have moved to Madagascar which is much cheaper. People in Mauritius no longer want to have 'dirty' factories. They want nice, clean, computerized electronics ones."

Sometimes Roy's work has placed him in the lead on important issues. For example, he often denounced and opposed child labor. "The IWS is totally opposed to the use of child labor and will take all the measures which are realistically within its power to eliminate this practice," he told a seminar at the All India Carpet Trade Fair in New Delhi in February 1994. His tough remarks appeared in the following month's issue of the *Asian Textile Journal.*

Roy left his base in England not by choice, but when his employer sent him overseas. In 1994, he arrived in Hong Kong. "It was a great promotion to take charge of operations in a much more important region -- China and Southeast Asia," he said.

Later a boardroom battle led to "a new man coming in

FANCY A GAME OF GOLF?
WHAT THE HELL? IS IT A UFO?
MAGIC CARPET

and wanting his own people". Although then made redundant, Roy soon joined another textile enterprise and resettled in Hong Kong.

In 2001, he tinkered with retirement. "Then the people at another company asked me if I wanted to work in Asia for them. Before long, a second company came along and said, 'Roy, how about doing some part-time work with us?' " His consulting days had started.

Straddling Two Continents

Repeatedly, Roy's regional duties have taken him to the Chinese mainland, Taiwan, South Korea, Japan and Thailand. Yet despite such a strong Asian focus, he keeps a steady presence in Europe too. "I spend about 60 per cent of my time in Asia and 40 per cent back in the United Kingdom," he said.

Is it really possible to straddle two continents effectively? "Yes," Roy said. "With conference calls and laptops, I can work away no matter where I am."

Roy talks with a strong regional accent. "Often people ask me exactly what language I speak," he said. "The answer is 'strong Yorkshire with a smattering of English'."

According to Roy, "There are good people everywhere. Those I managed always were great. Perhaps I was lucky, but actually I like to think that I can bring out the best in most people. My management style recognizes that others work with me, not for me. Obviously, each country has its cultural differences. The Muslims in Turkey would break off for prayers. In India, nothing like that happened. But the people that I worked with everywhere I went were outstanding. I can make no distinctions about their approaches to work and what they did."

Meals to Remember

Some of Roy's most memorable adventures have happened in restaurants. "Recently in Japan, I ate raw horse meat for the first time," he said. "The restaurant was chosen by ITC, our agents there, who also invited people from a knit-fabric manufacturer. It was a cross-your-legs-and-sit-on-the-floor place. The menu had a set meal, part of which was *sashimi,* the raw fish, other bits and pieces, and something dark, red and mysterious. It was shredded, as if having gone through a mincer, but in long strings, almost like spaghetti.

"I will eat anything so I tucked into it. The taste was nice and went well with the *sashimi.* Then I asked, 'What exactly is this?'

"The answer came back, 'Oh, that is raw horse. We wanted to wait until you had finished eating it before saying anything.'

"So I polished off mine. As for my American boss sitting beside me, oh, no way, he would not eat it."

Roy then recalls a "puppy-dog incident" from almost 20 years ago. "With the wool people, we had an office in Shanghai," he said. "Once, a group of us from there went out to lunch. We took along two marketing women who had come from Hong Kong, one a British-born Chinese lady and the other a French-Canadian.

"As the restaurant staff served the meal, out came what looked remarkably like a suckling pig, but with a pointy nose and a curly tail. So I knew that it was a puppy dog.

"Well, it had died already. What could I do? So I began to eat, and it tasted nice. But the British-Chinese and the French-Canadian women just freaked. They absolutely freaked.

"On the way out, I picked up a name-card for the restaurant, and the symbol on it showed a puppy dog. Our manager in Shanghai, **John Sheung,** purposely had taken us to a restaurant specializing in puppy dogs to see if he could freak out the *gweilo* director, me, which he did not."

Once in the late 1990s, Roy ate earthworms at a restaurant in Shenzhen, a special economic zone in China's southern Guangdong Province. "I had been at a Chinese factory, and its managers took me out to lunch at a place with lots of livestock outside – ducks, hens and snakes in cages," he said. "I saw a big pile of earthworms there too.

"Then during the meal, one dish had some veggies and white, stringy stuff that looked like noodles, but quite chewy – not noodles at all. The cooks had cleaned out all of the dirt from inside the worms, which then collapsed to look like thick noodles but with a point at each end. I ate those too, but if given a choice, I would not want to have them again. They amounted to pieces of chewy nothing, with no particular taste."

On the Home Front

Roy's wife, **Sandra,** stays at their British home in Topcliffe, a village in North Yorkshire. "All of her friends live near there," Roy said. "Sandra is a nice, unassuming person who enjoys pottering in the garden, cleaning the house and going out with her friends for lunches in the nearby villages. For me, she really has a calming influence. I call her every night (using Skype).

"Sandra enjoys travel too, but just for holidays. She has visited Hong Kong and loves it, but not to live. If she ever came to stay in Hong Kong, I still would travel all week and see her only on weekends. For the rest of the time, she would be stuck in an 800-square-foot flat on a high floor, probably with a lovely view but nothing else."

Both born and raised in Yorkshire, Roy and Sandra recently celebrated their 40th wedding anniversary. Typically, they marked the occasion by long-distance. "I rang her up and said, 'Happy ruby wedding anniversary.'

"She replied, 'What? Is it? Oh!'

"Being the one who remembered the anniversary earned me great brownie points. Ever since I put the date into my computer, it pops up each year to remind me."

In 2006, tragedy struck when Roy and Sandra's only child, **Samantha,** aged 32, died of cystic fibrosis. She had been waiting and hoping for a lung transplant when her time expired.

"The hospital was in Cambridge (England), two hours driving-distance from our home," Roy said. "Samantha held a local record after rushing there 12 times for a possible transplant. Each time, the available lung turned out to have something wrong, to be damaged in some way. The doctors always said, 'No, we cannot do it'. Sadly, she passed away before a 13th chance came."

Despite those dozen setbacks, Roy places no blame on British doctors. "It reflects the nature of the problem," he said. "Some people go for a transplant and get the first organ. Others go two, three or more times. You always receive the call and then start rushing down the motorway. Meanwhile, doctors examine the dead body, check the designated lung and make sure that it functions properly. The recipient will not know until arriving, until the last moment, if the lung is considered suitable. Problems are common. Maybe the organ-donor died in a motorbike crash, but turns out to have a cancer growth that no one knew about. A lung must be in perfect condition for any transplant to go ahead."

Big Fish Almost Terminates the Textiles Man

Roy has had his own life-or-death experience, a positive one, with British medical care. A few years ago when fishing (supposedly a peaceful, relaxing hobby) along a river near home, he hooked an 11.5-pound barbel-fish. "That is a really big fish for the area," he said. "As I went back to my car to get my camera to photograph it, chest pains hit me."

His excitement about the big catch had triggered a heart attack. "A helicopter came for me and created great public interest by landing in a village pub car-park," Roy said. "But apparently I was not stricken quite badly enough to ride in the helicopter, so the medics put me into an ambulance.

"Lying there wearing an oxygen mask, I remembered the fish still caught in a long net submerged near the riverbank. Using a mobile phone, I called a friend, **Geoff Cross,** who lived five miles away and pleaded with him, 'Would you mind going to the river to find the fish, weigh it and take a picture? It is a big fish. Please!'

"My wife, riding in the back of the ambulance with me, scolded, 'Roy, put that oxygen mask back on right now!'

"Luckily, my friend located the fish. He weighed it, took a picture and released it back into the river."

Roy recovered nicely, but if the heart attack had struck moments earlier he might have tumbled into the water, giving the mighty fish all the bragging rights to tell its swimming mates: "Once I caught a man. Oh, he tried to outwit me, but to no avail. He must have weighed about 150 pounds."

As for other hobbies, Roy enjoys photography, golf and beer-drinking. He marvels at "the incredibly high price of beer in Japan".

Cobra on the Course

With mediocre golf-skills, Roy looks unlikely ever to throw much of a fright into any of the all-time great players like **Jack Nicklaus, Arnold Palmer** or **Tiger Woods.** But swinging clubs at a tiny dimpled ball once exposed him to a decidedly unexpected hazard, one never yet seen in the entire 152-year history of the British Open Golf Championship back home.

"I like to hack around, playing golf with my friends," he said. "But one time I played with our company directors, **Geoff Blackburn** and **Tim Eynon,** in India. As usual, I hit my ball deep into the rough. Then I spent a long time in there hunting around and stamping about looking for it. Finally, I spotted the ball and off we went again.

"Suddenly a commotion started behind us. A big king cobra, upright and hissing, had appeared at the edge of the rough. Some caddies chased it off by throwing stones and sticks.

"But I thought, 'Gosh! I just finished stamping around in the grass there.' The next time when my ball went into the rough, it stayed there. I neglected to go in looking for it."

Three Favorite Places

Ultimately, Roy ends up liking places for the people he meets and the friends he makes there. If he could choose anywhere at all to live, his top-three picks would be England, Ireland and Hong Kong. Luckily, he already spends considerable time in all three.

Ireland looms large as Roy's favorite fishing destination and holiday-place. "The Irish people are wonderful, so friendly, welcoming and nice," he said. "You can make friends there so quickly. If a visitor from anywhere at all goes into a bar in Ireland, people instantly will say, 'Tell me now, where are you from? Can I buy you a pint? Tell me about your country.' I also love the fantastic Irish music and how the people play it in bars, maybe when just sitting around a table with a fiddle, a squeeze-box and a banjo."

In contrast, Roy has visited some other places where he has no desire to live. "I never would feel comfortable in Singapore," he said. "That place is too hot, too sweaty and much too clean. To me, it looks plastic, hardly even real."

Elsewhere, "Mauritius is wonderful. But as a laid-back

holiday island, it is not my ideal place."

Nor does he favor Bangladesh. "That must be the worst place I ever went," he said. "A few years ago, I spent a week in Chittagong. The traffic was unbelievably bad. The cars were all scratched and damaged with bumper-bars welded onto them. Craters filled the roads, and a 10-mile drive could take hours."

As for nearby India, "I like it, but would prefer not to live there. I love Indian food. I appreciate India as a place to buckle down and work. From south to north, it has an enormous diversity of scenery, food and people. But what bothers me about it is the massive poverty divide with the abject poor trying to survive in lean-to shelters near the high-rises and the rich guys. There are whole shantytowns, masses of them.

"Much of the time, I travelled out-in-the-sticks there," Roy said. "Industry was spread across the country. Typically, I would reach a hotel, spend a night in Delhi, go to the office and then head up-country to various places."

In the 1980s and early '90s, Roy's German boss, **Helmut Schumacher,** liked to send him on hair-raising journeys. Often that meant flying on Vayudoot, an Indian airline active from 1981 until 1997. "My boss took a great delight in giving me news clippings about Vayudoot," he said. "One that I especially recall told how the airline had grounded half of its planes to cannibalize them for parts to keep the other half flying.

"After one of my first trips, Helmut made a point to ask me, 'How did you like it, Roy?'

"I told him, 'Fine, but I really dislike that Vayudoot flight up to Ludhiana.'

"Then in his broad German accent, Helmut said: 'Well, Roy, there are three choices to go from Delhi to Ludhiana. You can take the train, but I must tell you that the trains frequently get stopped and attacked by bandits. You can go by road, but I must tell you that a recent survey has shown that most of the vehicles on the highway are trucks and that half of the drivers are drunk or on drugs. Or you can go by Vayudoot."

Pilot: 'We Have a Technical Problem'

One Vayudoot flight to Goa, when Roy travelled with the IWS English design consultant, **Geraldine Clarke**, seared itself deeply into their memories. "After the plane approached Goa, with no word of an explanation from anyone, it flew figure-eight patterns above the airport for 30 minutes," Roy said.

"Then the captain came out of the cockpit. Together, he and the cabin crew pulled up a carpet in the middle of the plane where they had a spy-hole window to look out, down at the undercarriage. The only words that the captain said to the passengers were: 'We have a technical problem. Please read the safety leaflets in the seat-pockets in front of you.'

"Next the cabin crew came around putting all bags off the floor into the overhead bins. A man behind me refused to relinquish his bag, and they argued like mad. The cabin crew loudly asked the guy: 'Sir, what is more important? Your briefcase or your life?'

"As the flight descended, the passengers decided that we should put our heads between our knees and brace ourselves. Twice, the plane came in at low levels but rose again. The third time it actually landed.

"Then the cabin crew calmly said, 'Welcome to Goa. For those of you travelling on to Kochi, please remain on board.' Amazingly, about half of the passengers stayed right there on that plane.

"The next day, I flew back and happened to see the same crew members in the departure lounge. When asked about the day before, they said that a light to indicate that the plane's undercarriage had locked properly into place did not come on and so the pilot had feared that the undercarriage might collapse on landing. Therefore, he had used up extra fuel in the air and then made some low-level fly-bys to allow people on the ground to see how it looked from below."

Tragedy on a Road to the Taj Mahal

A serious accident marred Roy's one and only visit to the Taj Mahal in Agra, India. Centuries ago, **Emperor Shah Jahan** ordered the building of this famous, white-marble mausoleum in memory of his wife, **Mumtaz Mahal.** She had died during childbirth in 1631. Roy's misadventure also involved a child.

"We rarely had any time off, but one Sunday, I told an Indian friend, **Peter Mukerjee,** that I never had seen the Taj Mahal," Roy said. "So he hired a driver and a car to take us there, a journey of several hours. On the way, a little boy, maybe 10 years old, ran onto the road and our car hit him.

"The driver tried to speed off immediately, but we yelled at him, 'Stop, stop.' Very quickly, people from nearby then surrounded us, beating furiously on the car. Unable to move, we had no choice but to stop."

Next the police arrived. "One policeman with a rifle got into the back of the car with me. Another rode in the front, and they accompanied us to a police station two miles off the main highway.

"We stayed there for hours, waiting in a tiny courtyard, while the police talked to our driver who also spent much of the time ringing up his boss to ask for money so that he could get the car back. He also needed to negotiate with the boy's parents about how much money they wanted so as not to press charges for their child being run over."

Roy never learned the extent of the boy's injuries. "For

a while, he just lay on the road unconscious. We kept asking the police about how he was, but got no reply. It was awful.

"Then the police released my friend and me, but still held the driver. There we were – about halfway between Delhi and Agra and two miles off the main highway. So we wandered the streets, found someone with a car and pooled our money to convince that person to help us.

"After having departed at 7 a.m., we eventually reached the Taj Mahal at 5 p.m. It closed at 5:30. So we had a half-hour to dash around the Taj Mahal and take some photos.

"Finally, we rode a train back to Delhi, returning dirty and sweaty to our hotel. After such a day, we badly needed some cold beer and went straight into the hotel bar. To our dismay, the staff told us, 'Very sorry. Today is the first Sunday of the month -- a dry day.' "

At times, Roy and his business colleagues experienced much worse, even "horrific", train trips in India. "The worst part could be trying to board the trains," he said. "People slept almost everywhere, using the train platforms as rain shelters. Passengers always needed to step over them. There would be lots of pushing and shoving. On the overnight trains, each passenger received a filthy blanket. It was as crowded as hell. The train toilets had a terrible smell. It all made for nasty, really uncomfortable journeys. Often the only comfort came from a six-pack of beer that we took along with us each time!"

Twin Pubs in Roy's Life

Roy's long-term plans call for returning full-time to Topcliffe. "I look forward to that," he said. "The village there has two pubs, a post-office and a church. I never go to the church or to the post-office, but I know the pub guys really well."

Thanks to Roy, his favorite taverns in England and in

Hong Kong have forged a "twin-pub" relationship. If regular customers from The Swan Inn, managed by **John Heidstrom** and **Carrie Ann Roberts,** in Topcliffe, ever visit The Junk Pub on Hong Kong Island's Jaffe Road, or vice-versa, they will receive a warm and rousing welcome.

"Two guys from my pub in England did pass through Hong Kong," Roy said. "Later they returned home talking in glowing terms about how great The Junk Pub is and how welcome they felt. In the perhaps-unlikely event that people from The Junk Pub happen to pass through Topcliffe, they can get a similar welcome."

Roy favors The Swan Inn "because it is a really nice country pub just 50 yards from my house," he said. "It has great local people and always organizes charity events, like a recent weight-loss challenge. Three guys, including the pub landlord, got weighed and the one losing the least weight had to have his body waxed and then run around the village while wearing a pink mankini (male bikini). There were no winners, just a loser."

Although The Junk Pub, in Hong Kong's Wanchai District, has vastly different surroundings, Roy senses "the same atmosphere. Something always is going off, I know everybody and the bar staff is great. It creates a nice feeling when you walk in and everyone greets you. Actually, the clienteles at the two pubs come from totally different backgrounds. Most of the regulars in Topcliffe grew up in the area and work on farms, at supermarkets, in other businesses or at schools. Those at The Junk are multinational and have much more diverse occupations. Yet the characters of the people in the two places, and the great fun that they have together, are just the same."

If Roy had worked only in England, he would have functioned within a much narrower scope, or none. "I probably would have become jobless long ago," he said. "In most of Europe and in the United States, the textile trade has tanked. Except for Italy and Spain, which still have decent textile industries, all the rest has moved to Asia."

Although Roy enjoys staying on the move, he hesitates to suggest that everyone else should do the same. "If that lifestyle suits someone, then sure," he said. "But it all depends on each person and on personal circumstances."

Expecting a 'Dig in the Ribs'

Roy's travels give him countless stories to share with his buddies, like the other beer-drinkers at The Swan Inn. "Maybe so," he conceded, "but I do need to be careful. In small communities like Topcliffe, you can be called a showoff for always telling personal stories. So I never volunteer my travel tales to anyone.

"Actually, my wife keeps me out of trouble in that way. If she hears me start to talk too much, she gives me a serious dig-in-the-ribs. That training teaches me not to tell too many stories wherever in the world I am – unless, of course, someone happens to ask me."

BEWARE OF GHOSTS, CORRUPTION AND TIGHT SQUEEZES

Peter Coombes Embraces the Business Challenges

Editor's Note: *Turbulence hits, problems arise and big adjustments become necessary when a business person turns into an expatriate who then needs the contacts and know-how to prosper in a new place. Peter Coombes, an Australian who successfully moved to the Philippines, considers the issues.*

THE PHILIPPINES – After settling down in a new country, Australian businessman **Peter Coombes** soon felt at ease enough to start an important task -- helping to spur the local economy. Having endured hazards and constraints since then, even once squeezing out of an unforgettable tight situation, he stands at the brink of his most important and lasting contribution so far.

In a joint venture with an influential partner, **Noel "Toti" Carino,** 60-year-old Peter has developed plans for the biggest hotel yet in Angeles City, his adopted hometown in the Philippines. Their 160-room facility, the Best Western Ritz, will become the city's "first branded hotel".

"It always is important to work with the right people," Peter said. "Toti Carino is one of the biggest property developers in the Philippines. He owns a lot of real estate in a lot of places and is very well respected.

"Of course, Filipinos always feel wary of foreigners at first. They screen you pretty well before even letting you through their doors. You need to prove yourself to them too, but once you are onside with them, then it becomes possible to do business. I happened to have the good fortune to meet Toti Carino, thanks to my good friend **Steve Polastri.** Even while doing this first joint venture together, we also discuss other business possibilities."

Originally from Queensland, Peter specializes in the financial details surrounding real-estate projects. He first visited the Philippines in 2000 and moved there in 2005. Earlier, he worked on property projects in Australia, where he last lived in Caboolture, just north of Brisbane.

'People Get Devoured Here'

Peter's international move temporarily confused him. "Business here in the Philippines gets done in different ways," he said. "Making the adjustments can be terrible, a treacherous thing. With so many pitfalls, definitely you make mistakes. Then if you survive, it becomes a matter of getting beyond all of the miscues.

"A lot of people get devoured here. They go into business and lose their money. When people arrive in the Philippines with a little money and want to place it somewhere to earn more, someone always stands ready to take it off them."

After wading through the problems and past obstacles, "there are opportunities to be found and profits to be made, but investors must be cautious and, most importantly, they need good local advisors, especially accountants and lawyers. Fortunately, I have found both. You must have the right advice and be in with the right people. When I first arrived, I had no one to advise me. As a result, I learned some hard lessons."

'White Ladies' on a Dark Night

An extra startling hazard afflicted one of Peter's earlier property developments after Pinoy workers had drilled foundation holes for a multi-floor building. "We employed guards on the construction site every night, which is normal," he said. "Otherwise people may get in and swipe the reinforced steel and whatever else they can find there.

"One night a guard contacted us (the developers) to say that he had observed 'white ladies', meaning ghosts, coming out of the holes, walking around and then descending into other holes. The guard also called his supervisor, a Filipino guy I know personally, who then went to the scene and watched the same thing. They both observed these 'white ladies' moving on the site and vehemently confirmed the sightings.

"After hearing about what had happened, our workers adamantly refused to continue on the site until we somehow resolved matters. So we invited priests from the Catholic Church to come and deal with the situation. They brought some chickens, cut the birds' throats and sprinkled the blood around, which seemed to work. No more ghosts appeared, and our work resumed.

"We later learned that one of the buildings knocked down to make way for our project had been a notorious abortion clinic. The laborers felt sure that the ghosts were restless spirits resulting from what had happened there."

Asked if he believes in ghosts, Peter sidesteps the question: "A lot of supernatural sightings happen around here. For some reason, Filipinos usually are the ones tuned into the phenomena. Other people rarely see the ghosts."

Peter makes similar observations about Filipino faith-healers, who allegedly can cure illnesses with their bare hands, draw blood and remove dangerous tissues without making incisions or leaving scars. Their magic appears to work mostly for Pinoys, he said.

Living With Corruption

Always, the biggest business hurdle comes from rampant corruption. "You have to live with corruption," Peter said. "That remains my constant number-one concern. On any worldwide corruption list, the Philippines ranks right up there among the worst places.

"Enough money can sort out almost anything here. If you run over a person on the roads, or do something else terribly wrong, then probably you can buy your way out of it."

Annoyingly, the locals assume that outsiders, especially white-skinned ones, command plenty of wealth. "If you are a white person, then for whatever you do, higher rates apply. Even when something is offered for sale at the side of a street, the price goes up the moment when you walk over to take a look. Often you must pay almost double what a Filipino person would. You get used to it."

Stuck in a Trike, Like a Cow in a Bog

In business dealings and beyond, Peter has gotten into a few tight fixes. One amusing example involves trikes, a normally reliable Pinoy transport mode ideal for quick scoots. Essentially a motorbike with a passenger seat attached, each such vehicle has a roof to protect the driver and passenger(s) from sun and rain. Any trike sometimes carries three Pinoys. Typically, two locals can fit into the passenger compartment and another may hop onto the bike behind the driver.

A bulky guy, Peter dwarfs most Pinoys. "My weight

is substantial," he said. "Some of those trikes are bigger than others, and I always tried to look for one the right size. What happened to me one time definitely was the trike's fault!

"In what turned into a really tricky situation, I got into the trike alright, but at the end of the journey had difficulty to get out of it again. Unfortunately, the trike had parked right outside of a cafe with large tinted windows. People outside could not see in, but everyone in the cafe could look outside."

There Peter sat, squirming, trapped -- stuck in the trike. "The trike-driver got off his bike, came around and tried to pull me out, like I was a cow caught in a bog." Even that failed.

Finally, "I had to put my legs out and gradually slide out horizontally on my back, almost like a contortionist, landing flat on the ground. As I got to my feet, I realized, 'This is embarrassing.'

"Hastily, I looked around and thought, 'Well, at least not too many people were here to see what just happened.' In fact, everyone in the cafe had watched. When I went inside, they all loudly applauded me."

Peter reacted to that confining experience by hiring **Nilo Globio**, a "good and reliable" full-time driver to guide him through the streets, typically to and from business meetings, in a red Honda C-RV (compact recreational vehicle). The C-RV has ample space.

Australian Barbecues Cook Up Consequences

Eleven years ago, Peter married **Bernadette,** a Filipina. They met in the Philippines, married there and initially lived together in Australia, where they had two sons, **Cameron** and **Clayton.**

"Earlier I used to hang around with a few guys who had Filipina wives," Peter recalled. "They invited me to barbecues. I always felt impressed by their relationships, how the wives were and how they cared for the guys. Honestly, I was not

ANOTHER TIGHT SQUEEZE IN THE PHILIPPINES!
Fields Ave
ANGELES CITY
ALL ROADS LEAD TO SAN MIGUEL

much good with the ladies. But when you meet Filipinos, they always have a cousin or someone in mind for you to correspond with – they try to hook you up so that maybe the other person can leave the Philippines. Through that process, I met my wife. We had a lot in common and started to correspond. I went to the Philippines a few times, that was it, and we got married."

The family's ultimate move to the Philippines began with Peter going to meet a potential business partner. "I had reached a stage in my career at which I could take some time off," Peter said. "Meanwhile, I thought that it would be good for my sons to spend some time in the Philippines.

"So I arrived to meet with **Larry Snider,** a retired builder from the United States. We decided to build houses together, and I did buy an apartment complex from Larry and stayed there for several years, during which time we further developed the property and named it the 'Bushman's Retreat'. Soon it became almost fully occupied by Australians."

Early in Peter's career, he had worked at an Australian bank before switching to loan-development companies. In 1974, he became a licensed real-estate agent. After several small ventures, he succeeded with a property project "right at the heart of Brisbane". Then for more than a decade, he operated from an office on Cavill Avenue, the main street in Surfers Paradise, Gold Coast. Overall, Peter now prefers the Philippines for business. "Selling things is harder in Australia. It costs more to do business. A lot of red tape and different approvals apply too. I found no corruption there, but other problems definitely persist."

Save a Child, Pay 'Compensation'

Constant exposure to poverty in the Philippines reminds Peter of the need for viable business projects to spur employment and build prosperity. Sadly, chronic poverty creates a distressing kind of desperation and greed. Peter tells of a heart-wrenching example. He knows a long-childless couple who heard about a tiny Filipino boy living near them who teetered near death. Worried and keen to help, they went to the boy's home and saw the child, gaunt and starving, placed prone beside a deep hole that his family had dug.

"The boy resembled a fish out of water, his mouth constantly moving in a struggle to breathe," Peter said. "His relatives planned to wait just until he died before tipping his body into the hole. They said that they had stopped giving him water so the end would come soon."

With consent from the fading boy's parents, the childless couple took him away, fed him, arranged for medical attention and nursed him back to health. Then they launched procedures to adopt the youngster.

The boy's biological parents and other kinfolks never once expressed thanks for saving the child's life, nor did they care to reclaim him into their own family. Instead, "recalling how much they had loved that boy", they constantly demand financial assistance, even "compensation", from the rescuers.

The Spirit of Robin Hood

Peter often receives invitations to join the Rotary Club, the Lions Club and other groups. Usually he declines for lack of the necessary time. But he does participate as a non-veteran member in Angeles City's sub-branch of the Returned and Services League of Australia and as a committee member for a local rugby club where his sons enjoy playing.

"The RSL does medical missions and lots of good things," he said. "Its members may be old fogies, but they go out and trek through the jungle to reach little towns to deliver cough syrups, vitamins and other important items."

In another charity effort, Peter and Bernadette have teamed with Manila-based husband-and-wife lawyers **Zeus** and **Lorelie Librojo** to create the "Kawayan Foundation" (the Bamboo Foundation), which helps to pay the education expenses for promising young people from poor families. "We seek funds from different sources," Peter said. "Then we make sure that the students involved really do stay in school. We cultivate contacts at the schools and receive school reports."

Successful business people can gain intense satisfactions by assisting charities. Allocating money from the rich to help the poor creates the best feelings imaginable, Peter said. It awakens a sense of almost resembling **Robin Hood,** the legendary medieval bandit who led a "band of merry men" lurking in England's Sherwood Forest to rob from the rich and give to the poor.

Peter's experiences as an expatriate add up to a "positive" total. "The Philippines has been a good home for me," he said. "For anyone who can sort out a cash flow, it becomes quite a livable place with the right kind of economics. You can buy all of your vegetables, fresh fruits and other food in the markets, all much cheaper than in Australia. The schools are good too. Overall, it makes a favourable family environment."

Any prospect that Peter will return to live in Australia appears to diminish daily. "The longer that I stay here in the Philippines, the less that I think about going home to Australia," he said.

STANDING IN FRONT: CLASSROOMS OF MANY NATIONS

Darren Turnbull Takes Teaching on the Road

Editor's Note: *Darren Turnbull, a technical training expert based in Doha, Qatar, left his native Australia in 1985 when he grew disillusioned with life there halfway through a mechanical engineering degree. Since then, he also has studied or worked in France, China, Papua New Guinea, the United Arab Emirates and Canada. He describes himself as constantly "seeking the expat lifestyle".*

QATAR – Not all classrooms around the world look exactly the same. In fact, they vary much more due to the students than to the teaching equipment, seats or wall colors.

Diversity governs more than two decades of teaching experiences for 48-year-old **Darren Turnbull,** an Australian-born educator who has taught in five countries after studying in two. On the latest job, he serves as an information-technology instructor at the College of the North Atlantic in Doha, Qatar. "I teach information technology (IT) because that is in strong demand," he said.

Darren has crisscrossed oceans and continents, always finding his way into classrooms. Since his own student days in Australia and France, he has taught in China, Papua New Guinea (PNG), the United Arab Emirates (UAE), Canada and Qatar.

'Australia Bored Me'

Despite Australia's well-deserved reputation for sun-drenched, pleasant lifestyles, Darren felt unhappy there. "Australia bored me," he said. "It has a backwards suburban culture that makes it insufferable to me. I could not stand it anymore so I left."

A chance to study in Lyon, France, as an exchange-student triggered his departure. Off he went, beginning an international odyssey.

After returning, Darren soon decided to join an American Field Services (AFS) six-week cultural exchange program in China. "So I went there. Then someone said, 'Why not stay here and work?' "

Darren's globe-hopping habits have given him an international family. His wife, **Shu Ping**, hails from Guangzhou, southern China's largest city. "Once you marry someone from a different culture, then the way that you think about the world changes forever," he said. "Your horizons widen. The most interesting people that I have met are those who have married outside of their own cultures."

The Turnbulls have a 13-year-old son, **Tarique,** born in the UAE, who attends the Canadian School of Qatar. "My son thinks of himself as a Canadian," Darren said.

Common Sense, Broken Bottles

When in China, Darren taught at the Changsha Railway Institute in Hunan Province and then at the Guangdong Institute of Technology in Guangzhou. "The best thing was that the students were very studious," he said. "The worst thing was that they often lacked common sense. In most places, people will use common sense to try solving their problems. In China, people instead tend to believe that there should be a certain method to do things and that no other way exists. I cannot blame them. The problem comes from institutionalized thinking."

In Guangzhou, Darren taught during a 1989 political "awakening" as nation-wide student protests erupted. Tens of thousands of young people soon occupied Beijing's Tiananmen Square.

"My students would place bottles with pictures of Chinese leader **Deng Xiaoping** (1904-97) on the classroom tables and then protest by throwing rocks and smashing the bottles," Darren said. "They acted en masse, believing that this was something they should do. They felt a duty to stand up and to oppose their government."

Darren, then aged 25, younger than some of the students, watched in fascination. "At first, I understood almost nothing," he said. "We lacked today's technology. There was no Internet. It was a closed situation. For a long time, I reflected on the events. Not until years later did I better understand exactly what had happened."

When China's military, the ironically named People's Liberation Army (PLA), cracked down hard using brutal and deadly force, Darren's students reacted in different ways. "Those from Guangzhou and elsewhere in southern China mostly just returned to their lives as usual," he said. "There the normal mindset calls for disregarding the government to focus instead on earning money.

"Many of the most anti-government students came from elsewhere. The northern Chinese felt more concerned about their rights. They certainly were angry, but the reasons why the protests began still puzzle me. Were the students angry because they believed that they were supposed to feel that way or because they really disliked the government?" Maybe both reasons held true.

'The Maddest Place on the Entire Bloody Planet'

Seeking new challenges, Darren and Shu Ping relocated to PNG. "A job came up there," Darren said. "I told my wife, 'Well, that must be almost the same as in Australia.' (PNG, not New Zealand or Indonesia, is Australia's nearest neighbor.) I never had been to PNG before.

"Oh, boy! Was I wrong? I remember when we first arrived in Port Moresby, the capital city. People there chew betel nut and spit out much of the juice. We walked out of the airport and saw red betel-juice stains everywhere. To us, they looked exactly like blood stains.

"A guy came to the airport to pick us up with a pickup truck and told us to ride in the back. So there I sat in the back of a pickup truck, having just arrived with my wife, who was asking, 'What? What? What's this? You took me here, and this is what PNG turns out to be like?' So I tried to reassure her: 'This is not like Australia after all, darling. This is PNG, an entirely different country.'

"Then I arrived at a place in Port Moresby to sign a work contract. As I stepped into an elevator, I saw a guy from a distant village sitting there in a corner on the elevator floor. He gave me a big smile. Later when I left, he still sat there, smiling while riding up and down. There are not many elevators in PNG. He was trying to get all of the possible experiences with the elevator so that he could return to his village and explain as best he could to everyone there

TODAY'S LESSON...
GIVE ME WINE, NOT A CAMEL ANY TIME.
DOHA DUNES
I CAN TEACH YOU A THING OR TWO ABOUT HOW TO HANDLE THIRST

exactly how it worked. He sat there for a few weeks – not full time, but coming daily to experience the elevator."

Quickly Darren reached a startling conclusion: "PNG probably stands alone as the maddest place on the entire bloody planet. You have tribal cultures, people who live in cities and those who actually conduct business, all of them totally different subcultures. It creates a completely bizarre place."

Penis Gourds Worn Proudly

To outsiders, nothing looks more unusual than PNG tribal men, mainly from the highlands, wearing only penis gourds. Each of these sheaths, typically made from dried-out gourd, fits over the wearer's penis, held in place by attached loops, one circling his scrotum and the other his abdomen. Men in the same cultural groups wear similar penis gourds.

Making penis gourds, like wearing them, takes certain flair. Designated gourds have weights tied to their bottoms to stretch them during growth. The curves come from strings that restrict and point the growth in certain directions. Once the gourds have been harvested, emptied and dried, the resulting sheaths get treated with beeswax or resins and perhaps decorated using paint, shells and feathers.

"Penis gourds remain prevalent in Iryan Jaya and remote parts of PNG," Darren said. "I never did see any in my classrooms though."

Then he confesses: "I tried wearing a penis gourd once, but my wife freaked out. She thought that it was meant to be some kind of strange sexual aid."

Darren worked for the PNG Education Department, teaching high-school physics, first in Aiyura in Eastern Highlands Province and then at Keravat in East New Britain. "There were four national high schools, quite an elite system. The idea was to bring together students from all of the tribal groups so that everyone could understand that other people were much different from themselves. PNG has hundreds of groups and hundreds of distinctly different languages, but everyone needs to get along. So the government always wants to convince the students that PNG consists of much more than just tribes – that it really constitutes a proper country. That may sound like a peculiar need, but the place only obtained independence (from Australia) in 1975."

Youngsters from the tribal villages faced major upheavals to move to the cities and study there. "They had lots of trouble," Darren said. "On the level of one person to another, most of the students resembled aliens to each other. They viewed one another as highlanders, as people from the coast or as those from a different province. With such different attitudes, they did not get along well with each other at all. Fights and problems erupted constantly.

"Then 'the white guy' (like teacher Darren) must attempt to sort everything out. Papua New Guineans tend to regard white-skinned people as being just another tribe. We are the white tribe with the regular task to sort out problems for the other tribes because we are neutral and outside of the disputes. Being from a different tribe, we are considered as good choices to arbitrate."

'My Most Remarkable Teaching Experience'

Successfully teaching physics in PNG presented some special challenges. "Culturally, certain icons that we use routinely to represent various concepts mean the opposite there," Darren said. "Then the more you try to explain things, the less that it works."

For example, when explaining about magnetism, Darren indicated the directions of magnetic forces by drawing arrows with distinct tails. "In the exam, my students answered almost 100-per-cent wrong," he said. "What had happened? Well, in PNG, most arrow-heads have feathers attached, making them resemble the tails that I drew."

Otherwise, the students performed surprisingly well. "I liked them," Darren said. "They recognized the important chance for an education and to advance their lives. They held a solid respect for their teachers and gave me my most remarkable teaching experience.

"In terms of physical wealth and goods, those people had nearly nothing. They were very humble, but with a big thirst for knowledge. For a teacher, the most satisfying thing imaginable is to find the classrooms full of students who really want to know exactly how the world works.

"Imagine being raised in a PNG tribe. You would receive very little formal education. Yet the students tried so hard and put their whole hearts into learning."

No Longer Recite, Recite, Recite

After the Turnbulls moved to the UAE, Darren taught IT at the Higher Colleges of Technology in Al Ain, a city of 370,000 people near the Omani border. "The educational medium was in English, but the students were Arab," Darren said. "I wonder if it makes much sense for a country to educate its people using a foreign language, but that is what happens.

"Certainly, the students were good people. They tried hard, but had slightly unhelpful backgrounds. People in the UAE have been limited by an Egyptian-based education system, similar to what all of the Gulf countries have. The students can achieve only so much in a college environment. They want to succeed, but their early education revolves around needing to recite, recite and recite. Then they get thrust into an English-language, Western-style system not about reciting, but about starting to think.

"Another big problem arises from the fact that most

governments in the Middle East dislike any possibility that the people may think for themselves or even question the status quo. That creates a huge dilemma that becomes difficult to manage. An instructor who happens to say anything 'wrong' in a classroom will be kicked out of the country. Usually, the instructors just sort of swerve around many sensitive topics, but this all poses a real challenge. You always want to do right for the students, and the right thing for them would be to question their bloody governments, like so much of the world does."

An Immigrant's Life 'Damn Tough'

Eventually, Darren applied to immigrate to Canada. "Having already been an expatriate, then I wanted to see what it would be like to live as an immigrant, and, believe me, it turned out to be damn tough!"

The family moved to Vancouver. "For months, potential employers told me, 'You have no Vancouver job experience,' or else 'You have no Canadian job experience.' A person can immigrate to a new country, but it may not matter much what his or her passport then says. Whenever I tried to describe myself as being from Vancouver, people would say, 'No! That cannot be true. Your accent sounds nothing like any Canadian one.' Other Canadians refused to regard me as being a Canadian. The issue relates not just to my documents, but also to attitude, lifestyle and all the rest of it."

At certain carefree moments, Darren liked Vancouver. "It can be a 'cool' city," he said. "Almost everyone comes from somewhere else. Lots of Chinese people live there."

On a one-time-only visit to Ottawa, Darren even learned a stern lesson, the details of which he never will forget, about the clout of fierce Canadian winters that rage beyond the mild Pacific coast. "In Vancouver, the temperature at the time stood at minus-two degrees," he said. "When I arrived in Ottawa, it was bloody minus-30. I saw icicles hanging off the buildings. My face turned red and numb from the cold. People had to shovel snow. What an unbelievable shock! The coldness! The freezing skin! Honestly, it was not a pleasant situation at all."

Canada, Australia Strangely Similar

Often Darren resented Canada for its similarities to Australia, albeit with much harsher weather. "Those two countries are so similar that it strikes me as really peculiar," he said. "In both places, everyone instantly needs a driver's licence, and the people really like to barbecue. Canada also can be boring with too much of a suburban lifestyle. People live on their little streets and focus on the future, thinking that when they retire, then they will take a big holiday and go around the world. But I already have travelled. I travel all the time. Why would people want to be forced to wait until age 65 to start enjoying themselves?

"Another problem, again like Australia, arises from Canada's high rates of taxation. You simply cannot get ahead in life.

"Plus any good house in Vancouver seems to cost at least Cdn $1 million. Sure, if you go far enough away, to another community entirely, you probably can afford to buy property there, but most of those places have too few jobs. In such huge countries like Canada and Australia, why must so many of the people always squash up together, being forced to live in Toronto, Vancouver, Sydney or Melbourne? So much more space could be available."

'Constant Marijuana Smell' Covers a College

Eventually, Darren taught at the British Columbia Institute of Technology. "That is a very good school, but the work was challenging because I never had taught in a Western country before," he said. "The students all knew everything about their rights and always wanted to argue with me to demand higher grades. They were like expert lawyers. If they actually had spent more of their time studying, and less time arguing, they might been more successful.

"Another thing that they consistently did was smoke marijuana. A constant marijuana smell hung all around the college. You could get off buses and immediately see people smoking. In my classes, I noticed so many guys sitting there, completely stoned, with really red eyes."

Ice-Hockey Fans Skate Deep into the Middle East

Before long, Darren was recruited when a Canadian college expanded from a small province all the way across the Atlantic Ocean to Qatar. As always, he welcomed a new adventure.

In Qatar, the college has 600 employees, all of them Canadians (a requirement to work there). These people and their families form a big ice-hockey-loving, Maple-Leaf-flag-waving cluster deep in the Middle East. Unlike Qataris, they easily can recite the names of history's best-ever ice-hockey players, the likes of **Wayne Gretzky, Gordie Howe, Ken Dryden, Phil Esposito** and **Jean Beliveau.**

Often Darren regards some of his colleagues' behavior as being silly. "How ridiculous!" he said. "People there try to recreate the conditions of 1950s and '60s suburban Canada in Qatar. They get transplanted from Canada and then hardly even need to think about being in a different country. Canada is a multicultural country, yet the college staff-list fails to reflect that pluralism."

So Much Arrogance

Darren's students hail from across the Middle East. Qatari nationals account for 25-30 per cent with the rest being expatriate Arabs from Jordan, Syria or elsewhere.

"Many students in Qatar show a tendency towards arrogance, unlike those I taught in the UAE previously," Darren said. "In the UAE, the young people whom I met felt proud of their culture and liked to organize weekend trips. Off we would go into the desert for a party, one without alcohol obviously, but with a nice picnic after we rode in four-wheel-drive vehicles across the sand dunes. But in Qatar, just once in more than six years did a student ever take me to meet his family.

"Then when I failed several students, they arrogantly told me that I might be deported because they have family connections to immigration officials. That has become the students' trick – to use family *'wasta'* (the equivalent of *guanxi* in Chinese) to get their own ways. Recently, the situation has improved with instructors reacting to such efforts with "no-nonsense" attitudes.

"There is so much arrogance. How bad does it get? Once when my Chinese wife and I visited a hospital in Doha, an Arab man came up, pointed at my wife and demanded, 'What this?'

" 'Excuse me,' I said.

" 'What this?' he repeated with disgust on his face.

"He meant, 'What could you possibly be doing with this Chinese person?' I get pissed off about such things, but my wife hardly cares. She handles those situations with so much finesse.

"Another thing is that my wife likes to drive. When she does, I can watch out the car-window and see the Qatari men we pass looking incredulous. They think, 'What? Woman driving car? Asian woman? Man not driving car?

Why?' And then they slap repeatedly at their brows in disbelief.

"Life can be like that most of the time. Truthfully, the Middle East hardly looks like a good region for Asians or for females."

Will Darren ever return permanently to Australia? Does he want to live there again? "I am not going back there to stay," he scoffed. "Nor will I go back to live in Canada again either."

Although international adventures still make Darren happy, not everyone back in Australia comprehends his motives or approves. "My mother fails to understand," he said. "She always asks me: 'Why are you not coming back to Australia? You are Australian. Come back here.' "

He simply cannot comply. "Strangely enough, I no longer even associate myself much with Australia," he said.

New places and experiences continue to educate this teacher. In that sense, Darren too has a mighty thirst for knowledge, one quenched mainly by staying on the move.

FROM KUNMING TO YANGON

By Darren Turnbull

(assisted by Steve Cray)

Editor's Note: *Here, Darren Turnbull, the same Australian-born educator featured in the previous chapter, tells about an enlightening journey from China to Burma across a border that everyone believed to be closed.*

BOUND FOR BURMA -- All good journeys start in a pub, and this one proved to be no exception. It was on a hot, 45-degree Doha day over beers in the bar of the Sherazad Hotel that my Canadian work colleague **Steve Monk** and I decided to set off on an adventure that would take us out of the stupefying suburbia that our employers had created for us.

It was April 2008 when we hatched the plan to undertake a mostly overland trip from Kunming in Yunnan Province, China, to Yangon, the former capital of Burma, a country now known as Myanmar. The 758-kilometer

(471-mile) trip would take us about three weeks, although the whole process from conception and visas to completed journey took four months.

In May, we contacted Magado Travel in Yangon to arrange special permits for the Ruili/Muse border crossing and were given the necessary permission on the condition that we did not involve ourselves in any political activities. We then travelled to Hong Kong in early July to apply for Myanmar entry visas, which remarkably were granted on the same day. It was a measure of how few people travelled to the unstable country then that the consulate in Hong Kong's otherwise crowded Wanchai District looked almost deserted apart from us. We were issued with visas that prohibited overland crossings (we were supposed to fly), but a call to our contact in Yangon reassured us that the situation would pose no problems.

We set off in mid-July, flying to Kunming, where we were scrutinised by immigration, security having been beefed up due to the imminent Beijing Olympics. Kunming is the city of eternal spring, according to guidebooks, and it is stunning, with mountains as a backdrop, friendly people and excellent food. We stayed there for three days, at the New Century Hotel, and were treated to a taste of typical Yunnan hospitality.

'We Are the PLA. Are You Afraid?'

One night, some People's Liberation Army soldiers eating dinner at an outside street restaurant confronted us with: "We are the PLA. Are you afraid?" Our response was to laugh (nervously), and we quickly received a hearty invitation to join them at their table. They paid for everything. In fact, we had trouble to pay for anything in Yunnan. Local people simply would not have it.

On another occasion, we encountered a bunch of

triads, obviously drunk, being dragged out of a disco by their comrades. They apologised to us for the condition that they were in, which we thought was odd given that they probably were the toughest lads in town. The fact that they were triads was confirmed to us by the disco manager.

In Kunming, we also discovered the secrets of the *da,* a feature of ubiquitous Chinese disco culture. A *da* is a bucket of 12 or 16 beers, the only booze available at a disco, the idea being that if you have a *da* on your table, then women are bound to be attracted to you. Well, that's the theory anyway.

After three days, we set off for the airport to fly to Mang Shi to catch a bus for the overland trip, and there the real fun started. After heavy rain that day, the airport was flooded with all the flights cancelled. We were told at the airport check-in counter that if we wanted to change our flight or get a refund, we would have to do it in Hong Kong because that was where our original tickets were booked.

'Where Do You Really Want to Go?'

For a few moments, it looked as if our journey had ended before it even started until, luckily, a taxi driver, initially taking us back to our hotel, came to our rescue. I cannot remember his name, but he was a typical Chinese opportunist looking to capitalise on every encounter.

Ever alert, the driver picked up on the obvious frustration in the back of his cab. "Where do you really want to go?" he asked us.

"Ruili on the border with Myanmar," we answered, not expecting much sympathy.

Amazingly, he promptly called his wife to say that he had two possible long-distance passengers. Next we agreed on a price of about 2,000 yuan (just over US$315), including accommodation on the way.

Once the price had been established, the taxi driver stood firmly on our side – and we got more than the deal for which we had bargained. As we stopped off at the Dali walled city, in Yunnan, for the night, he surprised us by arranging for girls to "keep us company". We politely declined.

The driver had checked us into a hotel using a bunch of Chinese ID cards that he kept for the purpose. He explained that the rate was cheaper if we were Chinese.

In Dali, we again encountered Chinese hospitality. A group of local tourists insisted on paying our bar bill because we were guests in their country.

After an eight-hour taxi journey from Dali, we arrived at Ruili on the China-Myanmar border. Ruili is an isolated town with a strange part of its territory across the Shweli River on the Myanmar side. We witnessed Myanmar people jumping across the border fence and the police doing nothing to stop them while the Chinese lined up to cross the border "officially". What struck me immediately was the honesty of the local people. It was just five yuan to go anywhere by taxi, for example, but the drivers would accept no tips.

'On the Floor Sprawled a Dead Body'

We sensed a cowboy-town element to the place – the wild east. After finding the Jing Hua Hotel, where we were booked, we hardly believed our eyes when entering the lobby, for there on the floor sprawled a dead body. The guy's head recently had been blown off with a shotgun blast or something similar. Blood and brains lay everywhere. Totally in shock, we were about to turn around and find somewhere else to stay when the flustered manager came up to us in a desperate bid to rescue what little business he had, reassuring us that the hotel was safe for foreigners.

"Don't worry," he said in faltering English and with no sense of irony. "We have 24-hour-a-day security."

Against our better judgment, we agreed to stay. So we clambered over the corpse to reach the reception desk while the staff members hastily cleaned up the mess, destroying crime-scene evidence in the process. A little while later, an ambulance arrived to take away the body -- without even covering it up.

Obviously, after the dead-body shock and being checked in finally, we needed stiff drinks and so set off to find a pub, only to learn that Ruili has none. For entertainment, the people there go to discos, which were about the only places where we could find any booze, although once we briefly crossed the border illegally to drink Myanmar beer, which is banned in China for being too strong.

A Most-Beautiful Woman

As the only foreigners in town, we provided quite a novelty and attracted ample attention, especially at a disco. There I met the most beautiful woman I ever saw. A dancing girl from some minority group, she looked so exotic that I still measure every woman I see against her beauty. Obviously, I was not entirely discreet in my admiration because the manager noticed and directed her to stand at our table. It was very unsettling, I tell you, which I must have conveyed because eventually she left.

At the disco, Steve came a cropper with help from the local beer. He had danced with no less than six local women when his drunken disco antics resulted in two destroyed tables, much shouting and a very painful broken finger. The women helped us back to our hotel, but Steve's finger needed medical attention.

In agony, Steve even suggested that we should give up and return to Kunming for treatment. The other options

Some people eat rats, you know.
But others eat dogs and snakes.

were to find a hospital in Ruili or to push on to Yangon.

I talked Steve out of returning. Remembering the headless body in the hotel lobby, we also decided to give the wild east's medical services a miss and to continue with our journey. Expertly, I treated his finger with sticky tape for the time being.

One morning, I received a panicked phone call from the staff at the hotel's reception desk asking me: "What has gone wrong with your friend? He is at reception with a towel in his hand."

"Okay," I said. "I will sort it out." (Steve does not speak Putonghua, but I do.)

It turned out that Steve innocently wanted a clean towel, but his state of undress had been misinterpreted as a request for sexual services. Little did we know that the adjacent building housed "professional" ladies. (That explained why our rooms were full of condoms, including bizarre battery-powered ones.)

'They Eat Rats Too'

We arranged to meet our guide, **Mr Shwe,** whose response to every question that we put to him was, "Yeah, yeah, yeah". But he came up trumps at the Ruili-Muse border post, and we successfully negotiated the checkpoint formalities for our trip to Yangon via Mandalay, the second-largest city in, and the last royal capital of, Burma.

A Chinese border guard, oblivious to his mistake, said, "You are the first Americans we have seen." Then he asked how many hours we would stay in Muse, and I joked that we would not return. Clearly fearing for our safety, he replied seriously, "Not coming back? You should reconsider. Myanmar people are very dangerous, and they eat rats too." We decided it probably best not to remind him that the Chinese regularly eat dogs, civet cats and snakes, among other wildlife varieties.

Having cleared Muse immigration, we stayed for one night in the city, rats or not, which proved fascinating for giving us a border perspective from the Myanmar side. Being dirty, polluted and crime-infested, Muse makes Ruili look like a paradise. No wonder that the Myanmar government appears less than keen for people to visit there.

The next morning, we set off for Lashio, the largest town in Shan State, about 190 kilometers from Muse and slightly farther northeast of Mandalay. Our guide still escorted us – “yeah, yeah, yeah” – and we had to pass through four checkpoints. Military personnel manning these posts were bemused, like the border guards, to see foreigners in their vicinity, but they let us continue without too much hassle.

We arrived at Lashio in the evening and stayed for several days. Populated by ethnic Shan, Chinese and Burmans, the town only can be described as characterless, hot, dusty and creepy. Suffering from long-time friction between the Myanmar government and armed tribes, it gets barricaded at night.

After Lashio, where a local man amusingly asked us to teach him how to drink alcohol, we set off for Mandalay, where we stayed for three nights. Hot all year, Mandalay has cheap Chinese-run hotels, restaurants and shops, having been invaded by Chinese opportunists. There is no love lost between the Mandalay Myanmars and the Chinese.

One night, Steve and I ventured to the Irrawaddy River “beer stations” to imbibe. There, with beer goggles firmly in place, I met a local young lady who accompanied me back to the hotel, where I speedily sobered up and reconsidered. It proved tough to disentangle myself from her and persuade her to leave. What a narrow escape indeed!

On to Yangon

Then we continued on to Yangon, where Steve finally had his finger X-rayed and bandaged. While there, we secured invitations to a reception for the recently appointed Australian ambassador. Other guests there could not believe that we had travelled from Kunming. They believed the border to be closed. We needed to show them our stamped passports to prove that we told the truth. We ended up staying in Yangon for a month.

Our journey ended, as it began, in a pub, or a beer station as the Myanmar people call it. There, on our last night, Steve and I reflected on what had been a phenomenal trip. Even the local people had difficulty to believe that we had done it.

As of early 2012, the Ruili-Muse border officially remained closed to tourists. I wonder – was it something that I said?

FAMOUS BOAT SAILS INTO SUNSETS AND PHOTO ALBUMS

About the Book's Cover

Duk Ling Captain
Cheung Man Fai

AT THE EDGE OF THE SOUTH CHINA SEA – Normally seen in tropical waters near Hong Kong, the *Duk Ling,* a uniquely restored Chinese junk, symbolizes the adventures and exotic sights of expatriate lifestyles. Happily, those lifestyles take place almost everywhere all the time.

Pictures of the 60-foot *Duk Ling* (meaning "clever duck"), the last original Chinese junk seen in Hong Kong's harbor, appear in magazines, tourism brochures and photo albums worldwide. Some people even choose this boat as a wedding- or birthday-party venue.

Commercials, movies, documentaries and television shows regularly feature the *Duk Ling* too. For example, it appears in a **Jules Verne**-based TV mini-series, *Around the World in Eighty Days* (1989) starring **Peter Ustinov,** in another mini-series *Noble House* (1988), starring **Pierce Brosnan** and based on **James Clavell**'s novels, and in the movie *Rush Hour 2* (2001) starring **Jackie Chan** and **Chris Tucker.**

'Breeze in Your Face'

People enjoy simply seeing such a remarkable vessel. If they can ride across the water onboard as its three batwing sails billow, then they never forget the accompanying flutter of excitement, sense of romance and thrill of adventure.

"You feel the breeze in your face and taste the salt in the air…," reports *Discovery,* the airline Cathay Pacific's magazine. "Wrinkles disappear like magic as the sails fill out, and the timber of the boat creaks comfortably. As wind and sails begin to work together, it's like settling into an antique rocking chair."

The *Duk Ling,* with its schedule closely supervised by operation manager **Dymond Tai,** carries up to 40 people at a time. Its captain, **Cheung Man Fai,** who took over at the helm more than a decade ago after his father held the same job, leads the five-member crew. Under contract arrangements that have lasted 23 years so far, the Hong Kong Tourism Board charters the junk twice a week. The other past corporate clients include Morgan Stanley, Goldman Sachs, Deutsche Bank, Sheraton Hotels, Adidas, Qantas Airways, Air France, Amway, Louis Vuitton and other global companies.

Nearly No Nails

Built as a Macau fishing boat in 1955, the *Duk Ling* consists of timber and sails, but nearly no nails. Little pegs and joints hold it together. For several decades, the boat served its original purpose. After being found derelict in the early 1980s, the *Duk Ling* received an extensive restoration. Two expatriates led the meticulous work: **Pierre Couderc**, a French adventurer now living in Chile, and **Alain Zaugg,** a Swiss man-of-the-world since settled in Malaysia.

"It was love at first sight when Pierre Couderc first saw the *Duk Ling* sailing into Stanley Bay (Hong Kong), where he was windsurfing…," reveals the same issue of *Discovery* magazine. "He remembers the excitement he felt in observing that the old lady still had her original superstructure, unlike virtually all of Hong Kong's fishing junks, which have long since lost their masts and undergone other undignified modifications in being motorized."

Couderc "realized straight away that the boat had big potential". Eventually he sold the precious and restored vessel to a Hong Kong corporation led by **Paul Watt,** an Australian expatriate businessman. The sale proceeded on the basis of an understanding that the buyer too solemnly pledged to treat the junk with respect and to maintain it diligently.

A Wet Wedding Party

The *Duk Ling* loses a little of its glamor only when the weather refuses to cooperate. Paul mentions an example. "Dymond, the boat's operation manager, has worked with us for about eight years," he said. "One day, I stood in the boardroom of our Hong Kong office. Through the window, I noticed the *Duk Ling* sailing in the harbor, but the weather was really, really pissing down rain, and looking very miserable.

" 'So I said to Dymond, 'Who chartered the boat for today?'

" 'It's a wedding party,' she told me.

" 'Goodness me, that sounds like a pity,' I said. 'Normally, for weddings, people use the boat for photo shoots. We need to offer these newlyweds two hours with the boat for free in the sunshine on another day so that they can come back and do things properly.'

"But Dymond tried to tell me, 'It makes no difference.'

" 'What? Why not?'

" 'They are only French,' she said.

" 'So we both had a laugh. I know what she meant by that. She is married to a British chap named **Martin.**

" 'I told her, 'You have picked up all of Martin's bad habits and opinions.'

" 'Well, I am British,' she said.

" 'No, you are not,' I told her. 'You are a Hong Kong Chinese.'

" 'Sometimes I am British, and sometimes I am Chinese,' she insisted," echoing a refrain often heard in Hong Kong, even a decade-and-a-half after China took sovereignty over the city.

" 'Of course, it is a well-known fact that the British do not like the French (and vice-versa, presumably), although they may not be sure exactly why."

In fact, the *Duk Ling* and its management do not discriminate against anyone. "That's right, exactly right," Paul said.

History on its Deck

More than most, this boat carries history on its deck. Back in the mid-20th century, authentic Chinese junks filled the harbors of Hong Kong and Macau. As the last original one left in Hong Kong, the *Duk Ling* stirs mental images of past taipans and opium traders.

These days, it qualifies as remarkable and special. That makes it very much like the people featured in *All Aboard! Planet Expat* – and like so many of the book's readers too.

MORE COMING SOON! DO YOU WISH TO BE PART OF A BOOK?

With one book completed, the Power Publishing Club intends to tackle many more. Upcoming projects include *All Aboard! Planet Expat, Volume 2*, maybe with the focus the next time on female expatriates. Among the other prospects are books about leading families, dynamic companies or fascinating places. Readers with remarkable true stories to tell, and who wish to become part of a future book project, are welcome to contact us individually or in groups. We invite suggestions and ideas about the endless possibilities. Also we seek distributors worldwide for all our books.

Contact: ***info@powerpublishingclub.com***

BOOK-LOAN RECORD

Billions of people love books. Most readers, bless their hearts, behave generously to share the pleasures of reading. They gladly lend their favourite books to friends. The Power Publishing Club enthusiastically encourages this, but far too many readers then neglect to return what they borrow. For kind lenders, that turns highly annoying.

When lending *All Aboard! Planet Expat,* why not make a note on this page so that the borrower cannot forget the obligation to return the book? If necessary, maybe the borrower should pledge a safe return by signing here too.

ONE LAST THING

The team behind *All Aboard! Planet Expat* leaves the following space mostly empty in case that some readers or other interested people wish to add extra words or artwork of their own.

ONE LAST THING

The team behind *All Aboard! Planet Expat* leaves the following space mostly empty in case that some readers or other interested people wish to add extra words or artwork of their own.

ONE LAST THING

The team behind *All Aboard! Planet Expat* leaves the following space mostly empty in case that some readers or other interested people wish to add extra words or artwork of their own.

A SPECIAL INVITATION

Has this book encouraged you to travel and to experience more of the world's wonders? Travel represents the greatest learning opportunity that anyone can experience. No one should fear unfamiliar countries, cultures or people. The publisher and production team hope that the book will inspire many people to seek new experiences in new places. If we have achieved this much, then it's mission accomplished.

ABOUT THE ARTIST

Sara Seneviratne, an award-winning cartoonist from Sri Lanka, has journeyed through much of Asia and beyond as a multimedia consultant and artist. His work appears in leading newspapers, magazines and online. A specialist in political satire, social issues and human rights, he won Amnesty International Human Rights Press Awards in 1996, 1997 and 1998. He also provides the creative spark and primary talent behind *Funworld* magazine.

ABOUT THE EDITOR / PRIMARY AUTHOR

John Cairns, a seasoned editor and author, has lived in Hong Kong since 1992 when he left his Canadian homeland. Born in the tiny province of Prince Edward Island, he resided in three other provinces – Nova Scotia, Ontario and Saskatchewan – before taking the plunge to move to Asia and become a full-fledged expatriate. Using the pen-name **Jay Scott Kanes**, he has three previous published books: *High Degree of Atrocity* (2004), *Dog-Gone Cat Case* (2005) and *Island Toes A'Tapping* (2006). He welcomes email **(at john.johncairns@gmail.com).**